Jack S.

Lacie W. R.I.

BURNOUT

Also by Jeannine Kadow

Blue Justice

BURNOUT

Jeannine Kadow

A DUTTON BOOK

DUTTON
Published by the Penguin Group
Penguin Putnam Inc., 375 Hudson Street, New York, New York 10014, U.S.A.
Penguin Books Ltd, 27 Wrights Lane, London W8 5TZ, England
Penguin Books Australia Ltd, Ringwood, Victoria, Australia
Penguin Books Canada Ltd, 10 Alcorn Avenue, Toronto, Ontario, Canada M4V 3B2
Penguin Books (N.Z.) Ltd, 182–190 Wairau Road, Auckland 10, New Zealand

Penguin Books Ltd, Registered Offices:
Harmondsworth, Middlesex, England

First published by Dutton, an imprint of Dutton NAL,
a member of Penguin Putnam Inc.

First Printing, March 1999
10 9 8 7 6 5 4 3 2 1

 REGISTERED TRADEMARK—MARCA REGISTRADA

Library of Congress Cataloging-in-Publication Data

Kadow, Jeannine.
    Burnout / Jeannine Kadow.
        p.   cm.
    ISBN 0-525-94464-8
    I. Title.
    PS3561.A36154B87   1999
    813'.54—dc21   98-33751
                                             CIP

Printed in the United States of America
Set in Sabon
Designed by Leonard Telesca

PUBLISHER'S NOTE

This book is printed on acid-free paper. ∞

For
Jules Bass
with admiration, appreciation, and love.

ACKNOWLEDGMENTS

Special thanks to Mitch Kadow for his invaluable technical guidance, to Jarl Secher-Jensen for his mountaineering expertise, and to Ray Coleman, Teton County Search and Rescue Team. Thanks too to the many others who gave so generously of their time and expertise in medical, legal, psychological, arson, and FBI matters. You know who you are.

Prologue

❧

Shooting the moon, Lieutenant Rick "Slammer" Bratton thought, drilling through the sky at Mach 1 in his F-18, up thirty thousand feet right next to Heaven. *Goddamn, Slammer, this is the life. Thirty million dollars' worth of fighter plane between your legs and one bright night to sail through.* The view from the cockpit was magic. Pure magic. A full moon hung belly-down on the black Bering Sea. Wisps of cloud skated across the horizon. The round Plexiglas bubble was his window on the world and he shared it with no one. North of the Aleutians, alone in the silver Hornet, snug in his seat. He could have stayed up there forever, but the practice mission was over and it was time to head back to the Nimitz-class carrier twenty miles south.

Bratton eased back on the throttle and started his descent. His eyes scanned the instrument panels. Digital numbers glowed green in the dark. Hydraulics, oil pressure, fuel flow, EGT, RPM. All normal. Dropping down through fifteen thousand feet, fifteen miles out, the air was clear and whitecaps were visible on the choppy sea.

Ten miles out, the carrier flight deck lights were shining brightly. Bratton grinned under his oxygen mask. He loved rough water landings. That's why they called him Slammer. He could bring a Hornet down in any kind of weather. *Slammer* Bratton always nailed the landing on the first try.

Down on the carrier flight deck, Lieutenant Commander Linda Severino stood with her face turned up, watching the sky. Her short blond hair whipped in the wind. Twelve squadrons were airborne, twenty-four planes, but only one interested her and it was flying approach, preparing to land now. The pilot was a young fresh-faced Texan named Rick Bratton. He had a hearty appetite and a big laugh. Severino knew he had a family. A wife at home, a baby in a crib. A fifteen-knot wind blew in hard off the water. Underneath her heavy flight suit, she shivered. But Linda Severino wasn't cold. She was scared. She wondered if Rick Bratton was scared yet. If not, he would be. Soon.

Bratton hooted. He was less than five miles out, eighteen hundred feet up in the air, drifting in at 180 knots, rock-steady and dropping down nicely.

Severino glanced at the men around her. Five young LSO's. Like her, they all had radios jammed up to their ears. Her commanding officer stood off to one side. He had a battered face that looked like stone and deeply tanned skin from years of flying right next to the sun. Severino turned away and looked out to sea, surprised none of the men saw her fear. Sweat rolled down her back. She gripped the radio. *Come on, Bratton. Phone home.*

One mile out, Bratton glanced down. Ocean swells were running eight to ten feet. The carrier in front of him was rocking and rolling like a fucking bucking bronco. He grinned again, ready for the fun.

Severino watched the F-18 gracefully drop into a clean glide slope.

"Four-Oh-Five, Hornet," Bratton radioed, "ball Six-Point-Five."

"Roger ball," Severino replied, eyes riveted on the silver Hornet coming in, dead on and fast, a half a mile away.

Bratton was in the groove, looking good, riding the centered ball down, focusing on the centerline lights of the landing area and the one all-important amber light he needed to guide him in. Suddenly, the master caution light on his instrument panel flashed on.

Bratton's grin vanished. The left engine fire light glowed red and a computer chip voice chirped: *Fire, left engine. Fire, left engine.*

"Fuck," Bratton swore, twisting around in his seat. He looked through the fiberglass bubble right into the mouth of the engine and saw billowing black smoke. "Fuck."

Severino saw the smoke too. She bit her lip. It was happening now. It was time.

Bratton keyed in the mike. "Slammer Four-Oh-Four. I've got a left engine fire alert and I see smoke."

Linda Severino held the radio mouthpiece tight to her lips. "Divert and eject, Slammer." Sweat pooled under her arms. "Now!"

"Roger." An eighth of a mile out, riding right up tight to the carrier tail, Bratton shoved the stick over and the throttle up, forcing the plane hard left.

"Eject, eject, eject," Severino chanted, watching flames spurting red-orange against the night as the Hornet swerved away from the landing deck.

Bratton twisted around in his seat again. Harness straps cut up high and hard into his thighs. Orange flames shot out of the engine behind him.

"Fuck." He turned back to the instrument panel, ready to shut the engine down, but there were no lights at all. The panel was black. His controls were dead. There was no up, no down, no east, west, north, or south. There was no power and no hydraulics.

He jerked the stick, already knowing the steering was out too. "I've lost all electrics and hydraulics," Bratton shouted into the radio.

"Eject!" Severino screamed. The thundering roar of afterburners kicked the air around her and she smelled the smoke. "Eject! Now! Now! Now!"

Bratton dropped his hand away from the throttle and grabbed the bright yellow handle on the side of his seat. He prepared his body for the coming shock and yanked up hard. Nothing happened. "Lower handle's dead!"

Impossible! Linda cursed under her breath. She hadn't touched the seat. "Upper handle! Pull, pull, pull!"

Bratton was already reaching up, wrapping his hand around the upper yellow handle and yanking down as hard as he could. Head thrust back against the seat, stomach muscles tensed, ready to eject, he yanked again. Nothing happened. The canopy didn't blow off, the seat didn't punch out with him in it, and he wasn't floating through the air with his parachute billowing out behind him. "Upper handle's jammed," he shouted, frantic now.

Severino gripped the radio, wishing she could reach right up into the sky and pull him down to safety. She wanted him to be okay. Something had gone wrong. She had rigged the fire, but the pilot wasn't supposed to die. The crewmen around her were frozen in place, watching the burning plane streak through the night. She felt the angry eyes of her CO on her, as if he knew that this was her fault.

"Jettison the canopy," she ordered Bratton, trying hard to contain her panic. But she knew the CO saw the sweat rolling down her face, her jaw trembling, body shaking, and he sure as hell saw the sick pallor of her skin as the nausea rolled up inside of her. Guilt. The CO saw her guilt. He knew, she thought, he knew what she had done.

Bratton gripped the canopy jettison handle and yanked. The canopy exploded off. Wind rushed at him, a hundred and fifty miles an hour, slamming him against his seat. Pinned, unable to move, Bratton struggled to climb out, but the hurricane blast was an invisible hand jamming him back as the plane hurtled along, rocking and weaving out of control.

He vomited into his oxygen mask. His body strained against the pressure. The plane plunged. The world went into slow motion. Tumbling down, all sense of direction was lost in his wild spiraling free fall toward the black surface of the sea. Howling wind and roaring engines deafened him.

Rick Bratton couldn't even hear his own final screams.

Linda Severino heard his screams. The radio shoved up next to her ear, she listened helplessly to Bratton crying, cursing and shrieking, begging for his life, as the burning F-18 swiveled down, flipping nose over tail a quarter mile out from the starboard side of the ship. She heard Bratton's deep guttural groan and then the ear-splitting crack when his plane hit water like it was cement.

The radio went silent.

A geyser of white sea foam flared. An explosion split the night and a bright orange fireball swelled up into the sky. Spilled fuel had sparked and blown. A fire on the sea. A fire on water. The strong wind blew smoke and ash back at her. Tears streamed down her cheeks. Someone was calling her name, shaking her hard. She looked away from the fire into the angry face of her CO.

"Severino," he screamed over the high-pitched whine of jet engines. "What the fuck happened?"

She saw his hard eyes, the unnatural pallor of his skin, and behind him, two rescue choppers rising, lifting off the flight deck, churning out to sea. It was too late. The pilot was dead.

How could she explain it? Who would believe her? Who would understand? *There had been no choice.* The whispering voice had found her there on the Great Bering Sea. It was always his voice, the same whispering voice, taunting her, telling her to do things. At first they were small things, but the game he played had escalated into this. A terrible understanding filled her. She would never be free of him. Never.

If she resigned, quit, changed her name and face and moved away, he would find her. He owned her. Didn't he? Wasn't this final proof of his power over her? Now she was a killer like he was. He would rejoice. He would whisper once again how they were inexorably bound, brother and sister, bound by blood, bound by fire.

"Severino!" The CO shouted over the roar of jet engines and the beating night wind.

"I did it!" she yelled, pointing out at the crash site. "I rigged the fire. He made me do it. I had no choice. No one was supposed to die."

"Pull yourself together." The CO moved to grab her by the shoulders. She lunged away.

The landing deck had no rails. She looked back once at the CO and then she jumped, springing high and wide away from the ship, falling rock-hard into the surging sea. She hit feet first and knifed straight down through twenty feet of water. Her flotation jacket punched her back up to the surface. The November sea was arctic cold, thirty degrees Fahrenheit and already sucking the life out of her. Her hands and feet went numb and her core turned to ice. She had twenty minutes. Maybe less. The cold would kill her.

Her flotation jacket held her head high above water. A cloud flitted across the sky, then was gone. The moon above seemed to be the great featureless face of God, the burning bush tossed high in the sky. The current sucked her dangerously close to the carrier. The cold made her crazy.

She eyed the endless flat hull rising out of the water. It was a steel cliff, high and slick, with no footholds to help a climber. But she was not a climber. She was a swimmer. She could swim to land, to the Aleutian Islands, take shelter in a lightning-split tree, scratch for berries and nuts. *He would never find her there.* Crazily, she rolled over and slapped tiny-handed and feeble at God's Great Bering Sea. Her arms were dead blocks of ice. She gave her body up to the swells and waited to drown, but the flotation jacket kept her stubbornly afloat, spinning her up face-first to the sky, to air, to life.

The moon seemed something pregnant and the sea was the first water of her birth. Her mind felt as large and dark as the north Russian sky, then the darkness snapped and she felt dreamy. The sea rocked her while the wind and waves whispered. There were voices, a chorus of sirens beckoning.

Come, come, her dream sirens sang.

Up above a rescue chopper hovered, rotors whipping. The belly of the chopper opened. A lifesaving harness spun down on a cable and hit the water, close enough to touch. She tugged her flotation jacket zipper down and shrugged out of it. Next, she wriggled out of her flight suit and held onto the rescue harness and the flotation jacket to stay afloat.

The white-hot searchlight lit her up. She squinted into the light and saw a red-clad swimmer, poised to jump, ready to come after her. She looked down and saw iridescent bubbles clinging to her pale frozen skin. A cresting swell lifted her. She pushed the harness away. Hanging suspended, naked in the water, she let go of her flotation jacket and went under. She sank fast, out of the spill of searchlight, into deeper dark water.

Her lungs ached, but instead of breathing or swimming or fighting, she closed her eyes and thought of the quiet and how the water was pillow soft against her cheek.

Chapter One

❧

The dream came that night, as it often did, scaring me awake to the sound of my own voice crying out, my heart slapping hard, my breath shallow and dry, my body shaking with fright. It was the face, always the face, the same nightmare face, pale thick lips, limpid eyes, thin copper hair hanging dull and flat to his skull, and the sour sick smell of his breath as he whispered to me, filling my head with his voice: *Lacie, touch the flame, reach out and touch the fire.*

I jerked to an upright position in bed and opened my eyes. I was alone. I had been waking alone for years, but when the nightmare came, I wanted someone there next to me, to stroke my hair, to shush and hold me, to rock the terror away. The sky outside my window was still dark, the bedside clock glowed 5:00. The sheets were a messy tangle, damp with my own nightmare sweat. I shoved them aside and got up.

The nightmare stayed with me through my shower and stand-up breakfast of tepid black coffee and dry wheat toast. I dressed quickly in a black turtleneck sweater, black wool pants and matching jacket, then stepped into a pair of glossy black crocodile shoes. The three-inch heels were too high for comfortable walking, but I didn't care. They put me over the six-foot mark, which gave me confidence. And I didn't plan on walking much anyway, just holing up behind my desk and losing myself in a three-part investigative story scheduled to air the following week.

I worked for WRC-TV, the NBC affiliate in Washington, D.C., anchoring the six o'clock news. I was one of the rare anchors who wanted to do more than just read the news. The entire process from start to finish was what thrilled me, going out and finding the news, hunting it down, digging it up, and then in pictures and words, telling my audience *the story*. The story was everything. I had a natural gift for anchoring and a passion for reporting, and was blessed with a lush new contract that guaranteed me both.

I grabbed a heavy wool coat, slipped on a pair of gloves, and stepped out into the dark November morning, locking the door to my town house behind me. A light dusting of snow covered the ground and heavy clouds above promised more. The cold stung my ears and eyes. Winter had arrived early. I picked my way down the walk, skidding across ice patches, swearing quietly, regretting my impractical choice of footwear.

I hailed a passing taxi, ducked inside, and gave the station address. We sped quickly across town, silent and alone on the snowy streets. In the east, the rising sun brightened clouds to the color of steel. Street lamps sputtered out. Fat wet flakes fell from the sky. The cab wipers slapped back and forth in a steady rhythm, and suddenly I felt tired, wishing the holiday weekend was over.

"Nice Thanksgiving?" the old black driver asked, sneaking a long look at me in the rearview mirror.

I was used to those secret looks. Most people in town recognized me even though I was relatively new to D.C. My face was plastered on fifty billboards in the metropolitan area. All the local papers had done profiles about me, chronicling my career and whatever tidbits they could dig up about my private life. There was enough there worth digging for, plenty of publicly documented tragedy that kept the tabloids pumping. Mine was the success-against-all-odds kind of Cinderella fable America craves.

The driver cleared his throat, and I knew he took my silence for rudeness. I smiled at him brightly. "I had a wonderful Thanksgiving."

"Turkey and potatoes, all the trimmings?"

"All the trimmings," I lied with my big fake smile.

It had been a lousy Thanksgiving, spent alone, eating a chopped salad in my office, reviewing the stories I would read on the late news. I had volunteered. There was no reason not to, no reason to stay home. My daughter, Skyla, was up in Manhattan for the holiday with her father, as we had civilly agreed so many years ago when I walked out on him for good, taking our baby with me. Jerry was a lousy husband. The list is a long ugly one, and I haven't trusted men much since.

Jerry turned out to be a surprisingly wonderful father, but like so many things, he was better at it part-time than full-time, and Thanksgiving was included in the part-time deal. All in all, things were working out well. I just had to suffer through the rough spots, the every-other-weekend thing, the two summer months, and the blasted holiday splitting that left me daughterless, alone, and unhappy.

My new town house felt too big and too quiet without Skyla's laugh and dazzling presence. Thirteen years old and she was *someone*. She was the best of Jerry and me—his effervescent ebullience tempered by my pragmatism—mixed into something altogether new and original. Thinking of her made me smile. Today was Saturday. Monday, she would be home.

With none of the weekday rush hour to contend with, the cab-driver made good time across town. He was still sneaking looks at me, his curiosity eating away at him. I could tell he was screwing up the courage to ask me the usual question. He pulled to a smooth stop in front of the station and turned around in his seat. His gaze dropped down to my hands, but they were gloved and hidden. Disappointment flickered across his old weathered face. "I read about them," he said pointing shyly.

I fumbled for my wallet.

His watery eyes were wide, fixed on my hands. "They hurt much?" he asked, with a kind of wonder in his voice.

"Sometimes."

"Can you really type?"

"Sort of," I snapped, holding out a ten.

"I don't mean to pry, Miss Wagner, but you're an inspiration. You remind folks how good we got it, just to be in one whole piece and all." He smiled at me shyly, and his big worn fingers brushed my glove.

My cheeks flushed. I paid the meter plus five for his sincere words and stepped out into the fast-falling snow, thankful to be out of the cab, away from sympathy and curious eyes. My hands embarrassed me. They were burned in a car accident fire when I was ten. My father was trapped in the car and burned to death that night. I was lucky. They say some passing stranger lifted me free in time to save my life, but not my hands.

My hands were and still are horribly, hopelessly disfigured. The flame ate all the way through to bone, then went on to chew away muscles and tendons too. Even after all the plastic surgery over the years, my hands are monstrous appendages. Shockingly hideous. They disgust me, but they are mine. I have never learned to accept them.

I am tall and slim. A hundred and five pounds stretched over a five-nine frame, so light sometimes I think I'll float away. My hips are narrow and straight like a boy's, and my long legs are hard from running. I like the discipline of the sport, the solitude of it. I run in every kind of weather, as if one day I'll run right out of my body into a new one, untouched by fire.

Until that impossible day, I live with my hands and my fear of fire. I do not stand near fireplaces or allow candles on the table. The tiny flames of birthday cake candles scare me, as does the strike of a match or a butane lighter's weak bluish fire. Charcoal barbecue grills, wood ovens, cherries jubilee served flaming at the table, crêpes suzette—even the sun. I prefer winter when clouds mask the sky and dim the sun to a soft watery gray.

I welcome cold and fear heat. I take tepid showers and drink cool coffee. In my new town house, I bricked up the four fireplaces and replaced gas stoves with electric. Even a tiny sputtering pilot flame scares me. Fire of any size takes me back to that terrible night of the crash, to my father's live body burning to death in the seat next to me. In a crazy attempt to pull him free, I plunged my hands into the flames. When I pulled them out, they were two torches glowing red in the black Massachusetts night. The smell of my own burning flesh still wakes me at night. When I see fire, I smell death.

The last three fingers on each hand will not straighten. They curl in, toward the palm, and are stubbornly stiff. My thumbs are stumps, amputated at the knuckle. My index fingers somehow remained whole and somewhat straight, though weak. Dozens of operations and painstaking skin grafts have failed to make my hands appear normal. The flesh there has many colors—vivid red, baby pink, snow white. The scars are numerous and vary in texture from rigid waves of puckered skin to translucent waxy smooth patches. Deep channels run across my palms in places where no amount of grafting and collagen implants could replace dead tissue.

Reconstructive surgery has progressed in the twenty-four years since my accident. There are new techniques now, improvements could be made, but I can't go through it all again—the pain of skin grafts, the long healing and the huge hope, then unwrapping my hands like gifts, watching bandages fall away, only to see ugliness where I'd hoped beauty might be.

Technically, I am handicapped. I cannot hold a pencil easily and rarely try anymore. I can type, in a manner of speaking, but it is not pretty to watch. I jab at the keyboard, using my two straightest fingers, alternating, left right left right, painfully stabbing the words out, letter by letter. In the beginning, it took me hours to type a paragraph, ten minutes to spell my full name—Lacynda Wagner. You cannot appreciate the manual acrobatics it takes for me to type those thirteen letters without looking and fast.

There is another female anchor out West with maimed hands, but she was born with hers. She was a Thalidomide baby. It was a terrible trick of medicine that twisted her palms and gave her flippers for fingers. Like me, she has been commended for her courage and determination in overcoming her disability. Unlike me, her hands do not embarrass her. She does not wear gloves. She displays her hands naturally on the nightly news, shuffling papers and clapping them together when someone on the set says something funny. *They are part of me,* she has candidly said, with her winning white smile.

I wish I could be like her, but know I never can. I do not display my hands, not for my loyal news audience or *People* magazine or even for my curious but well-meaning news director. I wear gloves in public and on the air. Always. Even in summer. I hide my hands from the world and mostly from myself. They are a bitter visual reminder of the accident and the man who, later, set out to destroy my life.

But that early November morning, standing in the falling snow on the last peaceful Saturday I would have for a long time, I didn't know of him and I certainly didn't know he had already started his deadly game. I lingered there on the sidewalk in simple ignorance, tasting snowflakes when I should have been tasting fear.

WRC-TV took up a sizable chunk of a city block in a somewhat respectable part of D.C. I admired the building for its Old World charm. It was white and pretty, with big bay windows and a peaked roof. A hundred years before, it must have been a graceful residence on a graceful street, but now there was nothing like it in sight, only a crowd of rust-stained office buildings and fast-food drive-thrus.

I walked carefully up the slippery walk to the station entrance and rapped on the locked plate glass door. The night guard shuffled over and let me in. The lobby was drawing room cozy with fine polished wood and overstuffed chintz sofas. Poster-sized framed pictures filled the walls showcasing NBC network series stars and the *WRC Action Six* news team.

I breezed by my own picture, tapped it once for luck, and wound through a maze of corridors, to the newsroom in back, humming as I went. I had been at WRC for six months. It was a significant jump from Norfolk, Virginia, and it was my big break. I hoped WRC would lead me straight to a network slot in New York, where Skyla could move easily between parents, and where Jerry Costello, Attorney-at-Law, would see my face on the network news each and every night of his egotistical self-centered life.

I grinned thinking about it. Jerry was a good man, he just wasn't good for me and his last words when I walked out proved it: *"Just wait, Lace. You'll be back, begging me to take you in. It's a hard world out there. You'll never make it on your own. You need me, you goddamn need me!"* He could never understand why I was consumed with finding my own identity when his was big enough for two.

The newsroom was empty. Computer screen-savers flickered in the dark, fax machines were still, telephones quiet, and the studio deserted. I switched the lights on in my spacious private office, hung up my coat, and logged on to my computer, expecting e-mail from Skyla. When she was up in New York, we exchanged five or six cyber messages a day, and talked in the evening when my news-cast was over.

I had spoken to Skyla on the Thursday of Thanksgiving and received two e-mails Friday morning but somehow missed talking to her later. I had called several times throughout the evening but got Jerry's answering machine. Assuming he had taken her to the the-ater or a late show, I left one last loving message Friday night, then fell into bed, into a restless troubled sleep until the whispering voice finally scared me awake.

Lacie, Lacie, do you remember the flames that night? Can you see them, touch them, feel them licking your skin raw?

I shook myself and scrolled through my new e-mail. There was nothing from Skyla. Still edgy from the nightmare, I grabbed the phone and dialed Jerry's apartment, not caring about the ungodly early hour. His machine picked up. I left a curt message for him, and tried his Hamptons beach house, where I got another madden-ing tape. *"Hi! Jerry's not here! Leave your message after the beep."*

I imagined his voice reverberating in the big empty rooms out there, the dunes sifting up in the wind, tight to the deck.

I left a second curt message and hung up, upset. Jerry *always* answered the phone. Even if he was in a dead sleep. Even if he was with a woman. Especially when he was with a woman. It was one of his power plays. He couldn't resist knowing who was calling him. The only reason no one answered was because no one was home.

He had probably whisked Skyla up to Vermont to ski for the weekend. He was impulsive and not always good about communicating, often taking her away and *forgetting* to tell me. I cursed Jerry, but when I thought of Skyla's long silvery blond hair billowing out behind her on the long run down the mountain, my anger faded.

I wrote Skyla a funny note with a new lawyer joke she could use on her dad, sent it zinging out into cyber-space, then settled down to work, hoping a good full day would calm me down.

I was wrong. Mid-afternoon, the newsroom was noisy and busy for a Saturday, with reporters milling around, phones ringing nonstop, the hum of fifty computer terminals, and faxes spooling in. It was loud and boisterous, but not loud enough to drown out the whispering voice of my dreams.

My phone rang at two. I picked up on the first ring, hoping it was Skyla.

"Lacie Wagner."

"Afternoon, Lace. Max here."

I put my feet up on my desk, leaned back in my chair, and smiled. Max was my uncle, my father's brother, and he was determined to help me any way he could. He was a high-ranking officer in a top-secret military division called the Delta Force. His position gave him access, information, and contacts throughout the government, not just the Pentagon. In short, he was my guardian angel and the perfect source. "What do you have for me?" I asked, tapping my pencil in anticipation.

"A story that hasn't been released yet."

"My favorite kind. Government?"

"Navy."

"Home turf," I quipped. Norfolk had an important Naval base, and during my years reporting there I acquired an excellent understanding of aircraft carriers and fighter planes. "When does everybody else get this?"

"In seven hours. You've got an exclusive for the six o'clock news."

"I'm all ears."

"An F-18 went down last night over the Bering Sea, north of the Aleutian Islands, midway between Russia and Alaska."

The Navy had lost a number of jets in the past year, not enough to be considered a scandal, but enough to raise a few eyebrows. "What was it this time?" I asked. "Faulty ball bearings? Shoddy maintenance? Or did a Russian MIG accidentally shoot it down?"

"Stranger than that."

"Define strange."

"A female officer on board the carrier said she caused the accident."

I dropped my legs from the desk and sat up straight, smelling several stories at once. "That's a loaded sentence, Max. Inferences of sabotage, not to mention the newsworthy gender thing."

"It gets better. After she confessed, she tossed herself overboard."

My stomach tightened. "What?"

"You heard me. She jumped."

"You sure she didn't fall in?"

"She *jumped*."

"They find her?"

"Nope, she's fish food by now."

"Max, please."

"Sorry. They found her flotation jacket. The jackets all have built-in life vests. If she'd kept it on, they might've been able to save her."

"You lost me."

"Linda Severino took her flotation jacket off, Lacie. She took her flight suit off too. She wanted to die."

"Start at the beginning."

He told me as much as the Navy knew. The carrier was on special assignment in the Bering Sea, well out of the normal season of passage through the strait. The flight deck carried a full regiment of aircraft flying nightly training missions. The ship was in what the Navy calls "Blue Water," which simply means it was out in the middle of nowhere. The closest piece of land was a tiny heap of treeless rock, one in the string of the inhospitable Aleutian Islands.

Weather conditions were abysmal, as they always are in the Bering Sea. An Arctic current runs down from the north and eventually smacks into warmer water rushing up from southern Alaska.

The two meet, creating great blankets of fog hundreds of miles across. If it's not the fog, it's the cold, drifting ice chunks big as football fields, or monster waves. The Bering Sea is not a gentle place, especially in November. The average water temperature dips to thirty degrees and the waves run ten to twenty feet high in calm weather. In storms, they become solid walls of water, forty feet high. There must have been some compelling reason for a Nimitz-class Naval carrier to brave the Bering Sea in November, but that was not the focus of Max's story.

The sky was crystal clear, Max said, and the sea rough with ten-foot chop. The accident occurred three hours into the routine flight operations of twelve squadrons rotating through the night. The F-18 was heading back in to the carrier, preparing to land, when an engine burst into flame. The controls failed and the ejection seat jammed. The pilot couldn't get out. A hundred and twenty sailors and officers on deck watched in horror as the flaming jet dropped out of the sky with the pilot trapped inside. The female officer claimed she had sabotaged the plane. She jumped overboard moments later. A rescue chopper was sent out to save her.

"I've got a copy of the carrier's air traffic control tape," Max said. "Listen to this."

Initially, the helicopter pilot's voice was calm as he radioed the ship: "Home base, this is Night Spotter One. We've got a home run. She's alive and moving. We're sending the harness down."

"Roger."

"Home plate, this is Night Spotter One. The harness is in the water and she's holding on. Our diver is standing by, ready to drop down if she needs help, but she's got the harness and looks A-OK."

"Good work, Night Spotter."

"Home plate, this is Night Spotter One." The pilot sounded worried now. "Something weird's going on here. She's still got the harness but she's taking her flotation coat off. No, she's taking her flight suit off too. But she's still hanging on to the harness."

The pilot's voice changed. He was talking fast and sounded incredulous. "Jesus Christ! I don't fucking believe it! She pushed the harness away and dropped her float coat! She's gone under! The diver is in. Repeat, Home Plate, the diver is in. He's going after her."

"Continue your efforts, Night Spotter!"

"Home Plate, this is Night Spotter One. The diver's on the spot she went under. He's searching."

"Continue your efforts, Night Spotter!"

"We're sweeping the area with light, but don't see her. The diver's up. He's empty-handed."

"Continue your efforts!"

The back-and-forth went on for twenty frantic minutes. Then, the tired voice of the helicopter pilot called in one last time. "Home Plate, this is Night Spotter One. There's no sign of her. We lost her. Repeat. We lost her."

The tape ran silent. Empty air and the hiss of tape heads.

Max came back on the line. His voice was low. "Do you understand what you just heard. Lacie?"

"She took her flotation coat off, just like you said, and she deliberately let go of the rescue harness."

"She wanted to die. Drowning's not a pretty way to go."

I couldn't think of any way to go that was pretty, but I kept that observation to myself. "Can you e-mail me the audio tape as a sound file?"

"Done."

"Good." I wanted to play a portion of the tape for my news audience. "Tell me about the woman."

"Thirty-four years old."

My age, exactly.

"She was a high-ranking officer," Max continued. "Lieutenant Commander in charge of all the Landing Safety Officers on board. It takes ten years' flying and a perfect record to win that job. Her name was Linda Severino."

"The name's familiar."

"It should be," Max said. "Her father's John Severino."

I whistled, remembering bits and pieces of political legend. In the late sixties, John Severino was a high-profile senator from Virginia. He was a dazzling political strategist and gifted speaker, a man so charismatic and popular, he could have been President one day. But something happened and he suddenly vanished from the public eye. I couldn't remember why.

There was another reason why I recognized Linda's name. "Max," I said breathlessly, "when I was a kid, that last summer at camp before the accident, Linda was there."

"Do you remember her?"

"Not well."

"Try," Max pressed. "It's a great angle for your story."

I closed my eyes and concentrated. The accident that killed my father and destroyed my hands occurred the night he was driving me home from that summer camp. Whenever I tried to think back to that summer, I went blank. It was a black hole in my psychic universe. Names and faces flashed by from time to time, but nothing more. It was as if my mind repressed everything associated with the accident.

"It's no use," I said, opening my eyes. "I can't remember much. Just that she was one of the girls there."

"Well, Linda Severino grew up into one hell of a woman. A chip off the old block. She was an F-18 pilot and the head of her squadron. Career Navy flyer. A gifted flyer too. She flew in the Gulf War and came home covered in decorations. Meritorious, bravery, you name it. She was one of the best and brightest officers the Navy had. Linda Severino was not the kind of woman to act crazy like she did last night."

"You said there were witnesses?"

"A dozen right there on the landing platform with her, including her commanding officer, Dick Johnson. Tough son of a bitch. He's the commander of the entire carrier air group. He said her exact words were these: *I did it. I rigged the fire. He made me do it. I had no choice. No one was supposed to die.*"

"*He made me do it.* What did she mean?"

"No one knows."

"What about family or friends? Any insight there?"

"Her father's an invalid and a recluse. Rumor has it he's got serious mental problems of his own. Mother's dead. No brothers or sisters, just her husband, Jeff Hoag. Linda kept her maiden name. Hoag was informed of the accident early this morning. From what I heard, he was totally unglued and mostly incoherent. A lot of gibberish about Linda suffering from nightmares full of whispering voices and repetitive dreams of planes exploding in midair. He calmed down enough to say Linda had post-traumatic stress syndrome from her combat missions in the Gulf War. He claims she had a lot of guilt from the killing she did over there. But, he swears Linda was totally competent and said there's no way in hell she would've rigged the plane to go down."

He was silent for a long moment. I pictured his big bearish face, the heavy cheeks and thick eyebrows scrunched up while he tried to understand Linda Severino's bizarre and seemingly inexplicable act. Max was a pilot too, and he certainly had an opinion about what had happened.

"Max? What are you thinking?"

"Lacie, I think she did it," he sighed. "I think she tampered with that F-18's fuel line, fixed it so it would catch fire. She had the access and the know-how. She wasn't counting on the ejection seat jamming. That was a freak occurrence. She figured the plane would catch fire, the pilot would get out, and the plane would go down."

"But why?"

"That's what you have to find out. Maybe she really was crazy."

"Or?"

"Or, if there was this mystery man who *made her do it*, then you have yourself a hell of a big story, Lacie. This could be the big one you've been waiting for."

We talked a while longer, then said good-bye.

Max was wrong. The big story was coming right at me. It was hours away and it wasn't the story of Linda Severino or her husband or the unfortunate pilot.

It was my story. All mine.

I settled down to work at my computer, keeping my gloves in my lap, as I always do, so I could slip them quickly on if someone came in. I spent the rest of the day making calls, searching archives, typing bare-handed and bold, working the Severino piece into something exciting. I snaked my way through the Navy bureaucracy, wheedling information out of reluctant officials and precious soundbites out of Linda Severino's friends and family.

Linda Severino was everything Max had said and more. She was highly respected by the men she worked for and by the men who worked for her. She had dozens of friends, and very little family. Like me, she was an only child. Her mother was dead, but John Severino was still alive. The *Washington Post* archives were full of information about the former senator. As the old news stories scrolled across my screen, I shivered.

In the early seventies, the Senator's car slammed into a cement wall, leaving him paralyzed from the waist down and covered with third-degree burns over ninety percent of his body. After the accident, the public man turned private, cut off all contact, and dropped out of sight. I was unable to find a phone number for him, or even a mailing address. James Severino did not want to be found.

Linda must have loved her father deeply. Friends said she kept her maiden name out of pride. Jeff Hoag, I learned, was a pilot too, career Navy like Linda. My source at the Navy told me Hoag resigned two years earlier and flew commercial for American Airlines out of D.C. The job gave Hoag plenty of time off to take care of their baby girl while Linda was at sea. One of Hoag's friends told me Linda had promised her husband this mission was going to be the last. She was going to quit flying, stay at home, and be a full-time mom.

Jeff Hoag was my last and toughest call. I hated intruding on the privacy of grief.

Hoag agreed to talk to me. He sounded shell-shocked, but contained—until I probed him gently about Linda's wild self-accusation. Then he exploded.

"Goddamn all of you! Nobody understands! Linda was under a lot of pressure, but I swear to you on our child's life, my wife was competent. One hundred percent competent. She wasn't crazy, she wasn't depressed, and there's no way in hell she would've rigged that plane to go down. No way!"

"Then why do you think she said she did, Jeff? And why did she jump?"

"I don't know," he wept. "None of us will ever know."

That was the sound bite I needed. I thanked him softly and said good-bye.

Next, I pulled the stock footage I needed to make the story come to life: video of Linda proudly accepting a medal of honor at the White House, shots of a Nimitz class carrier, courtesy footage from PBS of the Bering Sea in winter, and newsreel clips of Linda fighting in Desert Storm. An able editor spliced them all together and, finally, I recorded my narration.

When the piece was done, I raced out of the editing bay to the news director's office and rapped on the glass partition. Harry Worth was hunched over his desk smoking, red-lettering a story, and shouting into the phone at the same time, fueled by his usual high-octane mix of nicotine and coffee. He waved me in with the cigarette and signaled for me to wait while he finished his phone call.

Harry Worth was a lion of a man dressed in a custom-cut navy blue suit, red silk suspenders, and shirt so white it glowed. Thick white hair swept back from his high forehead. His powerful face showed his sixty-odd years of age, but on Harry age looked good. Sharp brown eyes missed nothing, lips were full and sensual, and his voice was memorable with a resonant low timbre. He was long and lanky, but had a paunch even his thousand-dollar suits couldn't hide. He spent too much time in the newsroom and not enough time playing sports.

Harry Worth commanded respect. He was one of the most talented and highly paid men in the news business, with a long and renowned network career. I admired his newsman's instincts, his work ethic, honesty, and everything else about him. After six short months at WRC, I considered Harry Worth a friend, and knew the feeling was mutual.

He cut the phone call short, smacked the receiver down, and ground his cigarette out. "What is it, Wagner?" He knew by the look on my face I had a winner.

"Tonight's lead. A WRC exclusive."

When I finished telling the story, Harry rocked back in his chair and sucked on his cigarette.

"People jump for three reasons," he mused. "Guilt, insanity, or despair. Hoag claims his wife wasn't depressed or crazy enough to kill herself. He also claims she wasn't guilty because he says she wouldn't have sabotaged the plane. But one thing's clear. Her jump is directly related to that plane going down. What if she did rig the plane? The big question there is why? Why on earth would she have done such a thing?"

"Two possible answers, Harry. Hoag could be wrong. Maybe Linda's experiences in the Gulf War did leave her unbalanced. Maybe sending a plane down in flames was a strange kind of symbolic act to purge her tortured soul. A final act before leaving the military."

"Or?"

"Or, someone really made her do it. Either way, it's a big story and we've got it first."

Harry grinned. "You're a one-woman rescue squad, Lacie Wagner. You're my dream come true. Have I told you that lately?"

"Yesterday, Harry. You told me yesterday."

Harry had reason to be appreciative. He had been brought in to fix WRC's local news, which was losing in the ratings to everything in town, including *Leave It to Beaver* reruns. Harry's first move was to hire me. I took the job with two stipulations. My hands, even gloved, would never appear on camera. And, I did not want a co-anchor. I worked alone. In a town of Barbie and Ken anchor teams, the *WRC Evening News* was all mine. Six months and one huge promotional campaign later, we were in first place. As far as Harry was concerned, the credit for first place was all mine too.

He pushed a sheaf of ratings across the desk. "The numbers just keep getting stronger every day." He leaned back in his chair and beamed. "You've done a hell of a job."

"Under your guidance," I reminded him. "You built a new set, hired a new team of reporters, and put better stories on the air than the other stations."

"It's not the reporters or the stories," Harry insisted. "It's you. You have the face of a star, and that's what this town wants. A star. The camera loves you. You're all cheekbones and eyes. Hell, eyes make the anchor. They convey a world of wordless emotion to the audience. Sympathy, outrage, indignation, empathy, mirth. An anchor's eyes are more important than the voice. But you've got the eyes and the voice, and the ambition to make it all work."

I had ambition all right. Success was a way of proving that despite my disability, I was strong and able. I was a loner and Harry openly admired that. Outside of weekly dinners with Harry, I never socialized with the news staff. I knew they said I cared more about winning than being liked. They were right. After leaving Jerry, I moved stubbornly forward, staying focused on two things: my daughter and my career.

"You're network material," Harry was saying, shaking the ratings at me.

"From your lips to God's ears."

I turned to leave, then looked back at Harry. Something in his expression stopped me. The lion was gone. For an instant, he looked deflated. His shoulders sagged and his head appeared too big for his rangy frame.

"Harry? You want to talk about it?"

"Ego," he mumbled.

"What?"

"My fucking ego. Watching you reminds me of my youth, Wagner, when I was the star anchor, shaking things up the way you are. I love news and I love running the newsroom, but I've got to tell you I loved nothing more than being on air. Sometimes I just feel old when all I want to feel is young—to shake things up like I used to. Guess I should just be goddamn glad I'm alive, right?"

"Alive is good, Harry." I touched his big hand with my half-filled glove, then wound my way through the newsroom to my own office. I closed the door, shutting out the newsroom sounds I loved, the radio static, the shouting, the clack-clacking of faxes, the snapping of computer keyboards, doors whooshing in and out, phones ringing.

I sat not knowing that one day soon I would think: *Harry! Shake up nothing!*

Sometimes the shake can kill you.

The weekend producer rapped on the door and pointed at the clock. It was ten minutes to six. I was needed on the set.

I opened with the Severino story. When it was over, I spoke with deliberate intimacy about the pain of loss and the difficulty of learning to accept the unacceptable. I hinted that there would be more startling surprises and shocking revelations in the search for the truth about what happened to Linda Severino. The story was strong, meat in an otherwise soft newscast. Thirty minutes later, I closed: "Lacie Wagner, WRC-TV Action News, wishing you a good holiday and a very good night."

The hot studio lights faded as the floor crew drifted out. I sat in the semidark, thinking about Linda Severino, wondering what she was thinking when she took her flotation jacket off. I wondered how long it took her to die and if, at the last minute, she fought to stay alive. Everyone I had spoken to told me how courageous and fearless she was. I wondered if she was afraid when she jumped, and I tried to guess what her thoughts were in the final moments, in the false sweet euphoria hypothermia brings.

I thought of her husband's statement. How he described her troubled sleep as racked with recurring nightmares and whispering voices. Were the whispering voices ripe with threat? Did coal-stoked eyes burn bright in her sleep while wide wet lips promised flames and death and the stink of freshly burned flesh?

Were her nightmares like mine?

I stepped out the rear studio door and walked without my coat, into the frigid night.

It was pitch dark, as black as a deep dreamless sleep; the kind I never had.

Chapter Two

❦

I called both Jerry's numbers twice more Saturday night and again early on Sunday morning. I paced and worried and cursed, at the same time feeling silly for my reaction to the unanswered calls. Nowhere in the custody agreement did it stipulate that Jerry or Skyla had to check in with me during their time together.

The day crawled by. I tried to read the Sunday *Times* and couldn't. I tried to eat lunch. Food tasted like chalk. I watched the clock and the steady snow sifting down outside, and waited for Skyla to call. At three o'clock, I gave up and went to the station. I fiddled around with the Severino piece, planned my follow-up for the week, and made a few half-hearted phone calls trying to drum up a fresh story for the show, but there was not much news in Washington on any Sunday, let alone a holiday Sunday. The newscast was going to be a dull compilation of week-in-review clips, frothy feature reruns, and tired footage from the annual Presidential pardon of the White House Turkey. Congress was recessed and the Western world was basically at peace. I wished I were.

Hungry for company and dinner after the newscast, I called Max, hoping he would join me for a BLT and cole slaw at our favorite pub. His machine picked up and his rich baritone voice announced he was out of town. Cryptic as always. He could have been on his way anywhere, from the North Pole to Bolivia. Max traveled the globe. He was out of town more often than not, and most of that time was spent in remote places teaching Delta Force recruits survival and combat techniques in the earth's most inhospitable places. I loved Max like a father and missed him when he was gone.

I wandered out to the lobby and watched long twilight shadows falling across the snow-covered streets. Snowplows hummed in the distance. I felt aimless, out of balance, worried about Skyla. I went back to my office and looked at the pictures of us together, our faces so much alike with pale translucent skin, almost pearl white, and sky blue eyes. Unlike me, Skyla was born with silvery blond hair that had never darkened.

Ironically, my own long hair is the color of flame, a riotous red-gold that stands out against the black clothes I always wear. I am not comfortable wearing color. Red and yellow are the colors of fire. Embers are orange and scars are pink. Bright blues and vivid greens are loud, joyous colors. I am neither loud nor particularly joyous. I like the calm of black, the stark discipline of it. Black suits me well. Black is the color of fire when the flames are gone.

I don't wear much jewelry either. I am not comfortable with heavy gold chains swirling around my neck or fat pearls bobbing from my earlobes. I never wear bracelets stacked on my wrist, rings, or a watch, nothing at all that might call attention to my hands.

Once, I had a silver charm bracelet made up of all the planets in the solar system. It was a gift from my father and I wore it every day and every night until the crash. In the years that followed, I carried it in my pocket where I could slip my ruined hand around it and roll the round planets through my stiff fingers like a rosary. When Skyla turned ten, I took the bracelet out of my pocket and gave it to her. I liked to see her stroking the charms with her flaw-less lovely hands. Skyla was the one perfect thing I had done. I loved her with my life.

At five-thirty, I grabbed the telephone and dialed Jerry's apart-ment. He answered on the second ring. I didn't bother saying hello.

"Where were you?"

"Happy Thanksgiving to you too," Jerry said. "Cindy and I went to Vermont for a few days. We just walked in."

Cindy was his latest bimbo. Skyla's description, not mine.

"Cindy, *Skyla*, and you went to Vermont," I corrected.

Jerry hesitated. "No," he said warily, "Cindy and I went to Ver-mont. Skyla stayed here in the loft."

My back went rigid. "You left Skyla alone?"

"Sure," Jerry said guilelessly. "She has plenty of cash and my gold card. After all, she *is* thirteen years old."

"That's the point, Jerry."

"She's not a child."

"She is a child."

"I beg to differ."

"Then tell me where our *adult* daughter is?"

"She's got lots of friends in the city," Jerry said coolly. "I assume she's visiting one of them."

"You assume."

He sighed. "You're overprotective."

"Am I?" My voice was shrill and my pulse was racing. "Did you call Skyla while you were away?"

"As a matter of fact, yes. Twice a day."

"Did you actually speak to her?"

He paused. "I left messages on the machine."

"Did she call you back?"

"I didn't ask her to."

"So let me get this straight. The last time you saw or spoke to our daughter was Friday morning when you and *Cindy* left for Vermont."

"You're interrogating me."

"Goddamn right I am." I was shouting now, distraught and panicked.

"For Christ's sake, Lacie, calm down. Like I said, Cindy and I just walked in. It's only five-thirty. Skyla's probably out with her girlfriends, at the movies, eating popcorn, having a great time. She's a responsible young woman and very mature for her age. You've said so yourself. It was her choice and she said she wanted to stay in the city. Why not? New York's wonderful."

"When you have Daddy's gold card it is."

"What does that mean?"

"It means a gold card is not an acceptable replacement for supervision, Jerry. Neither of us has spoken to her for more than forty-eight hours. Do you realize that? Two full days! Don't you get it yet?" My voice was rising again, my throat constricting, and my stomach rocking. I was overprotective, but I knew New York was not a place for a girl like Skyla to wander around in alone. I picked up her picture. *She was so pretty it scared me.* I took a breath and went on. "What the hell kind of father are you? You left your daughter at home alone so you could go off and play in the goddamn snow with Candy."

"Her name is Cindy."

"And Jane, and Suzie, and Hillary, and Wendi. Different vintages, different names, same product. Thirty-six, twenty-four, thirty-six and dumb."

"I don't have to listen to you."

"No, but you'll have to look at me. I'll be on your doorstep in three hours." I slammed the phone down, aware of the sweat rolling down my back.

Jerry exasperated me. He enraged me. He always had. He was unpredictable, a control freak, insecure, and frighteningly ambitious. He could also be monstrously childish and irresponsible. I wondered what I had ever seen in him. It was a rhetorical question. I knew. I fell for him because he was older, dynamic, charismatic, and he made me laugh. More important, when he first saw my hands he didn't flinch.

Jerry was a brilliant trial lawyer and a master salesman, but he couldn't sell me on his theory. Skyla wasn't at a movie or with her friends or getting a pedicure or using Daddy's gold card. No matter what Jerry said, how he wheedled and whined, one fact was clear: Skyla had not communicated with either of us for more than forty-eight hours. And that meant she was in trouble.

I shrugged into my coat, tugged my gloves on, and stormed out into the newsroom.

Harry saw me through his glass door and poked his head out of his office. "Where are you going?"

"New York," I said, moving rapidly.

Harry hurried after me. "But you're on in twenty minutes."

"There's a problem with my daughter."

"I appreciate that, Wagner," he said, following me out the door. "But who the hell's going to anchor the news?"

"How about you, Harry?"

He started to reply, but I was already running down the walkway, hailing a passing cab.

"What about tomorrow?" he yelled.

"I'll call you from New York." I ducked into the cab and slammed the door. Sorry, Harry, I thought, glancing out the rear window at his thunderstruck face. I didn't know about tomorrow or the day after. I didn't know what New York had in store for me.

Thank God.

Chapter Three

The shuttle landed in New York late on an ice-slicked runway. I raced through the empty terminal with my one hastily packed overnight bag, jumped into a waiting cab, and gave the driver Jerry's address. Slumped against the cold vinyl, swiping my gloved hands across my tear-stained cheeks, I wondered if I was crazy. Was I over-reacting? Skyla was a smart, together young woman. Hard as it was for me to admit it, she was not a child. She may have been stuck somewhere in between, but the scale definitely tilted more toward woman than child.

She could survive three days in Manhattan nicely in a pricey apartment with a full refrigerator, cable TV, video on demand, and an address book full of friends. As the cab rolled through the Midtown Tunnel, I felt stupid and considered turning back, sparing myself an embarrassing confrontation with Jerry and his bimbo du jour.

The cab stopped for a light. I watched a young girl strut across the street, leopard miniskirt high on her bare thighs despite the snow, stiletto heels skittering on ice, fake rabbit stole clutched tightly around her teenage shoulders, and my anger and fear returned. New York wasn't Disneyland, and that wasn't even the point. How dare Jerry leave her alone on the holiday weekend, when she could have been with me. The whole purpose of the split holiday thing was to give her an equal sense of family. Well, fuck him and his private daughter-less celebration. I was a little bit crazy, a lot mad, totally irrational, and I didn't care.

Jerry's new loft was on the outskirts of SoHo, close enough to walk to the trendy galleries, yet far enough away to be considered a speculative buy. The building was a newly renovated hundred-year-old beauty. The renovation was first-class, but the old buildings around it were not yet done. Some were veiled in scaffolding. Others were just gutted shells. Jerry's was the only building lit and occupied. I paid the driver and got out. A liveried doorman escorted me in.

"Mr. Costello's expecting you."

The lobby was smartly done with polished wood and beveled mirrors. An art deco clock dominated one wall. One of the two elevators was open and waiting. I stepped in and let it whisk me up to ten, remembering Skyla telling me how there was only one loft on each floor. The elevator opened onto a softly lit entrance hall. I crossed it in two steps and rapped sharply on Jerry's designer door.

He answered, smiling sheepishly. A jolt of hope ran through me. I waited for his next words, the ones with which he would explain how Skyla had come home and how he had tried to call me. I waited for him to step aside and show me Skyla, grinning and bashful, full of apologies and hugs.

"Lacie," was all he said.

I pushed past him into the vast open living area. Ten-foot windows ringed the room. The Empire State Building glittered uptown in the distance, the twin towers of the World Trade Center sparkled downtown, much closer. The loft itself was magnificent. Natural wood floors gleamed. Two twelve-foot leather couches sat at opposite sides of a wide glass coffee table. An immense oriental rug squared out the living area. Rich oil paintings filled the walls. Jerry's taste had changed. The works were all surprisingly classic and obviously expensive.

Hidden speakers piped in a piano sonata. A graceful bar looked inviting with crystal decanters, fine wine bottles, and Baccarat glasses on display. Candles flickered in a dozen different places. I went around and blew them out.

I marched down a long wide hall, checking the rooms left and right, peering into an empty but splendid kitchen full of butcher block, marble, and copper pots. It had a breakfast nook big enough to seat a party of ten. Jerry's office was next, a sumptuous room with a huge mahogany desk, floor-to-ceiling bookshelves, and every kind of electronic wizardry. I checked Skyla's cheerful room, then the one nicely appointed guest suite, and finally the master bedroom, where I ran into the infamous Cindy. She was nineteen years old, bare-legged in a short black skirt suit, busily tossing shoes and socks into an overnight bag. Her suit was Armani. I wondered, viciously, who had paid for it.

"Hi," she squeaked, stealing a look at my gloved hands. "I was just leaving."

I followed her back to the living room and waited until she was out the door. Then I turned and looked at Jerry, comfortably elegant in black slacks and a red cashmere sweater. "Where's Skyla."

"She hasn't come home yet," Jerry said quietly, looking dwarfed by the enormous space around him.

"Then where is she?"

He shifted uneasily from side to side and tugged on the cuff of his sweater. "I don't know."

"It's your job to know." My knees felt weak. All the energy anger gave me suddenly left my body. I sank down onto one of the couches and put my head back. I felt the soft leather give as Jerry sat down next to me. His cologne was something spicy and good. He put a tentative hand on my shoulder.

"You look tired, Lace. I mean you look wonderful, but tired. Really tired."

"I am," I said in a dead voice. We had not seen each other in a long time. Three years, maybe more. A clock chimed somewhere. I counted ten bells.

"I wanted to call around to her friends," Jerry explained, "but I don't know where she keeps their numbers. Do you?"

"In her computer, where else?" How could anyone so smart be so dumb.

His hand dropped away. "I didn't think of that."

"Obviously."

I followed him down the hall to Skyla's room. She had a big IBM with all the bells and whistles. Skyla could program it in her sleep. It was her pride and joy. The screen-saver was set to a virtual fish tank. I touched the mouse and the fish disappeared. Her address book was easy to access, and straightforward. Jerry and I worked two phones and split the list.

Her best Manhattan friend, Dana, was my last call. "I talked to Sky on Friday morning," she explained. "She said her dad was going skiing with some new girlfriend Sky didn't really like. She said she was going to stay in the loft, watch reruns of the *X-Files*, and eat ice cream. She said she'd call me Saturday to go to a movie, but she never did. I figured she'd changed her mind and gone skiing after all."

I hung up and studied a fact sheet I had worked up. Jerry and

Cindy left the loft at seven o'clock Friday morning. Skyla's e-mail log listed two outgoing messages to me, time-stamped at nine and nine-thirty. The phone call to Dana followed at ten. Then, nothing— nothing but Jerry's voice and mine on his answering machine tape, rattling along as if Skyla were listening, thinking she would hear what we said. We had been talking to air.

"We have to call the police," I said.

"Lacie, it's midnight."

"That's the point."

"There's one thing we've overlooked. Skyla might have fallen in love. She might be out with some cute young guy. She expected me to be gone until tomorrow morning. I came back early because of the blizzard warning. Yes, that's it," Jerry said, standing, convincing himself, "she's in love. You'll see. Nine a.m. She'll show up, laughing at her fuddy-duddy old-timer parents. You'll see."

"Don't you have rules around here?" I hissed. "You find the thought of Skyla bed-hopping at thirteen years old *amusing*?"

Jerry shrugged. "It wouldn't amuse me. I'd try to talk her out of it. But kids grow up fast. I've always been more liberal than you, Lacie. And Skyla's a woman already. All you have to do is see the way men look at her to know that."

"Maybe that's what this is all about."

He eyed me, warily. "I'm not following you."

"Maybe you're uncomfortable around Skyla. Maybe you see her from a male point of view instead of a father's. Or, maybe you don't want her around because she reminds you too much of your ridiculously young girlfriends."

He punched the wall. "I'm a good father. You know that." His voice was hoarse, his face creased with anger. "But you just can't bring yourself to admit it. You've created some imaginary competition. In your game, there's only room for one good parent, not two, and the one good one is you. You can't see me as anything other than a great horned male monster you ran away from because I didn't live up to your *childish* expectations. And, I broke your heart."

He walked over and tipped my face up. "Tell me, Lacie. What do you see when you look at me now? A forked tail? Horns? Cloven hooves?" He dropped his hands, turned away. "The fact that I wasn't a good husband doesn't make me a bad father. I am a good man and a much better father," he said doggedly.

"It's easy to be good when it's part-time, Jerry."

He whirled around. "You wanted custody. I gave it to you. I would've kept Skyla with me, happily."

"Some life she would've had with you full-time. An endless parade of women running around in g-strings."

"Would that have been worse than the sterile, man-free zone you've got her in? If she's out bed-jumping at thirteen, maybe it's your fault. Maybe your *Keep All Men Out* policy had the opposite effect on her."

My shock, my hurt, must have been raw and visible on my face. Jerry took a step toward me. "I'm sorry," he said. "I had no right judging your personal life. I guess I never understood how much I hurt you with all my fooling around."

I stood up.

"Where are you going?" he asked.

"To the police."

"Stay." He quickly added: "We'll call Missing Persons from here. The guest room's made up. You'll be here when Skyla comes home. We both love her. Nothing can change that. Stay. It makes sense."

I didn't disagree with anything he said, and I was so tired. I sat down at Skyla's desk. "I don't want the guest room. I'll stay here."

He just nodded, his eyes bright with worry and something else. Something that reminded me of how he used to look at me when he loved me. When I loved him.

"You're too slim," he said, giving me a long intimate look. "You should put on some weight. But, Christ. I have to say you're more beautiful than ever. And, you've done so well. From small-town reporter to big-city star. I'm proud of you."

He spoke softly, and I thought I heard regret in his voice. I looked up at his eyes again, catching the last flicker of the old expression, the old love, then he shut down, crawled back inside of himself, straightened his back, smoothed his dark hair.

I turned to Skyla's computer and logged into my WRC mailbox, half hoping to find a message from her. There was one new message, sender unknown, from a place called the Cyber-Café.

"Do you know where she is, Lacie? Is she warm sitting by the fire? Is she watching the flames dance and dart? Is Skyla playing with matches, Lacie?"

I turned to call Jerry over, but he was standing behind me, reading those damning words, all the good mountain color draining out of his face.

"The police," I managed to say.

"I know the chief of detectives," Jerry said, reaching for the phone. "He'll send me his best men."

I sat on Skyla's bed while he made the calls, trying not to look at the damning words glowing on the computer screen. *Is Skyla playing with matches, Lacie?*

My daughter was everywhere around me and nowhere at the same time. Her desk was crammed with books—legal thrillers mixed in with solid classics. The four-poster queen-sized bed was rich-looking with expensive pale pink French sheets. As young as she was, Skyla had taste and style. She understood money. What it could buy. Where it could take you. And how it could protect you. Jerry taught her that. His own memory of poverty was never far away.

A vintage rocking chair sat bedside, filled with a heap of clothes. Skyla often tried on ten different outfits before deciding what to wear. I sifted through the Fair Isle sweaters, the cheerful wool cardigans, and the slim long slacks. Skyla was tall already like me and still growing. She hoped to reach six feet, play basketball, and be the tallest trial lawyer in the history of law. She wanted to follow in her father's footsteps, but wear a bigger shoe size. She towered over him already.

One of her violins was propped up in the corner next to a music stand filled with sheet music. Bach. Of course. Heavy drapes cloaked the windows. I pushed one aside and looked out at her view. Snow blew in circles, and I watched the wind play with an old newspaper page. I removed a glove and lay the palm of my hand against glass, so cold it burned.

Jerry wrapped up his call and hung up. He printed out the strange message and touched me lightly on the shoulder. "Missing Persons will be here soon. I'll make coffee. It's going to be a long night." He left me alone, in Skyla's room.

I opened her drawers, peeked in her closet, checked under her bed, and in her bathroom cabinets. There were no surprises. It was all the Skyla I knew. I lay down on her bed and stared up at the ceiling, at a poster of Brad Pitt. He grinned down at me, buff and happy. It made me smile.

I remembered Skyla as a newborn. The way her tiny feet, four inches in length, stuck out at right angles. How her tiny legs bunched up, knees pulled to chest from fetal memory, tiny baby fists crunched up tight, one stuck in her bow-tie mouth, the other moving in a dream reflex, swiping across her perfect cheek. I thought of her soft flannel nightshirt riding high, revealing her infant belly, round and pink, with a small pinch of umbilical cord still attached, browning and crusting, shriveling, preparing to fall off on the seventh day of her new free life outside of me.

Her damp silky hair lightened to a pale blond as the days passed, but her eyes never changed from the deep sky blue after which she was named. Now, looking at the cookie crumbs on the nightstand, the Wonder Bra tossed on the floor, the Sony Walkman on the pillow, I wondered, achingly, where in the world she was.

I thought of Polly Klass, Adam Smith, and all the stories of missing kids I had reported on over the years and felt afraid. The long vigils and searches that went on for years. Hope fading as days and nights went by. The heartbreaking Internet bulletin boards filled with cries for help: *Have you seen our son? Have you seen our daughter?* Five years old, eight years old, seven, thirteen, fifteen—an endless scrolling screen of school pictures neatly labeled with the date and time of disappearance. I thought of the agony of waiting. I thought of Skyla's face on flyers, milk cartons, grocery sacks, and on the evening news. *Have you seen this child?*

The strange e-mail message mocked me. *Where is Skyla, Lacie?*

I held my hands up and studied my palms. The lifelines were obliterated, burned away. My hands appeared portentous, foretelling the future, reminding me of the past, disrupting the present. I pictured Skyla's hands, how her lifeline was strong and deep and clear. Unbroken.

Jerry appeared at the door. "The police are here."

The chief of detectives sent over the head of the Missing Persons Unit, a sad-eyed lieutenant named Hodge. His light brown hair was wispy and shot through with gray, though his body was still youthful, rangy, and lean. The chief had clearly called Hodge at home and rousted him out of bed. He was unshaven and hastily dressed in a rumpled gray suit with a dark tie knotted wrong and mismatched socks.

He sat down on one of the living room sofas and flipped open a small black notebook. He spoke quietly, watching us closely, his green eyes bright with interest as we gave him times and dates. Jerry showed him the printout of the strange e-mail message. He leaned forward, nodding his head, chewing on his pencil as if this was what he had been waiting for.

"Anything significant in his reference to fire?" Hodge asked, not knowing.

I looked away, let Jerry explain.

"Lacie was injured badly in a fire, when she was a child. Her hands." Jerry let the rest of the sentence hang.

Hodge's eyes skated over my gloves. He nodded to himself again, made a note on that small smart pad.

"Are the words a threat?" Jerry asked. "A warning? Does he have her?"

"The message could mean something, or nothing at all," Hodge said. "There's no ransom request. No direct threat. That strikes me as strange. First thing we're going to do is put a tap and trace on your house lines here and your office too, Mr. Costello. If whoever sent this e-mail took Skyla, he might be letting time go by, letting you get good and worried before he surfaces with his ransom request."

"What if he doesn't use a phone?" Jerry asked. "What if he uses e-mail again, or sends a letter?"

"Let's cross that bridge when we get to it," Hodge said. "I've been working Missing Persons for twelve years. It's been my experience that most kidnappers have an overwhelming need to connect one-on-one with the parents. They're giddy with power and need to gloat. If a ransom request comes by letter, there's still a good chance the perp will make some personal contact with you. I want to be ready. I need your okay to order the tap and trace."

"Fine," Jerry agreed, handing Hodge the phone. "Get it started now."

Once Hodge had his tap and trace set, he studied the e-mail message again, then dialed information. There was one business listing in Manhattan under CYBER-CAFÉ. Hodge noted the address. He looked up at us. "This is a place where you rent Internet time by the hour. The Cyber-Café specializes in anonymous services. You can go there, rent computer time, write up as many e-mails as you want, and program them to go out any day and time you want. The day it was sent doesn't mean that's the day he was there. Do you know if your daughter went there? Was she into computers?"

His use of the past tense annoyed me, as if Hodge had already decided Skyla was dead. "She has her own," I said, emphasizing the present tense.

Hodge blinked. "I see."

Jerry had left the front door open. A team of five uniformed cops appeared and hovered on the threshold. Hodge waved them in.

"First part of the search team," Hodge explained. "They'll start with the loft."

"She's not here," Jerry argued. "That's why we called you."

"I understand. But it's procedure for us to look anyway." Hodge closed his notepad, tucked it in his jacket pocket, and addressed the cops. "Thirteen-year-old girl was staying here alone while father was out of town. Last time anyone talked to her was Friday morning. Her name is Skyla. Skyla Costello."

The cops nodded and spread out into the loft.

Hodge turned back to us. "Fifteen more patrolmen will report downstairs. That'll give us a search party of twenty. That's more than usual on account of the bad weather. If your girl's out there hurt somewhere, we want to get to her before the full force of the storm hits. Also, if there's been foul play, we want to be able to find evidence before the snow covers it up."

I glanced at Jerry, at the muscle working at his jawline, and knew he was as scared as I was.

Hodge went on. "When these cops here finish with your place, they'll work the building over, checking the fire stairs, the roof, and the basement. They'll do a door-to-door canvass of your neighbors, make sure no one's seen her, make sure no one acts suspicious. From there, they'll move outside, to the alleys and empty buildings around us. By then, the outdoor team will already be well into the neighborhood search, working block by block, checking cars, parking lots, trash bins."

I inhaled sharply.

Hodge paused. "I'm sorry, Ms. Wagner. That was insensitive of me." He turned to Jerry. "I could use recent pictures of Skyla. As many as you have. I'll post a detective at the Cyber-Café. He'll talk to all the regulars throughout the day and evening. See if anyone there recognizes Skyla's picture."

The patrolmen reappeared and waited at the door. Hodge stood. "I'll get these boys started in the building, then I'll pitch in and work the exterior area with my own car. Storm looks bad. We'll need all the help we can get."

The request was clear. Jerry rose. "I'll come with you. Just give me a minute to get you those pictures."

"Good. Ms. Wagner, you wait here by the phone in case there's some sort of contact. If there is, keep him talking as long as possible, then call my cell phone." He put his card on the table.

I nodded.

Jerry returned.

Hodge moved to the door. "Okay," he said. "Let's go."

With those two simple words, the search began. Hodge and Jerry and the silent uniformed men filed out.

I went to the window. Ten floors down, squad cars jammed the street. Two more units sailed in, roof lights spinning. A fleet of cops racing against the weather, looking for a shoe, a parka, something that might be hers, or even Skyla herself. They were searching trash bins and alleys expecting to find a dead body.

Wouldn't I know if Skyla was dead? Wouldn't I feel it? Didn't mothers have instincts like that?

It was now one o'clock in the morning and the snow was falling fast.

My thoughts drifted back to the day I met Jerry. I was eighteen and wondering what to do with my life. Both my parents were dead, I was terribly self-conscious and shy. Men terrified me. But Jerry fascinated me. He spotted me in a bookstore and hounded me until I agreed to join him for coffee.

He was fifteen years older than I was, short and barrel-chested, with a hawkish face, a great sweep of thick black hair, arched jet black brows, and a wide sensuous mouth. Jerry was not handsome but he was incredibly sexy. It was the spark in his eyes, the rogue smile, his take-charge style, and the steady warmth of his hand on my shoulder steering me along through the bookstore, and later through life.

Jerry was a slum kid who had made his own way. He had seen atrocious things growing up, and that day he boasted how there was nothing left that could shock him. I boldly took my gloves off and held my hands out. Jerry just shrugged and said: "You'll never play the piano. So what? There are players and listeners. Nothing wrong with being a listener." Then he folded his hands over mine and swore he would make me fall in love with him.

Three months later, we married, and for a long time I was content to let Jerry run our lives. It was really one life with two bodies. His life, our bodies. He wanted a traditional home life, and I tried to play the role, but he couldn't play husband to my wife. It wasn't that he didn't love me. He did. He just couldn't love *only* me. Jerry loved women. All women. The more the merrier. Jerry was addicted to women.

I didn't want to see the signs of trouble, but they were hard to miss. Late nights out, coming home at three or four in the morning, and sometimes not at all. Jerry tried to lie, tried to say the late nights were *work*. He was wily and careful about his exploits, but he wasn't careful enough. He came home too many times with damp hair at midnight, smelling of French soap that wasn't ours. And, he could never hide that tomcat look in his roaming eye. Deep down inside, I felt sure it was my fault. It was my hands. Who could blame him for wanting a whole woman?

One night when Skyla was a baby, Jerry came home at midnight with that telltale damp hair. I tipped over the edge.

I was in the kitchen, stacking dishes, and quietly getting drunk. Why? For all the spoken and unspoken reasons, all the written and unwritten reasons, which all together were nothing more than simple unhappiness. It wasn't just his affairs. I was unhappy with Jerry, with our life, or more accurately, *my life,* which did not really exist at all, swallowed up as I was in his. Getting drunk freed my rage. *Wake up, Lacie!* My drunken alter ego whispered. *He's fucking another woman*. I slammed a pot down.

"Lace?" Jerry called out from the living room. "Keep the noise down. What the hell are you doing in there?"

I threw a dish across the room and sang out in a cheery wifely way, "Sorry, Jer, more grease than usual." Or some dumb thing like that.

I stood in the kitchen crying, tossing vodka back in straight shots, and when the vodka was gone, I leaned against the sink, clenched my monster hands into little ferret fists, and made a decision. Enough is enough. I swept a stack of dishes off the counter. They shattered on the floor.

"Lace?" Jerry shouted. "What the hell was that? Are you destroying the kitchen or cleaning it?"

"Oh, nothing serious," I called out.

I heard the smart snap of his newspaper, then his pigskin shoe heels tapping up against the good lacquer of our new coffee table. "Lace, leave that stuff. Come on out and keep me company."

I turned the kitchen light out and drifted into the living room, where I kissed him on the lips and tasted another woman's sex. I sat on his lap anyway and played the adoring wife thing one last time, thinking of Skyla, of how I didn't want her to grow up with this as an example of what a woman was. Of what a man and woman were together. I could do better. I didn't know how, only that I could.

The next day, I packed and left, leaving a handwritten note that said: *Jerry, we're not good for each other, and that means we're not good for Skyla. You'll hear from my lawyer. Lacie.* No *Love, Lacie,* or *regrets,* or *thanks for the memories,* or *always yours,* or *never yours,* just *Lacie.* I didn't even sign it *Good-bye,* because in old English it means God Be With You. I hated Jerry so much for cheating on me that I didn't have the good human decency to want God to be with him at all. I didn't. I wanted God to be with me. I needed him more.

I took Skyla on a Greyhound bus and headed south into our new future. With my forehead pressed to the chilly bus window and my arm curled possessively around my child, I watched the highway rushing by and made silent promises to her that sounded more like promises to myself: "You will have a better life. You will learn to be your own woman. Strong-minded."

We would learn together, I thought, kissing her sleeping face.

"You will never be a victim," I promised her, not knowing it was the one promise I would not be able to keep.

At two o'clock in the morning, I was still standing at the cold living room window, wondering if time was racing Skyla toward death or away from it. Across the city, a tower clock glowed bright in the night. Was the secondhand sweeping her closer to death, or was she already stilled, silenced, and cold?

I thought of time, of all the clocks ticking, flapping, turning, spinning, clicking ahead, of the glow-in-the-dark bedside dials, alarms set, triggered, readied, of kitchen clocks and watches. I counted clocks in the loft. The VCR clock, the oven digital, the tiny computer clock, the round clocks, the square ones, the tall free-standing grandfather, the graceful art deco timepiece atop Jerry's fine fireplace mantle. I thought of the watches, Jerry's collection of antique classics all ticking away in his sock drawer, buzzing, hissing, sweeping me forward into time while my child, my sweet-faced daughter, was swept away from me into timeless death.

The tower clock hand ticked over to three o'clock and two hours later it ticked over to five. I pressed my lips to the frosted glass eye-to-eye with my own lonely face, and tapped five times with one bent finger. Five taps. One for each letter of her name.

S-K-L-Y-A. *Skyla, Skyla, Skyla. The five o'clock hour is ours.*

Are you out there watching the same white-faced clock, counting to five like me? Or are your eyes closed tight in fear, hands bound tightly behind your back. Or is it that you can't count. Can't see. Cannot even breathe.

Are you out there in the night, waiting for the sunrise?

Count to five, Skyla. Then to six. Then to six thousand. Keep counting. I am coming to find you. To save you. I will bring you into the world for the second time. I cannot—will not—accept your death. I cannot imagine you speechless and breathless and lifeless, cannot imagine you chilled and bent, your willow body jackknifed to fit into a newly dug hole, some shallow pit crudely cut into the winter earth. I cannot think of the damp December soil seeping into your ivory ears, crumbling between your bloodless lips, sifting down, filling the air pockets and the gaps between your stiff fingers where your hands spread wide to ward off the death blow. I cannot think of how your body curls into a brittle arc, an immobile fetal position, while the weight of grave dirt presses down.

Five, Skyla. Count to five. Then six. Then six thousand. I am going to find you before the frozen earth thaws and turns to mud.

Jerry shook me awake. The sky outside was light. The black hands on the tower clock marked seven sharp. I had fallen asleep, curled on the floor next to the window. My left leg was numb. My hands throbbed with the cold and my eyes scratched from the short two hours' sleep.

He shook his head no before I could ask the question.

Jerry guided me gently down the hall, one hand steady on my hips, the other firm on my shoulder, steering me back into Skyla's room. He slipped my shoes off and settled me fully dressed under her covers, stroking my forehead as if I were the child and not the mother, the wife, the former lover. He cupped my chin, kissed my forehead, then was gone, a black form moving down the hall away from me.

My skin tingled from the touch of his lips.

I looked over at Skyla's bedside clock. It was seven-thirty. I wondered if she was counting.

Chapter Four

❧

I awoke at eight-thirty to the sound of someone humming. I opened the bedroom door and found myself face-to-face with a huge black woman dressed in pink and carrying a breakfast tray. "Who in heaven's name are you?" she asked.

I was too old to be mistaken for one of Jerry's girlfriends. "Skyla's mother," I said, brushing sleep-tangled hair out of my face.

Her eyes grew wide when she saw my bare hands. "Tulah," she said with an island accent. "I am Tulah. Mr. Costello's house-keeper. I was bringing Skyla her breakfast. She's always up with the birds, fooling around with that computer of hers."

"She's not here."

"Oh." She looked at the tray and then at me. "You hungry?"

I was surprised to realize I was.

Tulah swept past me into the room.

"Skyla eats all that?" I asked, looking at the eggs, potatoes, buttered toast, and granola.

"I scare her into it. If you don't mind my saying so, she's too skinny. Now I see where she gets it from. You're a bony thing too." Her voice was kind. She wore her hair knotted up on top of her head. Despite the weight, her ebony face was finely chiseled with full lips and high, strong cheekbones.

She set the tray down next to Skyla's computer. "Where is the little lady?"

I told her as much as I knew, and asked when she had last seen Skyla.

"Mr. Costello gave me four days off for the holiday. Thursday through yesterday. I haven't seen Skyla since last Wednesday."

"Oh." It was all I could think of to say.

Tulah crossed herself, then backed out quietly and shut the door.

I used Skyla's computer to log into my WRC e-mail box. There was an angry note from Harry followed up with a contrite apology followed by an exuberant note telling me that the network ran my Severino piece on the national news. Harry was ecstatic. I wished I could share the feeling.

I called his private line at the station and got his answering machine. I left a long apologetic message giving him the phone number at Jerry's loft and telling him about Skyla. The spoken words sounded strange to me. It was the first time I had said them out loud. "Skyla is missing. My daughter is missing."

I ate breakfast watching the snow falling outside. Parked cars were invisible now, fully covered. A few hearty owners were trying to dig out, but the snow seemed to fall as fast as they could shovel.

I showered and dressed quickly. It was nine-thirty on Monday morning. Skyla had not come home. My hands ached.

Jerry slumped in his office chair, talking on the phone. Dark circles rimmed his eyes. He had not slept and I knew he had been crying. He hung up when I walked in.

"Who was that?" I asked.

"Hodge."

"He thinks she's been kidnapped."

"Good a guess as any. Frankly, he's surprised we haven't had some kind of call already. None of the hospital emergency rooms within a hundred-mile radius have Skyla or any unidentified girls who fit the description, so she wasn't in some freak accident. The search last night came up dry. Hodge sent a fresh team out this morning to search Central Park."

He tapped an unlit cigarette on the desk. Jerry remembered my fear of matches, flames, and even smoldering cigarette butts. It was the smoke. Smoke is smoke, and to me, all smoke smelled like death.

He swiveled around and looked out the window. "Mother Nature's not helping much. They're predicting three feet by nightfall. Hodge is doing his best, but he won't get much done today. I told him I'd handle the building staff here. We can talk to the doormen who worked from Friday to last night. There were five or six different guys rotating through the weekend. We'll get the names and home numbers and find out who saw Skyla last."

Six doormen. Six different kinds of memories. I knew from interviewing people for stories, memories are short. Imperfect. Easily muddled. Unreliable. Jerry knew that too. Criminal defense lawyers make their fortunes on the imperfection of memory.

"Your lobby has security surveillance cameras," I said.

"So?"

"They may not erase the surveillance tapes every day. If we go through the past three days, we'll see Skyla. We'll know exactly what time she left the building and if she was alone. We'll know how she was dressed too. The more information we give Hodge, the better chance we have he can help us."

He flashed me an admiring smile. "I see why you're a good reporter."

A half hour later, the building super was at the door handing Jerry a cardboard box full of videotapes.

"They're all labeled with masking tape," the super said. "We write the date and the hours of the day on each one. I keep them for a week as a rule, then erase them, tear the masking tape off, and start all over again. Six hours on each video, recorded on extended play. Hope you find something helpful."

Jerry carried the box into his office. "We'll start with Friday morning."

"My last e-mail from her was at ten o'clock."

Jerry found the tape marked with Friday's date and the hours 6:00 A.M. to Noon. He slipped it in the machine and used the remote to zip through on fast forward.

"There she is," I whispered.

She walked off the left-hand elevator, alone. Her hair was loose and full, falling around her shoulders, to her waist. She tossed it back and pulled a fake fur hat over her head. She stopped in front of the mirrored lobby wall, tugged the hat lower, and made a face at her own reflection. Jerry took careful notes as we inched through frame by frame, watching Skyla move through the lobby. The lobby clock on the wall read 11:03.

She wore blue jeans, a pair of black L.L. Bean knee-high snow boots, a bright pink alpine parka, and a long pink scarf. She stopped again to pull a pair of beige sheepskin gloves on while she chatted with the doorman. There was no sound on the tape. Her back was to the camera. We watched the doorman listening, and tried to guess what she was saying. Was she telling him her plans? Where she was going? Jerry noted the doorman's name. I hoped he had a good memory.

The doorman held the door wide for her and she skipped out into the snow, disappearing from view before we could see if she turned left or right. Left or right. In a city the size of Manhattan, left or right meant nothing at all.

We let the tape run on the chance Skyla went in and out several times over the weekend. Jerry and I sat side by side on his plush couch, waiting to see the face of our girl again. Families came and went, dozens of dogs were trotted out and back in again, Chinese food arrived, flowers, boxes, baskets, all arrived. Strollers, pizzas, the thousand different activities on a holiday weekend. We stopped at the last tape of Sunday night, when Jerry saw himself walking in with his arm around Cindy.

The screen went black. Jerry and I sat in the quiet. Tulah hummed somewhere down the hall. Jerry put his head in his hands. Looking at his curled defeated shoulders, the weight of his guilt, I felt tender toward him. As much as I tried to hate Jerry, I couldn't. He was Skyla's father. A small part of me would always love him.

My thumbs throbbed as they sometimes did, the stumps burned and itched.

"We have to talk to the doorman next," I said doggedly, as if I were tracking a story. "Then, we'll get this to Hodge."

Jerry nodded.

Tulah appeared at the door. "Mr. Costello? Mail's here. I got to go ahead and leave now. If I don't, I'll get stuck in the storm for sure." Tulah handed him the stack of mail. "This envelope on top's marked urgent. It's addressed to Miz Lacie." Tulah turned her big body around and ambled out.

Jerry gave me the envelope. My name was in black block letters across the front. It was not addressed to Mrs. Jerry Costello, but to Lacie Wagner c/o Costello. I stared at it dumbly. The postmark was stamped Saturday, New York City. I was sitting in the newsroom on Saturday. Who would have known I'd be here Monday? I hadn't even known that myself.

My hands were more unsteady than usual opening the envelope. Inside was a plain generic black VHS videotape, the kind available in drugstores, supermarkets, and video shops all around the country. The label was marked with the same black block lettering as the envelope. It said simply: FIRE.

My blood ran cold. I felt dizzy. The tape fell out of my hands. I began to shake uncontrollably. My stomach twisted.

"What is it?" Jerry asked, wrapping his arms around me, trying to calm me.

"Fire," I whispered, pointing to the label.

I had never seen Jerry afraid. Now, fear drained the blood from his face and his hands shook. He picked the tape up with a tissue, walked like a robot to the video machine, and dropped it in. He sat down next to me and punched the remote control. The tape deck lit up.

Black screen. The scratch of a match. The sound of someone breathing a cigarette to life. Orange glow of a cigarette tip, a small burning ember in a field of black.

A male voice whispered, *"Fire."*

The cigarette tip moved closer. It filled the screen.

The disembodied voice whispered again: *"Flame."* The whisper was scratchy. Hideous. *"Reach out and touch the fire, Lacie. Fire burns, doesn't it, Lacie?"*

Cut to a shot of a blue eye. A single blue eye wide open. Skyla's eye.

She blinked. Her eye darted left, then right. "What are you doing?" Skyla's voice. "Don't do that!" Her eye squeezed shut. She screamed. "Don't burn me! Please don't burn me!" The eye blinked a dozen times fast. Tears welled and spilled, her expression changed. Hysteria now, as she cried over and over: "Don't burn me. Please don't burn me. I don't want to die. I'm afraid. I don't want to burn."

The camera cut to a wide shot. It was night. I guessed the cameraman used car headlights to light the scene. Patches of white snow against dark wet earth. A small heap. A flicker of flame on the heap. The camera zoomed in. The heap was pink. A pink ski parka, hood pulled over covering the head. The body lay facedown. Arms tied behind the back. The fire started at the bare bootless feet and fed on jean denim, snaking up, to the pink parka, curling along the hemline, growing strong and fast. The flame became a bonfire, a human bonfire. Pink nylon melted, jeans shriveled back, the fire raged, eating Sky, burning Sky, charring and smoking my beautiful Sky.

My nightmare voice whispered. *"Skyla's burning, Lacie. Did you ever think Sky would burn?"*

I choked her name once, then fell mercifully into black.

There is a violence to birth—blood and searing pain and primal fear—but when I gave birth to Skyla, I refused all painkillers. The pain was sweet to me, I wanted every second of it.

Now, I couldn't bear the pain of witnessing Skyla's death or even the pain of knowing she was dead. I dropped into a dark soundless place and stayed there for three days and nights. I woke up once crying Skyla's name. Jerry sat on the bed next to me, staring at the floor.

"Tell me she's here," I said in my new hoarse voice.

He lifted his red-rimmed eyes, raw with grief, and looked at me. "We lost her."

I sank back into the black.

I drifted in and out of consciousness, dimly aware of Tulah's starched presence, her warm fleshy hands bathing me with a sponge, or holding my head while she forced me to swallow soup, water, orange juice. Uniformed policemen hovered outside my door. I heard Jerry's loud angry voice. Detectives wandered in and out, wanting to talk to me. Hodge was long gone. This was a homicide investigation now, run by a short sweaty detective named Martinez. He had a list of questions, but when he tried to ask them, I closed my eyes and shut him out, waiting for the blessed doctor, for the fistful of Valium and the deep black sleep that followed.

I woke in the night, in the dark, and felt Jerry sitting next to me on Skyla's bed. He stroked my wild knotted hair and whispered promises and assurances. *You're going to be okay.* How I wanted to believe him.

Skyla? Do you know how afraid I am now? Of living alone without you?

Alone. That's what I was without my daughter. I had been ready for many things in my life. I had been ready to fight, to work like a dog, to crawl and kick and inch my way up, but I wasn't ready to be alone. Not now. Not tomorrow. Not ever. I wasn't ready to live without Sky.

With Jerry there, I didn't feel alone. Even though I blamed him for what had happened, my grief was stronger than anger. I let him hold me. Our bodies were old friends after all, and like small frightened animals in winter needing warmth to ease the terrible chill, we clung to each other. I found comfort in the scratch of his unshaven cheek against my face and in the taste of his tears. We were held together by an unspeakable pain.

When I woke up again, Jerry was in a deep sleep. I watched the rise and fall of his chest as I used to watch Skyla when she was newly born. Back then, I was so scared something might happen to her. I lived in dread that I might drop her or not feed her enough. I was afraid I might accidentally drown her in the bathtub or find her smothered in her crib. I was certain that the second I turned away, she would fall out the window or over the balcony or dart in front of an oncoming car. Suddenly the whole world seemed treacherous. Every room in the apartment was a potential killing field. I was afraid some inadvertent stupid negligence of mine would result in her injury or worse.

I was afraid of accidentally killing her.

Now, my worst nightmare had happened: I had let Skyla out of my sight. I let her go, looked away for a split second, and in that second she died, as surely as if I had accidentally drowned her.

The grief was going to be a roller coaster ride for me. I knew that. My emotions were often that way, a problem I held tightly in check. It began after the accident. A swift and sudden rush from high to low, a pendulum swing from light to dark. The doctors agreed it was one more terrible side effect from the accident and that, like my nightmares, it was a psychological trauma that might or might not last a whole life long. From that point on I was carried helpless in the tick to tock, the side to side sway, the up and down roll of my unpredictable emotions.

There was only one period of time after the accident when my emotional swings and nightmares stopped all at once. It was, ironically, when I was pregnant with Skyla. In those nine perfect months, I lived in balance—not too happy, not too sad, no dark nightmares to shake me up. I felt nothing but the steady beating of two hearts in my one body, an invisible metronome, a measure of hope. I slept totally happily every night, with Jerry wrapped around me on the outside and my child growing on the inside.

I crept out of bed and went down the hall to Jerry's office. He was the quintessential nineties dad. Materialistic, media-mad, driven, divorced, caffeine-dependent, and he had his child's life documented on video. Every event was recorded and labeled: *Skyla's Fifth Birthday. Skyla's First Day on Skis.* Twenty tapes altogether, going all the way back to the moment she was born. Now he had a gruesome final entry to the video album. The perfect horrible bookend to the video of Skyla's bloody, bawling, kicking arrival into this world—her crying, kicking, flaming departure into the next.

I watched all the tapes that night, one after another, starting with her birth. The doctor heroically holding her up by her feet. My own face, dazed and ecstatic. The nurse handing me Skyla for the first time. I moved on, fast-forwarding through the rest of the tapes. Skyla zipped by, growing as I watched, laughing and dancing and playing the violin and running around in the frenzied fast-forward pace of a cartoon character. The sound zipped along too. It was a high-pitched gibberish, a parody, a comedy—until I dropped the last tape in.

I put it on slow motion and played it back frame by frame, sick from my own horrible need to see it again.

I watched Skyla being born. Now I watched her die. I watched Skyla burn.

Chapter Five

❦

They found her," Jerry said to me the next morning, which was three days after her murder, three days I spent delirious, three days lost to me forever.

I was sitting on the couch in his office. He was at his desk, staring at the phone, as if he had imagined the call. "Where?"

"In a box in an alley next to the First Precinct house."

The sky outside was the color of lead.

I shut my eyes. "How do they know it's her?"

"Her wallet was in the box."

"I want to see her."

"No, you don't."

"I have to see her." The natural human reaction to death is denial. The tape was not enough. Part of me believed it was a terrible joke, a compilation of clever special effects. I fantasized that Skyla was out there somewhere, alive. "I have to see her," I said again, looking at Jerry's stricken face.

"I won't let you."

"I'm the legal guardian. It's my right."

"There's nothing to see."

I knew what fire did. I saw what was left of my father when they pulled him from the flames. "I want to look at my daughter and say good-bye."

Jerry broke. "Dammit, Lacie. There's nothing to look at."

"I don't care."

"I do care." He dropped to his knees and shook me, looking hard at my face. His eyes were wild with shock and rage. "The fire wasn't enough, Lacie. He wasn't finished with her. He cut her up in pieces. He sent some of her to the station and kept some for himself."

I pushed Jerry back, not believing his lies. "You're just saying that to keep me away. I don't believe you. I have to see Skyla. I have to say good-bye."

The chief of detectives picked us up with his car and driver. He was a big man with a fleshy face and bear-brown hair he kept cropped short and tight to his head.

"Thank you, Garrett," Jerry said. "I appreciate your coming in person." Jerry was plugged into the city. He was a prominent citizen, a colorful public figure. The vicious murder of his daughter was an outrage. He got special treatment. "Garrett, this is Lacie Wagner. Skyla's mother."

"I'm sorry for your loss," the chief said, extending a damp meaty hand.

I was ungracious and ignored him. He shrugged and ducked into the front seat of the car. I ducked into the back, where I sat glaring at the rolls of fat on the back of his neck, wondering what this man could possibly know about my loss.

Jerry slipped in beside me.

I turned my head away from them both and blew a circle of steam on the window. "A wallet doesn't establish legal identity," I said to anyone who cared to listen. "Someone could have found Skyla's wallet, thrown it in the box."

"We found this with it, Ms. Wagner. Did this belong to Skyla too?"

Garrett reached over the seat back and dangled a plastic evidence bag. Inside, was the silver charm bracelet, all the planets in the solar system. It was streaked black in places from heat and flame.

I nodded once curtly, turned away, and watched the city sail by. The blizzard had stopped sometime during my three days of delirium. Streets were plowed down to a thin film of slush. Snow piled high to each side in six-foot banks was already gray from city dirt.

The M.E.'s office was uptown, housed in the same building as the city morgue. Our car eased to a stop in front of a grim brick building with the City of New York seal embossed in gold on a double glass door. Underneath were matching gold letters: CHIEF MEDICAL EXAMINER. Jerry sat next to me, silent and stiff.

Somehow the media had found out we were coming. Dozens of reporters and photographers were leaning against news vans, fiddling with equipment. When Garrett's car pulled up, they jumped. I was the big story now. My father, my hands, and now my daughter. The triple tragedy of Lacie Wagner. Some kind of karma. Cameras tracked us like one-eyed barracudas. Jerry hurried me up the walk.

"Mr. Costello!" reporters cried.

"Just leave us alone to grieve."

The Chief ushered us inside, through the lobby, and down to the M.E.'s office. It was a surprisingly cheerful space, with Broadway theater posters on the walls. I imagined the M.E. had to have it that way to keep from going crazy.

He was an older, kind-looking man named Feldstein. He came around from behind his desk, put his hand on my shoulder. "Ms. Wagner, I'm sorry for your loss."

Where did they learn that expression?

I wanted to turn away, but his gentle brown eyes held me.

"This viewing is unnecessary," he explained, patiently, as if to a child. "The remains are not in the kind of condition where a visual ID can be made. There's nothing to be gained by exposing yourself, by compounding your pain. We'll establish legal identity through a matriarchal DNA test. The matriarchal test is always conclusive. The patriarchal test is not. A specific strand of DNA is carried from generation to generation, mother to child. In females, the DNA is one unbroken line stretching as far back in time as we can find DNA to read. It's the way the Romanov children were identified. It's indisputable. One hundred percent accurate. I can take a sample from you today, here, and that will be the end of it."

The room was quiet, waiting for my answer.

"I'm sorry," I finally said. "I have to see my daughter first. I have to see for myself what he did to her. What that monster did to her."

The M.E.'s eyes shifted from me to Jerry and back again. "I work with death every day, Ms. Wagner. I understand your need to confront reality before you can let go. But you must trust me. This is beyond what any of us should ever have to confront, as a parent or otherwise. I'm pleading with you to reconsider."

I shook my head.

The M.E. dropped his hands. He turned to Jerry and shrugged. "She has the right."

"Like hell she does," Jerry warned. "I won't allow it."

The chief of detectives took Jerry by the shoulders. "Calm down. It's her choice. You can wait in here."

"No," Jerry said, brushing the chief away. "I'll go with her."

We followed the M.E. out of his office, down a long hall, and into a small glassed-in viewing room made for visits like ours. A heavy drape covered the observation window. Jerry stood behind me, close, touching my arms.

The chief tried one more time. "Please don't do this, Ms. Wagner."

My eyes bore into the drape, trying to see through it. "I have the right to see my daughter. I have the right to say good-bye."

The M.E. sighed heavily and looked from Jerry to the chief, then he pulled the drape aside.

Jerry stumbled back, away from the window, sagging against the wall, face in hands.

I moved forward, laid my gloved hands against the thick glass, and stared at the grisly image on the steel cart. I spoke to Skyla in my mind, as if she were alive.

I'm here, baby, thinking of the way you looked dressed in white chiffon, the fabric like you, pale and fragile and gossamer thin. You were five and dressed as an angel for Halloween, complete with delicate wings framed in wire. I can hear your laugh: Look, Mommy, look! I'm very beautiful, don't you think?

And you were. I scooped you up in my arms and held you tight. There wasn't much to hold. Fifty-two pounds of all my hopes and dreams and love stretched into your rail-thin body. Even though I tried to fill you with puddings and candies and pastas, you stayed light. You were light as the whisper of your breath on my cheek. There was something ethereal about you. I wanted you to be heavier, stronger, more durable—more like your father, less like me— but I guess I failed in that too. Even when you grew into a young woman, even then, with your height and your thirteen years, I was afraid to hug you too hard. I was afraid I'd break you in two.

But now I see someone else has done that to you intentionally. He sawed you in half, hacked off the top of you, the bottom of you, and the arms at your sides, leaving me only the middle. I'm standing here trying to find something in the charred chunk of torso, a sign that this is you, but there's nothing left in these blackened remains.

I can't touch your lips or your feather-soft skin. I can't hold your hand or touch your feet. I can't see the length of leg that made you tall. I can't hold you or cradle you in my arms or put my face next to your lips to be certain your breath has stopped. There's nothing here but the middle.

A somber voice said: "Ms. Wagner?"

My eyes were locked on the place where her neck ended and her head ought to have been. "Skyla?"

And it wasn't. It wasn't her. It couldn't have been her. It was a creature, a funerary totem, a nightmare in the middle of day. I was screaming now and pounding the observation window, scratching the glass with my useless gloved fingers, trying to reach her, and Jerry was screaming, *"Jesus, I told you not to allow this,"* and the chief was shouting back at him: *"I'm sorry, Mr. Costello, but she's the legal guardian and she has the right."*

"Like hell she does," Jerry cried, pulling my body away from the window, pushing my face around away from the glass, pressing it deep into the plush wool of his jacket, folding his strong hands over my ears, then carrying me out, out, out, away from the one butchered piece of Skyla left to me on this earth.

Chapter Six

Cremation.

It was a hard decision for me, but Jerry wanted it. He said it wasn't right burying Skyla, leaving her like that for all time. Jerry warned: "Every time we go to her grave, we'll be thinking about how just one piece of our little girl's down there, not the whole of her. It will sicken us. The grave will never give us peace or solace. So why have it."

Cremation.

The word frightened me. I knew about it—I knew every detail—the exact dimensions of the incinerator, the length of the sliding steel table inside, the precise temperature of the fire, the length of combustion, the order of physical destruction, how the flesh falls away from bone first, then how the bone marbles, cracks, pops, changes color, sifts down to ash, and finally, horribly, how the skull explodes. Skyla, ironically, would be spared that.

Cremation, Jerry insisted, was the only option. He handed me the brochure.

$240.00 for ages ten to adult. $150.00 for children one to ten. Infants free. Ash will be placed in a cardboard box unless the family purchases an urn. The cost of the urn . . .

I tossed the brochure back at him.

"We'll set her free, Lacie. We'll throw her to the wind and sea, and set her free from her terrible death. We'll go out to Montauk. I know a captain there, a priest with a boat who does this kind of thing."

I looked up into his sad intent eyes and nodded. He was right.

Jerry went down the hall to call the M.E.'s office to arrange for the release of Skyla's remains. I paced from window to window in the living room, listening to the quiet hum of him talking. Suddenly, he was shouting, pounding his fist on the desk. I walked into his office at the same time he was hanging up.

"Jerry? What's wrong?"

"The Park West funeral home showed up at the morgue last night to pick up a teenage girl who had been killed in a car wreck. Somehow the paperwork got mixed up, and they got Skyla's body instead. The M.E.'s office hadn't taken tissue and blood samples. Her remains were cremated early this morning."

"Therefore what."

"They want to send the ashes to a specialized lab for analysis. There's a small chance there's a bone fragment left that they can test for a DNA match to establish legal identity. But that will take time. Months. Even then, they may not be able to reach a conclusion. They won't give us her ashes until they do."

I absorbed his words, then leaned across the desk and touched his cheek. "I have never asked you for anything, Jerry. Never. Now I am. I want the last small dignity of giving her a Christian burial. I won't wait days or months or years to do it. Get her ashes. Call the mayor, the police commissioner, the governor, if you have to. I want to bury my daughter."

Jerry made the phone calls.

We had Skyla's ashes by the end of the day.

I awoke the next morning to the cry of gulls, and the sight of them dipping and milling over a satin sea. Jerry wanted me to stay with him, but I needed time alone, so I spent the night in an old hotel in Montauk, out at the eastern end of Long Island, a half hour's drive from Jerry's swank beach house.

My room had a huge window facing the beach. Thunderclouds hung low in the sky. The sea was quiet, ominously still, and I wondered how long the calm would last. Long enough, I hoped, for our mission. I wanted to be done with it—to bury Sky—to be free of Jerry and his long sideways looks full of pity and worry. I wanted to be alone, to tunnel into myself, to drift back to a time when I was free of pain, to a time when Skyla's laugh woke me—not the sad cry of seabirds cartwheeling over my daughter's ocean grave.

When I was showered and dressed, Jerry called. "Bad news, Lace. The captain says we have to wait for the storm to pass. Could be a few hours, could be all day."

"It's so calm now," I protested, knowing I had already lost.

"Proverbial calm before the storm," he quipped. "We can go

into town and get coffee, maybe even visit the lighthouse. The view is something."

I told him again, as nicely as I could, that I wanted to be alone.

"Okay," he said gracefully. "Whatever works for you."

I pulled an extra black sweater over my black turtleneck and black jeans, and set out. Roaming the deserted beach, I picked up a smooth length of driftwood and used it as a walking stick. I wandered far, to where there were no houses or hotels, just sand dunes and sea grass growing wild. Then I ambled down and walked the tide line.

From time to time, the surf cast objects out on the wet-packed sand. Soda cans, tires, baseball caps, and even an angry purple man-o'-war. I poked at it with the stick. His tentacles quivered, the angry purple-blue sac pulsed. I imagined how it would feel to be attacked by a man-o'-war in the water, the hundred stinging tentacles burning my face.

Furious that there were things that could burn even in water, I pierced the purple membrane with my driftwood stick. The purple sac collapsed. I jabbed it over and over again until the jelly inside had all oozed out. I stepped over it and walked on down the beach with the wind hard in my face. The satin sea was gone. The storm had arrived, kicking the sea into a white-capped froth.

I walked recklessly in the shallows, not caring that my pant legs were soaked and stuck to my ankles, or that my hair was wet. When the first fork of lightning split the sky, I was glad. The rain washed down, fat hard drops slung at me sideways by the gale force wind. It was dark as night and I was glad that God was crying for Skyla.

Eastern thunderstorms either blow themselves out quickly or linger for days. This one swirled, cracked, and blew, but by two o'clock the rain was a soft sweet patter and the wind had calmed to a breeze. By three o'clock, the sea was satin again and the rain had stopped.

I returned to the hotel, showered and dressed for the second time, then walked down to the harbor, to the boat. Jerry was already on board, drinking a root beer and talking easily with the captain. Jerry saw me and stood up. He was impeccably dressed in elegant dark wool pants, shiny calfskin loafers, a dress shirt and tie, and had a thick dark cashmere sweater tied easily around his shoulders. He helped me on deck and steered me over to the captain.

The captain was a startling man, strong-jawed and handsome. Thick silver hair curled around his tan face. He had a brilliant smile and the powerful body of an outdoorsman. Too handsome for a priest, I thought shyly, taking in the clerical collar he wore with his black cable sweater. He wore old faded jeans and beat-up sneakers. Despite Jerry's expensive clothes, he looked the poorer of the two men. The captain's eyes were rich with belief. Jerry's were hollow, emptied by grief.

The captain folded his hands over my gloves in a gesture of sympathy. He had the good taste to skip the bromides. "Folks call me Captain or Father. I'll leave it to you."

"God and I are at odds now, so you'll understand if I just call you Captain."

His green eyes bore into mine. "I understand. There's hot coffee below. Help yourself."

I did. His coffee was good. I lingered in the small galley, stirring sugar into my cup while I studied the smart, tight lower-deck quarters. Captain had clearly spent time in the military. The bed was tightly made and the gear neatly stowed. It was a tiny space arranged with jigsaw-puzzle perfection.

A bookcase was filled with religious books, bibles of many sizes, and plenty of philosophy. Posters filled the walls: grinning porpoises, cartoon-lipped blowfish, ribbon-bodied black eels twisting in the current, carnival-striped parrot fish schooling along. Captain's sea was a peaceful place. A good place for Skyla.

I rinsed my cup and wandered up to the deck. We had motored out of the harbor and were hitting the first choppy swells of open sea. The town behind us was shrinking by the minute, the rolling sea in front of us was still gray and stirred up from the storm, but the sky was clear. I hooked my arms around the rail and widened my stance, enjoying the tilt and sway of the boat, the good sound of the motor working, and the feel of ocean spray on my cheeks.

Jerry sat at the prow with the urn cradled in his arms. He had put his sweater on against the ocean chill. Captain stood straight and tall at the wheel, checking his instruments, squinting at the sky. He looked over at me. His eyes were bright with love. For an instant, I felt his faith and smiled.

Forty-five minutes later, when the shore was just a featureless stretch of sand, Captain cut the engine and let us drift. In the sudden quiet, I heard new sounds—old boat wood creaking, flags snapping in the wind, boat belly groaning, and water slapping against the prow. It seemed right, marking her end like this, returning her to the very beginning, to the sea. The sky had turned a brilliant blue, as startling as the color of Skyla's eyes. This was a good place for me to say good-bye.

Captain was suddenly next to me, offering a lush bouquet of red roses. Jerry appeared at the rail. Captain pulled a small dog-eared black bound bible out of his coat pocket. He opened to a marked page and began to speak.

I closed my eyes, let his voice fill me. It was deep and steady, a full-throated rumble. He read slowly and clearly. I glanced at him once and saw his own eyes were closed. The bible was limp in his hands. He recited from memory. A gold cross glinted at his collar.

"We return Skyla to the elements and to the God that granted us the gift of her life, however brief it was, a gift so splendid and bright, we are blinded and humbled and forever marked by her. Her music was the music of angels and it will play for eternity."

Captain touched my elbow lightly. I dropped the roses overboard. Jerry looked at Captain, seeking approval and confirmation that it was time. Captain nodded slightly. Jerry opened the urn and leaned out over the rail. He hesitated long enough for me to notice. Then, he tipped the urn and Skyla's ashes poured out.

One pound of powdered ash, grayish in color, the consistency of silt. My hope, my dreams, my strength, my child, reduced to one powdery pound. I hated her killer most then, watching the ashes spread. I hated him for leaving me one pound instead of two, for cheating me out of burying my daughter whole. I hated him for leaving me to wonder where in the world the rest of her was.

Her eyes, her full cheeks, her hair and legs, long like mine. Her splendid hands, ten perfect fingers, nimble enough to make music from a violin, strong enough to hold me tight. Where was the rest of her? The question remained unanswered.

Jerry went on pouring.

A sudden winter wind came in from the west, blowing the ashes back at us. Some caught in my hair, touched my lips, settled on my shoulders. Jerry shook the urn, until it was empty. Then, he simply dropped it into the water and let it disappear.

Captain let the boat drift a long while. We watched the ashes fan out, earth staining sea. Sometime later, the engine kicked over. The boat swung slowly around and headed for shore. I stayed at the rail facing open sea as we motored away, watching the drifting ash stain.

Jerry appeared next to me. "Lace, do you ever think we should try again?"

"Try what?"

"Us. Maybe we've both proven everything we need to. Maybe we would be good together now. We could help each other. We could start over. I love you so much."

His eyes were so sincere. Skyla's death had changed him. Grief ravaged Jerry, gave him a new solemnity.

"Lace?" he prompted softly.

I was tempted. Jerry was that way. He made me feel like I was the only woman in the world. He made me feel protected. As much as I wanted protection now, I knew Jerry was wrong. We couldn't start over. We could only move on.

I kissed him gently on the cheek. "You've got it all backward. You want me as a way to hang on to Skyla. You don't understand. She was the link that connected us. Without her . . ."

"I see," he said, even though he didn't. "I misinterpreted the other night. So then. Where are you going from here?"

I shrugged. "I'm not ready to go back to Washington. I may stay in New York until I sort myself out."

"Take the loft. Stay as long as you want. Tulah's off for a few weeks. If you want her to come back sooner, all you have to do is call. I'm staying out here. I've got a lot of thinking to do." He ran his hands through his hair. "Jesus. I've got to rethink my whole life. I can't go back to work. I can't defend anyone. I've lost faith in the oath I took, in the fact that everyone deserves a fair trial. I'm not thinking clearly, or maybe it's that after all these years I'm finally thinking clearly. I don't know which. I need time. Goddammit, I need a lot of time."

I put my arms around him. He deserved that one small comfort.

"Can I drive you back to the city?" he asked.

"No. The hotel manager's taking me in tonight."

"Okay then." He hooked a stray strand of hair behind my ear. "Okay. Our girl is gone, Lacie. Our girl is gone. There's nothing left to say."

He turned away on his small dapper feet, good gabardine slacks snapping in the wind, cashmere sweater clinging to the soft flesh handles at his waist. Jerry turned back once, flashed me one quick smile full of regret, then he was moving across the narrow walkway and onto the pier. He shoved his hands in his pockets and headed for his white Mercedes. The afternoon shadows fell long, the first chill of night blew in off the sea. I turned away and listened to the thunk of a car door slamming, the jump of the big German engine, the crunch of gravel as he pulled away, then to silence when he was gone.

I returned to the city late that night and holed up in Jerry's loft, not bothering to check my e-mail or my voice-mail or respond to any one of the dozens of condolence letters the doorman handed me when I walked in. Instead, I crawled into myself, wondering when I would feel like living again.

Time compressed. A day ran by like an hour. I let it run. The first day became the second, the second quickly the third, then suddenly it was the tenth, followed by the eleventh. Hours and minutes slammed into one another, days were ivory on an abacus. Telephone messages reeled in and I just let the machine blink while the digital number ticked up hourly. Fifteen messages, eighteen, twenty-nine, thirty-two, and then the little micro-sized tape snapped and the whirring of the empty tape heads drove me mad. I jerked the plug out of the wall and threw the answering machine against the floor.

On the fifteenth day, someone appeared in the bedroom doorway. I stirred from a heavy dreamless sleep, eyes unfocused, wondering who it was. The shades in Skyla's room were pulled down tight and I had no idea if it was day or night, morning or evening. The figure stepped across the room and jerked a window shade. It snapped up. Sunlight streamed in.

It was Tulah, bigger and blacker than I remembered her, in a spotless white starched dress. Her bosom was huge, her arms heavy, her waist barely discernible in the round rolling mass of her body. She looked me over and shook her head.

"You are a sorry sight," she admonished, shocked and repulsed by the mess I had made of Skyla's room. Cracker boxes littered the bed, mugs of stale coffee were stacked five high on the rocking chair, and empty wine bottles left wet rings on good wood. The bed was covered with empty tranquilizer bottles and clothes were wadded up on the floor. The air was stuffy and ripe with the smell of careless living.

Tulah folded her round arms across her breast. "Miss Lacie," she thundered. "Shame on you."

I pulled my knees to my chest and rubbed my sleep-crusted eyes. My stomach rocked from too much wine and not enough food, my head pounded from the sedatives.

Tulah scooped me up in her able arms and carried me into the bathroom. She set me down on cold porcelain and twisted the faucets on high, testing the water with caring hands, somehow knowing I couldn't take things too hot. When the tub was full, she rubbed me down with a washcloth, scrubbing behind my neck, under my arms, the bottoms of my dirty feet, behind my ears, then she worked a fistful of shampoo into my scalp.

She dunked me twice, rinsed my head in a stream of fresh cold water, pulled the drain, and lifted me out. I let her wrap me in a full-size pink bath sheet, one with Skyla's own initials. She rubbed my head and back, wrapped me in a robe, and steered me into Skyla's vintage rocker. She came back five minutes later with four pieces of buttered toast, and watched over me to make sure I ate.

Then she started to clean. She was a black dervish pushing the vacuum with a fanatic's precision. When she finished, she went around collecting cups, crusted plates, empty wine bottles and carted them away. She was back in no time, stripping the bed, changing the sheets, plumping the pillows. She opened windows, ordered in groceries, and made me a ham and cheese on rye. Finally she unpacked my suitcase, ironed my wrinkled clothes, and hung them carefully in the closet. My long black slacks, black shirts and sweaters looked sad next to Skyla's brightly colored clothes. I felt sorry for myself all over again.

Tulah folded the fresh bedsheets down and pointed. "Get in."

I did.

She pulled the top sheet up and tucked it tight around my shoulders. Then she gathered her coat, hitched her purse strap over her broad shoulder, and wagged a finger at me. "It's time to pull yourself together, Miss Lacie. It's time to move on, let the grief go some."

"What the hell do you know about grief?"

"Plenty," she said in a voice so sad it shut me up. "Plenty."

Her purse slid off her shoulder. She set it down and sat on the bed next to me. "I lost my two boys. It was a long time ago. The hurt's always with me, always fresh, but I'm living and they're not.

You're living, and for whatever God's reason, Skyla's not. I can't tell you about God's ways, about why things happen that seem unjust. But I do know plenty about surviving, Miss Lacie. I been there, trying to lose my hurt in bottles cheaper than your fine French wines, but no less effective. I know all the wine and the pills in the world won't make the hurt go away. You just got to get up and learn to live with it. Get on with your life. You can miss her, you can hurt for her, but you got to live. It's time to move on."

"I can't," I said in a small strained voice. "I can't."

She reached for me and I let her. I found comfort in her full island arms, listening to her rich voice sing Trinidad lullabies. I cried until I cried myself out. Then, I slept.

When I woke, she was gone. The sky outside was dark. I stumbled out of bed, went barefoot down the hall to Jerry's office. He had given the original tape of Skyla's murder to the police, but made a copy for himself. I was glad now he had.

I dropped the tape in and watched, mesmerized by the frightful images of my daughter's death—the screaming, the tears, the hysteria of knowing what was coming next, the panting, the wrestling, the heaving breaths, then the eyes—sky blue after which we named her—*Skyla with the sky blue eyes*—those eyes widening in horror, squeezing shut in denial, the beautiful blond head shaking *no-no-no*, and the full peach lips begging for her life, then her eyes widening in a new horror, focusing on the instrument of her impending death, and finally, the burning. I watched the flame catch on pink parka nylon, and I listened to the voice.

Sky is burning.

The whisper.

The ragged hoarse whisper.

Reach out and touch the flame, Lacie.

The ragged hoarse whisper on the tape.

Sky is burning.

The ragged hoarse whisper of my nightmare voice.

Reach out and touch the flame, Lacie.

Sky is burning.

My grief shifted and turned to rage.

I walked to the window and looked out at the great sweeping view of the city. The Empire State Building, the neat grid of streets, the rivers flanking Manhattan, frozen now with ice. I pulled my robe tight. Night washed out in the first light of day. He was out there, with his hoarse whisper and his murdering heart. He was out there with his cold calculating mind and his clever ways. He knew my name, my addresses, my face, and my hands. His tape was a grizzly performance, the continuation of a dialogue begun in sleep.

My sleep.

This was not a random killing, a chance encounter, or plain bad luck.

I recognized the voice. It was the raw ragged whisper I heard in my dreams. It was the voice of my nightmare face.

Now, I knew the nightmare was real, the face was flesh and blood. Thick lips, limpid eyes, thin copper hair hanging dull and flat to his skull. The sour sick smell of his breath as he whispered to me, filling my head with his words—*Lacie, touch the flame, reach out and touch the fire. Sky is burning.* The same whisper. The same man.

I curled my deformed fingers and smacked my fists against the glass.

"Goddamn you," I whispered, staring out into the cold winter dawn. "God fucking damn you."

If I could find the voice, I would find the man who killed Skyla and the man who haunted my dreams. They were one and the same, and I knew somehow he was the key to me.

Chapter Seven

❦

I showered and then fixed myself breakfast for the first time in fifteen days. Food tasted good. I was ravenous, starved, and now I needed all my strength. I ate eggs and bacon, buttered toast with jam, sweet crunchy granola, and a jelly doughnut. I went into Jerry's office and sat at the desk. A business card was propped up against the telephone: *Detective Dan Martinez, NYPD, First Precinct, 10 Elizabeth Street, New York, New York, 10004.* There was a phone number too, but I didn't bother to call. I put my coat and gloves on and left the loft.

Striding through the lobby and out the doors, my head felt clear. My daughter was dead, but my maternal instinct was alive and kicking. With Daniel Martinez's help, I planned on finding her killer. *And then what? Would the full weight of justice be justice enough?* I pushed the question out of my mind, stepped off the sidewalk and hailed a cab.

I had been in police stations hundreds of times, but always as a reporter. Now, swinging through the double doors of the First Precinct house, I was a citizen and a victim. Inside, telephones rang, hand radios buzzed, uniformed cops milled in and out of the station. A plastic Christmas tree leaned in the corner. The paper angels and red glass balls made me sad.

I flashed Martinez's card at the desk sergeant. He nodded and pointed.

"Up two flights then turn right. You'll see the door marked Homicide."

A pair of cops wrestled a handcuffed junkie up the stairs behind me.

"You going to get at least ten this time, Humper," one of the cops shouted.

"I want my lawyer," the junkie called Humper shouted back.

"Lawyer ain't going to help you, Hump. Only God can help you now."

I ducked into the Homicide squad room and flashed Martinez's card at the receptionist. She had the telephone in one hand and an unlit cigarette in the other. She squinted at the card, pointed to a hefty man across the room, and mouthed the words, "That's him."

He looked familiar, then I remembered him as one of the three detectives who hung around Jerry's loft waiting to talk to me when Skyla was found.

He recognized me too. He stood up and stuck a hand out in greeting. I ignored it. "Mind if I sit?" I asked, to deflect the unwanted handshake.

"Sure thing," Martinez said, sinking back into a squeaky rolling chair. "So you finally woke up." His attempt at a joke fell flat. I let him squirm. "I mean, we was waiting around for you, but finally I just left a card and told Mr. Costello to have you call us. You waited quite some time, Mrs. Costello."

"Wagner. My name is Ms. Wagner. Mr. Costello is my ex-husband. I didn't keep the name."

"Sorry. Jerry Costello, Skyla Costello. I just assumed, that's all. No offense meant."

"None taken." I smiled brightly to make up for my sharp manner. I wanted Martinez on my side, even though I didn't like him. His hands were pale and chubby. He had one thick index finger stuffed into a fat gold high school ring and the other index finger shoved into a skimpy gold wedding band. Fluid retention could puff fingers up sausage-thick, and daily heavy drinking was probably the cause for Martinez's retention problem. He was a young man, in his late thirties, but he was going downhill fast.

His breath smelled of tuna fish even though it was ten in the morning, his hair glistened with an oily patina, and he wore dime store musk. The combined effect was wholly unpleasant. I wondered how Mrs. Martinez suffered his embraces. A framed snapshot had center stage, next to the nameplate, right within my reach. A fat baby, dressed head to toe in powder blue, grinning at the camera.

Martinez sneezed and buried his nose in a well-used Kleenex. He honked twice, then smiled sheepishly and stuffed the shredded tissue in his shirt pocket. "I have a G-D cold. My kid gave it to me."

"I'm here to talk about the case."

The sheepish grin vanished, he was all business. "Ms. Wagner, I'm afraid there's not much to talk about. First, on behalf of the Department, I'm sorry for your loss."

That again.

"Next, allow me to assure you that your daughter's murder has been the number one priority around here."

"Your use of the past tense makes me nervous, Detective Martinez. *Has been* the number one priority?"

"Yes, ma'am." He began to work the class ring, twisting it right, then left, then right again. "You see, three weeks have gone by since your daughter was killed. The more time that passes, the less likely our chances of getting the perp."

"The perp."

"The whacko who killed her. That perp. Anyway, the thing is, we don't have a lead. He just snatched her up somehow, took her off somewhere, and killed her. We've been upside down and inside out of Mr. Costello's business as well as your own, looking for someone with a reason for doing this. Other than a few of the usual petty gripes folks get against each other, nothing shook loose. Nothing that could point to a motive for murder, anyways. To make matters worse, we don't have a witness, a weapon, or any other thing to help us out."

"What are you trying to tell me?"

He got a wide-eyed aw-shucks look on his face. "I guess what I'm saying is, the case is pretty much closed." He squirmed again. "As far as an ongoing investigation goes, that is."

"Closed."

"Well, not officially. Not legally. It's open until such a time as we apprehend the perp."

"Her killer."

"Yeah, same difference."

"No, it's not, Detective Martinez. There's a subtle semantic difference I wouldn't expect you to appreciate."

He scratched his throat, gave a nervous cough.

"How many murder cases would you say you work each year, Detective?"

"Wait a minute now . . ."

"How many of those cases involve minors, children under the age of eighteen?"

"Ms. Wagner . . ."

"Who is it around here who decides when a case is closed? You? Your supervisor? All of you together?"

"Now, just hold on here. You're talking to me like a G-D reporter." His eyes went skinny with suspicion. "Is this an interview? 'Cause what I tell you isn't for TV or any other G-D press thing. I was talking to you straight. Cop to parent. And here you are stirring it up like a story."

"It is a story, Martinez. It's my story. My daughter. I want you to find her killer."

"Well, now, I told you we're real sorry about what happened, and we've done our best, but I'm not God! I can't just snap my fingers and make the perp appear! I need information, clues, leads, witnesses. I got shit. What else can I say? This is going to be one of those cases that just don't get solved. Not unless there's a miracle, or not unless the perp hits again with the same MO and we get him. Until then, this case is going nowhere. I'm shooting straight with you. Better to know the truth than to walk around full of false hope."

I grabbed the framed picture of his son and leaned across the desk. "Turn the tables. A psycho snatches your son and sends him back to you a week later chopped into pieces and burned to a crisp. What do you do, Martinez? Do you spoon-feed your wife bromides? Do you reel off statistics while she weeps in the dark? Your son is in a dozen pieces and some of them the *perp* didn't even bother to send back to you. What do you do, Martinez? What do you do?"

He slammed a meaty fist down on the metal desktop. "I'd find the bastard and kill him."

"We finally agree on something." I dropped the baby picture, stood up, and walked away.

When the intent of my words seeped through Martinez's dullard brain, he rolled through the squad room after me. "Ms. Costello!"

"Wagner," I shouted back at him. "My name is Wagner."

He stopped me at the top of the stairwell. I heard the junkie called Humper screaming somewhere down the way.

Martinez's eyes bulged. His bloated face was flushed. "You leave the police work to us."

"Well now, that's a real problem, isn't it? The detective in charge of the case just told me the *police* have no reason to continue an active investigation. My daughter is dead. That's reason enough for me."

"Ms. Wagner," he shouted, "we don't advocate vigilante justice!"

I was long gone, moving down the stairs, out the door, and across the street. I looked back at the station house, at the cop cars parked at odd angles, the uniformed cops rushing in and out. "My daughter is dead," I said out loud, to the air.

Finding her killer was up to me.

I went back to the loft determined to learn all I could about her last days in New York.

She kept a calendar and schedule in her computer. I clicked into them and started to read. Skyla recorded all her activities meticulously. Her violin lessons, what pieces were played, where she went for dinner, what she ate, what movies she saw, which books she read. She once told me it was her way of hanging on to experiences so she wouldn't forget.

The NYPD had already gone through her computer looking for a line to follow. And, just like the NYPD, I struck out. Skyla had marked the Friday, Saturday, and Sunday following Thanksgiving with big bold type: TO VERMONT TO SKI WITH DAD. And Monday afternoon was marked with the same bold type: FOUR P.M. SHUTTLE BACK HOME TO WASHINGTON.

If Skyla had changed her plans, she would have marked the calendar. My brain felt sluggish. The oversight didn't fit. It wasn't Skyla's way. Finally, unable to figure it out, I closed out of the calendar and went on-line to check my WRC e-mail box for the first time since Skyla was found.

The list was long. A hundred and five messages scrolled down the screen. Many were from colleagues in the news business, anchors and reporters scattered across the fifty states, most of whom I had never met. The outpouring of sympathy moved me.

Harry had been sending daily e-mails. They were all short notes filled with kind words. He wanted me to take as much time as I needed, and to know my job was waiting whenever I was ready to go back. Max had given up trying to call. He sent through five e-mails in bold block letters, urging me to contact him. I felt badly about the selfishness of my mourning. Max had loved Skyla too.

I wrote a long reply and sent it out into cyber-space knowing it would get to him wherever he was, then went back to sifting through messages. There were five from Linda Severino's husband,

Jeff Hoag. He said he was anxious to talk to me in person about his wife. There were things that I should know. I copied down his address and phone, put him at the top of my call sheet, and continued scrolling through my messages, acknowledging each one, thanking people for their kindness.

Max called in the middle of my work. Skyla's computer was equipped with a C-Phone. Max had one too now, wherever he was. It enabled us to carry on a telephone conversation and see each other on the computer screen. The resolution wasn't great, but Max's face looked good to me.

"Holy Christ, Lacie, I've been worried about you." His great bushy brows scrunched together. His hazel eyes were dark with sadness.

"Me too, Max."

"From what I can see, you look pale and skinny."

"Hell, Max. I look like hell because I've been through hell."

"I know you have. I talked to Jerry. I wanted to come. But he told me to stay put. Said you'd asked for time alone. I'm halfway around the world right now, Lacie, but all you have to do is say the word and I'll be there."

"Thanks, Max. I still need to be alone right now."

"One day you'll learn you can't do everything alone," he admonished, frowning. "You've got people like me who love you. Once in a while you ought to let us in. Now, enough of my speeches. When are you going back to work?"

I hesitated. "I don't know. I'm taking time off."

"How much time?" he asked, suspiciously.

"I don't know."

"I know you too well, Lacie. You're the kind of person who buries herself in work when things are bad." His eagle eyes narrowed. "What are you up to?"

"Nothing," I said guilelessly.

"Is that so." He was unconvinced. "What do you plan on doing with your *time off*."

"This and that," I said weakly.

"Level with me," Max ordered. His mouth tightened. "Dammit all, you're going after him."

"Who?"

"You know damn well who. The monster who killed Skyla. Your reporter's instinct is a world-class compass when it comes to trouble, and the direction it points to now is Skyla's murder. Leave it alone, Lace. Get on with your life. Skyla was in the wrong place at the wrong time. It was a random freak occurrence."

"No, it wasn't," I said, my voice so low I wasn't sure he heard.

"Why do you say that?"

"It sounds crazy."

"I'll be the judge of that. Now, talk to me."

I told Max about the strange e-mail I'd received, then how the voice on the video was the same as in my dreams.

"He's out there, Max. He's out there grinning and singing, happy about what he's done. The way he crafted the tape. The things he says. It's all directed at *me*. I'm scared, Max. I'm scared it's just the beginning, that Skyla was the start of some sick game he wants to play with me. Even if I pack up and go back to D.C., something tells me this won't be over. So, I might as well stay close to where Skyla disappeared, close to where she died." There was a beat of silence, then I said: "I'm going to stick around here and hope he surfaces. I didn't want to tell you. I thought you would try to stop me."

"Why the hell would I try to stop you? I want to *help* you, Lacie!" Max leaned in close to the camera. I could see the fire in his eyes. "I want to buckle the son of a bitch into the electric chair myself."

"We have to find him first."

"Write this name down," Max ordered. "Stein. Jack Stein."

"Who's Jack Stein?"

"One of the best men I know. He's with the Bureau. He can help you find the man who murdered Skyla."

"I'm not sure I want his help." Martinez's bloated face popped into my mind. "I don't trust cops, Max."

"Jack Stein isn't a cop. He's a federal agent. He's the right man. At the very least, go see him. You'll change your mind when you meet him."

"I'll think about it."

"You need him, Lace."

I didn't think I needed anybody. I liked to work alone.

Max went on. "Trust this man. Give him everything you've got."

I changed the subject. "Where on earth are you, Max?"

"Somewhere cold. That's all I can say. It's goddamn cold here."

I smiled. "Take good care of yourself."

He scowled at me. "It's you I'm worried about. I'll be in touch."

I blew him a kiss and watched his image disappear. The screen went blank. It was four-thirty in the afternoon. I went back to my e-mail. A new message had zapped in. I opened it.

"Did you watch Skyla burn, Lacie? Did you see the flames lick her skin? I'm watching you, Lacie. I've been watching you all along. I watched you at the beach, walking in the rain. I watched you while you slept, alone in the old beachfront hotel. I watched you walk with Skyla's father, and waited while he folded you in his arms. I'm your love, Lacie. I am fire, and fire is your lover. Our love burns, Lacie, yours and mine. It burns. Skyla's dead, but the game has just begun."

I fumbled for the phone and called Jack Stein.

Chapter Eight

❦

An hour later, I was pacing in the nondescript waiting area at FBI headquarters downtown. It was an austere room with gray industrial carpet, black vinyl folding chairs, and a cheap chrome coffee table. No one could accuse the FBI of excess. A few old magazines cluttered the table. A metal ashtray overflowed with cigarette butts and the air smelled stale. A bulletproof locked glass door gave access to the long central hallway where men in nondescript gray suits hurried in and out of offices.

From what I had seen, the Bureau was still a conservative male bunker. That was okay with me. I wanted the reassurance of a seasoned agent, one with three decades or more of Bureau experience. I looked forward to authority, a stern face, graying hair clipped short.

I carried an envelope with printouts of the two e-mail messages and a copy of the videotaped murder. The original tape as well as the envelope it came in were officially the property of NYPD Homicide Division and unavailable to me. Certainly, I thought, one of Max's grim gray agents could cut through it all, make fingerprints appear where the NYPD found none, run the details through VICAP and find a string of similar murders, ones with evidence. I hoped with the turn of a key, the feds could ID the man, find the monster, and blow him away.

Before he came after me.

Before he killed me.

The door to the long corridor swung open. I looked up. Jack Stein leaned easily against the doorjamb, looking at me boldly from head to toe. He waved me in.

"Sorry you had to wait," he said, not sounding sorry at all.

He steered me into an office on the right. It was small and there was nothing personal about it. None of the usual pictures, no shots of Jack Stein shaking hands with the President or even the head of the Bureau, no smiling kids or charming wife, no plants on the sill or books on shelves. There was just a square metal desk and a chair on either side. The desk surface was organized in an orderly manner with an IBM notebook computer, a thick manila folder, and a black telephone that was, at that moment, ringing.

Jack Stein didn't offer to take my coat, so I kept it on and waited, standing in front of his desk, feeling for all the world like a schoolgirl while he took the call. His side of the conversation was mostly one-word answers to questions I couldn't hear.

"Yes."

"Sure."

"Maybe."

"Sounds right."

He watched me while he talked. I didn't like his casual manner and the amused twist to his mouth, as though he were just waiting for me to express my surprise at how he looked. I stubbornly decided I wouldn't give him the pleasure.

The fact was, Jack Stein didn't look anything like an FBI agent or a cop or anything else that had to do with the law except, perhaps, breaking it. I wondered how he did any kind of undercover detective work, as memorable as he was. He was broad-shouldered and built like an athlete, with the kind of size you don't easily forget. In my high heels I topped six feet; Stein towered over me. I guessed he was six-six. He was too big for the confines of the tight Bureau office. The metal desk seemed dinky and cheap, the chair beneath him flimsy.

His hair was longer than any agent or cop I'd ever seen, and I had to admit to myself that it was beautiful—thick and silky, rich honey in color. It curled at his neck and around the sides of his rugged tan face. He had deep lines to either side of his mouth and enough finer lines fanning out from the corners of his eyes to put him somewhere in his late forties. He wore faded blue jeans and a chambray shirt and had blue eyes. They locked with mine and I saw the blue was a deep sapphire color, velvet almost, and darker than my own.

I blinked away and quickly took in the rest of him. His shoes were solid hiking boots with red laces and rugged soles. His belt was thick fine leather and worn from years of wear. A brown leather holster fit snug at his trim waist, revolver tucked neatly inside. He wore no watch or ring. His hands were the same deep tan as his face, and his fingers were long and fine. Other than the few copper hairs curling at his wrists, the skin on the backs of his hands was smooth. His nails were carefully clipped and clean. A bright red alpine parka was draped on the back of his chair and a black nylon backpack sat on the floor, the kind students carry.

Jack Stein paced back and forth with an easy athletic grace and flashed me an occasional smile while he talked on the phone. He made me uncomfortable. He was too sure of himself. He looked too different. He was too virile. More important, I was certain Max had made a mistake. Max had steered me wrong. I didn't believe Jack Stein could help me find my daughter's killer and I planned on telling him I wanted to go elsewhere in the Bureau. Higher up.

I wanted the standard senior agent—gray suit, white shirt, rep tie, pale skin, hair clipped close and neat. I wanted a serious Bureau man with a big corner office, someone who had come up through the ranks the proper way, a tried and true fed who had a whole team of men working for him, not this rugged giant who looked like he climbed mountains before breakfast.

"You must be Lacie," he said, when his phone call ended.

"Ms. Wagner," I corrected, feeling combative.

He raised an eyebrow and sank down into his chair, motioning for me to sit.

I stayed on my feet, ready to leave.

"I'd know you anywhere, *Ms. Wagner*," he said. His voice was richly timbered and low.

"I don't believe we've ever met," I said, "or if we have, I've obviously forgotten." Wanting to imply he was forgettable. Which he wasn't.

To my surprise, he laughed. The sound of it filled the small room and embarrassed me. "No, we haven't met," he said, "but I've seen your face enough to feel like we have. I shuttle back and forth between New York and D.C. When I'm in D.C., I watch WRC. I admire your talent and your work."

I ignored the charm and the compliment. "You know Max?"

"In a manner of speaking. We met once."

"I thought the two of you were longtime friends."

"Sorry to disappoint."

"Frankly, from the way Max talked about you, I expected you to have the kind of position and leverage here it takes to get things done." I looked around the small cramped space and shrugged. "Obviously, I was mistaken."

"Maybe you should go out and come in again." He was grinning again, the muscle in his cheek twitching.

"Pardon me?" I expected to be dismissed, not invited back.

"We seem to have started off on the wrong foot, *Ms. Wagner.* Let's try again." He swiveled his chair around to face a bare wall. He counted to ten out loud while I looked at the back of his head, at the honey curls dipping over his collar, then he turned around and stood up. "Ms. Wagner, my name's Jack Stein."

I had to admire the fact he hadn't tried to shake my hand. Max must have tipped him off.

"I'm an expert in many areas of value to the Bureau and to you as well. I've been with the FBI exactly fifteen years, three weeks, five days, and six hours, and I plan on staying another fifteen years. I work alone. No teams or staff or secretaries or backup. My computer is my office without walls. I just borrow space here when I have meetings like this one. I'm good at my job, the best some say, and that's earned me the right to dress as I please. I hope I can help you."

He was so cocksure it annoyed the hell out of me. "Why?"

"Max asked me to help. I don't want to let him down."

"Again, why?"

"Because I owe Max my life," he said without skipping a beat. He sat down and touched the manila file. "I've been watching the news. I knew about your daughter before Max called."

I stiffened, ready for the standard cop bromide—*I'm sorry for your loss*—and promised myself I'd walk out on him the minute he said it.

He opened the file to a picture of Skyla on the front page of the *New York Times.*

Here it comes, I thought.

He touched the picture and said in a quiet voice: "I'm sorry for your loss."

I was ready to bolt, but then he looked up at me and his blue eyes locked with mine. I saw something stirring inside him, a sadness as powerful as my own. It hit me. Jack Stein really was sorry. I decided to stay and hear what he had to say.

"Thank you," I managed, meaning it.

Jack blinked and his expression changed. He shut the folder, slid it into his backpack, and stood up. "I hate this place. It gives me claustrophobia. Mind if we talk somewhere else?" The question was rhetorical. He was already shrugging into his parka, sliding his computer into its carrying case, slinging the backpack over his shoulder, and moving toward the door.

His take-charge manner got me mad all over again. He looked like a mountain man in the red parka, big hood flapping in back and a jumble of used ski lift tickets hanging off the zipper. I needed a cop, a detective, a federal agent—not ski patrol.

I hurried down the hall after him. He was greeted by name by most men we passed, and I noticed a number of them looked at him with a strange expression. Something close to awe. Just my luck, I thought sourly, a living legend. I imagined him setting up spy satellites in places like the North Pole. He walked right by the elevator to the stairwell. We were on the twenty-eighth floor. He glanced once over his shoulder to make sure I was there. "I hate elevators," he explained. "Besides, going up and down stairs keeps you strong."

He loped down them fast, almost as if it were a race. As good a shape as I was in, I had to run to keep up with him. At the first floor, he pushed through a door, cut across the wide main lobby, and spun through a revolving door that put us outside and on the main entrance steps to the building.

White snow dazzled in the late-day sun. Jack put a pair of sunglasses on, the small round kind with reflective lenses. He turned to me and I saw my own face staring out of the little mirrors. I was glad. His eyes unnerved me.

I was out of breath.

He looked at me again, from head to toe. "Sorry if I went too fast. Max said you liked to run."

"Oh, really," I said, turning from him and loping down the steps. "What else did Max tell you?"

"He said you hate men."

I knew without looking back, Jack Stein was smiling.

"Looks like you and Max covered everything," I said, more calmly than I felt. "I thought this was going to be a murder investigation, not a profile on my personal life."

"First rule of a murder investigation, Ms. Wagner, is to find out everything you can about all the players." He fell into step beside me. "It's the black Range Rover, parked at the curb." He took my elbow and steered me that way.

I shook free, wondering how he could park in a no-parking zone. When we got closer, I saw the plates. They were MD tags. Jack Stein was a doctor. He could park anywhere he damn well wanted.

"You didn't tell me you're a doctor."

"You didn't ask."

"What kind of doctor are you?"

"A good one." He unlocked the door and held it open.

Suddenly it occurred to me that Dr. Jack Stein didn't like me any more than I liked him. Before I could stop myself, I said it out loud: "You don't like me."

"We don't have to like each other, Ms. Wagner. We're working, not dating." He slammed the door and went around to the driver's side.

We drove in silence for a long while, moving slowly in the rush hour traffic. I kept my head turned, pretending to look at the city outside, hoping he wouldn't see the color in my cheeks. Why had I said such a stupid thing? Why was I acting this way? Something about Jack Stein knocked me off balance. I lost all my usual poise, the camera cool that made me a good reporter and an even better anchor.

He brought out the worst in me.

Night fell quickly. Suddenly street lamps were on and the sky was dark. I glanced at him. The sunglasses were off and he was looking straight ahead, intent on winding his way through the traffic-clogged streets. We inched uptown. There was a Santa on every corner and brightly lit trees in every store window. It was Christmas. Somehow, I had missed the transition to December. Tears stung my eyes.

"I climbed in Switzerland once," Jack Stein said, out of the blue, "with a blind man. We were a party of five and we climbed linked together by ropes, the blind man in the middle position. We made our way up the mountain, shouting instructions to him—*Reach higher, stretch, left, right, there. Hold!*—locating the hand- and footholds for him with our words. We were his eyes.

"He was an experienced climber, but the blindness was new. Darkness was new. It took us eight hours to scale the face of that mountain. We reached the summit by sunset, in time to pitch camp for the night. The blind man felt his way out to the edge of the plateau. He turned to the setting sun, knowing where it was by the feel of the last warm rays on his face. *It's a magnificent view,* he cried, lifting his arms to the sky. *Thank you, God, for the gift of sight.*

"He was learning to *see* in a whole new way, with all of his other senses. He tracked the sunset by the warmth of the sun on his face, and knew when night arrived by the sounds of night creatures and the feel of the chill night wind. He swept his hands over grassy slopes, touching the fields, and located flowers by smell. He inhaled the great rush of clear high altitude air and he saw the river by tasting its water on his tongue and hearing the sound of it rushing over rocks.

"The next day, we climbed down the same way. Two in front of him, two behind, shouting out the coordinates for his holds. When we reached the bottom, I suddenly didn't know who had been braver: the blind man for trusting us to lead him, or the four of us for letting ourselves be tied to the blind climber by a rope on that sheer mountain face. If he had missed a hold, a step, a grip, if the blind man had fumbled or faltered or panicked, if he had fallen, we all might have gone down with him. The moral of the story, Ms. Wagner? Teamwork takes trust. Second rule of a murder investigation."

He pulled the Range Rover in next to the curb and cut the engine.

"I thought you worked alone."

"Max said I'd have a hard time keeping you out of it."

"Max was right again," I said, climbing out and dropping down onto the sidewalk. My high heels slipped on ice. I steadied myself and picked my way slowly across the sidewalk, careful not to ask for help.

Jack waited for me at the door to a restaurant. His backpack and computer bag were slung over his shoulder. I wondered if he went anywhere without them.

The room was warmly lit and paneled with polished wood. Sofas and easy chairs crowded a cozy bar area. Jazz played softly. The smell of food made me hungry. We left our coats at the check and moved along. Jack was obviously a regular here. The staff greeted him by name. "Hi, Jack!" "Hey, Jack!" "Good to see you, Jack!" coming from all directions. The bartender looked me over as we walked by and winked at Jack. My bad feelings deepened. Jack Stein was obviously a ladies' man, and the fact that I was mistaken for his date annoyed me.

We wound around to a corner table for two. A small votive candle burned in the center. I blew it out.

"Too romantic for you?" Jack quipped.

"I don't like candles."

Jack's eyes flickered over my gloved hands then away, to the waitress. He ordered a large bottle of Perrier with lime. I needed something stronger, a vodka on the rocks with a twist. It made me feel like a grown-up again.

"Serious drink," Jack said.

"I'm not driving."

When the drinks arrived and the food ordering was done, he stretched his long legs and settled back. "Tell me about Skyla."

My voice caught in my throat. I had been so busy hating him, I'd forgotten why we were together. "How far back do you want me to go?"

"Let's start with the weekend she disappeared."

I talked. The vodka loosened me up enough to work through the chronology of events, starting with the last time I had spoken to my daughter and moving forward through the following days and my rushed trip to New York. When I got to the part about the videotape, my words slowed, my voice cracked, and suddenly I couldn't speak at all. Jack reached over and lightly touched my arm. His hand was warm. I went on to tell him about the video.

"I brought you a copy. The police kept the original."

He just nodded, so I went on talking. I skipped over my three-day delirium as much as I could, but he read between the lines. That expression was back in his eyes. It was dark as night and heavy with sorrow.

I finished the vodka and had another. It made me honest. I told him about the ceremony at sea for Skyla and how, after that, I had holed up in Jerry's loft for fifteen long days and nights, hiding from the world, hiding from the truth, from the twisting pain of my own new and terrible emptiness. I told him how the loneliness weighed on me like stone, how I felt gutted, hollowed out inside, and then I tried to tell him about the voice.

"I have nightmares," I started. I stopped and started again. "What I mean is, I have had a series of nightmares. They started when I was ten, after the accident."

"Tell me about the accident."

"Max didn't give you all the gory details?"

"I want to hear it from you."

I flushed, fiddled with my silverware. Talking about the accident didn't come easy.

"My father was driving me home from summer camp," I finally said. "He was driving fast. Something happened. The car suddenly swerved off the road, hit a tree, and burst into flames. He was trapped. The fire killed him. I was luckier." I lifted a gloved hand. "The fire just destroyed my hands. The nightmares started soon after that. My doctor said they were part of posttraumatic stress syndrome. He promised they would go away, in time. It's been twenty-four years. They have not gone away."

I hesitated.

"Go on," Jack urged.

"There's a face in the nightmare, always the same face, a nightmare face. He's watching me through a window. His face is very close. I can see the color of his eyes, the sweat beading above his lips, and the texture of his lips. He's saying, *Come, Lacie, come. Walk with me into the fire. Reach out and touch the fire.*

"Other times, he's standing at the edge of a forest, in the shadows of the trees, waving to me. *Come, Lacie, come. Follow me into the flames.* Still other times, I'm in a ring of fire. He stands off to the side, watching, and even though he's whispering, I hear his voice over the roar of the fire. *Touch the flames, Lacie. Reach out and touch the flames. Feel them lick your skin, feel them burn. Burn, Lacie, burn.*

"In the dream, I do reach out and touch the fire. Flesh falls away, I watch my hands shrivel and char, and all the while he's whispering to me. I can't stop his voice, and I can't refuse him. I do what he says. I watch myself burn."

I took a long swallow of vodka, savoring the searing taste of it. I swirled ice cubes in the cocktail glass, listened to them clink. I put the glass down, picked up the videotape, and looked at Jack for the first time in the telling of my story.

"The voice on this tape is my nightmare voice. It's exactly the same voice I've been listening to in my dreams for twenty-four years."

Jack Stein didn't say a word, but skepticism showed on his face.

"I'm not crazy," I said, feeling defensive again.

"I didn't say you were."

"The police have given up," I said, turning the discussion away from me. "They say they can't find a killer when there's no trail of evidence to follow."

"The cops are wrong," Jack scoffed. "Behavior tells us about personality, and the killer's been talking to us with every little thing he does. He's telling us all about himself and he has been from the start, from the moment he wrote your name and address on the envelope and sent you the videotape." Jack took a color photograph of the envelope out of his pack and placed it on the table.

"Where did you get that?"

He ignored me and leaned forward. "Look at the writing. The letters are large and neat. The killer is calm, confident, and controlled. Not likely to slip up. Consider the postmark date. He was thinking ahead. This was sent by someone who knows you well enough, or who has studied you long enough, to know you'd go to New York when you didn't hear from your daughter."

He had my attention. "Go on."

"Nothing about the crime appears random. We're not looking for some drugged-out punk who pulled Skyla into an alley on a whim. The videotape and the e-mail were meticulously planned follow-ups. This killer is highly organized and computer literate." Jack put the photo away and sat back. "Now, tell me the rest."

"I think killing Skyla was just the beginning." I handed him a printout of the e-mail. "I got this today. That's when I decided to call you."

"There are a lot of psychos in the world," Jack said when he finished reading it. "This could be the equivalent of a crank phone call, someone who picked up details from the news reports and wants to stir you up."

"It's from the killer. Those are similar to the words he used in the first e-mail and on the videotape of the burning. And, some are the *exact* words I hear in my nightmares. The transcripts of the videotape and the first e-mail were never released to the press. The tape itself was played for a select group of NYPD homicide detectives. Even so, there's absolutely no way any one of those detectives could possibly know about my nightmares, let alone *exactly* what's said in them."

"What about your husband—I'm sorry—your ex-husband. Skyla's father."

"What about him?"

"Did you ever tell him about your nightmares?"

"Of course."

"In detail?"

"Yes."

"The exact words?"

"Probably."

He tapped the e-mail printout. "Could this be from your ex-husband?"

I knocked my cocktail glass over. Ice cubes rolled across the tablecloth. "What an insane thing to say."

"Is it?" he said, matter-of-factly. "We have to consider every possibility. When a child is murdered, ninety-two percent of the time it turns out to be a relative. Statistics don't lie. You told me yourself the tape was mailed Saturday, a full day before your last-minute decision to come to New York. Wouldn't Jerry Costello have known you'd show up after three days had passed and you weren't able to reach your daughter? And who else could possibly have known enough about your fear of fire and your nightmares to deliver a tape that was clearly designed to torture you?"

Jack leaned forward. His voice was soft, but his expression was hard. "Does your ex-husband have psychological problems? A violent temper? Was he an abusive father? Did he go too far one day, then have to cover up his mistake? Did he hit her too hard, accidentally kill her, and then dress it up like murder?

"Does he hate you, Ms. Wagner? Or more likely, does he still love you? Is he filled with rage? Didn't you walk out on him, take the child with you? Isn't it possible you left him with a festering anger that finally exploded? Isn't it possible that Jerry Costello had some kind of personal motive for wanting to hurt you? And isn't it true that the most effective way to hurt you would be to hurt your child?"

Tears stung my eyes for the second time in the few hours since I had met Jack Stein. I thought of Jerry's sagging shoulders, the way he held the urn, how grief had punched him hollow. "You have no idea how wrong you are, Dr. Stein. Jerry's a lot of things, not all of them good, but he was a wonderful father. He worshipped Skyla." I laid a gloved hand on his arm. "Jerry worshipped his daughter. Do you hear me?"

"I heard you the first time."

"I'm not sure you know what the words mean."

Jack's jaw tightened. The food arrived. We ate in silence. From time to time, Jack studied the e-mail message as if the killer's name was encrypted there. He didn't speak again until dinner was over and the plates were cleared.

"Do you still love Jerry Costello?"

"Sometimes," I said, honestly, remembering Jerry's warm embrace, his dark eyes, and our shared sorrow.

"He's the father of your child," Jack said. "It's natural for you to want to give him the benefit of the doubt. But you have to understand. I hunt child killers. That's what I do. I don't have the luxury of giving anyone the benefit of the doubt. I've seen terrible things over the years—children maimed, beaten, burned, suffocated, handcuffed to water pipes—by one or the other of their parents. You don't believe it until you see it. It happens in rich homes. It happens in poor homes. The killers are fathers, uncles, brothers, cousins, mothers, sisters, aunts. They're Catholic, Protestant, Jewish—every race and religion known to this earth.

"Only eight percent of child murders have nothing to do with a relative. They're serial killers who specifically go after children, random psychos who choose children for their victims. But that's not what Skyla's murder feels like to me. I don't think it's random, and it doesn't feel like the first in a series of killings. It's too personal. The videotape, the e-mail, his choice of fire as a murder weapon and the significance of fire to you. Whoever it is, the killer definitely has a personal connection to you.

"I assume the worst in human nature. Anything short of that I take as a pleasant surprise. So, in my book, Jerry Costello's a suspect. I'm going to investigate him vigorously. I'm going to dig and snoop and scratch for every detail of his personal life and when I'm done, you'll know so much about your daughter's father, you'll feel as if you had married a stranger."

"Why don't you investigate me while you're at it?" I snapped.

"I already have." He looked smug. "And I did a hell of a lot more than talk to Max."

"How dare you."

"Because I'm working for Skyla first, and for you second. And, like I said, looking out for you is a favor to Max."

"You're serious," I said, incredulous.

"I know everything about you," Jack said in a satisfied way. "You started as a go-fer at a TV station in a crummy no-name town in the heart of Alabama, earning a hundred and twenty dollars a week. You got the job because you were a single, pretty, physically challenged girl with a baby at home. The news director felt sorry for you.

"You ignored the sympathy and took the job. Six months later you were delivering news stories instead of coffee. There wasn't much news to speak of in the town outside of local elections, cookie drives, and zoning disputes, but you covered those cookie drives like they were congressional budget battles, and the dinky mayoral race like it was the American presidential campaign.

"I saw your tapes, Ms. Wagner. The news director saved them all. He was proud of you. Said he knew you'd be a star one day. Your hard news style got you noticed by a news director in a bigger town a few hours away. He offered you a hundred dollars more a week than you were making and a full-time job as a reporter. You took it.

"The station was still small. You had to horse your own camcorder around, tape your own stand-ups. But there was only one direction for you and that was up because you have a gift. When you look into the camera, it's as if you're talking one-on-one with each and every person in the viewing audience. You break down the third wall. You report the news as if you care.

"That gift and an incredible work ethic pushed you along through four more cities in a straight line up the Eastern seaboard—Knoxville, Asheville, Raleigh-Durham, and then Norfolk, where you anchored the noon news and finally got your big story. A dead body washed ashore two miles south of your station. If the body had drifted down to the next town, you would've lost out.

"Luck works in mysterious ways and nothing was more mysterious that day than the bloated, naked, white-bellied floater that washed up with the rope noose still around his unlucky neck. There were signs of torture. Cigarette burns on the feet. The victim was a Naval officer. You were one step ahead of the police. You interviewed every enlisted man who had been under his command. You worked quietly, consistently, and figured it out. A young recruit had cracked under the pressure. He tortured the man who had tortured him in training.

"You got his confession on tape. His monstrous crime got him the death penalty, and then you snagged the one and only interview with him before he died. Not *Current Affair* or *Barbara Walters*, but Lacie Wagner—because the killer liked you. He said he trusted

you. He said you had a beautiful and empathetic face. Your interview was a masterpiece. I watched it. The network picked it up and
suddenly you were hot enough to land an anchor slot in Washington, D.C.

"Your past and present colleagues describe you as a *loner, worka-
holic, aloof.* News directors and station managers are more generous. They agree with those three adjectives, but hurry to sing praises
about your *telegenic gift, quick mind, vigorous reporting, incredible work ethic.* Their words, not mine. Nothing you don't already
know. WRC wouldn't have offered you the deal they did if you
weren't everything the news directors said and more."

He paused, arched an eyebrow at me.

"Good work, *Agent* Stein," I said sarcastically. "Do go on."

"Call me Jack." He launched in again. "Other than Max, who
is really family, you have no close personal friends. Your D.C. town
house cost a hefty four hundred and thirty-five thousand dollars.
You plunked down seventy-five thousand dollars—your life savings, money you got from your father's life insurance policy—and
financed the rest thanks to a sterling credit status and a juicy salary."

I tried to interrupt.

Jack held a hand up. "Incidentally, just for fun I found out your
salary sets a new high in D.C. No other local station anchor in the
market has ever made as much as you."

He went on, reciting a litany of my shopping habits, down to the
size clothes I wore. He knew the brand of sheets I slept on, the kind
of coffee I liked, and the last ten books I had read. It was uncanny.
Unsettling. Scary.

"According to your divorce papers, Jerry Costello was an *irresponsible philanderer with compulsive promiscuous behavior.* After you left him, you had no men around, no dates, and you sure as
hell didn't have any slumber parties for two. If you ever saw a man
outside of professional circumstances, it was incredibly discreet. I
couldn't dig up a single man who said he had so much as kissed
you chastely on the cheek, let alone had an affair with you.

"Even though you had only two thousand dollars in your personal bank account when you walked out on Jerry, you didn't accept a dime of alimony and you didn't touch your father's life
insurance money until you moved to D.C. You paid your own way,
but you did hit Jerry big for child support. You used it to make sure
Skyla had private schools and twenty-four-hour round-the-clock

supervision. Whatever you didn't spend went into Treasury Bills in Skyla's name.

"You created a perfect biosphere for your daughter. When she was younger, her nanny always took her to school and picked her up, shuttled her to violin lessons, dance class, and basketball practice. You had Skyla's daily life scheduled down to fifteen-minute increments. You controlled everything. You were the New Age supermom who did it all and still managed to have her hair look great at the end of the day." Jack crossed his arms across his chest and smiled at me.

"You have no right to inspect my personal life, let alone judge it."

"Oh, yes, I do, Ms. Wagner, because your daughter was murdered. Nothing, I repeat, nothing and no one is going to be off limits to me. That's the third rule of this murder investigation. If you can't accept that, let's end this now."

"You learned a hell of a lot considering I only called you this afternoon."

"I had a pretty good head start. Max called me the day he heard Skyla had been murdered. He wasn't satisfied with what Jerry had told him about the NYPD investigation, so I started looking into it."

While I was cowering from the world, Jack Stein had been methodically going about his job.

"You know anything about fishing, Ms. Wagner?"

"No."

"A smart fisherman doesn't drop one line into the water. Not if he needs that fish for his supper. He sets up a bunch of lines and he works them all at the same time. You use different lures, different types of bait and hope that out of all the goodies you drop in, one will be attractive enough to make the fish bite."

"That's a simplistic metaphor. We're talking about torture and murder, not trout."

"Life and death are more simplistic than you may think."

"I don't think there's anything simple about the way my daughter died."

"Of course not. You've misunderstood me entirely."

The check came. We fought over it. I lost. He paid in cash, then pushed his chair back and stood up. "Let's go. We have work to do."

I followed him out and into the Range Rover. Clouds slipped over the moon. The air tasted of snow and a rush of wind had the feel of a fresh storm coming. Jack pulled away from the curb and went around the block, then headed downtown. We did not speak.

Suddenly in the middle of our strained silence, he laughed. "It's my turn now to ask the question: You don't like me, do you, Ms. Wagner?"

I didn't bother to answer.

"Tell me this. Is it because I'm a man or because I don't fit your predetermined idea of what federal agents act and look like?"

"I object to you because you're arrogant."

"I'm direct. I'd think, as a newswoman, you'd appreciate that." He sailed down an empty Fifth Avenue, timing the lights well, hitting a string of green. "And, arrogant or not, I'm your best bet, Ms. Wagner. You don't know it, and you certainly don't know why, but I'm the only one who has a shot at nailing Skyla's killer and keeping you alive all at the same time. The bottom line is this: I'm not asking you to like me or approve of me or to even be civil to me. I am asking you to trust me."

"Like your blind man on the mountain?"

"Exactly." He stopped in front of Jerry's loft. The door locks popped up. I dropped out of the warmth onto the icy pavement and slammed the door as hard as I could. Jack Stein caught up with me at the door, carrying his computer, backpack, and a duffel bag.

"That's a no-parking zone," the doorman said.

"The car stays put," Jack said, flashing his shield.

"Yes, sir."

"Any new tenants in the building in the last six months?"

"No, sir."

"Any renters or house guests?"

"Not that I know of, sir."

"You sound like a military man."

"Marines, sir. Eight years."

"Good. Are you armed?"

"All the doormen here are, sir. We're hired out by a private security service. I carry a nine millimeter semiautomatic with a full clip. It's a high-security building. The owners want it that way."

"Good. I see you've got two elevators here."

"They both service the whole building, lobby to penthouse. There's one loft per floor and we've got ten floors."

"What about basement access?"

"That's separate. You go down the stairs or through the alley door. You can't get into the upstairs from the basement, not without going through here first."

"I want the left elevator shut down. Reserved for me. No one else uses it. Can you set it up that way?"

"Sure."

"Excellent. I don't want any unexpected visitors." Jack handed the doorman a card. "I carry a cell phone. If anybody wants to go up to that loft, you call me, whether I'm there or not, any time, day or night."

"Yes, sir."

"No one goes up to *check the cable box*, or *fix a phone line*, or *work on the plumbing*. Just to be clear, absolutely clear, no one is authorized to go up to ten. And that includes Mr. Costello."

"But that loft belongs to him, sir."

"Mr. Costello wants to come up, you call me on my cell phone."

"I guess so."

"Guessing so isn't good enough. In case you didn't hear, some psycho burned Skyla Costello to death. I don't want her mother to wind up in the same condition. No one goes to ten."

"Yes, sir."

"What kind of security tie-in do you have with the police?"

"My desk has an alarm button set into the floor. It's activated by foot and rings right through to the precinct house. And, the cops drive by once every half hour or so because this is the only occupied building on the block at night. It's isolated. The precinct doesn't want any problems. We lock the front door after eleven. I only let in people who live here. Otherwise, I talk through the intercom while they wait outside."

"Good. When does the shift change?"

"Nine tomorrow morning. Super comes in then too."

"I'll be down at nine to speak to them personally. Stay alert tonight."

"Yes, sir."

We stepped into the elevator. On the ride up, I was aware of Jack towering over me, and I felt ridiculously small. The doors whispered open. We stepped out into Jerry's entry hall. I unlocked the front door. Jack followed me in and bolted it behind us.

He walked into the living room, whistling through his teeth. "Jerry Costello has very good taste."

He dropped his duffel bag, set his backpack and computer case on a side table, then crossed over to one of the huge framed windows and opened it. Gripping the sill with his hands, he stretched his torso all the way outside. He looked right, left, up, and down, then dropped gracefully back inside.

"What are you looking for?"

"Fire escapes, neighboring balconies, or any other means of possible access to this loft. I'm also checking the distance to the roof and the distance between this and other buildings. This loft's fairly isolated up here. Someone could possibly access the roof from the vacant building in back. And if he did, he could conceivably rappel down from the roof and try for a window entry, but that would be difficult. Your husband . . ."

"My ex-husband."

"Jerry Costello paid a lot of money for these double-paned soundproof windows. You'd need to throw one hell of a hammer blow to get through them. It's unlikely anyone would try, but not impossible, depending on the skill of the potential intruder. You've got just that one building in back and nothing but air to either side. The loft fronts the street. I'll take a look out the rest of the windows, but from what I can see, you've got a pretty safe nest up here."

He repeated the high-wire act in eight other windows, and went on to systematically search the loft. I trailed along as he peered behind the furniture, into closets, under beds, behind doors, in bathtubs. When he finished, he took one last spin through the living room, closing drapes and double-checking window locks. "We still have a lot to go over," he said when he finished. "Details about Skyla's life, her friends here, her friends in D.C. I have to know everything about her."

The tape of Skyla's murder was heavy in my shoulder bag. I was drained, unable to do more than sleep. "Tomorrow," I said simply.

"You're tired." His voice had softened. "Tomorrow's fine." He stretched out on the couch. "I'll be right here if you need me."

I am a private woman, used to running my own life and looking after myself. I wanted his help, but I certainly didn't want to live with him. It was an issue of pride and control. I hated feeling helpless, dependent. Chalk it up to the Jerry days. Having Jack Stein stay the night made me feel dependent.

"You're not staying here tonight," I announced.

"Sure am."

"I don't need a bodyguard."

"Max seems to think you do." His eyes flickered over me. "I'm beginning to think you do too."

I went to the front door and opened it. "You said so yourself. I have a nice secure nest up here and an armed marine downstairs. That's good enough for me. You can come back tomorrow morning. There's no need for you to stay. Good night, Dr. Stein."

He flashed me a smile. "I'd make you that uncomfortable here?"

"Nothing personal, but yes."

"Okay." He shrugged, opened his backpack, and took out a thick coil of what looked like telephone jack cords. He yanked one of Jerry's phone jacks out of the wall and plugged his own cable in, then snaked it across the floor, out the front door, and into the hall.

I watched him drop his backpack on the ground, set his computer next to it, and make a cushion out of his red down parka. He sat cross-legged on the parka and looked up at me. "Like I said, I'll be right here if you need anything."

I tried to think of a smart retort, but found myself speechless. Jack stuck the modem cable in his computer and booted up. Seconds later he was tapping at the keyboard, dialing in, logging on to who knows where, doing who knows what. I was as stubborn as he was. If he wanted to stay in the hall, let him.

As I was closing the door, I paused. "You neglected to tell me something."

"What's that?" he asked, without looking up.

"What did you conclude after your admirably thorough investigation of me?"

"You were an excellent mother. You loved your daughter. Very much. She meant the world to you."

I shut the door, locked it, and went to Skyla's room, where I tried to sleep. I tossed and turned, stared at Brad Pitt on the ceiling, and thought about Jack Stein. When the clock flipped over to 2:00, I pulled on a pair of black sweatpants, black sweatshirt, and black gloves, tiptoed out to the front door, and peeked through the peephole.

He was still sitting straight up, punching away at the keyboard. His face was relaxed and he was smiling to himself.

I opened the door.

He looked up. His smile disappeared. A hard curtain dropped back down over his features, turning him to stone. "Yes?"

I thought you might be hungry. Or thirsty. Or wanting to sleep in the guest room. I didn't feel like saying any of it now, but I had to say something. "What are you doing?"

"Playing poker. I'm at a table in a virtual casino. There are six other players from all around the world. There are sites where you can play for real money. This one's just for fun."

"Do you often play poker at two in the morning?"

"Do you often wear gloves at two in the morning?"

I slammed the door, bolted and chained it, then swept the peephole open and watched as long as I dared, not breathing, not blinking. He was relaxed again, intent on his computer, although I felt certain he wasn't playing card games. He was working. Dropping fish bait out into the great cyber-pond, waiting to see if something or someone bit.

I clicked the peephole shut and drifted back down the hall to Skyla's room, to bed.

I fell asleep sometime after three. Jack Stein's red parka glowed brightly in my dreams.

The nightmare came later that night. It was the same face, the same voice, but new, different words.

Was it fun watching Sky burn, Lacie? She asked for you, called your name, begged for you before she burned, Lace. Your guard dog is useless. He can't keep me from you. I am going to touch your ivory breasts and kiss you between the legs. I am going to know and touch and feel every part of you before you burn. We were meant to be lovers. Your guard dog is useless, Lacie. He can't keep you from me. Jack Stein's a giant, but he can't keep you from the fire.

I woke up to the sound of my own screaming. The telephone was in my hand, and Jack Stein was pounding on the front door.

Chapter Nine

The nightmare began the same," I explained, huddled on the couch, struggling to put images into words. "It was the face, as always, but this time I saw his body too, bare and ruined by fire. He placed my hands on his scarred chest. Our skin was the same. I couldn't tell where I ended and he began. He was whispering terrible things to me in my dream when the telephone rang. I answered and heard his voice. He said: *Your guard dog is useless. He can't keep you from me. Jack Stein's a giant, but he can't keep you from the fire.*"

"What else?" Jack asked.

"Nothing," I lied, not wanting to tell him about the sexual threats or the erotic promise heavy in the whispering voice. "He knew your name. How could he know your name?"

Jack did not answer. He was standing by one of the big windows, looking at the clock tower outside. The sky was black, but morning was not far away.

"He knows because he's watching me, isn't he?" I asked. "He's been following me and now he's following us."

"It's still early," Jack said as the clock hands ticked over to five. "Try to get some sleep."

"I can't."

"Okay." He turned around. "Then we might as well start in."

Jack showered and changed in the guest suite. I took my time in a long tepid bath, then dressed in black slacks and a cable-knit sweater. I left my hair loose and pulled my gloves on.

Jack was in the kitchen, sitting on a stool at the butcher-block island, toasting bagels and brewing coffee. The curtains were drawn. I pinched one aside and saw the pink glow of sunrise in the east. I dropped the curtain and studied Jack. His hair was still damp and he was freshly shaved. He wore a pale yellow button-down shirt with the sleeves rolled up. Jeans were faded and the soft denim revealed a swell of powerful thigh muscle. His gun was in the holster at his hip.

"I found these in the freezer," he said, dropping a hot bagel on a plate.

I sat on a stool next to him and reached for the butter. There are things I cannot do with gloves on, like opening pop-top soda cans. There are things I can do but find embarrassing. Eating buttered bagels with my black leather gloves on embarrassed me, but I did it anyway.

"Butter's hell on leather," Jack observed.

"I don't care," I said, stubbornly.

"Take your gloves off, Ms. Wagner. Pretend I'm not here."

He was so big next to me, the freshness of him, the size of him, I laughed. "Right."

"What are you afraid of?"

The flinch. The automatic recoil. The disgust.

"Drop it, Jack."

He was about to reply, thought better of it, and poured me a cup of coffee instead. "The contact this morning proves he's close, Ms. Wagner. I'll find him."

"The police had a team of detectives working the case and they couldn't find a single witness or a shred of evidence, let alone the man. How are you going to succeed where they failed?"

"They don't have my training, determination, or stamina," Jack said, matter-of-factly. "I don't give up and I don't fail."

We ate in silence. Jack finished, pushed his plate away, and turned to me.

"The police had a case without a lead," he explained, "a killing without a clue. No murder weapon. No witnesses. No motive. The detectives worked hard, but not smart. And finally, they just gave up. Even so, technically, the case is still theirs. It doesn't come under FBI jurisdiction, and since the NYPD didn't ask for federal help, I have no legal right stepping in."

"Therefore?"

"I want you to understand that what I'm doing isn't sanctioned or official. I'm way out of line. The Bureau knows and will look the other way as long as I don't step on any toes in the NYPD. So far, I haven't. I've been the perfect gentleman, much as that may surprise you. Homicide hasn't agreed to let me go through their case files, but they did give me a verbal rundown on their investigation as well as a set of the crime scene photos from the alley where Skyla's remains were found. More important, they gave me the original videotape of the bonfire and the envelope it came in."

"And?"

"I sent them down to the lab in Quantico for analysis. The tape was edited, but the images themselves were not digitally enhanced. The camera recorded exactly what it saw. The narration was laid down later. No voice alteration devices were used. His whispering disguises any regional inflections he might have, but we can tell from the syntax, the way he stacks his words, that he's an educated, literate Caucasian, probably middle-aged."

"What about the envelope?"

"Useless. It's been passed through too many hands to get any meaningful prints, which doesn't surprise me."

"What does surprise you?"

"The fact that no one saw anything. Homicide says they didn't get a single call, not even a crank one. Skyla walked out the door and no one saw her after that. Your daughter had the kind of face and hair and height people remember. How is it she walked right out the front door and vanished?"

I slid off the stool, carried cups and plates to the sink, and gingerly rinsed each item. Careful as I was, water and suds ran down my gloves.

"Dish soap's hell on leather, too," Jack observed.

I ignored him.

Suddenly he was next to me, slipping my gloves off, gently uncurling my hands, coolly reciting a litany of medical observations:

"Third-degree burns through the epidermal, dermal, and subcutaneous layers. Evidence of fourth-degree burns that damaged bone, muscle, and tendon resulting in the amputation of the right and left thumbs at the joint, and stunted growth in the left index and ring fingers. Vascular and nerve damage was most likely severe, creating heightened sensitivity to heat and cold in some areas, lack of sensation in others. Reconstruction was a long painful process. It must have been hell and I'm sorry for that, for what you went through."

Straightforward and sincere. The Jack Stein way.

He let go of my hands. "I'm glad that's out of the way. You have nothing to be ashamed of, Ms. Wagner, especially around me."

I was stunned silent, shocked speechless, and by the time I could speak, Jack was gone. I pulled my gloves on and went down the hall ready for war, but when I got to Jerry's office, I saw Jack at the desk holding the videotape of Skyla's burning and my rage disappeared. All I felt was tired and sad. And very, very afraid.

Jack Stein's a giant, but he can't keep you from the fire.

"Tell me about Skyla," Jack said, turning the tape over and over in his big hands. "What kind of girl was she?"

"Don't you know the answer to that?"

"I talked to her teachers, her coach, and some of her friends, but I want to hear it from you."

"She was ambitious. Bright. Top of her class."

"Shy?"

"Hardly. She was a talker."

"Popular?"

"Yes. She was captain of the basketball team. First chair violinist in the school orchestra too. She bounced through life with a wonderful inner joy and found the voice for her joy in music."

"Did she want to be a professional musician?"

"No. She wanted to be a lawyer like her father."

"Did she have boyfriends? A lover?"

"She was thirteen years old!"

"Almost fourteen."

"You sound like Jerry," I said, disgusted.

"Teenage girls do have sex, Ms. Wagner. It's an unfortunate reality."

"Don't lecture me. My daughter did not have sex."

"How do you know?"

"As you so poetically put it, I created a biosphere for her. And, we were close. I would have known. She thought boys were good for a game of basketball and not much else."

"Are you sure? There's a poster of Brad Pitt over her bed."

"Brad Pitt's not a boy. He's a man."

"Maybe she was seeing a man in secret."

"Impossible. I knew where she was every minute of every day, with the exception of the time she spent with her father. And I certainly didn't encourage her to think about men."

"I'm sure you didn't."

I glared at him.

"Were you overprotective?"

"You've already decided I was, so why ask?"

"I'm just trying to understand Skyla's environment."

"She didn't get killed in *my* environment."

"So you blame Jerry."

"Are you a shrink?"

"No. Answer the question. Do you blame Jerry?"

"Of course. At first." I took a deep breath. "But not now."

"Why?"

"Now I know that Skyla's murder wasn't a random event. Nothing Jerry could have done would have made a difference." I stood up. "The man who killed her would have gotten to her somehow, no matter where she was."

There was a long beat of silence. I settled back into my chair.

"The questions I ask when a child is killed," Jack finally said, "are the same questions you ask when you go after a news story: *Who, What, Where, When, Why, and How. What* is always the murder itself. In Skyla's death, we know the *Where, When,* and *How,* and they tell us a lot about the killer's mindset."

"Such as?"

"*Where.* He waited until Skyla was in New York to take her. That tells me he wanted her away from you, out of your control and in his. He's a control-oriented man. *When.* He took her on Friday morning, but didn't kill her until the night hours between sunset Friday and sunrise Saturday. It was not a blitz attack. He spent time with her before he killed her.

"Then, he mailed the tape Saturday knowing you wouldn't get it until Monday. He made you wait and hope, wonder and worry. He played with you. You were his toy. He controlled what you felt by how much information he gave you. He's organized and methodical. Are you following me?"

"Yes," I said, fascinated, despite myself. "The *How* is fire."

"Right. He chose fire because of you. This was a very personal crime. Feels to me like it was driven by hate or revenge. The burning and vicious butchering that followed totally obliterated Skyla's identity. Those are acts of rage. He delivered the tape to you and the remains to the police so he could be sure you saw what he had done. Those are cold, calculated acts. He's full of rage, but it's very controlled."

"We're down to *Why* and *Who.*"

"The question to focus on is *Why*. The *Why* almost always leads to the *Who*."

"Why would anyone want to kill Skyla?"

"To devastate and terrify you. To get back at you. She was the victim, but you are the target. I've taken a deep look at your professional life and unless you tell me otherwise, nothing you ever did made anyone mad enough to destroy you or your daughter. Am I right on that?"

"Yes."

"Did Skyla know about your nightmares?"

"I had to tell her."

"Why?"

I hesitated. It was such a thin line to walk, giving him the information he needed without revealing too much of myself in the process.

"Ms. Wagner?"

"My nightmares scare me." The way Linda Severino's scared *her*.

Linda lingered in my thoughts because I was haunted by her husband's description of her troubled sleep; how it sounded eerily like my own. Linda and I were tormented by whispering voices in our dreams and unspeakable tragedy had fallen on us both. I was silent for a long while now, thinking that her death had been portentous, a warning of the horror waiting for me.

Jack was patient. He let me be.

"I scream in my sleep," I finally went on. "I had to explain my behavior to Skyla."

"What did you tell her?"

"The truth. When she was old enough to hear about the accident. When she was old enough to understand and not be frightened."

"Was Skyla afraid of fire?"

"Isn't everyone?"

The question hung there between us.

Jerry's clock chimed eight. Jack tapped the videotape. "We should run this now. Make sure there's nothing we've overlooked."

My throat tightened. Tears welled up in my eyes. I folded gloved hands across my face. "Hell of a way to start the day, Jack."

He came around the desk and lifted my hands away. He was crouching next to me, inches away, with that dark look in his eyes again. "I need you to do this," he said softly. "I'm sorry."

"Me too."

* * *

It was one thing to watch the tape with Jerry, Skyla's father, or alone in the dark as I had twice before. It was quite another thing to share it with a stranger. Death is so personal. So terribly personal. I turned my back as if that defiant action alone could erase the images, but I was still left with the sound. The spark of a match igniting, the whump of fire catching, the crackle of it feeding on nylon and hair, the unmistakable hissing sizzle of flame devouring flesh.

Jack stopped the tape several times, asking questions and making notations on a legal pad. Sometimes he drummed his fingers for minutes before running the tape again.

Reach out and touch the fire, Lacie.

"Are you sure the words are identical to your dream?"

"Yes."

Skyla crying: *What are you doing? Don't do that!*

"Does Skyla sound natural to you?"

"Of course not. She sounds scared. Hysterical."

"Yes, but does she sound like she's reading a script? Like it's a performance?"

"No. Absolutely not."

Skyla screaming: *Don't burn me! Please don't burn me!*

His fingers drummed, the pen scratched across paper, then the spit and hiss of Skyla burning filled the room again.

I left the room once to be sick. I brushed my teeth afterward, wet my face with cold water, and went back in. The screen was blank. Jack had stopped the tape.

"Let's finish this," I said.

He hit play.

Skyla's burning, Lacie. Bright in the night, flames shooting high, lighting the sky.

"Are you sure you know the narrator's voice?" Jack asked.

"I told you. It's the man who called this morning, the same voice as in my dreams."

"Is it? Have you ever heard Jerry whisper?"

"It's not Jerry!" I insisted, exasperated. "How can Jerry possibly be a suspect when I've been hearing the killer's voice since I was a child?"

Jack stopped the tape. "You're not going to like what I have to say."

"I'm getting used to that. Say it anyway."

"The night your hands burned, you witnessed your father's horrific death. One or the other of those events would have been deeply traumatic. Both of them together was more than your ten-year-old psyche could deal with. Psychological fallout was inevitable. The nightmares were triggered by your accident as a psychic release for your fear. Your subconscious manufactured the face and voice. Your young mind created the nightmare man. Stress triggers his reentry into your psyche. He drifts in and out of your dreams proportionately with the amount of stress you're under. Now, you've subconsciously linked the nightmare voice with the voice of the man who killed Skyla, making them one and the same."

"You don't believe me," I said flatly.

"I believe a man murdered your daughter. I believe that man is after you. Do I believe the killer is your nightmare man? That he walked out of your dreams and into Manhattan? No, I don't. He's flesh and blood and he has a name." Jack punched play. "Listen to the background. What do you hear?"

"Nothing. Silence. Wind."

"Listen again."

I heard it. A hollow hoot. "An owl?"

"Exactly. There aren't any owls in Manhattan. There are cars and sirens and the rumble of trains. This tape was made in the country. He transported her out of the city, alive and in one piece. We know he has a car. It's not so easy to grab a girl her age off the street in broad daylight without anyone noticing. I think Skyla chose to go with him."

"She never would have gone off with a stranger," I said with certainty. "Never. In a million years. She was too smart."

"Right," Jack said, quietly. "He either created the illusion of trust, or he was someone she knew."

"Back to Jerry?" I complained.

"Until my investigation proves otherwise," Jack promised.

"Poor Jerry. Guilty until proven innocent."

"In my book, yes."

"Your book is wrong. He was in Vermont when Skyla died."

Jack rewound the video to a wide shot at the start of the bonfire. "Are you certain those are Skyla's clothes?"

"That's what she was wearing when she left the loft." I told him about the building security tape.

"Do you have it?"

"Yes." I changed tapes and hit play.

It started early that Friday morning. Jerry and Cindy, with matching Vuitton overnight bags, walking through the lobby and out the front door. "So much for your Jerry theory," I said in a self-satisfied way. I scanned ahead to Skyla's appearance, then gave the remote to Jack.

He watched intently, zipping back and forth over the short sequence: Skyla coming out of the elevator, stopping in front of the mirror, adjusting her hat, turning her back to the camera and chatting with the doorman, then walking out the front door and disappearing from view.

He stopped the tape on the final image of Skyla stepping outside, hair whipping in the wind, right hand letting go of the door, feet in motion, warm breath smoking in the cold morning air. Jack was mesmerized by that last sequence. He played it over and over again, willing her to turn around and tell him where she was going and who she was going with. Willing her to turn around and go back inside to safety. To life.

"Did she tell the doorman where she was going?" Jack asked.

"No. No one knows where she went that morning, so where do we start?"

"With Dr. Grace Levitt," he replied, tapping Jerry's desk calendar. "Jerry's psychiatrist."

"Psychiatrist?" I asked, unable to hide my surprise.

"He sees her twice a week. Her office is on the Upper West Side, not far from the Cyber-Café the e-mail was sent from. She may be able to give me a better understanding of who Jerry is."

"Why don't you meet him and see for yourself?"

"I will, Ms. Wagner. But the third rule of a murder investigation is your number one rule of reporting: Have all your facts together before you do the face-to-face interview."

The innuendo in his voice infuriated me. I shot out of my chair. "Facts? What facts do you have other than your handy murder statistics? Jerry couldn't have done it. He was in Vermont."

"No, he wasn't."

"What?"

"He lied," Jack said, simply. "I have a problem with a man who lies to the police in the investigation of his own daughter's murder.

And I have a problem with a man who lies to the mother of his dead daughter. Makes me wonder what he's hiding."

I sat down, shocked. "You saw him walk out the door with Cindy Reese."

"They walked out together, but she went to the airport and Jerry didn't. I talked to the car service that picked her up that morning. Cindy got in the car alone and the airline manifest proves she flew alone. Jerry wasn't on the plane like he said he was. He didn't go to Vermont until Saturday night, on the six o'clock flight from La Guardia Airport."

"There must be some mistake."

"There's not. He lied to the police and to you."

Jack crossed over to Jerry's video library and looked at the hundred cassette boxes, all clearly marked with Skyla's name. The accusation was unspoken, but I heard it loud and clear. Jerry was obviously obsessed with recording his daughter's life, and although I had not noticed it before, I saw now that the brand of videocassette used by the killer was the same as those that filled Jerry's wall: Sony, 120 minutes, extended play. Rainbow boxes, all marked in indelible black ink on the spine.

"He's her father," I said, softly. "It's just not possible."

"Isn't it?" Jack said, spinning around. "Think it never happens? Or that it happens rarely? Each year more than five hundred children are killed by one of their natural parents. The average is neatly split. Half those kids are daughters, and fifty percent of the time, the father's the killer.

"Consider last year: A hundred and thirty-three girls were killed by their own fathers. Not a stepfather or a neighbor or an uncle or a stranger walking down the street. The biological father. You could fill up a jumbo jet with a hundred and thirty-three girls, blow it out of the sky, and the nation would weep. Most of those murdered daughters got no national attention at all. Filicide is America's ugly little secret.

"And you can't shrug it off as a *black* thing, or a *scared teenager killing an unwanted baby* thing. There's no racial or age bias to these killings. The murdered daughters range from newborns to sixteen years old. The fathers, from nineteen years old to sixty-one, and the majority of the murdering fathers are white. There's an interesting pattern to the killings. Babies up to the age of two, the fathers tend to use their bare hands. Toddlers two to four, they use blunt objects, hammers, bricks, whatever is handy and within reach at the time. From age four on up, you see every kind of weapon imaginable: mallets, screwdrivers, ice picks, rifles, shotguns, pistols, kitchen knives, hunting knives, homemade bombs. And fire."

"Fire?"

"Last November, a thirty-five-year-old white father in Charlotte, North Carolina, dunked his eight-year-old girl in a tub of gasoline, then tossed a match and watched her burn. In April, a forty-eight-year-old father in Daytona Beach, Florida, knocked his fourteen-year-old girl unconscious, set the house on fire, and ran. He thought it was the perfect crime, but the fire was put out before her body turned to ash. The medical examiner found the hammer blow on her skull, and when he did the autopsy he saw that she had burned alive. The smoke damage to her lungs proved that. Want me to go on?"

"No."

"There isn't anything I haven't seen, Ms. Wagner. I promise you that."

He changed tapes in the machine and watched the burning one last time, as if the camera would miraculously spin around, away from Skyla, and show us her killer's face.

"Why?" Jack asked. "Why tape the murder? A killer who does this usually wants the tape as a souvenir so he can sit in a dark room and relive his act over and over, ad infinitum. But this tape was made for you. He's mad at you. Full of hate and rage."

I looked at the incandescent flames bright against the night sky, taped for me, just for me, only for me. How could someone hate me so much?

"Jerry loved me," I insisted.

"Maybe it turned to hate somewhere along the way. I can't exclude him because of what he used to feel for you a long time ago. I can't exclude him for any reason. He lied. We owe it to Skyla to find out why."

The investigation had to go backward before it could move forward. Fire was my past. Now it was my present, burning bright on Jerry's custom screen. Past and present were linked. I would have to look back to try to understand where or when or how I had wronged someone. How far back? A year? Two? Ten? Thirteen? Back to Jerry's hands firmly, possessively on mine? To his intent eyes, wide open when we made love, and the solemn hard promises he spoke—*You'll always be mine, Lacie*—*Don't ever leave me,*

Lacie—Reach out and touch me, Lacie—while he moved steadily in and out of me?

Reach out and touch the fire, Lacie.

Jack hit eject. The tape popped out. He took it and reached for his parka. "Let's go. Grace Levitt is expecting us."

Chapter Ten

❧

Dr. Grace Levitt had a grandmother's face, silver hair pulled back in a neat bun, wire-rim glasses, and full soft cheeks. Her clothes were simple; a long denim skirt and white blouse buttoned high on the neck.

She was the mother confessor incarnate and I understood instantly why Jerry had chosen her. He would not have opened up to a man. And with any other kind of woman he would have been male first, proud and posturing, unable to expose his inner self. But a matron was a safe haven. A mother figure was loving, tolerant, forgiving of all excesses.

Her office was on the first floor of a prewar apartment building. Floor-to-ceiling bookshelves lined the walls. An oriental rug was a pool of Prussian blue against parquet floors. Two deep armchairs faced her broad cherry wood desk. A television set and VCR were on a portable cart in the corner. Logs crackled and glowed in the fireplace.

When the introductions were over, I settled into one of the armchairs with my back to the fire. Grace Levitt sat in her leather desk chair. Jack remained standing. He gave a brief rundown on his Bureau specialty as well as his background in medicine, and thanked her for agreeing to see us.

"Don't thank me yet," she warned.

"You know about Skyla Costello's murder," Jack said.

"Of course." She turned to me. "My heart goes out to you, Ms. Wagner. A friend of mine is a highly talented counselor in Washington. If you need guidance through this difficult time, I can arrange a meeting." She looked at Jack. "Now, down to business. Why are you here?"

"I want to talk to you about Jerry Costello."

"As a doctor yourself, Agent Stein, I'm surprised you bothered to ask. My office is a privileged setting, and what is said here is protected under doctor-patient confidentiality."

"There are exceptions," Jack countered. "Specifically in the area of warning. If you believe a patient presents a serious danger to someone or has threatened someone, you're permitted to inform the potential victim as well as a law enforcement official."

"I don't need a refresher course in New York state law and psychiatry," she shot back. "I am certainly aware of what my professional rights are, but I fail to see how they could possibly be of interest to either of you."

"Keep the warning exception in mind when you watch this," Jack said. He dropped the bonfire video into the VCR and hit play. Skyla's face filled the screen.

Levitt watched, transfixed and horrified. When the pink parka ignited, she jumped up and turned the tape off. "I've seen enough. What does this have to do with Jerry Costello?"

"I want to satisfy myself that he didn't kill her and that he's not coming after Ms. Wagner next."

Grace Levitt turned away, but not fast enough to hide her shock. She walked the length of the room, fussed with her collar, tucked a stray hair behind her ear.

"Skyla's murder was an act of rage," Jack explained, "directed at Ms. Wagner. This tape was made explicitly for her. The crime was personal, driven by rage, perhaps even revenge."

"And for that reason alone you suspect Jerry Costello?"

"No. He lied to the police about where he was when his daughter died. That's reason enough. In the absence of hard evidence, behavior is all I have to go on. I'm looking for motive, for a psychological footprint to match up with the killer's. I need a map of Jerry's mind and you're the only one who can give it to me."

"I'm sorry," she said, shaking her head and sitting down.

Jack pushed the VCR play button. The sound of Skyla's burning body filled the office. "Just because the idea of a parent killing a child is morally repugnant doesn't mean it never happens. Talk to me. For Skyla's sake."

"No," she said, with far less conviction than before.

"No because you don't know anything that would be useful," Jack asked, "or no because you do know something and you're afraid to talk?"

She steepled her hands and took a deep breath.

"What do you know?" Jack pressed. "There's plenty of leeway under New York law for you to decide what constitutes a threat. Jerry's state of mind would be enough. You know that. If Jerry ever made threats against Ms. Wagner or if his mental state could be considered threatening, you are legally permitted to disclose."

Grace Levitt absorbed this.

"If you don't talk to me," Jack said softly, "I can and will subpoena your files, Dr. Levitt. Rest assured of that. Skyla Costello is dead. Ms. Wagner is in imminent danger. The killer called her this morning and promised that he will burn her too."

Levitt looked up at the monitor, at the picture of my kicking, screaming, flaming daughter. "These are very special circumstances," she conceded. "The threat to Ms. Wagner is obvious on the tape. It's new information to me and, in light of it, there are things you should know."

"Thank you," I said.

Jack stopped the videotape.

"Tell me about Jerry," he said, sitting down and leaning forward, his blue eyes bright with interest.

"To understand the possible threat, you must first understand the man. He's been a patient of mine for twelve years. He had never been to a therapist and, as many people are, he was uncomfortable in the beginning. He was afraid to open up. The first year was not productive. He treated our time together like a trial, as if he had to convince me how talented, clever, and articulate he was.

"Each time I tried to zero in on the issues in his life, he veered away. It became more like a skillful verbal fencing match than therapy. When I tried to move our discussions to a deeper, more meaningful level, he blocked me. Finally, I told him I could no longer accept him as a patient. *Most people pay you to be a lawyer,* I said. *You pay me to let you play lawyer. This is a ridiculous waste of time for both of us.* From that moment on, he changed. He talked honestly."

"About what?" Jack asked.

"His compulsions. His anger. His fears." Her brown eyes were sad. "He has so many fears, more than you would ever guess."

"What is Jerry Costello afraid of?"

"Death, among other things. He's terrified of growing old, of losing his masculinity, of being unable to perform, of women finding him unattractive. At the core of this tremendously successful charismatic man, is a self-conscious insecure boy. He suffers from obsessive-compulsive disorders. When he goes out to buy a cookbook, he buys ten. The same with clothes. If he needs one pink shirt, he buys eight new pink shirts.

"He's equally compulsive about sex with women. Jerry wants a monogamous relationship, wants it desperately, but he just isn't capable. And, as the years go by, he craves sex with young women. Twenty years old. Nineteen. Eighteen. Maybe less. He has never confessed to crossing that delicate legal line, but admits he's been tempted."

"The younger the woman, the more powerful and sexually potent he feels?" Jack asked.

"Exactly," she replied. "Jerry gets his sense of manhood from a woman's dependency on him. He needs to be the stronger of the two, needs desperately for women to revere and admire him. That is complicated by his compulsion to seek out multiple sexual encounters. He will often have several different women in the same week.

"The only time he could manage his compulsions was when Skyla was with him. Jerry believed there were just two things he did right in life: practicing law and being a father to Skyla. Nonetheless, Skyla's growing up absolutely terrified him. He felt confusion and guilt about his fixation on young women. He said watching Skyla change from a child to a woman proved that time was passing. If she was getting older, that meant he was too. He felt powerless to stop or slow or evade the inevitable march to death. The only thing that scares Jerry Costello more than death is the loss of control. And that fear is the very basis of his feelings for Ms. Wagner."

"Which are?" Jack asked.

"Love and rage," she said looking at me. "Jerry's need for other women is totally at odds with his obsession with the one woman he wanted—the one woman he had but couldn't keep. You, Ms. Wagner. He started therapy because you left him. He was confused and depressed, but mostly he was angry. Even though his own behavior drove you away, he was furious at you for leaving him. In his own way, Jerry loved you desperately, and he still does.

"His obsession with you has never been resolved. The fact that you were—are—handicapped is very important to him. He was fascinated with your hands, with what the fire did to them. It was proof that you needed him. You were his broken bird. He didn't believe you could ever fly without him.

"When you left, he was convinced you would come crawling back. He thought you wouldn't be able to make it alone. You proved him very wrong. You not only survived, you flourished, and the more successful you became, the more it upset him. He has always felt your success diminishes him as a man. It proves he was, and is, disposable.

"This year, when you made the move to Washington and it became clear you'd be a star, his anger manifested itself in a terrible way. Jerry began to have episodes of impotency. He blamed you. He said sometimes when he tried to have sex, he saw you instead of the girl he was with. He imagined that you mocked him. Made fun of him. It was totally irrational, but it rekindled his latent anger. He experienced terrible mood swings as a result."

"Did you put him on Prozac?" Jack asked.

Levitt frowned. "I know where you're going with that line of thinking. I'm more than familiar with the track record of the drug."

"Then you know what the adverse reactions have been."

"Sudden, inexplicably violent acts by people who have never been violent before. As I said, Agent Stein, I know the casework."

"It was a yes or no question," Jack said. "Is Jerry Costello on Prozac?"

"Yes. I prescribed it at his request three months ago."

"Did it have side effects?"

"A doctor can only rely on observation and the honesty of the patient. I can't swear his experience with Prozac was or is problem-free. Jerry's a convincing actor. He lets me know what he wants me to know."

"What else has he let you know?"

"That his feelings—his anger—for Ms. Wagner scare him."

"How is Jerry dealing with his daughter's death?"

"I wouldn't know. He stopped therapy the week before she died. He said he needed a break. I haven't see him since."

"Dr. Levitt, in your opinion, is Jerry Costello capable of committing an act of murder?"

"Each of us is capable of unimaginable acts. Each of us has a combustion point. Most never hit it, thank God. How can I tell you what another person is or isn't capable of when I can't answer that question as applied to myself? None of us knows. Not a single one of us. The people we think we know best turn out to be strangers, and we are often strangers to our own selves."

"Is it at all possible that Jerry Costello could have committed filicide?"

"I've been peering into the darkness of the human psyche for thirty-two years and I've learned one thing above all, Agent Stein. Anything is possible. Even the unthinkable."

"I need to be alone," I announced outside when it was over, craving time and motion to absorb what I had just heard. I walked away from Jack. I didn't want to see the conviction in his eyes, the satisfaction, the cool *I told you so* set to his broad shoulders.

"Ms. Wagner . . ."

I spun around. "Do me a favor. Don't talk to me about it. Don't say a word. Not one word. Not now. Just leave me alone."

He didn't. He followed me, doggedly, honey hair glinting in the sun, block after block after block. He was always there, an arm's length behind. I faked composure, shoved my hands deep in my coat pockets, and walked fast. The sun was warm on my face, but I was bitterly cold inside. I hated Jack for taking me to hear those words.

In his own way, Jerry loved you desperately, Ms. Wagner, and he still does.

Jerry had been crazy with jealousy when I first left him—an odd reaction for a philanderer. He used to call me at one, two, three in the morning. Bed checks. *Are you alone, Lacie? Is someone there with you? I know someone's there with you!*

When jealousy got him nowhere, he tried remorse and all the sorry promises of an addict: *I'll change. I'll be better. I'll be different. I'll get counseling. I'll never look at another woman again. I swear. Please come back. Try again. I miss you. Oh God, Lacie, I miss you.*

And finally, *I hate you.* He said it a lot in the first year after I left him.

Love had turned to jealousy and hate, and somewhere along the way, anger had turned to rage.

Anything is possible, Grace Levitt had said. *Even the unthinkable.*

Who else could possibly hate me so much? Who else knew how truly terrified I was of fire? Who else knew my nightmares word for word?

Jerry did it. Jerry did it. Jerry did it.

I considered Grace Levitt's summary of his sexual problems. Sex had always been a game to him. *Sex is fun,* Jerry used to say, ticking off a hundred other reasons why he couldn't keep his hands off other women. Sex was sporty, recreational, casual, therapeutic, but mostly it was *fun.* Now I knew it was an uncontrollable compulsion. It had nothing to do with love or marriage or, certainly, procreation. Skyla had been an accident. One he had not been happy about—at first. His words came back to me.

Pregnant! How did that happen?

The usual way, I answered, wishing sarcasm were poison.

Why would you possibly want to bring a child into this shitty world? What's wrong with you?

You.

What?

You're what's wrong with me. I wheeled around and left.

Jerry tried to find me. He called every hotel in Manhattan, traced my credit cards, called my friends, few as they were, and he would have called Max too if he had been on the same continent. When I appeared weeks later, gaunt and sad, he folded me into his arms and cried. *Don't ever leave me again.* He swore he wanted the baby and when she was born, I finally believed him.

He was spellbound by the tiny wriggling child we had created. He fed Skyla, rocked her, changed her diapers. He bought her a glow-in-the-dark globe and told her tall tales of our round world. He learned how to mix her formula and wash her baby-fine hair. He set up trust funds and college accounts, bought her a basket of blue-chip stocks, and held her on his lap while he read the *Wall Street Journal* aloud. When it came to Skyla, Jerry was committed, devoted, and honest. Everything he wasn't with me.

Now, walking swiftly up the West Side, I remembered his first angry words: *How could you bring a child into this shitty world?*

You were right, I thought. *But was it you? Did you do that to her?*

Jerry had a temper. It was swift, sudden, and surprisingly violent. I remembered the night a careless driver rear-ended Jerry's brand-new Jaguar. Jerry exploded. He jumped out, pulled the man from his car, and hit him once, hard enough to break three teeth. Later, contrite, he paid off the man to drop the lawsuit. Had I glimpsed a dark side to Jerry that night, one he had kept well hidden all these years?

Jerry did it, Jerry did it, Jerry did it.

Then, I remembered Captain's boat, the misery in Jerry's eyes when he emptied the urn. Our shared sorrow. And the voice. The whispering voice wasn't Jerry's. It couldn't be Jerry's.

Could it?

Jerry did it. Jerry did it. Jerry did it.

Back and forth. Guilty. Innocent. Guilty. Innocent. The verdict changing with every other footfall.

I glanced behind me. Jack was still there, trailing along. I walked faster. He matched my pace.

"You don't have to follow me," I called out.

"Yes, I do."

"I'm quite capable of taking care of myself."

"I'm sure you are."

"You don't have to stay with me tonight."

"Yes, I do."

I spun around. "Don't you have somebody waiting for you at home?"

Bull's-eye. Jack Stein closed down cold. His face darkened, his body tensed. He crossed his arms over his chest, but he did not leave.

I moved ahead again, happy I had hit him where it hurt. The mountain-climbing doctor was made of flesh, not stone, and I had driven a nice sharp arrow in somewhere deep. He followed me anyway, his footsteps tapping out the accusation.

Jerry did it. Jerry did it. Jerry did it.

Jerry was a convincing actor. He could convince a jury that a guilty man was innocent; he made his fortune doing that. Was he the guilty man playing innocent now, with crocodile tears and trumped-up grief?

Impossible? Grace Levitt didn't find it impossible. Nether did Jack and he had thousands of fat facts to prove the point. Case histories. Filicide. It happened in rich homes. It happened in poor homes. Had it happened in Skyla's home? The thought made me sick. Filicide.

Jerry did it. Jerry did it. Jerry did it.

"You're wrong," I said, tossing words into the air, hoping Jack would hear.

Jerry did it. Jerry did it. Jerry did it.

"You are wrong!" I announced again, moving swiftly ahead, afraid that Jack was really right.

I marched along, block after block, until the boots in a shop window stopped me. Reminded me. Broke my heart. Ankle-high, four-inch stacked heels, glossy black calfskin, side zip. *The Avenger Boot*. Emma Peale. Adventure and intrigue.

"Hardly your style," Jack observed, close behind me.

"Skyla wanted a pair," I said, smiling sadly. "They're the *in* thing for teenagers. She saw them one day in Georgetown, in a window like this. Before I knew it, she was inside trying them on. The change in her was staggering. The Avenger Boot walked her right out of adolescence. She was suddenly leggy and sure, stalking around the store like she owned the world, so grown-up it scared me.

"I told her she couldn't have them. I lied and said they made her look cheap. Her confidence disappeared. She put her Reeboks back on and turned into a young girl again. I'm as guilty as Jerry. I didn't want Skyla to grow up too fast. It wasn't the age thing that bothered me. I was afraid of losing her. But I lost her anyway, didn't I? I should've bought her the boots." I put my forehead against the chilly display window glass. "I should've bought her the goddamn boots."

A gust of wind kicked up, blowing candy wrappers and old newspapers around my ankles. My coat hem whipped my legs and I felt hollow, popsickle-stick brittle and light, as if the wind could slap me into walls, lift me into the sky, spin me away like a dry leaf. Of course I was light. My child was gone. Where there had been two of us, there was now one. My second pair of sky blue eyes was shuttered forever.

Jerry did it.

Jack's hands settled on my shoulders. I leaned back and let him hold me earthbound, out of the wind.

When the feeling passed, we walked.

"How much do you know about Prozac?" Jack ventured.

"I did a three-part series on it a while back, *Prozac: Promise or Poison*. Crushed the competition with a forty-five share. Prozac's hardly your run-of-the-mill antidepressant. Some consider it the wonder drug of the nineties. People use it to change their personalities the way women change their hair color. Introverts suddenly become extroverts. Shy people become incredibly confident and outgoing."

"Did your story include the side effects?"

"Of course. *Uncontrollable violent behavior,* just as the good doctor said. There are hundreds of case studies to back it up. A powerful consumer group in D.C. is pressuring the FDA to take Prozac off the market."

"Jerry has serious psychological problems. Maybe the drug pushed him right over the edge."

"I don't buy it."

"You really want to believe in him, don't you?" Jack's eyes were unreadable behind the mirrored glasses.

"Yes. You don't know him."

"Neither do you. Twelve years ago he wasn't the man you thought he was. Maybe that's the case now."

I stopped walking. "You really want him to be guilty, don't you?"

"No," Jack said icily. "You couldn't be more wrong. I want Jerry Costello to be innocent. I want Jerry Costello to come up a paragon of virtue. A man of honor. I want to find out he was a Norman Rockwell kind of dad. But for the moment, all I know is he lied and I'm going to find out why."

"How?"

"I'll ask him, Ms. Wagner. Then I'll watch his face."

Chapter Eleven

We stayed in that night, both of us exhausted by a day that had started before dawn. Jack used the computer and his federal clout to grimly troll for information on Jerry Costello. I ended up in Jerry's bedroom, poking through his things as if a man could be judged by his possessions.

Jerry had three walk-in closets. I opened them all and touched his fine Italian slacks, the gold buttons on his cashmere jackets, the collars of his shirts. I inhaled the scent of new rich leather and counted thirty-nine pairs of Italian shoes. I flipped through the tie racks, touching silk, remembering the cavalier way he knotted his ties, so cocksure and proud, loving the ritual of dressing in good clothes.

I stepped into his oversized marble bathroom and opened the cabinets. Jerry was a control freak, and if my own live-in experience and Grace Levitt's testimony weren't proof enough, this was. Everything was alphabetically organized. A for Alka-Seltzer, B for Benadryl, C for Codeine, D for Dexedrine, E for Excedrin, and so on, all the way to V for Valium.

From what I saw, he had trouble sleeping, staying awake, digesting, eliminating, relaxing, breathing, even making love. I found all kinds of sex toys and the lubricants to use with them. Poor Jerry. When we had been married, he slept like a kitten, ate like a Hun, and made love like a teenager with a tireless inventiveness that relied on our own two able bodies, not prepackaged toys.

I had loved Jerry all those years ago. Why? Because he loved me. Simple as that. He was a successful man, the most successful, and there I was, young and insecure with my poor burned hands, feeling lucky to have any man at all. I loved the pride in his voice when he introduced me to his partners: *Lacie Costello, my bride,* those words falling off his lips like milk, sweet warm milk.

With Jerry I was no longer the fire-maimed freak. He gave me sanctuary, accepted my deformity, washed it away with his generosity, his extravagance. Jerry thought spending money would buy him love and it bought him mine, for a time. Having no other way of measuring my own self-worth, I let his gold standard do it for me. I loved his extravagance. I loved the naked adoration in his eyes, the way he made me feel beautiful, the way he made me laugh. Then I found out he was an incurable liar and cheat, and I grew up fast.

Now, I picked one of his shirts out of the hamper and buried my face in it, smelling his cologne, his sweat, his ambition, his energy. I considered Jack's question. Why did I want to believe in Jerry? I suspected it was because he was Skyla's father. I loved her so much, it ran over and spilled onto him. Was that blinding me to the truth?

And the truth was, Jerry had lied.

I tossed the shirt back in the hamper and went to see what other damning evidence Jack had dug up.

He looked up when I walked in.

"Jerry's American Express statement for the month of November," Jack said, tapping the ThinkPad screen. "On the Friday after Thanksgiving, he rented a car from Hertz here in Manhattan. Hertz records show he checked the car out at eight-thirty Friday morning. He returned the car to La Guardia at five o'clock the next night with a quarter tank of gas. Speedometer readings show he traveled a hundred and forty miles."

I turned my back on him and walked out.

Not knowing what else to do, I went into Skyla's room, sat down at the computer, and dialed into my WRC e-mail box.

There was a long message from Harry promising me an unlimited paid leave of absence. He was anchoring the news while I was gone and, reading between the lines, Harry loved it. The phone on the desk rang. I picked up. It was Harry.

"I got tired of waiting for you to phone home," he complained gently. He went on to give me all the usual newsroom banter, brought me up to date on the ratings, the lead stories and general station gossip, then he zeroed in on the reason for the call.

"Lacie, I'm calling as your friend."

"I'm listening."

"Don't take this wrong, but I think you should come back to work. It would be good for you."

"I can't do that just yet."

"They say staying busy helps with the grief, the adjustment."

"Is that what they say?" My voice was colder than I intended. I warmed up and started again. "Sorry, Harry. Nothing in the world's going to help me adjust. Nothing."

"What about your career?"

"What about it?"

"What I'm trying to say is that you still have your whole life in front of you, your whole *career*, and it's a brilliant one. You know I'm on your side. I'll give you as much time as you need and want. If it's six months from now, well, fine by me. But that wouldn't be a good choice for *you*, Lacie. Sooner is better than later."

"I wish I could agree."

"I'm worried about you sitting up there all alone in New York. What do you do all day?"

"I'm working on a story."

"A story? You lost me."

"Trust me. Wait for me. I'll be back when I'm ready."

He sighed. "Stay in touch."

"I will." I hung up.

Max called next. He used the old-fashioned telephone. I asked him why.

"Because I'm somewhere unpleasant at the moment where I can't carry my computer. I'm using a cell phone instead. God's gift to mountain men. Speaking of which, I hear you found Jack Stein. How is he?"

"Abrupt. Direct. Speaks his mind. A little rough around the edges with me, although he's absolutely charming to the rest of the world. He's an excellent guard dog, Max. Very committed. I tried to call him off. He wouldn't budge."

"Good," Max said, his gruff voice rich with satisfaction. "You told me you were scared. I've never heard you use that word in your life. Stein stays." The connection began to break up.

"Max?"

"Lacie? Lacie?" His voice dropped in and out, and then he was gone.

I hung up and went back to my e-mail.

There were a dozen messages from members of the national support group Parents of Murdered Children offering words of comfort and inviting me to local chapter meetings.

I politely declined. I have always been a solitary woman, never the kind to commiserate, to reach out, or make my pain public. I could not imagine sitting in a circle with grief-stricken parents and soft-faced counselors urging me to share my sadness. I didn't want bromides. I wanted action. Revenge. Justice. My mission was my own. I had to find the man who killed Skyla. I wanted to see the monster, touch him, feel his heartbeat. Then, I wanted to kill him myself.

Even if it was Jerry.

Especially if it was Jerry.

The last message was from Jeff Hoag. He wanted to talk to me about Linda Severino's death. I wanted to hear what he had to say. Linda was more than a story to me, and I welcomed the distraction from thinking about Jerry. Hoag's area code was 202—Washington, D.C. It was still early enough to call.

He answered on the first ring.

"You know, Ms. Wagner, I can't accept the fact she's gone. We met in the Navy eight years ago. We flew together, sailed together, saw the world together." He paused. "I never thought the day would come when we wouldn't be together."

"Jeff, there were some disturbing allegations made about Linda." I tried to be as gentle as possible, to draw him out. "Her behavior that night, her wild statements."

"Yeah. The tabloids have had a hell of a time. They call her *Crazy Linda.* TV reporters camped out in front of my apartment for weeks. They wanted to know how I felt about what she did. I just flipped them the bird and said, *No comment.* Truth is, Ms. Wagner, you're the only one who handled the story with dignity. I wasn't very helpful to you back then, but now I want you to understand Linda. What she was going through. Maybe you can find out what really happened on the ship that night. Set things right by her somehow."

"I'd like to try."

"Can this be off the record?"

"Yes."

"Okay," he said. "Here goes. Linda had psychological problems.

We tried to keep them a secret. We were afraid she'd be considered unfit for active duty. Truth is, she had problems when I first met her. They went all the way back to her childhood."

"What kind of problems?"

"Dreams. Nightmares."

I sat straight up in my chair. "Go on."

"Sometimes they went away for a month or two, but they always came back. She thought she was crazy, schizo."

"Why?"

"Because she heard the same voice over and over in those nightmares. She used to wake up crying and screaming. Sometimes it took hours for me to calm her down. She'd go around and double-check all the doors and windows, make sure they were locked. *He's coming to get me,* she'd say. Just like a little girl. Like there was some big bad man out there. *He's coming to get me.*" Jeff laughed bitterly. "She got herself in the end, didn't she? Took a flying leap into the Bering fucking Sea, and it wasn't guilt that made her jump."

"What did?"

"I have some crazy theories, but I'd rather hammer them out with you in person when you're back in D.C. and have the time."

"Fair enough," I replied. "Tell me this: Was Linda afraid of anything?"

"Other than the nightmare voice?"

"Yes."

"Sure. Linda was afraid of fire, Ms. Wagner. She was afraid of burning to death."

I hung up feeling dizzy, sick. Three lives converged: Linda's, Skyla's, and mine. What was the thread tying us all together? Fire and the voice, the whispering voice. How could Linda's whispering voice be the same as mine? And if Linda heard the voice too, how could it possibly be Jerry's?

I suddenly felt overwhelmed, unable to make sense of the senseless, too fragile from my loss to deal. Grief is heavy. The weight of it dragged me down.

Were you afraid, Sky? Did you feel the fire?

The vision of her charred butchered torso popped into my mind. *Were you afraid, Sky?* My own fear stitched tight around my heart and squeezed me breathless when I considered the final minutes of Skyla's life, the pain she must have felt. *Did you feel the fire?* I wanted to curl up on the bed, crawl back into the black hole of booze and self-pity and dark drugged sleeps. I tottered into the bathroom, fumbled in the cabinet for my Valium stash.

Linda was afraid of fire. She was afraid of burning to death.

A bottle of bubble bath tipped over and shattered on the floor. The sweet noise of destruction set me off. Perfume bottles were next, five jars, a tall crystal vase. The pendulum had swung. Tick had turned to tock. I slammed the hair dryer into the mirror. Suddenly there were a thousand wild-eyed Lacies and a thousand honey-haired giants in back of her.

Jack loomed in the doorway.

"Leave me alone," I said, sagging against the counter. My body felt brittle and my brain was an old film projector speeding images across the screen: Linda jumping, Skyla burning, Captain praying, Jerry pouring ashes, the nightmare face whispering, and Lacie weeping—weeping, weeping, weeping. The earth was sliding right out from under my feet and this time it did not stop. Jack caught me before my body hit the glass shards on the floor.

He carried me out to Skyla's bed, thumbed the Valium open, dropped the pill into the back of my throat like a dog, and made me swallow. I struggled and wept until the drug took hold. Jack stayed with me, pressing my face into the warm slope of his neck, riding it out, letting me fall apart in the practiced professional comfort of his doctor's arms.

I must have cried myself to sleep. When I opened my eyes, hours had passed, and Jack was gone. I got up and moved down the hall, cocking my head, listening to silence, thinking he had left, that I had scared him away.

I heard the faint sound of a violin and followed it to Jerry's office. Jack was sitting in the dark, watching one of Jerry's home videos on the wide-screen TV. It had been made recently, at the end of the summer, out at the beach. Skyla was wearing a white summer shift and standing barefoot in the sand, playing the violin. Deep music. She played from the heart.

Jerry appeared in the frame. He swiped the violin and fiddled a country jig. Then, he dropped it and swept Skyla into his arms. He waltzed her across the sand, dipping and whirling, humming a crazy dance tune. Skyla's swinging dress, her hair shining in the sun, her laughter ringing out. She was so very alive. Father and daughter waltzed down to the tide line and away, until they were tiny against the horizon.

Jack made a sound. Tears wet his cheeks. A new interest stirred in me. When I saw the raw unedited emotion on his face, my feelings for Jack Stein began to change.

The next morning, I rose at dawn. The loft was quiet. The mirror was still shattered, but the rest of the bathroom had been cleaned up. I showered and dressed, then walked down the hall, checking rooms, sure that Jack had slipped out in the night.

I found him in Jerry's office, sitting behind the desk, staring at the computer screen. He wore a fresh navy turtleneck under a blue chambray shirt. His eyes were swollen and a fine gold stubble coarsened his cheeks.

"Jack?" I wanted to thank him for his professional courtesy and for not embarrassing me. Mostly I wanted to thank him for not deserting me. I needed him. In the light of day, I realized that. There wasn't anyone else. NYPD was out. Jerry was clearly out. There was just me, and I knew I didn't have the resources or the experience to do this alone. This wasn't the same as lugging a camcorder around southern Alabama. For once in my life, I had to admit, I needed help. Jack Stein was my best and only hope.

He was looking up, waiting for me to finish my sentence.

"I'm glad you're still here," I finally said.

"Service with a smile, Ms. Wagner."

"Lacie. Please."

"Lacie," he repeated, with a wry smile.

"Since Skyla died, this feeling hits me out of nowhere from time to time. The ground drops out from under me. Sometimes I catch myself. Sometimes I don't. Last night I didn't."

"Happens." He said it casually, but his expression was troubled. "There are support groups that can work you through this."

"Group support. Like your mountain climbers. All tied together, right?"

"Something like that. Trust, sharing the experience with others who have been through it, helps."

"It's not who I am. I'm a loner, Jack, and despite your good mountain talk, I think you understand that." I leaned across the desk. "You're not supposed to watch your child die. That's not how it's supposed to work. Nothing will help me through this or over this. Nothing. Especially if it was Jerry. I want to find out why he lied."

"So do I," Jack said, pushing his chair back and rising. "Let's take a ride out to the beach."

Chapter Twelve

❧

We raced east on the Long Island Expressway, away from Manhattan, into the rising sun. It was only six o'clock, but Jack wanted to get there early, to catch Jerry unprepared, with his defenses down.

There is much to be said—everything to be said—for the surprise visit. I knew that from reporting, from shoving mikes into the faces of condemned men, grieving widows, sole survivors, Olympic winners, Herculean losers. *What happened? How did it happen? How does it feel? Why did you do it? What made you do it?* Truth is revealed in vulnerable moments. I had built a career on that premise, capturing the truth when it was raw and real and new. No one was exempt from my shotgun questions. *How does it feel? Tell me how it feels.*

Hadn't I been the first one to talk to Jeff Hoag, to capture his grief on tape for the whole nation to hear? Hadn't I always pushed my way through the pack of reporters, eager to get to the victim first, convinced that I was more compassionate because I had once been a victim too? Hadn't I been even more eager to leap on the guilty? Hadn't I always been there in my smart black blazers and camera-ready face wanting to pry the God's honest truth from a surprised, unprepared subject?

It was Jack's turn now.

Why did you lie, Jerry? Why did you lie?

The question was an accusation and it would be thrown at him before he had wiped the sleep from his eyes. If Jerry answered right, he was free. But if he panicked like one of his hostile witnesses on the stand, if Jerry slipped up or fucked up or tried to lie his way out of the lie, Jack would nail him.

We traveled in silence. I glanced at him from time to time, wishing he hadn't seen my emotional free fall the night before, surprised that I cared what he thought. Then, I remembered his quiet sorrow, the tears on his face, and I wondered who they were for.

Sixty miles out, Jack turned off the expressway and cut northeast toward the shore, topping seventy on long empty stretches of country road. A half hour later, the ocean splayed into view across flat expanses of old farmland blanketed in fresh deep snow. A high night wind had whipped the sky clean. The gentle winter sun sat low, the water sparkled.

I cracked the window and inhaled tangy salt air. Jack slowed. He made a series of right turns, then followed a narrow straight road that dead-ended at the beach. One huge house stood alone with the vast blinding snowfields on one side and the wide open Atlantic on the other.

The mailbox was marked, *Costello*.

Jack whistled. Grudging admiration shone in his eyes.

The house was three terraced levels of glass and wood with sweeping windows and skylights. Sand dunes tumbled away from the main deck. Tall sea grass swayed in the wind. Jerry's white Mercedes was in the drive. Jack pulled in behind it. We dropped out of the Range Rover, moved upstairs to the front door, and rang the bell.

Jerry's voice crackled out of the intercom. "Who is it?"

"Lacie," I said.

"Hey! Nice surprise! I just got out of the shower. I'll throw something on. Give me five minutes."

He opened the door in three. His hair was damp and he was dressed in his idea of casual: thick cashmere sweater the color of butter, knife-pressed chinos, and soft leather loafers, no socks.

"Lacie and friend," he said, sizing Jack up, taking in his hiking boots and unshaven face.

"Jack Stein," Jack said. "Hope we didn't catch you at a bad time."

"It's early, but what the hell. Come on in. Check out the view while I get coffee. How do you take it, Jack?"

"Black, thanks."

Jerry left us in the living room. It was an enormous space with high vaulted ceilings, skylights, and bleached wood floors. The furniture, like the house, was oversized and richly upholstered in earth tones. Massive classic seascapes were artfully placed, but the real showpiece was the beach view. One wall was all window, ten sliding glass door partitions that opened onto the front deck.

I cracked one open and listened to the pounding surf. A gust of wind picked up sand and tossed it my way. Gold glitter against the glass. I closed the door and counted seagulls. One in particular caught my eye. His fat body was bright white against the hard blue sky, his wings were spread and motionless. He was drifting, letting the wind do the work. An orange flare shot up high into that cobalt sky and the next second my great white winged friend was plummeting down, feathers burning, smoke trailing from the impact point in his belly. Wisps of burnt down spiraled away on the breeze. The smoldering bird hit water.

Jerry had seen it too. "Damn kids," he complained, walking in, setting a tray on a side table. "Nothing better to do on the holiday than hang around the beach and use gulls for target practice."

I wanted to believe him, but felt somehow that gull was an omen meant for me.

Silly Lacie. Finding hidden meanings in children's pranks.

Jerry gave me my coffee, then handed Jack a steaming mug. "You two just happen to be in the neighborhood?"

"Not exactly," Jack replied, moving casually through the room touching fabrics, studying the man, his objects, his home. "I'm with the FBI, investigating your daughter's murder."

"FBI? You sure don't look like a federal agent, if you don't mind my saying so."

"Not at all, Mr. Costello."

"Jerry, please." Still friendly and easy, sipping his coffee. "I didn't know this had moved out of NYPD Homicide. Chief of detectives is one stubborn man. It takes a lot for Garrett to call in the feds. Frankly, I'm glad he did. What are we looking at, some kind of serial killer? You got other cases like this one?"

"No. We ran the crime specifics through VICAP. There were no matches."

"Doesn't mean there won't be." Jerry started pacing. "Fucking nut, running around out there loose as we speak, looking at young girls, choosing his next victim. Who knows when he'll kill another innocent kid?"

"He won't," Jack said flatly.

Jerry stopped pacing. "You lost me."

"He isn't a serial killer. This crime was personal, very personal, and Skyla wasn't the target at all."

"Oh, wow. Now you've really lost me, Jack. You've airlifted me right into the woods and dropped me without a parachute. How can you possibly say Skyla wasn't the target?"

"Burning Skyla was a warning to Lacie. Lacie's the target."

"Lacie?"

"Yes."

"Well, that's a hell of a theory and I hope you're wrong. What can I do for you?"

"Fill in some blanks."

"Didn't know there were any. Homicide did a crack investigation. They turned everything and everybody inside out and upside down, didn't they?"

Jack sidestepped the question. "What time did you get to Vermont that Friday?"

"Jack. Buddy. You came all the way out here to ask me my flight schedule? My full statement is in the police reports."

"I want to hear it from you," Jack said lightly. "It's a thing I have when I move into an investigation at the halfway point."

"Halfway point!" Jerry exclaimed. "You're a lot more optimistic than Garrett. Last I heard, he was ready to call it quits. Tough call for a proud man. Then again, I guess that's why he brought you in."

"When did you get to Vermont?"

"Friday morning. Ten o'clock. We were on the mountain by eleven. Five hours of kick-ass skiing over the kind of bumps that remind a guy that his knees aren't twenty anymore."

"Even if his date is?"

"Very good, *Agent Stein*. You did your homework."

"Did you have dinner or spend time with anybody other than Cindy Reese while you were in Vermont that Friday?"

Jerry walked away from Jack. "What's that got to do with my daughter's death?"

"These are just routine questions."

"They don't sound routine to me," Jerry said evenly. "They sound like Bureau bullshit."

"Just doing my job."

"Your job." Jerry sipped his coffee. "Are you checking me out, Stein? Sneaking around peeking into my private life, my business life? Are you investigating me?"

"These are routine questions, Jerry."

"Costello," Jerry said, pointing. "You call me Mr. Costello. Routine questions? You would've used the phone. No, you're not here in person to ask a few piddly-shit questions. You could've saved yourself a long drive, which makes me wonder: Why did you come all the way out here? I'll tell you why. You're here because you're checking me out. You want to see for yourself where I live, how I live, who I live with. The Bureau's got balls, Stein, sending you waltzing right up to my doorstep."

"Jerry," I attempted.

"Stay out of this," he ordered, eyes locked on Jack.

"Jack just wants to nail down where everyone was the day Skyla disappeared, that's all."

"Thanks for the news summary," Jerry sniped.

"Who did you have dinner with Friday night in Vermont?" Jack asked again.

"My girlfriend, that's who," Jerry said. "I had dinner with Cindy Reese."

"You have a receipt?"

"No. I paid cash. Now, the real question is this: *Why* are you checking me out? Tell me that, Stein."

"You're smart. Figure it out."

Jerry blinked. Comprehension spread across his face. He flushed. "You son of a bitch. Now, Stein, you put this down for the record. I loved my daughter. Worshipped her! *Worshipped her!* Got that? Now get the fuck out of here. Both of you."

"If you loved your daughter," Jack said, "why did you lie?"

"Fuck you."

"No, Jerry, you're the one who's fucked." Jack walked up close to Jerry, crowding in on his personal space. He used his size to intimidate and made his voice hard. "You weren't in Vermont at dinnertime, you weren't in Vermont at all that Friday. You didn't fly up until Saturday night. People lie when they have something to hide. What are you hiding?"

"Get out."

"Not until you answer my questions."

"Are you charging me with something here, Stein? Should I call a lawyer?"

"Do you need one, Jerry?" Jack let it sink in. "You have a brand-new white Mercedes parked outside. What in God's name were you doing driving around in a black, four-door, full-size, Hertz rent-a-car in New York City on the Friday Skyla disappeared?"

"Get out."

Jack flipped his cell phone open. "Guess I'd better give your buddy Garrett a call. Tell him you're refusing to cooperate with a federal agent. Tell him you lied in a police investigation." He started punching numbers.

Jerry was trapped. I watched a fever light grow in his eyes and sweat dot his forehead. He had no chance now to concoct a new story or to set an alibi other than the one he had and thought was airtight. No time to rewrite his *closing statement*, that being the one on file with the police, no time for a *side bar* with the judge or a *temporary adjournment* to prepare for the next day. Jack was smart doing it like this.

"Put the phone away, Stein," Jerry finally said, all the bravado stripped and gone. "Sit the fuck down and listen to me."

Jack snapped his phone shut but remained standing.

Jerry looked small next to Jack, and dwarfed by the huge room around him. He ran a hand through his hair, sank down on the couch. "Fuck." He shook his head. "First thing you've got to understand is that Skyla asked to stay in the city. I didn't desert her. She was a responsible girl and she had an armed guard downstairs. I thought she was safe. I never would've left if I didn't honest to God believe she was safe. Jesus." His voice broke. He took a deep breath.

"Truth is, I've always felt Lacie was too strict with her. Over-protective. I believed my job was to balance that out, give Skyla some extra freedom, let her run some and grow to understand the responsibility that comes with having freedom. She earned my trust in a thousand little ways over the years. We built up to her being able to spend some time alone. I had left her on her own for one night a couple of times before."

"She never told me that," I said, panicked that I hadn't known.

"We knew you'd freak out," Jerry explained. "Anyway, like I said, she earned my trust. I wasn't frivolous about leaving her that weekend. It was two nights instead of one. So what? I knew she could take care of herself. And, if she needed me, I was always just a phone call away. I carry a cell phone."

"The Jerry Costello approach to parenting," I said bitterly, unable to help myself, hoping that was the worst thing he had done. "A gold card and a cell phone. I thought you were so much better than that."

"Lacie," Jack warned.

Now was not the time. And, all those careless transgressions were meaningless compared to the enormity of the larger crime.

"Skyla wanted to stay," Jerry argued, losing composure. "She asked to stay. So I said yes. I left her in the city, but I didn't go to Vermont. Not right away." He rocked on the edge of the couch and tried to pull himself together. "My Mercedes was in for repairs. You can check that out with the dealer in Manhattan. I rented a car because I was taking a drive to the country."

I thought of the owl on the tape. Jack's observation: *This tape was made in the country somewhere.* I knew that Jack was thinking that too.

"Where did you go?" he asked.

"Bear Creek Inn up in the Hudson Valley, near West Point. An hour from the city."

"Why?"

"I was meeting a woman there."

"You have this," Jack said, gesturing to the house. "Why did you need a hotel? You had Cindy. Why did you need another date?"

"It's hard to explain."

"Find a way."

"I was fooling around with one of those sex chat rooms on the Internet and met a woman. She was uninhibited, to say the least. Things got heated up, much as they can on-line, and the next thing I knew she was challenging me to spend a day and night together at this country inn. *It will be a feast,* she promised. *I'll bring everything. Champagne, caviar, lobster salad, and my own body. If you have any guts, you'll be there, ready for a personal adventure.* I'll spare you the rest.

"I told her to name the day and time. A couple of weeks went by, I didn't hear back. But that Friday morning, when I checked my e-mail, there was a message from her telling me I would find her in bungalow eight at the Bear Creek Inn. I couldn't resist.

"I told Cindy something had come up, that I'd meet her in Vermont the next day. She went up ahead of me. I rented the car and drove to the inn. My mystery date had registered under a phony name, Tania Kaplan, and she paid for the room in cash. The bungalows were separate from the main building. No one saw me go in or out. I got there at ten in the morning, spent the night and the next day with her, then drove out to the airport to catch the six o'clock flight to Vermont. I told Cindy what to say to the police, but I didn't tell her why. That's it. That's the truth."

"Then you won't mind if I check your story out here and now."

Jerry punched up the speaker-phone sitting on the side table. "Go right ahead."

"One more question before I start," Jack said. "You want to explain why a call from the killer to Lacie yesterday morning traced back to your cell phone number?"

I whirled around. Jack hadn't told me that.

"Impossible," Jerry swore. "Fucking crazy."

"Is it?" Jack said. "Homicide never lifted the tap and trace on your loft phone on the odd shot Skyla's killer would make some kind of contact with you or Ms. Wagner. The call came in at five-thirty yesterday morning. AT&T says the call was made from your cell phone." Jack pulled a fax out of his pocket and dropped it on the coffee table.

Jerry glanced at it. "I didn't make the call, so do what you have to do to check out the rest of my story and then get the fuck out of here."

Jack sat down and started dialing.

Jerry's eyes were hard on me, his full lips were tight with anger, and the blood was high in his cheeks. One good shoe tapped the floor, counting out the charges against me. *Lacie, how could you.* I watched his shoe go tappity-tap, foot bare in soft Italian leather, then I watched the emotions shift across his face. Fury, wonder, amazement, betrayal, love, and, yes, there it was. Hate.

How much do you hate me, I silently asked, waiting for Jack's verdict.

I turned away, stared out the window. I listened to the rumble of Jack's voice and felt Jerry's eyes burning into the back of my head.

Then, Jerry was standing behind me.

"How much do you hate me, Jerry?" The words slipped out.

"In general or just right now?" he asked, drawing the curtain of hair away from my face, holding the mass of curls gently in one small hand.

"In general."

"Some. But not as much as right now. How could you ever question me?"

"Circumstantial evidence. Your own false testimony. How could I not?"

"I see," he said, even though he didn't. "I want you out of the loft by next week."

I nodded once and went back to counting seagulls. Jerry dropped my hair and drifted away.

Jack worked the phone. The speaker let us hear it all.

The Mercedes dealer vouched. So did the owner of the country inn. He kept a log of the license plates of cars that stayed overnight in his parking lot. He had Jerry's rental car listed for that Friday night. He also remembered the young woman who rented the cabin. He got her phony name out of the guest register, Tania Kaplan, and described her with a variety of spicy adjectives.

Naturally he was interested in sneaking a peek at the man who joined her. He gave an accurate description of Jerry, right down to his black shearling coat and Vuitton overnight bag. He was more graphic in detailing the girl's physical appearance, but couldn't give the license plate or credit card Jack wanted to track her with. The Miss came and went in a cab, and paid for her room in cash.

Jack put Jerry on the phone with Cindy and ordered him to tell her to talk straight. Cindy admitted she had lied and that Jerry told her what to say. Jack hung up. The verdict was in. *Thank God,* I thought. I could not have lived with that.

"Why did Cindy agree to give you an alibi?" Jack asked.

"Cindy does what I tell her to do."

"Why did you ask her for one in the first place?"

"Garrett ran the investigation. He stood by procedure and said he needed to know where I was and who I was with the Friday Skyla disappeared. He's a stickler for details like that. Given our friendship, Garrett wasn't the pit bull you are, but he did want my story corroborated. I had to lie to do that."

"Why?"

Jerry hesitated.

"Why?" Jack said again.

"Because the woman I was with turned out to be a girl. Clever, advanced for her years, but underage." He laughed bitterly. "Having sex with a minor is a felony in this state. It's enough to get me disbarred. I couldn't risk having her testimony sitting in a police record for everybody to see."

"I need to talk to her," Jack said. "You'll just have to live with the consequences."

"*Live with the consequences.*" Jerry's eyes were bright with tears.

"While I was fucking a seventeen-year-old, my thirteen-year-old girl was dying. I get to live with that, Stein. I get to live with that for the rest of my life. I'm not giving you her name. You got the truth you wanted. You're not getting my license to practice law too. Do whatever the hell you want, but you're not getting her name. Now the two of you can get the fuck out of here."

Jerry followed us out to the deck and waited for us to leave. We swung into the Range Rover. Slammed doors. Wind beat against the windows. Jack turned to me.

"I'm sorry, Lacie. I had to do this." His tone of voice and expression told me he wasn't sorry at all. Neither was I.

"Jerry brought it on himself."

Jack's cell phone rang. He picked up. "Jack Stein." Color drained out of his face. He tipped the phone so I could hear.

"Well, well," my nightmare voice whispered. "I watched you call on the old lady doctor yesterday. A doctor of the mind, revealing secrets. And the last I saw you were heading east, into the rising sun, to the grieving father, perhaps. His girl is dead and you think he did it. You're wrong, Jack, wrong as fire is hot. I'm the flame thrower, the fire eater, the setter of bonfires burning bright."

I looked up at the house. Jerry was still standing there in a combat stance, dark hair rippling in the wind, tears streaming down his cheeks, watching us while the whispering voice carried on.

"Jerry's an innocent pawn—not a knight or castle or king. Who am I? Where am I on the board? Am I black or white? Tall or short? I'm nameless and faceless, just a whispering voice, but know this: I'm a master of illusion. Clipping Jerry's cell phone number's proof of that. I'm smart and I like to play. I thought it was a game for two, for Lacie and me, but three will work nicely. It's more interesting with a new player on the board. You haven't missed much, Jackster. The fun has just begun."

Chapter Thirteen

Jack drove fast, speeding away from the beach, back to the city, steering with one hand and making calls with the other, working the Bureau resources. He ordered a tap and trace on his cell phone, and then requested background checks into all the residents in Jerry's building, looking for someone who hated me, who wanted me dead.

He had crossed Jerry off the list and was moving on, thinking out loud, discarding all the profiles that didn't fit—pedophile, kidnapper, rapist, serial killer—trying to glue one of his own together from the precious few pieces left behind. His brain was running at top speed, clocking along, rearranging the information, fitting new data into old, mentally feeling the wall in front of us, groping for a fissure, a loose rock, a crack, a place to start.

Most men in Jack's profession rely on hard evidence—fibers and hairs and ballistics, footprints in the mud, fingerprints at the scene, ligature marks on the body—physical data that lead the agent along a rational factual road to the truth. Jack had few facts and no useful evidence other than the killer's own behavior.

"He's organized and technically bright," Jack said as we soared down the expressway. "He wants to communicate. It's part of his thrill. I have to know how he got to Skyla. Jerry said Skyla asked to stay in the city. Why didn't she want to go to Vermont?"

"She told a friend she didn't go because she didn't like Cindy Reese."

"Ring true?"

"Now that I think about it, no. Skyla thought Cindy was a bimbo, but a nice one. They got along. And Skyla was crazy about skiing."

"When did Skyla talk to this friend?"

"Late that Friday morning. Aside from the doorman, she was

the last person to talk to Skyla before she disappeared. Her name is Dana Margolis. She's Jerry's partner's daughter and Skyla's best friend."

"Where does she live?"

"Eighty-second and Fifth."

An hour later, we were standing in Dana's living room, looking west over Central Park, at skeleton trees and white frozen ponds. The December sun slanted through the windows, lighting Jack up with a golden glow. He was big and virile in the daintily decorated room, hiking boots sturdy on soft flowered carpet, red parka bold against ivory walls.

Dana was slouched on the couch, staring at Jack like he was the Holy Ghost. We were alone with her, which was the way Jack wanted it. Her parents were out Christmas shopping. The Spanish maid had taken one look at Jack's federal ID and vanished down the hall. Dana was in awe of Jack, but felt safe with me, like I was family.

She used to visit Skyla in D.C. once a month. I had loved those weekends, the way the house was filled with music and laughter— the way it was filled with life. The girls were kindred spirits but physical opposites. *Mutt and Jeff,* Skyla used to kid, throwing her arm around her tiny dark-haired best friend, towering over her.

I looked at Dana now, demure in a pink fuzzy sweater and white skirt, and saw the sadness etched on her delicate face. Skyla's death had marked her. Her long hair was tangled and matted. Violet circles shadowed her eyes. I guessed she lay awake at night like I did, thinking of Skyla on fire. *I miss her, Ms. Wagner,* she said when we walked in the door. *I do too,* I had whispered back, hugging her tight.

Now, Jack was giving Dana a winning smile and asking for her help.

"I'd do anything to help," she gushed, dark eyes fixed on him, wanting him to like her. "I already told the police everything."

"I'm not the police," Jack explained. "I'm a federal agent and I like to hear things for myself."

"You don't look like a fed," she said shyly. "Your hair's too long."

"That's part of my secret," Jack laughed, tucking a sun-streaked curl behind his ear. "You seem like a smart girl, Dana. Pretty and smart. Great combination."

She blushed. "I do okay in school."

"Do you like sports?"

"Sure. I'm not tall enough for basketball, but I kick pretty good on the soccer field."

"Takes leg power to kick. You like to ski?"

"Sure, who doesn't?"

"Have you ever tried climbing?"

"No. Do you climb?"

"Summer and winter. The biggest mountains I can find. Hey, have you ever seen a frozen waterfall?"

"No. Sounds awesome!"

"One of the great wonders of the world," Jack promised. "A thousand feet of falling water stopped cold. With the right gear, you can climb straight up it. The ice is translucent. You can see pebbles and feathers and leaves, even fish that were in the falling water when it froze." His smile disappeared. "Skyla will never see that, will she?"

"Of course not," Dana replied, confused. "She's dead."

"Ms. Wagner tells me Skyla called you that Friday morning."

Dana looked at her feet. "We talked for a few minutes. What's going on, how we binged on too much dessert at Thanksgiving dinner, stuff like that."

"Why didn't she want to go skiing?"

"She didn't like Cindy. Sky just felt like hanging out in the loft and playing her violin."

Jack walked to the window. "You talk about anything else?"

"Movies, that's all," Dana swore, wanting Jack to believe her, which he didn't.

"Tell me the truth now, Dana."

"I am."

"I'm disappointed," Jack said, turning around. "You're lying."

"Am not." Defiant.

"You said Skyla was your best friend."

"She was." Sincere.

"If my *best friend* was murdered, I'd sure tell everything I knew about where she was going, who she was going with, and what she was thinking."

"I did," Dana insisted, looking at the floor, her hands, the window, at anything but Jack or me. "I swear I did. I told you everything I know."

He dropped to his knees in front of her. She had to look at him now.

"Let me tell you what happened to your *best friend*. She was tortured, Dana, burned alive while her killer taped it for our viewing pleasure. After that, she was hacked up and part of her was sent home. If you know anything that you're not telling us, then you're an accomplice. *You!* You're responsible for her killer walking free, drinking milkshakes and eating cheeseburgers while your best friend Skyla is spread out across the Eastern seaboard like some goddamn human puzzle—an arm buried here, a leg tossed there, a hand dropped in the river. Skyla was a talker and you're the last one she talked to. I know you know something. I want you to talk to me. Now."

Dana broke. She buried her face in her lap and cried. Jack fished in his pocket for Kleenex and settled on the couch next to her. He stroked her hair and talked softly about how he guessed she was scared, but how she had to talk, she had to trust him. He was sorry to be harsh, but murder was serious business, the most serious, and he needed her help.

"I didn't think what she told me would really matter," she said, still hiding. "It wouldn't make her alive again. I'm afraid."

"What are you afraid of?" Jack coaxed.

Dana hesitated.

"I'll protect you," Jack promised.

She shook her head.

"Work with me on this, Dana. Trust me. Talk to me. Get it off your chest. It's hard to keep fear all to yourself. Tell me what you're afraid of first and we'll go from there. One step at a time and you can stop any time you're too afraid to keep talking. Okay? How's that for a deal?"

Jack's curious combination of fury and charm worked. He won her over. She looked up at him, wide-eyed and wet-cheeked but trusting.

"I'm afraid my name will get in the paper or on TV, Agent Stein. He'll see it and come after me next."

"Your name won't go anywhere. This is between you and me. What did Skyla tell you?"

"She said someone sent her an e-mail on Thanksgiving claiming to know stuff about her mom, stuff Skyla should know. That's why she didn't go skiing with her dad. She was going to meet the person who sent the e-mail. I was afraid for her. I told her not to go! I swear, I tried to talk her out of it!

"She told me not to worry, that they were going to meet in a public place. She said there wasn't anything scary in the message. The person just wanted to talk. She even laughed and said she felt like an investigative reporter, like her mom, on the trail of a big story with secret sources." Dana rolled her eyes. "Skyla had such an imagination."

"Where did they meet?"

"I don't know. She said he was going to e-mail her instructions. She promised to call me at the end of the day. I never talked to her again."

"Did you go through her computer?" Jack asked, pulling a chair up to Skyla's desk.

"Of course. So did the homicide detectives."

Skyla used America On-line for e-mail. Mail was automatically deleted after seven days unless the user saved it to the personal filing cabinet. Jack checked. The cabinet was empty. He clicked back to the main Windows 95 screen and double-clicked on the Recycle Bin, which was the computer equivalent of a wastebasket. All deleted documents went to the Recycle Bin and stayed there until someone "emptied" the bin by deleting the documents again. It was a neat backup system.

Jack scrolled down the list. The bin had no chronology. Documents from three months ago were mixed in with more recent files, and the bin was full with sixty deleted documents. He found it somewhere in the middle.

"You forgot to look in the wastebasket," he said. "Take a look at these."

Two documents titled *Mom1* and *Mom2*. The time of deletion was 10:45 A.M. on Friday, November 25. Skyla had saved the messages to her hard drive, then changed her mind and deleted them. Jack restored the documents and opened them up. The first was dated the day before Thanksgiving.

I know your mother, Skyla. Do you know the truth about her hands? I'm sure she told you things, but did she tell you the truth about what really happened that night? There are things you should know and I'm the one who can tell you. You must meet me Friday. If you love your mother, you will keep this a secret. I will send you a message Friday morning telling you where to find me. It will be a public place, so you need not be scared. I want to help you, not hurt you. You must trust me. This will be your one and only chance.

It's time you know the truth, Skyla. You're old enough now to know the truth.

Jack glanced at my gloves. " '*The truth,*'" he quoted. "What does that mean?"

"I don't know," I said lifting my hands. "I just don't know."

"The message came from a cyber-café," he said. "Same place your e-mail came from. Hundreds of people drift through there every day. It's a cash business. There's no way to track this message."

He scrolled down to the second e-mail, dated the Friday of Skyla's disappearance:

Today is the day of truth, Skyla. Trial by Fire always ends in truth. Go to the Tilman Gallery on Wooster Street, at noon. Look at the pictures. Meet me outside when you are finished.

An old issue of the *Times* was on the desk next to us. Jack flipped to the entertainment section and found the ad at the bottom of the third page: *Trial by Fire. Vintage Black and White Images of the Triangle Shirtwaist Fire. November 20–December 30. Tilman Gallery. 120 Wooster Street, Soho.* Here was the address, the place, the physical space where my daughter met the man who killed her.

The gallery was a ten-minute walk from Jerry's loft. Stepping out, I couldn't help but think of how Skyla had set out that Friday morning with the same destination. Now we knew she turned right. We knew where she was going. The information was a tiny dot of color on a giant blank screen.

We moved swiftly, boots crunching on brittle snow crust. City snow looked dingy after the bright white fields in the Hamptons. Our warm breaths hit the cold and turned to mist. Night had fallen. The empty buildings around us were gutted cavernous pits of black. Clouds lay low in the sky, slipping apart from time to time, revealing a skinny curve of moon.

In the heart of Soho, the smell of roasting chestnuts filled the air. Christmas shoppers crowded the narrow sidewalks and separated us briefly. I found myself alone, surrounded by happy strangers. I envied their glowing faces and pictured all the homes filled with trees and lights, family and gifts, and pictured my own empty house in Washington. How could I ever go back? A drop of rain hit my shoulder. It was too cold for rain. Ice melting from a rooftop, I thought, brushing my sleeve.

Chapter Fourteen

He sidestepped back, hugging the wall. She walked by patting her shoulder as if she had felt something there—a leaf, some falling snow. She was close enough to kiss. Her heady perfume drifted his way, dizzied him, and for an instant he imagined he was infused with her, that he had swallowed her up whole with one deep inhalation, that they were finally one and the same, that she lived inside of him.

Then, the instant was gone, and Jack Stein was next to her, resting his hand lightly on her shoulder where his own fingertips had just been. Jack Stein, huge in his red mountain parka, steering her through the crowd, offering her false shelter in the cove of his shoulders, the curve of his arm, the wall of his solid, fit body. Shelter. Shelter. As if shelter alone could save her.

Jack Stein was shelter and guardian and soldier brave.

Jack Stein was dead. He just didn't know it yet.

Chapter Fifteen

We turned out of the main shopping district and down a quiet side street lined with old warehouses that had been converted into lofts and galleries. The sidewalks were deserted. There were no restaurants here, and most of the galleries were closed for the night. The Tilman Gallery was in the middle of the block, next to an alley. We went up three steps, through an iron door, and up a flight of stairs to the second floor.

The exhibition space had twenty-foot ceilings and exposed pipes. Dramatic lighting spilled across frightening black and white pictures hung on stark white walls. I took my heavy coat off and draped it across the reception desk. A guest register lay open next to me. I flipped back to November 25. Skyla's name swirled across the page in vivid purple ink.

"Is that her writing?" Jack asked.

"Yes. She had a thing for purple ink. Carried a purple pen wherever she went. She wanted to be unique."

A woman appeared, long and lithe in an orange jersey dress. She wore her hair slicked back in a sleek chignon showing off her striking face. Ebony skin and something of the orient mixed in, I guessed, judging from the high angled cheekbones and tilt to her eyes.

"Lacie Wagner," she said, recognizing me, surprising me. Sometimes I forgot that I had been a front-page story. She touched my shoulder in sympathy. "The whole city cried for you, Ms. Wagner." She looked at Jack and liked what she saw. Her smile brightened. "Naomi Tilman. I own the gallery."

"Jack Stein," he said, producing Bureau ID. "Were you working on Friday, November twenty-fifth?"

"Thanksgiving weekend. No. That would have been my daughter Mimi."

"Where can I find her?"

"Katmandu."

"Katmandu?"

"She went trekking. She left the Saturday after Thanksgiving and won't be back until New Year's Day. Mimi believes in abandoning the civilized world on a regular basis. She won't even travel with a cell phone for emergencies. I tried to convince her to take one. *What if something happens to me?* I said. *What if I die?* Mimi just laughed. *Mama, if you die, you won't be able to talk to me on a cell phone. They'll keep you on ice until I get home.*"

Jack smiled. "Mind if we look around?"

"Let me tell you what you're looking at. A hundred and forty-six women died in the Triangle Shirtwaist Building fire in 1911. They were poor immigrant sweatshop workers who were kept locked in during working hours. When the factory went up in flames, they couldn't get out. That one fire changed union laws forever, but the price for the change was horrendous, as you will see."

Jack thanked her and led me into the main exhibition room. "Look at the pictures, Lacie. Tell me if anything seems significant."

"What could possibly be significant? The building burned long before any of us were born."

"Nonetheless, you have to look."

The pictures were numbered one to fifty and moved the viewer through the story in a counterclockwise direction. I tried hard to keep my good journalistic objectivity, but waves of nausea rolled over me as I walked through the collection.

The terror, the agony, the fire.

A woman hanging from a window ledge, flames shooting out above. Three teenage girls leaping, skirts billowing, arms outstretched to break the fatal fall. Desperate young women in mid-flight, twisting and turning, women who chose to jump thirty stories to death rather than burn alive.

And then, those who burned. Exposed bone. Blistered skin. Smoldering bodies carted away on stretchers, sometimes swathed in white sheets or fire blankets, usually not. The dreadful search through wreckage for bones, teeth, wedding rings, tiny artifacts, evidence of life. Ash sifted, fallen timbers pushed aside, and one by one, the blackened pieces carried out.

I stopped in front of the last shot: A girl, Skyla's age, lifted from the rubble by a young man in tweed. Brother, father, cousin, friend? She lay slack in his arms, burned face in full camera view, charred hands hanging down. Crow claws, mangled and raw, just like mine must have been.

"This is the one," I said, my eyes fixed on the final horrible image—on her wretched hopeless hands. "This is what he wanted Skyla to see."

I spun away from the picture and ran out of the gallery, taking stairs two at a time. The iron door weighed a thousand pounds. The three gentle steps felt steep. Pictures of fire did that to me, made me crazy afraid and terribly sick. The Lacie Wagner cocktail, Fire and Fear, giving me a hangover before I even had a drink. I stumbled around the building corner and fell to my knees in the alley. My stomach turned itself inside out.

Jack's hiking boots appeared next to me.

"Lacie," he said gently, reaching.

I pushed him away. "Leave me alone. Please."

He stayed where he was.

"I want to be alone."

Jack stepped back but he did not leave.

Snow seeped through my wool pant legs. My mouth tasted sour and dry. My head reeled. I threw up again. Bile now. Nothing solid left. "I'm cold," I said, pressing my hands against the wall, shivering. "I can't make it upstairs. My coat's inside."

Jack hesitated, then said: "I'll get it."

I heard his boots move along the sidewalk and up the steps. The big iron door creaked open, clanged shut, and Jack was gone.

I rocked on my heels, waiting for the lingering nausea to pass. I closed my eyes and listened to city sounds muted by the falling snow. Horns. Sirens. And something else close, right there, behind me. A cigarette lighter snapping open. The rub of a thumb against metal clicking it to life. I smelled butane, heard the hiss of a flame, then the flame was next to my cheek, warming my skin.

"Fire," the voice whispered, hot in my night-chilled ear. "Reach out and touch the fire." His free hand gripped my neck, kept me from turning my head to see him. "You're alive, Lacie. I feel your pulse pounding. You saw the picture. The girl with the monster hands died. You could have been her. You could have had a face and body to match your hands. You don't. Do you ever wonder why? Didn't you ever want to know the truth, my beauty? My beauty with the paws of a beast."

The smell of him. The heat of him. The brush of his flesh against mine. The feel of his teeth on my ear. The taste of his sour sickly breath. Primordial fear spiked up my spine in a long thin line, radiating out to my limbs, my toes, my ten wrecked fingers, paralyzing me while the beast himself went on whispering humid erotic promises. One hand held the lighter to my face, the other roamed my body, cupping my breasts, right then left, trailing down over my ribs, my hips, clutching me hard between my thighs, clutching and kneading and threatening, his voice hoarse with desire, panting with intent while the tiny flame flickered.

He could have had me there, he could have taken me fast and killed me, but he swore he would wait.

"We will couple by the light of the great bonfire," he whispered. "I'll have you then, Lacie, when the Dead Time comes."

His wrist jerked. The flame scorched my cheek. It was that nightmare feeling of fire, only this time the blistering pain was very real. Then, the hot press of his body against mine lifted and he was gone. I whirled around looking for him in the alley shadows, but tears and fright blinded me and if he was running, I couldn't hear. I was screaming, screaming, screaming, and scrambling out of the alley when Jack came flying through the iron door and down the steps. He pulled me up off the icy cement and saw the wet hot streak seared on my face—my white Rossetti face burned red.

His cell phone rang.

"Some kind of guard dog, Jackster." He wasn't whispering now. No, he was boasting and gloating, giddy and free. "I could have taken Lacie then and there, whisked her away, right from under your federal nose. I've always been close, a step behind or in the next row. You can tap me and trace me, but you'll never hunt me down with the usual tools of your trade.

"My cell phone numbers are cloned. I use a number once, then throw it away. I've been a hundred different people in my one lifetime, changing names and jobs like shirts. My identities are borrowed, stolen, and invented, so how do you track someone who doesn't exist? How do you get a grip on smoke? I'm nothing but smoke and while we play, you won't see my face, the shape of my skull, or the color of my eyes. You won't bother putting heights and weights and descriptive detail into your fat federal database. You'll put one word in—*Fire*—and that will be me. It's the only face you'll see until the Dead Time comes and I reveal myself to you.

"But there's much fun to be had before that final day. There are die to cast and chips to toss, cards to deal, and chess pieces to place. I'm glad you're in the game, Jackster! I've been learning all about you and there's plenty there to learn. Men revere you. You're a legend to them all, a mountain climber and killer-hunter hunting killers like me. And women? They're more impressed still! You're huge and handsome, a girl's walking fantasy, the great outdoorsman with a mega-watt brain.

"But you don't fool me. The more I learn about you, the more certain I become. You're a sham, Jack Stein, a liar and a cheat, leading Lacie on, letting her think you can keep her alive. I know your track record inside and out, and it's flimsy in places where it should be strong. You've failed once before, you'll fail again. The burn on Lacie's face is proof of that.

"For now, know this: I won't fit into any of your standard profiles, so it's a waste of time to try. I'm like no man you've ever met or dreamed or feared. And smart as you are, you're not smarter than me. Swill your wine, Jack, and swill it well. The day's soon coming when Lacie burns in Hell."

Chapter Sixteen

Snow was falling hard, slanting sideways on a strong wind. Jack hailed a passing cab and hustled me in.

"I shouldn't have left you," he swore, ashen-faced and stricken. "I'm sorry, Lacie. I'm so very sorry."

Beyond fear, beyond terror, I was frozen in a fetal curl. He had found me, the nightmare face had found me and licked me with a tongue of fire. He had burned and scorched me, and now I was his. It was a just a matter of time. The pulsing sting on my branded cheek was a promise of worse things to come.

The cab sailed downtown and stopped in front of Jerry's building.

Jack paid the driver and helped me out. I stood on shaky feet in the swirling snow. Icy flakes hit the ribbon of my fire-stripped flesh. Cold against hot. Jack ushered me up the walk, arms locked around me, shielding me with his own massive body. We were a perfect target in the entrance lights. Jack's bright parka as red as a matador's flapping muleta.

He could be anywhere, I thought as I scanned the shadows, pressed tight to a building wall, cloaked by darkness, ready to hurdle out in a blitz attack, shouting a string of new threats, rhyming and sly. How could we play a game we didn't understand? What were the rules and where was the playing field? More important, who was the opponent?

We ducked inside. Jack cross-examined the night guard, who swore no one had come by looking for us, no packages had been delivered.

Upstairs, the living space was as we had left it. The alarm had not been triggered. The steady glowing light promised no one had broken in. Jack kept me at his side while he searched closets and bathrooms, checked window locks and under the bed. Finally, when he was sure we were secure, he rummaged in his duffel bag for a first aid kit and led me into the guest bathroom.

I waited with my back to the mirror. I didn't want to look. I didn't want to see. I didn't look at the burn, but I did feel it. Tentatively. Slowly. I took my right glove off and ran one bent finger along the length of it. The trail of fire began at the upper rim of my right cheekbone near my eye and angled down to the soft fleshy swell just above my lip. Narrow, the width of a finger, the length of one too. A raw red slash. I knew the feeling of red—the stinging of red—the hot blistering feel of skin freshly split open by fire.

"It's a second-degree burn," Jack observed, swabbing ointment on my skin. "This topical creme will prevent infection. I've mixed in Vitamin A and E to prevent scarring." He stretched white gauze over the red channel and taped it gently in place. His big hands were shaking. The burn was an accusation. *You failed,* screamed in bright red blood. He snipped the last piece of tape and stepped back.

I turned slowly and looked. White gauze again. My hands had once been wrapped in this same sterile white. I fingered the bandage, top to bottom, side to side, and studied our faces in the mirror. Jack's, unshaven, fatigued and shocked. My own, pale and stricken. We the hunters were now the hunted. Jack watched me carefully, waiting for me to fall apart. Instead, I touched his arm. "I need a drink."

Jack nodded. We went to the living room, to Jerry's wet bar, where Baccarat tumblers were lined up like lead crystal soldiers ready to take me into battle. He poured me a straight shot of vodka. I tossed it back in one neat move and held the glass out for more.

Jack arched an eyebrow but skipped the speech and poured. I tossed the second shot back as easily as the first. The cold inside me melted some and the throbbing pain in my cheek lessened to a dull thud beating in counterpoint to my pulse.

Beauty with the paws of a beast.

I dropped down into the deep leather couch, closed my eyes, and listened to Jack checking the tap and trace. When he hung up, I looked at him. He shook his head.

"He's using a cell phone clone," Jack said. "The number traces back to a banker in Iowa who was here on business last week. Tonight, the banker's at home in Iowa, having dinner with his wife and kids. The records on his cell phone show calls from both Iowa and Manhattan, in the same five-minute time frame. The tap and trace is useless."

Jack traveled from one end of the big room to the other, body alert, back tense and waiting, anticipating. He paced, left to right, right to left, hand ready at his hip, brushing the hard leather holster, feeling the grip of the gun. Jack. My massive night watchman. Dipping a drape aside, watching the white snowy night, double-checking the alarm and touching the gun. The gun, the gun, the gun. How do you fight fire with a gun, Jack? Tell me that.

"So, what does his behavior tell you now?" I mocked. "That he has good aim? That he's never far behind? That I'm a fool for thinking I'll get out of this alive?"

My words were crueler than I had intended. Hurt skipped across Jack's face.

"I'm sorry," I said, meaning it. "It wasn't your fault."

"Of course it was." He strayed to the window, tightened a drape. "Did you see him?"

"No. He came from behind."

"What did he say?"

"That I could have died like the girl in that last picture. I could have had a face and body to match my hands. He asked me if I ever wondered why I didn't. If I ever wondered about the truth."

"The truth. The same word he used to lure Skyla out." Jack tapped his holster. "Lacie, what happened the night your hands burned?"

"I don't remember much."

"Tell me what you can."

I got up and poured myself a fresh drink. "On the last day of summer camp, my father came to pick me up. It was late and getting dark. He came straight from his office and was still wearing his lab coat. He was happy to see me."

Lacie! My girl! Picking me up, whirling me around. Laughing. His fine loving laughter. *I missed you, princess.*

"What then?" Jack prompted. "What do you remember about the car trip?"

"Bits and pieces. Sitting in the front seat of my father's big Cadillac. His handsome profile. The spice of his aftershave. The radio playing low. He drove fast. I remember sticking my head out the open window, feeling the rush of summer air against my face."

"What else?"

"I don't remember how or why we went off the road. I don't re-member the crash. Just the fire, and even then it's only snippets of imagery. My father screaming. His hair on fire, his arms, then his eyebrows, then his face. I reached into the flames to try to help him. Everything's a blank after that. I woke up in the hospital. They told me a week had passed. They told me my father was dead." I tossed back the last of the third shot. My throbbing cheek now, like the rest of my body, was pleasantly numb.

Jack paced, heavy hiking boots surprisingly quiet on the glossy wood floor.

"What are you thinking about?" I asked after a time.

"Him. How he has stopped whispering. The game has changed. He feels confident, in control, in the driver's seat. There's no longer any need to hide his voice. He used the whisper as a terror tactic from what he knew about your dreams. Now, he doesn't need threat and implication to scare you. He's moved on to physical contact, direct communication. He's an intelligent, somewhat older man."

"How do you know?"

"It took patience, time, and effort to set the stage for snatching Skyla. And, it took sophistication, finesse, and control to take her in broad daylight. He drew her out to the gallery, and somehow es-tablished trust. He may have posed as a doctor or policeman, some authority figure that would make Skyla feel safe going with him. It took cunning to do that. He played with her mind, just as he's play-ing with yours.

"He has studied you, your life. And Jerry's. He's a rigid, orderly individual. These traits don't fit the profile of a pyromaniac or ar-sonist. He's not your average bed-wetting, cat-killing, fire-setting psycho. Did you see him tonight?"

"No, but I smelled him. Listened to him. Felt his touch. He's the same man as in my dream." I saw the look on Jack's face. "You still don't believe me. You think I'm crazy."

"I never said that," he said carefully. "I'm a man of science. I don't believe nightmares come mysteriously to life."

"How can you scientifically explain the fact he speaks words from my dreams?"

"Skyla."

"Skyla?"

"She knew about your nightmares. He spent time with Skyla be-fore he killed her. He got the information from her."

"Goddammit, Jack!" Frustration mixed with booze made me angry and bold. "The voice in the tape, the voice on the phone, the voice in my ear tonight are the same voice as in my dreams. I'm tired of being told that what I know is wrong. *I am right.* The man in my dreams is flesh and blood and he's hell-bent on killing me. I don't care how you decide to rationalize it, but you have to believe me. Find the scientific logic you need and find it fast."

Jack had stopped moving. He was watching me, surprised.

"You have to believe me," I said, suddenly feeling tired and spent. I sank down to the couch and lay my spinning head back. "The voice in the alley tonight was the same voice as in my dreams. I swear. I dreamed him and now he's alive. Explain that to me."

The liquor knocked me out.

I woke hours later, curled up on the couch, to Jack shaking me gently.

"It's the same man," I mumbled, stubborn even in sleep.

"Yes. It is."

"Don't patronize me."

"I'm not. Your nightmare isn't a dream, Lacie. It's a memory."

I sat up. The warm vodka buzz was long gone. I felt dead sober and cold. "Go on."

"The nightmare is a memory fragment from the night of the accident. Something else must have happened. Something you don't consciously remember." Jack unfolded a map of the East Coast. "Show me where the camp was."

"Ashley Lake," I said, pointing to a place in the Berkshire mountains, high on the northwestern edge of Massachusetts. "Two and a half hours from Boston. Three hours from New York."

"And the accident?"

"In the country, somewhere near the camp."

"Pack a bag," Jack said, marking Ashley Lake with an X. "We'll take a run up to the Berkshires tomorrow. Try to find out exactly where the accident happened."

I shivered. I had never been back. And now, after all the years, going back scared me.

Chapter Seventeen

❦

A mass of Arctic air blew down from Canada overnight, hitting the Northeast with thirty-knot winds and chasing temperatures below zero. The Range Rover was drafty and cold, even with the heater blasting on high. I kept my coat on. Jack drove in his parka. He searched every inch of the car before we left, looking for tracking devices. Then, he took a crazy route out of town, circling blocks, turning right then doubling back, checking the rearview mirror as we went. When he was sure no one was following us, he moved on to the highway.

Forty-five miles out of Manhattan, we picked up the narrow Taconic Parkway and wound our way north into the country, passing empty rolling fields and clusters of winter-bare trees. Jack slowed once and steered around a dead doe. Her amber hide was wet with blood, almond eyes were wide open.

They say car headlights at night will freeze a deer, stop it dead in its tracks. The deer will just stand and stare at the oncoming lights, immobilized by fear. I am that way with fire, I thought, looking back over my shoulder at the furry hump and the white snow smeared red. The night before, the tiny flickering flame froze me. Fire is fire, no matter how small, and all fire burns. I touched the bandage on my cheek.

Two hours out, Jack turned east off the parkway onto a two-lane road we had all to ourselves. We passed dingy white clapboard houses with sagging porches and big American cars on blocks.

Deeper in, the landscape changed. Well-kept farmhouses popped up, bright and spry on generous parcels of well-tended acreage. This was picture-book New England. Old red barns and silos standing high. Ivy green pickup trucks. Working land with horses and hay. Fields of snow banked off to the left, dotted with skinny barren birch trees, ghostly white and skeletal.

We passed old graveyards, stone pillars and vaults and weeping angels keeping watch. Headstones were legible despite a hundred years of sun and snow: Kiley, Shannon, Fallon, Temperance, Blythe. Old New England names.

A lemon yellow pick-up truck lurched across an unpaved side road, and we rode even for a while, eye-to-eye. The driver wore a red parka like Jack's. His face was leathery from the sun. He lifted a hand in greeting and smiled. His teeth were dazzling white against liver-colored lips.

Jack slowed on the main run through country towns. Places did not change much in the Berkshires. I would know instantly if a town was familiar. The first five were not. We cruised the rural routes. Little by little, I began to recognize things. A country store. A horse farm, the training rings and fenced-in meadows. An alley of mature elm trees flanking the road for several miles. My heart-beat picked up.

Trees whipping by, one after another. Then fear and fire.

An old dairy farm, *Tate's—Since 1926.*

"This is it," I said, touching Jack. "I remember the dairy farm. These trees. I'm sure we crashed near here."

"The camp's another hour up the road," Jack said. "You would have been driving in the opposite direction."

"Yes."

He made a U-turn and inched slowly back through the alley of trees.

The rush of sweet summer air against my face as I hung out the passenger window, grinning open-mouthed like a hound, waving my arms in the night. Racing past the dairy farm, tall silos lit up at night, thick smell of manure and hay. Counting the trees out loud— one, two, three, fifteen, twenty—There are so many trees, Daddy! His quick smile, white teeth gleaming, sleeves rolled up to his el-bows, glint of gold watch at his wrist. My skin prickly from the hot summer night, thick heavy hair damp at my neck. Fireflies sparking in the dark. Sticking my hands out, ten perfect fingers wiggling, as if I could catch those fireflies. As if, as if, as if . . .

The memory stopped with the firefly wish, went black and still.

At the end of the elm tree alley, the road shoulder to my right gave way to a steep ravine. Beyond, the land rolled gently for miles, spare and clean, but it was the ravine that interested me. The clus-ter of trees down there. Fat old trees.

I saw it. "Stop!"

Jack braked and pulled over on the soft shoulder. We got out. The wind hit me hard. I tugged my wool hat tight over my stinging ears and hurried down, stumbling once in a deep snowdrift. Jack offered me his arm. I led him a few hundred yards down the steep slope, into the gully.

The old trees had thick trunks almost as wide as a man is tall. Now, in winter, with their branches stretched out bare against the sky, the trees were ugly. In summer, they must have been lovely, but I did not remember the canopy of leaves or carpet of thick green grass, just the one unmistakable trunk.

"Here," I cried, slapping bark. "Right here!"

The gouge was huge, a living scar in dead wood. This tree had burned that night. All that was left was the blackened dead body, old burned wood scarred by fire like me.

"This was the place my father died," I said softly, remembering the sound of shattering glass and the *whump* of flame.

Jack walked away, pacing out the distance from tree to road.

My boots were lined with fur, but the bitter cold went right through. My toes went numb. My hands ached.

Jack moved back to my side. "Did your father hit another car that night?"

I looked around. "I don't remember."

"It's a long straight stretch through the alley of trees. Five miles at least. You said he was driving fast. If he was speeding through the straightaway and swerved to avoid something in the road—a deer, a dog, another car—he could have lost control. If he blew a tire or hit another car, he could have spun out off the road. Maybe he hit someone here in the glade. A camper. A pair of stargazing lovers. A hitchhiker. A runaway kid. Maybe someone else died that night and that's what this is all about. A lover, a father, a brother out for revenge."

"I don't remember."

"The closest town is Stockbridge. If an accident report was filed, that's where we'll find it. Let's go."

We hiked back up to the Range Rover. As we were pulling away, I took one last look at the glade. Jack was right. I suddenly felt sure there had been someone else in the grove that night.

*   *   *

The quaint town of Stockbridge was dressed for Christmas in red ribbons, wreaths, and twinkling lights. We passed bakeries, boutiques, antique shops, and found the police department at the far end of town, in a white-columned building set back from the road. A simple sign listed the offices inside: *Tax Collector, City Hall, Police*. Jack parked next to a black police cruiser and we went inside.

The police department was a cramped two-room office crowded with filing cabinets and cheap swivel chairs. The officer on duty lounged at a desk with her feet propped up, filing her nails and snapping gum. She wore a royal blue uniform and hiking boots like Jack's. Mouse brown hair frizzed around her plump face. She had small lips, a button nose, and carried twenty pounds too many on her five-foot frame.

We walked in. She picked the gum out of her mouth and dropped her feet.

"You spin out on the road?" she asked, noticing the bandage on my cheek. "Winter's a bitch 'round here. This time of year, we double as highway rescue. Hank's out there right now yanking somebody's fancy new sports car out of a ditch. The city folk come and buy million-dollar country homes so they can feel *rustic*. Only thing is, a lot of them are stubborn or dumb or both and they try to motor on up here in a Porsche or a Jag or some other high-ticket vehicle that doesn't have four-wheel drive. They all go off the road, one time or another. There are plenty of tow truck services in town, but when there's two cars involved, we've got to be there to take statements for the insurance company."

She rubbed her hands in front of a little space heater and grinned at Jack. She liked him. "Officer Gleason. Hell, call me Kitty. We're not formal here. I talk too much. Your turn now."

"Jack Stein." He showed ID.

Kitty's grin vanished. "You don't look like a fed."

"Thanks," Jack said, amicably.

"What brings Big Brother to a little place like this?"

"A car accident. One that happened a long time ago."

She folded a new stick of pink gum into her mouth. "How long's long?"

"Twenty-four years."

She snapped the gum and whistled. "Lordy, that's ancient history. We sure don't have records that far back up here. We're short on space, as you can see."

"Where would they be?"

She shrugged, picked at a hangnail. "Who knows. The old station house burned down about ten years back. Probable arson. Bunch of no-account high school kids with a bug up their collective ass about authority. Anyway, the place burned to the ground. Hell, it was a blessing if you ask me. The place was draftier than this and had enough critters living in it and under it to shake you up some. Rats, mice, gophers, termites, daddy long-leg spiders. Kids did us a favor, burning the old place."

"The archives burned too?"

"They must've. I wasn't part of the recovery team. The fire department boys went digging through the wreckage, salvaging whatever they could. The file cabinets were steel. Some of them might have made it. Maybe we still got something around here."

"How soon can you know for sure?"

"Those old files would be downstairs in the basement somewhere. There's so much junk down there, stuff jammed into boxes, half-burned stuff packed away. Nothing's really marked. Might take me the better part of the day to root around. I can't start looking until late this afternoon. I'm the only one here, holding the fort such as it is. Come back around six. I'll know better what we got then."

"No way to do it sooner?"

"Nope. But listen, Agent Stein. You might pass some of the down time chatting with old Ben Freeman. He was old when he was the police chief back then. He's even older now, but you never know. He might just remember something."

"Where can we find him?"

"He lives out on his family farm. Seventy-three and still trying to keep that big place up by himself. His wife died last year and his sons are both living in New York. Stockbridge was just too quiet for them." Kitty Gleason sighed. "Fact is, most all of the younger local men went off to New York. Maybe I should too." She picked up a ballpoint pen. "Now tell me what you know about the accident. Names, dates, that kind of thing."

Jack filled her in, then asked her to draw a map to the Freeman farm.

It was a forty-minute trip from the center of town and, judging from the size of the fields surrounding Freeman's tidy yellow farmhouse, the former police chief was rich in land if not in hard cold cash. It was a well-kept place but simple. Smoke curled from the chimney, a cobalt blue pickup sat out front. We went up to the front door and saw a pair of men's snow boots drying on the porch. Someone was home.

Jack rang. A dog went wild barking inside. We waited. The door cracked open, and Ben Freeman glared at us. He was six feet tall and powerfully built, dressed in a red flannel shirt and jeans. White steely hair was buzzed down tight to his skull. His jowls were loose, his skin creased, but his eyes were fox bright and clear.

"Who are you?" he boomed, holding a big golden retriever by the collar.

Jack showed his ID. "Jack Stein, FBI. I'd like to ask you a few questions."

"You don't look much like a Bureau man," Freeman snorted, snatching the ID. "Hair's too long." He compared the picture to Jack and tossed it back. "Come on now. No sense standing in the cold."

He opened the front door wide, let the dog out, and ushered us in. The living room was comfortable with Early American furniture and evidence of the recently departed Mrs. all around: white lace doilies on polished end tables, china figurines displayed on a shelf, cross-stitched pillows sporting gentle homilies scattered on the couch. Keepsakes crowded the fireplace mantle. Blue ribbons from cow shows were mixed in with framed newspaper clippings of Ben Freeman the police chief in a royal blue uniform with a badge on his chest. A fire burned in the grate.

"Have a seat," Freeman ordered. "You want coffee? I can only offer you instant. My wife died last year and I found out in a hurry how much about day-to-day life I just didn't know. I can till a field, help a cow give birth, grow flowers here in the dead of winter, but I can't make a goddamn cup of coffee. You want some anyhow?"

"No thanks," Jack said.

"All right then," he said, flopping back in his easy chair. "What on earth do you want to talk to an old man like me about?"

"Back in the summer of 'seventy-five, a car went off the road and burned out near Tate's Dairy Farm. A man died. Kitty Gleason said you might remember it."

Freeman pulled on his ear and nodded. "Who could forget? I was on duty that night. Got the call around nine."

"Who from?" Jack asked.

"Don't know. Some passing motorist must've seen the fire and called it in from a pay phone. The crash site's about twenty minutes from the center of town. That's twenty minutes if you're driving real fast and you know the road. More like thirty to most folks who drive it at night, and forty to nervous folks who don't know the road at all. We made it out in ten."

"Who's we?" Jack asked.

"My partner Jim Higgins and me. Jimmy moved away from Stockbridge a while back. Last I heard, he's out west in Vegas working security for one of the big hotels. Said he'd had enough of East Coast winters. Anyway, we were the first ones there. Stockbridge had just one ambulance back then. We didn't have a hospital—still don't—so the ambulance was run out of Kelly's funeral home in town. Made it neat for them business-wise. But the ambulance was pretty beat-up and it broke down all the time. When it was in for repairs, old man Kelly wouldn't think twice about using his big black hearse instead. Made plenty of people nervous, I'll tell you that. Folks don't want to ride in the funeral wagon until they're good and dead. It's creepy otherwise. Plain creepy."

He ran a hand over his bristly hair and shifted in his chair. "Anyway, like I was saying, that night of the accident, I knew the ambulance was on the blocks. The only hospital with any kind of burn unit was more than two hours away, out in Worcester. Old man Kelly's hearse was slow as a snail. Didn't make sense sending anybody alive off in it, so I left Jimmy at the scene waiting with the wreck and the one dead body while I shuttled the one living body to the hospital myself. Sometimes five minutes makes all the difference between life and death, and I figure I saved an hour's time making the trip in the police cruiser. It was new and had plenty of juice under the hood."

"What did you find at the accident scene when you got there?"

"A car, can't remember what make it was now, but it was a big fancy one, smashed headfirst into a big elm tree down in the gully off the main road. It was burning. Christ, you could see the flames from miles away. Somehow that car lit up and took the tree with it. We couldn't get our patrol unit down there, not without risking getting stuck ourselves. So we parked up on the margin of the road and hiked on in.

"First thing I remember's the smell: cooked human flesh. Once you smell that you never forget it. Next thing I smelled was gaso-line. I figured the tank had gone and busted. What troubled me was it must've been a hell of a lot of gasoline to make a fire as big and hot as that one was. Well, we took one look at the fire and knew whoever was in that car was dead."

"Was there another car in the glade?"

"No, sir. Just the burning one. But as I was walking through the tall grass in the glade, I tripped right over the body of a little girl. She was lying a good distance from the wreck. Fifty yards, give or take a few. I figured she'd been thrown somehow, but the way she was laid out, so careful like, hands folded across her little chest, made me think someone had pulled her out of the wreck. Hell, I thought she was dead too. Her face was covered with blood like she'd gone right into the windshield, maybe even through it. And she was so still. I leaned down to take her pulse just to be sure."

Freeman cleared his throat. "Sweet Jesus, I'd seen lots of things between farming and policing, plenty of bad things, but I'd never seen anything like that little girl. I couldn't take her pulse at the wrist the usual way, because her little hands were burnt right through, they were almost gone. Blood and bone was mostly all that was left. Her arms were burned some too, up the forearm, but nothing like those little hands.

"I felt at her neck instead and found she was alive, so I made a sling out of the emergency blankets we'd carried down from the squad car and wrapped her in it. She weighed nothing, I carried her out of the gully myself. My partner hung back sweeping the area with big flashlights in case someone else was laying out there hurt.

"I radioed the night operator, told her to send the fire trucks on out, and to rustle up two more of our men to help Jimmy. After that, I drove that little girl in to the Worcester Hospital, hoping she'd still be alive when I got there. Back then, Worcester didn't have a chopper or we could've saved some time flying her in. I drove steady around eighty miles an hour and got her there pretty quick.

"Jimmy told me there was only one other body recovered that night. A man, in the driver's seat. Wasn't much left to pull out after the fire. We all prayed he'd died before the fire took hold, but there's no way of knowing for sure. The girl turned out to be that man's daughter. I heard later that Worcester Hospital transported her out, back to Boston on account of those poor little hands.

Don't know whatever happened to her, but I thought about her a lot over the years."

"Because of the burns?" Jack asked.

"Sure, they stayed with me. First, because they were so horrible. Second, because they were so strange. How come just her hands were burnt up like that? Why not her arms or face? There was something else I just couldn't get off my mind. How did she come to be laying there in the grass so far away from the wreck? She couldn't have gone through the windshield, because the car was buried nose-first in the old tree, and she was laying way off to the *side* of the car, neat and proper as if her own mom had laid her out. I tell you, I chewed on that puzzle for a long while."

"What did you decide?" Jack prompted. "How do you think she ended up where you found her?"

Freeman shrugged. "Far as I could ever figure, someone *put* her there. It's the only dang thing that makes sense. I guessed someone pulled her out of that car seconds before the whole damn car blew and put her a safe distance away. Someone saved her life."

"Did that person ever come forward?"

"Hell no. And I never could answer that part of it. We never found out who called the accident in and we never found out who pulled that little girl out of the fire."

"Was there an investigation?"

"None to speak of." Ben pushed himself out of the recliner and moved to the fireplace. "It's a small town and a smaller police department. We don't have any detectives out here. Never did. Today, Stockbridge PD's got six full-time officers. Back then, we only had four, including me. That was it. Nobody had the training or experience to do any kind of forensic work. I guess we could've called in Boston PD, but there was no reason to.

"We had a couple of unanswered questions, but nothing suspect. Gasoline was the cause of the fire, so we figured the man had been hauling some gas cans in the backseat. People in a rush sometimes forget to screw those caps down tight. If he was hauling cans with loose caps, they could've leaked or opened up. The life insurance company didn't even come poking around. Too lazy, I guess, to make the long drive out. They accepted the accident report without question. The widow never pressed, so we just let it go."

"And you're sure the car didn't hit anything else out there?" Jack asked. "Another car? Campers sleeping under the trees?"

"Oh, I'm sure about that. I went back out the next day and searched the site myself. Even crossed to the other side of the road to see if a car or motorcycle had spun off in that direction. Didn't find a damn thing." Ben Freeman pointed a finger at Jack. "You think something funny happened out there, don't you, Agent Stein."

"Jack."

"All right, Jack, you think there was some kind of foul play that night, something we missed?"

"Maybe."

Ben Freeman tossed a fresh log on the fire. Wood snapped and cracked. I watched the new log burn.

Ben Freeman followed us back out to the glade in his old blue truck. Jack wanted to see for himself where I was in relation to the car. We scrambled down the steep gully for the second time that day. Tiny snowflakes whirled around us in a sharp north wind. Ben zipped his hunter orange parka up, put a hand over his eyes, and squinted at the sky.

"Storm's ahead of schedule. Snowfall wasn't supposed to start till late tonight. The boys at the National Weather Service say it's another blizzard blowing down from Canada. Glad to see you've got a sensible set of wheels." Ben clapped his hands against the cold and pointed to the blackened tree. "Car was there, nose-first, like I said. That's what made the big gouge. Came at it a little bit sideways from the looks of it." He crossed the open space and jogged up to the tree. Jack and I trotted after him.

Ben picked up two old branches and paced out a short distance from the old trunk. "Car tail would've been about here," he said, planting one branch in the snow. He turned his big body to the left and paced out a second, longer distance. "Fifty yards. That's about right here," he yelled out, planting the second branch. "This here's where that little girl was."

Jack frowned. We walked over.

"Quite a distance," Ben said, when we reached him.

"Bothers me too," Jack agreed.

"Well, I reckon that's all I can tell you," Ben said, watching clouds skate across the sky. "I can't help but worry if I did the right thing taking the little girl in. There's a part of me always afraid that moving her had hurt her in some way. I'll always wonder if I did the right thing."

I touched his arm. "You did, Ben. I was the girl."

His eyes flickered down to my gloved hands. I tugged one part-way off, feeling a strange need to show him.

His ruddy face paled. "God bless you, girl." He took me by the shoulders and kissed me lightly on the forehead. "I prayed for you. Now I know God was listening. God himself was looking after you that night. Well, I best be heading back now."

He trudged up the incline, sturdy and strong for a man of his years, a bright spot of orange against the white winter landscape.

I didn't believe God had been looking after me that night at all. The hands that had reached in and pulled me from the fire were not the hands of God or any of his army of angels. They were human. I lay down in the snow, face up, on the spot where Ben Freeman had found me. Wet snow slipped under my collar and dripped down my neck. I listened to the shrieking wind and the soft whisper of the new falling flakes.

Someone else had been in the glade that summer night. Who? I asked myself. And why?

Jack crouched next to me. "Can you remember now what made your car go off the road?"

I closed my eyes and tried, but all I saw was fire.

Kitty Freeman greeted us at six, somber-faced and subdued. "I found the file you're interested in. Hell of an accident. Christ. Gives me the willies."

Jack followed her into the police chief's private office. I lagged behind, reluctant to see images my own mind had so totally wiped out.

Things are forgotten for a reason.

Kitty dropped a thick manila file on the desk. "You're lucky. Those old steel cabinets kept the fire out, not to mention the water from the fire trucks. You'll find photos from the scene, couple of detailed police reports, including one signed by Ben Freeman himself. Letters from Mr. Wagner's life insurance company, our replies, and the hospital admittance record for Wagner's daughter—a little girl named Lacynda. If you need anything, just holler."

She looked at me with new interest as she strolled out. She had been so focused on Jack, she had not thought about who I might be.

Jack opened the file. He went to the photographs first and dealt them out like playing cards. I closed my eyes, not feeling ready, knowing I would never be ready.

"Lacie? These may help you remember."

I savored a few more seconds of darkness, then looked. The photographs were eight-by-ten black-and-whites, and grainy the way the specialized film used for police work used to be. The first picture established the scene. A wide-angle view of the glade, the blazing tree, the Cadillac barely recognizable, a raging fireball against the summer sky. The following shots moved progressively closer to the tree. Finally, the photographer was as close as he could get to the burning wreck. Through the smoke and flames, a blackened human form was visible, slumped over, one arm hanging uselessly out the driver's side window.

The photographer moved around the car, capturing the fire from all angles. Then, abruptly, the subject changed. The car and burning tree were no longer visible. The photographer had walked away from the car and found me.

As Ben Freeman had described, I was stretched out on my back in the long summer grass, legs straight out, white sleeveless summer dress tucked primly around my knees, white leather sandals on my feet, ruined hands folded peacefully on my chest. I had never seen what they looked like before surgery.

"You don't have to see these," Jack said, dropping an arm around my shoulder.

I shook him off. "Yes, I do."

White bones bared, sinew exposed, blackened flaps of flesh hanging, my silver bracelet a black circle in the raw tissue at my wrists, blisters bubbling up my forearms, blood and fluids staining the front of my singed summer dress. I looked at my face next, cut and bruised and bloodied, but miraculously untouched by fire. My waist-long hair had been singed down to three-inch tufts, and my eyes were closed against the nightmare. Blessed unconsciousness.

The next series of shots documented volunteer firemen fighting the blaze. There were a dozen different angles, the photographer working quickly and well, capturing the tension on one young fireman's face, and the drama of water geysering high in the sky over the glade. Ben Freeman had told us how they were afraid the whole field might ignite. That countryside, he said, was parched from a long summer drought. There were miles of dry brush surrounding, ready to spark.

When the fire was out, the photographer carefully documented the burned-out carcass of the Cadillac. Tires were melted flat. Paint had been seared off. The windshield had melted down, as had the steering wheel and dashboard. Then the photographer moved inside. These were the photos I did not need to see, but I couldn't help myself. My eyes were riveted on the apocalyptic image of my father's blackened brittle remains.

I almost missed what the camera had inadvertently picked up.

There, on the extreme edge of the frame, a figure was crouching in the glade. It would have been invisible, but a stray beam of a high-powered night lamp spilled a slash of light just bright and broad enough to see the silhouette. It could have been a passerby, an innocent spectator, but something stirred inside me and I knew it wasn't.

"He's there," I said. "Ben Freeman was right."

Jack picked up a magnifying glass. The heavy grain of the high-speed night film obscured detail. Magnified, it was still nothing more than a crouching faceless figure.

"There's no point running this for computer enhancement," Jack said, studying the image. "There's no detail in the shape. None at all. Why is he hiding? If he pulled you out of the fire, why didn't he come forward?"

Looking down at my father's ravaged remains, I shook my head sadly. "I don't know, Jack. I just don't know."

Chapter Eighteen

While Jack signed release forms for the file, I walked out to the car. Heavy snow sifted down, night was falling fast, the cold stunned. I swung up into the Range Rover and turned the heat on high. The worst of the chill was inside of me, in a place heat could not reach. It was the cold heavy weight of my heart low in my chest and the sad shiver of loss snaking down my spine. A daughter should not see her father burn, a mother should not see her daughter torched. I had seen both, and now I had seen myself when my flesh was still hot from the fire, how I lay rag-doll still, unconscious but safe while my father turned to ash.

Jack crossed the snowy lot and slipped in beside me, the file fat in his hands. "I want to read over those insurance and police reports again. Something bothers me, but I can't pin it down." He eyed the sky. "We'll never make it back to the city tonight, so we might as well stay. There's an inn not far from here. It caters to what Kitty calls the *city crowd*. Guess that's us. I called ahead."

Jack drove slowly through town, straining to see words on street signs in the heavy snow. A mile out, he turned left up a steep hill. We passed a white church. Tolling bells carried on the air. Jack turned right and the church disappeared.

The Maiden Lane Inn sat alone up on a hill, five miles from town, surrounded by fields and woods. It was a postcard-pretty rambling farmhouse with bay windows and a wraparound porch. I imagined wicker rocking chairs and slow-moving fans there in summer, guests sipping long ice teas flavored with mint. Now, the porch was stacked with firewood and snow shovels. A hanging wood sign flapped in the wind.

We passed a stable, then drifted up the long curving drive and parked next to a Jeep, the only other car in sight. Jack collected our bags and we hurried up the walkway in the gusting snow. At the top of the wide verandah stairs, we stomped our boots and shook our coats. Jack opened the front door. I stepped inside.

The main room was a city person's country ideal with chintz sofas, deep easy chairs in expensive fabrics, and good oil paintings on the walls. Not a farming magazine or cow show prize in sight. A woman appeared on the landing of the facing stairway. She was small but sturdy, and wore her long gray hair tied back in one thick braid. Her clothes were classic country: a blue cable-knit sweater and Levi's, solid Timberland boots.

"I'm Hannah," she said. "You must be Jack Stein and Lacie Wagner."

Jack shook her hand. "Thanks for taking us at the last minute."

"You're the only guests here tonight," she explained, leading us upstairs. "Christmas is usually a busy time for us, with folks coming up from Boston and New York, but they won't start piling in until the day after tomorrow. I gave my service girls the night off, and my husband and son are in Boston, so I'm afraid you're stuck with me. The good news is that I'm the cook around here, so you won't starve. And, I've given you the best suite we have." She opened the door. "Make yourselves comfortable. Dinner will be ready in a half hour."

The suite was spacious, two bedrooms linked by a sitting room with thick damask drapes and quality antiques. In the bedrooms, king-size brass beds were inviting with eiderdown duvets and a jumble of fat pillows. Bathrooms were huge with deep old-fashioned tubs and brass fixtures. Fluffy towels were draped over warmers.

I was too tired to protest the intimacy of a suite. We dropped our bags and took off damp coats. Jack changed the dressing on my face. The color of the burn was dark red now. The sting had turned to a throb. Jack taped fresh gauze in place, and we went downstairs.

The dining room was small and had its own fireplace. A fresh fire was burning. I chose a table by the window and sat with my back to the flames. Wind howled outside. I felt as if we were utterly alone in the storm, shut in, out of reach, out of sight. Safe.

Jack must have felt that too. He was relaxed for the first time since I had met him. He chatted easily with Hannah about local winter sports, hunting and mountain fishing, then ordered a good bottle of Cabernet. Hannah left and came back a few minutes later with the wine, hot rolls, and steaming bowls of thick minestrone soup on a silver tray.

We ate in silence, lost in thought, letting the hot soup and rich wine warm us. Hannah swept our plates away when they were empty, then served generous portions of roast lamb and scalloped potatoes. Jack was hungry. He asked for seconds. When he was finished, Hannah left us a wedge of cheese and fresh bread to enjoy with the wine.

Jack leaned back in his chair, stretched his long legs out, and swirled the Cabernet in his glass. The fire picked up highlights in his hair. He smiled. "Lacynda."

"Old-fashioned and Southern," I said. "I was named after my father's mother."

"Who turned it into Lacie?"

"My father, thank God."

"Tell me about him."

"He was a neurologist. He went to Harvard Medical School and stayed on for a long time doing research. Just before I was born, he left Harvard to go into private practice."

"What did your mother do?"

"Take care of my father. It was her sole mission in life. They were both born and raised in Atlanta. Childhood sweethearts, married at eighteen. She was thirty-five when she had me. I'm sure I was an accident. She never wanted children."

"No brothers or sisters?"

"Don't you already know the answer to that?"

"I do. You were an only child. Go on."

"My father loved his work. And, he loved me."

"You were close to him."

"Very." I remembered the weight of his arm heavy across my shoulders, fingers curled at my ear, tugging softly at my hair. *Lacie with Rapunzel's hair.* His broad hand sweeping over my face, closing my eyes, covering my ears, holding me against his chest so I could listen to his heartbeat. *Listen, Lacie, listen! That's the sound of life.*

"What was your mother like?"

"The opposite of my father. He was tall and thin. She was short and full-bodied. My father was quiet and understated, my mother was loud and flamboyant."

I thought of the wide bands of glittering rhinestones at her wrists, the square sapphires on her fingers. Thick gold chains, three at a time, roped around her neck. Earrings snapped smartly in place, bright scarves worn with a flourish. Bold print dresses, heavy perfume. Red lipstick and pink nails. She was a blinding rainbow of color. But under all the hot color was an ice-cold woman.

"She died when I was twelve," I said. "Max appeared one day at the boarding school she had put me in and told me to pack my bags. My mother was dead and I was going to Washington, D.C., to live with him."

"Were you scared?"

"I was happy. I hated boarding school. And I adored Max. He was gruff and eccentric, but I knew he loved me like my father had."

"Delta Force is hardly a nine-to-five job. Combat aviation, high-risk search and rescue, and so forth. Max certainly couldn't have been home much."

"No, but he had a wonderful live-in housekeeper who looked after me. He popped in and out. Called me every day from wherever in the world he was. He told me he trained new Delta Force recruits. That's the most he would ever admit to. I've always suspected he does more than just train, but I stopped prying a long time ago."

"How did your mother die?"

It suddenly occurred to me that Jack knew my life story. He had to. His background work had been too meticulous, too exact. The only reason he was asking questions that he already knew the answers to was that he wanted to study me, watch my face, measure my reactions, gauge my feelings. "Why don't you tell me, *Agent Stein*?"

"Okay," he said. "Two years after your father died, your mother washed a bottle of barbiturates down with a fifth of vodka. The cleaning lady found her. Some say it was an accident. Others say she knew too much about medicine to make that kind of mistake. I want to know what you think."

"Everything my mother did was deliberate."

"Why did she do it?"

"My father meant the world to her. I meant nothing. Especially after the accident."

"That implies she behaved differently before the accident."

"Before the accident, she loved me in her own way."

"And after?"

"She couldn't stand to look at me. My hands disgusted her."

"Why do you say that?"

I don't know what came over me, how I chose that night and why it felt right. Maybe it was the wine, or Jack's new easy way, something warm in his eyes. Maybe it was the safety I felt there in the country, with the blizzard all around. I wanted Jack to know how that one fateful summer night had changed my life and the woman I would become. How in a rush of fire, a burst of flame, that fire was a foundry that molded me into someone new. I wanted Jack to understand me.

I opened up. I described what my hands were like before they healed. How they were bent and weak, sparrow frail and twice as ugly with fingers curling in, thumb stumps sticking horribly out at right angles. Seared skin was hot pink and wet, nail beds were puffed and raw, and my gouged palms always felt like they were on fire.

I told him how my mother flinched when she looked at my hands, her nostrils flared, her lips rolled down and out. After the accident she never touched them, not even to rub in healing creams.

I told him how I lacked the simple dexterity to open those tubes of prescription ointments, how painful it was twisting the tiny caps off. I described the clumsy way I worked, using the back of one hand to rub cream into the other, and how I wrapped my hands in night mitts of white gauze to keep blood off the sheets. The white gauze glowed in the dark.

I told Jack that after that I would never wear white. White was medicinal, a hospital color, the color of sickness. Thinking of the white lilies on my father's grave, his pure white lab coat going up in flames, I had decided that white was the color of death.

Black was life. I wore it like an icon.

I fell silent for a long while remembering those feather-light white gauze mitts and the horrible oozing ugliness beneath them. I removed a glove and looked at my hand.

"Lacie?" Jack said gently when I had been quiet too long.

"The children at school considered me a monster. A freak. An outcast."

"You're not ten years old anymore," Jack said in that matter-of-fact doctor's way of his. "You're a woman and a beautiful one at that." Matter-of-fact again, nothing personal.

"So I've heard," I said, slipping my glove on. "It's the first thing writers say. *Lacie Wagner looks like a woman in a Rossetti painting, only she is slimmer.*"

"What do you see when you look in the mirror?"

Jack's soft expression encouraged me to go on. I told him things his investigation would never have revealed. How my face in the mirror always surprised me—that it was unblemished and clear, the features perfectly arranged. I expected scars and blisters, black soot. And, despite the heavy weight of my hair on my neck, I expected to see it singed down to the scalp. I told him how I was afraid to look at my own body. How Jerry once dragged me over to a full-length mirror, late at night, and shoved my nightgown down. *Look!* he ordered. *Look, Lacie! You're beautiful. You're goddamned beautiful! Don't you see it?*

All I saw was the uneven coloration on my forearms from the lesser burns, and the dark patches sweeping high across my thighs and belly where tissue had been excised for grafting. My skin was smooth and perfect everywhere else, my body slim and well-proportioned, but all I saw was a patched-up rag doll. A monster. A freak.

Graft scars had expanded as my body grew; the amazing elasticity of live skin. My breasts filled, my legs lengthened, my young body stretched tall, but my fire-eaten hands never changed. They were little-girl fists on a grown woman's body, squirreled and small, out of proportion to the rest of me.

I told Jack that as bad as my hands were, the worst scars were inside, and confessed that my view of myself had been shaped by years of ridicule. The children at school had done a good job brainwashing me. I never stopped hearing their vicious voices shouting, taunting, teasing: *Fire girl, fire girl, show us your hands—your daddy's dead and your skin's turned red*. I told Jack how I bowed my head in bitter shame, how my knees wobbled when I ran from them, how I never forgot the wall of hostile faces, the fierce shining pleasure in their eyes, the satisfaction and rich delight they took in throwing words at me like stones.

Those attacks took a psychological toll. I acquired a tick—a nervous hitching up of one side of my mouth. It had a life of its own, jerking up and down, out of control. The tick gave kids another reason to hate me, another reason to torture me with insults. With time and effort and supreme exertion of willpower, I retrained my mouth, but it took years.

"You know how I got through, Jack? Every day I promised myself I would show them. I would show the world. I would make myself into someone."

"You've done that," he said softly.

"Yes. Now with Skyla gone it doesn't mean anything to me. I failed her. I didn't keep her alive. How can anything feel good or right after this? Tell me that."

Silence was his answer.

"What's the hardest part?" I asked some time later in that long country night, when the wine bottle was empty. "What's the hardest part, Jack Stein, about hunting child killers?"

"The hours of uncertainty," he said, "before the child turns up dead. The fragile hope. False belief washed away by truth. I hate the press then too. The reporters. How the cameras eat the parents' grief."

I bit my lip. *How does it feel?* The newsman's mantra.

He went on. "I hate the accusation in a mother's eye when the killer isn't found right away, when she thinks I'm failing. But what I hate most happens when the killer is caught. It's the look of satisfaction on the parents' faces when the conviction comes in: Justice has been served. Arrest, prosecute, lock up, and destroy. Only thing is, the parents walk out of the courtroom as childless as they walked in. There is no justice. That's what I hate the most. There is no justice."

I was ready to ask personal questions next, as if revelation and soul baring were quid pro quo. He sensed what was coming, pushed back his chair, and stood.

"It's been a long day, Lacie. I'm going to take another look through those files. You should try to get some sleep."

He walked away.

My reporter's instincts tugged at me. I looked at Jack retreating, the square of his shoulders, the hair curling over his denim collar, the proud set of his head, and a new interest stirred in me, quiet as the falling snow outside.

When I returned to the suite, Jack was on the couch with the police reports spread across the coffee table. The irony struck me.

Once again he had no forensics report to help him. A proper investigation had never been made. He was left with grainy pictures and an old man's memory because my own was black.

"This is what bothers me," he said, tapping one of the reports. "The car hit the tree head-on. In a Cadillac, the gas tank is in the rear. The tank couldn't have blown up when the *front* of the car hit the tree. Anyway, Ben said the fire was way too devastating to have come from the gas tank alone. He said your father must have had gas cans in the backseat. But that's just conjecture. Guesswork.

"If the investigation had been properly done, we would know for sure. There would've been evidence of the cans. We don't know what was or wasn't in your father's car. Moreover, no investigation was done on the car itself. We don't even know *why* your father went off the road. Was he driving too fast? Did his brakes fail? Did he swerve to avoid a deer? Another car?

"There would have been skid marks we could have measured. If an animal had been hit, there would have been blood on the highway. If another car had been hit, we might have found glass. There was no investigation, so we can't begin to make any qualified decision about what really happened. We can only guess."

"I don't believe any of those things happened."

He looked at me for a long moment. "Why?"

"Because none of them explain why a man pulled me out, then hid in the bushes. How did he get there? Why didn't he identify himself?"

"Maybe he was a vagrant living in the woods. Maybe he had a reason to fear the law."

I examined the shot of the figure in silhouette.

Sounds rushed back at me out of my silent memory.

The cracking of glass and metal against wood. A long silence. Footsteps moving through grass. Liquid being poured. A match striking. The whump of fire catching.

I dropped the picture. "The gas was poured, Jack. On the car, on the tree, in the grass next to the car, on my father." I went to the window and pushed the curtain aside. The world was wiped out by snow.

"The man in the picture is hiding because he did it," I said in a new dead voice. "He pulled me out, but he wanted my father to die. He has come back to finish what he started all those years ago. He took Skyla. Now he's going to take me."

I felt fear there with the night pressing in, black night turned white, the color that scared me most. The color of death. I dropped the drape and left the room, leaving Jack alone with those horrible pictures. I left him with the puzzle pieces, the problem, and the one burning question I couldn't answer: Why? Why would anyone want to turn my father into a flaming totem and then come after me twenty-four years later?

Why, Jack, why? I thought, falling facefirst into the pillows, too tired to undress.

Find the why, Jack, and we'll find the who.

I stirred once in my sleep, eyes fluttering wide open from a nightmare. I saw light spilling out of Jack's room and heard the keyboard clacking. Awake and working at 3:00 A.M. He was an agent stripped bare. No whorling fingerprints to feed into hungry federal databases. Only a strange symmetry: My father and Skyla, up in flames. And me. Hands folded across a prepubescent chest. Virginal white summer dress streaked with blood and dark bits and pieces of my own charred flesh.

Why, Jack, why?

I slept with my gloves on that night, fists buried under my chin, dreaming of a stranger's hands lifting me high, lifting me free from the great billowing bonfire that ate my father alive.

Don't play with fire, Lacie. You'll always get hurt.

Chapter Nineteen

❧

Morning arrived crisp and bright with a shocking blue cloudless sky. Looking out from my bedroom window, I saw hills and bare-branched trees cloaked in white and black birds soaring in the new clear air. Snowplows hummed in the distance. A snowmobile drifted on the far-off edge of a field and disappeared into the woods. Kids out early, I guessed, having fun in the fresh snow.

I showered and dressed quickly, packed my one small bag, and went looking for Jack. He was sitting downstairs in the main room next to the big bay window, eating breakfast and chatting with Hannah. She jumped up when I entered, plied me with croissants and rich-smelling café au lait.

Jack was dressed in gray sweats and hiking boots. He looked tired. "Morning, Lacie."

"Jack. Sleep well?"

"Well, but not long. I got your hospital records from Worcester and Boston General faxed over. There was nothing surprising. I went through the profiles of the residents in Jerry's building too. One loft to a floor. Ten lofts. Everyone comes up clean. I had looked at them all pretty closely before, but I thought I'd look again, just to be sure."

I nodded and stirred my coffee. "What now?"

"We'll drive back to New York. I want to find Jim Higgins, the cop who took the pictures that night in the glade. Maybe he saw the man. If he can describe him, we can put a face to the voice."

"You don't need Jim Higgins to do that."

"Am I missing something?"

"I know what he looks like. My nightmare's a memory. I've been seeing his face for twenty-four years."

Jack lit up. "We'll get a sketch done in the city this afternoon. I'd like to get a quick run in before we go. When I skimp on sleep, exercise always gives me an extra jolt of energy. I don't want to leave you here. Come with me."

The boots I wore didn't have thick waffled treads like Jack's. Mine were made for shallow city snow, not deep country drifts. And, I had no sweat clothes with me. Just cashmere sweaters and wool slacks. "No, thanks," I said. "I don't have the right gear."

"Then drive alongside in the Range Rover," Jack insisted.

"You checked your car for tracking devices. And we're certain nobody followed us out here. He has no way of knowing where we are. He's in the city waiting for me there."

"I'm not going to leave you alone."

"I'm not alone. Hannah's here. From what I heard last night, she has plenty of hunting rifles in the house and she knows how to use them. I'll be fine."

Jack glanced at the bandage on my face.

"I'm safe," I promised, believing I was. Hannah's house was a sanctuary. The night had passed uneventfully. No one knew where we were. I felt secure. "Go, Jack. He's in the city. He's not here. Go."

Jack stood up reluctantly and tossed me the car keys and cell phone. "If you change your mind, you'll find me on the main road running east. I'll do a two-mile stretch there, then come right back. Four miles. Twenty-five minutes. Tops."

"Hell of a pace for a tired man, Jack Stein."

A whisper of a smile flickered across his lips. He slipped his parka on. His sweatshirt lifted enough for me to see the gun at his hip. I had tried to learn how to shoot a gun once, but my hands made it impossible to do it in a way that would ever save me if I needed saving.

"Twenty-five," he guaranteed, moving out the door.

I watched him lope down the broad verandah steps and across the drive. *Turn around and look at me,* I thought, needing to see his face and not knowing why it was suddenly so important.

Jack turned. I raised a hand slowly. He nodded and waved back, then swung down the road. He ran at a good pace, long legs reaching wide, knees high, arms loose and easy at his sides. I could almost feel him taking the good morning air into his lungs and how at home he was with open country all around. I imagined how the sun felt on his face, and how if I put my hand on his cheek it would be warm to touch. His red parka was cheerful, but there was something sad about Jack.

What made him such a solitary man? In the days and nights we had spent together, I had never heard him make a personal phone call. And, he seemed as oblivious to the Christmas holiday as I was. *Who are you, Jack Stein?*

My idle curiosity was changing. I really wanted to know. I had to know. I watched until he was a tiny speck of red against the snow. Then, he disappeared.

Hannah came in, shrugging into a lambskin coat. "I'm going into town. If you leave before I get back, just lock the front door and drop the key in the mail slot. There's more coffee in the kitchen. Make yourself at home."

She touched my arm and breezed out. A door slammed, an engine turned over. I watched her Jeep roll down the drive and turn right, traveling in the opposite direction from Jack.

I went back to my breakfast. When I looked up next, Hannah had vanished from sight. The countryside was empty. Suddenly I felt very alone. A flicker of fear stirred in my stomach. My cheek throbbed. The quiet around me seemed sinister, not calm. The keys to the Range Rover lay on the table next to Jack's backpack and phone. As I reached for the keys, the cell phone rang. I answered, hoping it was Ben Freeman calling with some new detail from the night of the accident.

"Did you learn anything in the glade, Lacie?" the nightmare voice asked. "Did you see the black tree and remember it burning? Did you remember me? I was there. I lifted you out and carried you free because I loved you. I still love you. I've always loved you. I've been with you all these years, a step behind, a step in front. Close enough to touch you from time to time, when you were not aware.

"I have locks of hair, clipped at opportune moments, and the best is the one taken from that summer night. The fire took most of your hair, but I took some too. I've held it and stroked it over the years, at the same time that I've held and stroked myself.

"I will eat your hair tonight, Lacie, I will stuff that precious tuft in my mouth and suck it. It's the color of fire and tastes of it too. The taste of fire is still on it. The taste of smoke, of burned flesh and ruined bones, the taste of your father's death is sweet to me."

I gripped the phone and searched the empty horizon for some sign of Jack. "Who *are* you?"

"The man who saved you. If I hadn't saved you, if I hadn't lifted you free, you would have burned there in the seat beside him—you would have been black and brittle too. I watched him carried out. The firemen were fooled. They thought his black carcass was whole, but it fell to pieces in their own helping hands. Some men threw up. Some turned away. One wise man found a small broom and swept the charred bone, ash, and cooked flesh into a bag. That's what they buried when they buried Richard Wagner."

The world outside was empty and white. Jack was nowhere in sight. Panic rode high in my chest. "What do you want?"

"You. You're my bride. I chose you that night. You'll feel the flames again, Lacie, with me. I'm going to kiss you long and hard and drive my own burning parts into you, then I'll lead you into the fire and we will burn as one."

His voice, silk then sour, running the scales of terror and taking me on the ride, turning sharply, swerving from veiled innuendo to raw threat. His words caressed, then dropped suddenly into a harsh hating whisper where the promise of pain left me breathless in an adrenaline rush, ready to get out, ready to run. I paced as he talked. My hands tingled. I wanted the voice to stop. I wanted it to never stop. I wanted him to talk until he said something that would help me find out who he was.

"Lacie, Lacie, burning bright, you have the face of a beauty and the paws of a beast. Burned and ruined since the tender age of ten. Did the children laugh at you? Run screaming in disgust? Do men now cringe when you touch them, turn their eyes away? Can you love a man with hands like that? A man won't want you to touch him. A man won't want to look at the scars on your belly, the gouged ugly skin at your thighs. A man won't be able to love you. He will be sickened, unable to perform."

His was the voice of the schoolyard bullies. He was one of them now, jeering, torturing me with words.

"Is that why your mountain man left you? Did he see your scars? Did the touch of your fingers sicken him? I won't cringe or vomit or flinch. Do you love yourself, Lacie, while you're waiting for me? Do you touch yourself in the dark with those pitiful hands? Can they give you pleasure? Can they move just right, down there, where a different fire burns? Or are you waiting for me?

"I watched Jack Stein running fast and hard away from your country inn. Doesn't he know how vulnerable you are? Doesn't the new burn on your face prove it? Touch the burn and think of me.

You are right in my reach. You always have been. I can take you the way I took Skyla. I can do it now."

I moved away from the bay window.

"Are you really alone there in that big rambling house? Or am I inside with you, on the floor above, in the next room?"

I grabbed Jack's car keys and ran to the front door, clutching the phone to my ear.

"Am I sitting in the Range Rover? Did Jack leave it unlocked? Did he forget to set the alarm? Or am I walking up to the back entrance? Did Hannah leave the service door open?"

I ran out the front door and down the stairs.

"Run, Lacie, run! But where? Is there a place you're certain I'm not?"

Too afraid to go to the car. Too afraid to go back in. Wishing there was safety in open space. The inn loomed behind me, three levels of windows, watching eyes.

I bolted down the long winding drive.

"Run, my beauty, run," he laughed. "The chase is thrilling because I know how it will end. I've spent years making plans, getting it just right. Today's not the day, but it will be here soon. The Dead Time's coming, Lacie. The Dead Time's almost here."

He hung up.

I stopped and listened to silence. An eagle soared above.

Seconds later, an engine kicked over. *Where? Left? Right? Where?* My pulse raced. I looked up at the top of the drive, at the Range Rover sitting right where Jack had left it. The keys were still in my hand. I stood, watching and listening, not knowing which direction to run.

The engine revved. *Left.* I spun around. A snowmobile whipped out from behind the stable. He was on my left and coming fast, slicing across the field, a plume of snow spraying out high and white in his wake. I sprinted for the Range Rover. He got there first and cut me off. In one neat turn, he accelerated and came dead on, engine shrieking. I was an easy target there in the wide open space. He reached me in seconds, swerving around, circling fast and tight, kicking up snow, showering me with white, looping in a dizzying whirl. I saw him in fragments, strobing by.

Ski mask over his face. Black gloves. Black boots. Black clothes. A fat red canister strapped to his back. Rubber hose running from canister to trigger nozzle. One gloved hand steering the snow-mobile. The other hand gripping the trigger and aiming the nozzle at me.

Flamethrower, my brain screamed. *An assault weapon built for war.*

The first burst of fire hit the snow at my feet.

I jumped.

He laughed, skidding and circling in a nice tight curve, working the trigger. Flame pulsed out, hitting snow then air, bright orange whips of fire streaming like water from a hose. Left, right, left, right, over me, at my feet, side to side—hot bursts that turned the snow around me to slush. Fire roared. The engine whined. His high crazy laugh rang out above it all. I dropped to the ground, covered my head, and waited for a flamethrower burst to turn me to ash.

The snowmobile skidded to a stop right next to me, engine idling at a steady hum. He jammed the trigger nozzle up under my chin.

"Touch me, Lacie," he said softly in my ear. "Reach out and touch me."

I shook my head.

"Do it! Now!"

I lifted my hand, blindly. He caught my wrist. Pulled my glove off. "Reach out and touch the fire, Lacie." His voice was heavy, thick with desire. He wrapped my hand around him. The soft thing swelled, hardened, and throbbed.

"I knew it," he whispered. "You alone can make me a man. The Dead Time's coming, Lacie. It's almost here."

He let go. The engine revved. Slush soaked me and he was gone, skimming across the fields, engine whine fading, disappearing into the woods.

Jack found me, curled up small, clawing the ground, panting with fear, knees pulled up to my chest, clenched against a blast of fire I felt and heard and smelled, but that somehow, miraculously, wasn't there.

It was eight-thirty in the morning.

Hell of a way to start the day, Jack.

Chapter Twenty

A half hour later, the Maiden Inn parking lot was jammed with cars. All five official Stockbridge police sedans, Ben Freeman's cobalt pickup, six state police cruisers, four U.S. forest service snowmobiles, and a dozen different makes of four-wheel drives belonging to volunteers. Maps were spread across hoods, the chief of police organized search teams.

Jack, shocked and shaken, sat on the verandah steps next to me while a sheepish Kitty Gleason kicked at the snow and explained how *the whole damn thing was her own damn fault.*

"The call came in last night," she said. "I was alone, working a double shift. Hell, if somebody else had been there, if Harv had taken the call or Buddy or Bill, none of this would've happened. Hell."

"The call," Jack prompted.

"Yeah. It came in around eight o'clock. A man said he was with the New York headquarters of the FBI and that he was looking for an agent named Stein who might've been by asking about the old Wagner accident. I said you sure had been by and that you were stuck here on account of the snow. He asked if I knew where you were staying. I told him. Didn't seen any reason not to."

The police chief called Kitty's name.

"Go on," Jack said. "He needs you on the search."

She bent down and touched my shoulder. Her lips were bunched up and I thought she was going to cry. "I'm very sorry, ma'am. I had no way of knowing."

She left. Ben Freeman approached. He knelt on a step and put his broad hands on the tops of my knees. "We'll find him."

No you won't, I thought. *He's too smart.*

"We'll find him," Ben Freeman swore, then he was gone, striding across the lot, hopping into his truck and roaring away, the golden retriever riding shotgun next to him.

"They'll follow the snowmobile tracks as far as they can," Jack said watching the search parties split up. "Cruise the back country. Set up some road blocks. But he's long gone. He had a car parked out there in the woods. He was long gone before any of us got here."

Yes, I thought, he was out there, giggling and pleased, laughing at me, at my fear, at his own clever game, at how I jumped and screamed and hid my face from his whips of fire. My mind kicked into gear, dredging up facts from memory and reciting them out loud. Keep a nice objective reportorial perspective, or else go crazy with fear.

"Flamethrower," I said. "Invented in World War One by the Germans. Perfected in World War Two by the Nazis. They strapped portable units filled with napalm on their backs, and went swarming into foxholes spewing flames, wiping out French and English soldiers like ants. Burning them off the face of the earth.

"That's what flamethrowers do. They burn people off the face of the earth. Standard backpack-style units have a range of about forty-five yards. Nothing exotic about the components. A fuel tank filled with oil or thickened gasoline. A flexible hose runs from the tank to the trigger nozzle. Pull the trigger and watch the fire fly.

"His looked homemade. A fire extinguisher turned into a weapon, just as deadly as the real things. I covered a story in Norfolk once about a man who burst in on a junior high school with one of those homemade deals strapped to his back. He killed five kids with it. Burned them to death. Like the soldiers in the foxholes, only these were just kids. Moral of the story? Homemade flamethrowers are just as deadly as the official ones built for war. And he had one pointed at me."

Thank God for rage. Afraid, I was frozen. Mad, I could move, fight, hunt. Stay alive.

"I can arrange to put you somewhere," Jack said, his cool veneer cracking, "far away, in a safe house. I can get you secure transport out. I think it's best."

"You think it's best for me to hide." I looked out at the fringe of woods where the snowmobile had vanished from sight. "I'm not hiding, Jack Stein. That wasn't the deal. It's me he's after and you need me to find him. The only place I'm going is to New York City with you. Now. As planned. One of your ace artists is going to put his face down on paper. Isn't that what we agreed?"

Jack looked at me for a long moment. "It is indeed." He must have seen my resolve and my anger too. He smiled slightly, as if he was proud, and helped me to my feet.

Chapter Twenty-one

Oh! The joy of hunting Lacie! The fun of making her jump and scream.

The morning before this one, he watched her step out of Costello's building with the stony-faced fed. She must have sensed him there in the shadows, because she looked over her shoulder more than once. From his clever vantage point, he watched the fed search the Range Rover for tracking devices, then pull away from the curb and accelerate down the street.

He saw the fed's eyes locked on the rearview mirror, hunting for some kind of quick movement, watching parked cars for a sudden flare of flesh, a head ducking under the dash, out of sight. The fed drove with the windows rolled down too, listening for the choke of an engine firing up, or the hurried steps of a man running, or the hiss of tires over slush. The fed expected to be tailed, not understanding that his opponent was a master of the game. Why bother following when there was only one place they could be going? And, it had been easy to find out where they were staying.

It was tough driving in heavy snow, but he made it out to the country that night. He moved around the old inn unseen, counting cars, and when the fed's light finally went out, he slipped the back door lock and crept down the halls, counting people inside. There were only three. With the blizzard blowing around, he guessed the fed felt safe. Careless mistakes are made when a player feels safe; he lets down his guard, takes his eye off the ball, and odds were Jack Stein would do just that. Oh, it was sheer luck all right, but they played right into his hand. As smart as a gamesman is, he never looks down on old-fashioned luck.

He had smiled and hummed that morning, hiding out behind the stable, and he was humming now. It was a beautiful day, bright and sunny. The highway was empty, he sailed along, fingers drum-

ming on the steering wheel. There was so much to be happy about. The sun dancing on snow. The crisp fresh country air whistling in through his open window. Precious cargo stowed safely in back. It was a lovely day, the finest, the best. A perfect day to build the perfect fire.

His new video Walkman sat on the seat next to him. He hit play and her face filled the screen. Lacie Wagner, she said in that smooth cool way. Lacie Wagner, with the evening news. She had a cigarette voice, though he knew she didn't smoke, rich and throaty, with the looks to match. He kept one eye on the road and the other on her. Bold arched brows, full ripe lips stained crimson and glossed, high-flying cheekbones in a slender porcelain face. He dropped a hand in his lap and stroked, remembering the touch of her one burned hand.

Oh! He would've given anything to have been there when the fed finally found her, shaking and crying in the cold morning air. He would've given anything to have seen the look on that one man's face. Stein. A fed undone by fear.

Chapter Twenty-two

It just doesn't look like him," I complained, looking at the computer screen as FBI specialist David Chang worked to make the face come alive.

"Don't worry, Ms. Wagner," he said. "We'll get it. A face is the sum of all the parts. So let's go back and take it part by part."

Chang was in his twenties, but his totally bald head made him appear old and wise. He was patient with me. We had been sitting in his windowless office in the Manhattan bureau for hours, trying to get it right. As clear as the face was in my nightmares, I had trouble describing it.

"His forehead is higher," I explained. "And his nose more aquiline."

Chang elongated the forehead and trimmed the nose.

"Is that better?" he asked.

"Yes."

"Good. Now, the eyebrows, Ms. Wagner. Are they right?"

"Yes."

"Good. Now, is his mouth right?"

"No. It's too thick."

"The lips alone can change a face. They are very important. The proportion, the style of them." He sketched in the changes. The face looked better. Not exact, but better. "Now, what about his bone structure? Look carefully."

"His cheekbones should be more defined."

"Good." Chang made the changes. The image morphed in front of us. The proportions were correct now: thin lips, pointed chin, cheekbones winging up and out, nose long and sharp, eyebrows black slashes above narrow hooded eyes, and the forehead, a high bare expanse of skin with a vein at the temple bulging dark against parchment-colored skin. In my dreams, I could see the vein pulsing.

"Is that our man?" Chang asked.

"That's him," I said.

"Ugly sucker," Chang observed.

"He was in his late twenties when she saw him," Jack said. "He'd be in his early fifties now."

Chang nodded. His fingers flew across the keyboard. The face on the computer aged five years at a time in front of us. The hairline receded, the flesh under the chin dropped, tiny wrinkles warped his skin, eyelids drooped. "Assuming he didn't pack on a lot of weight or get plastic surgery," Chang said, "this is how he probably looks today." He printed out a hard copy and handed it to Jack.

Jack nodded, pleased.

"Hope I've been helpful," Chang said, standing and stretching.

"You have," Jack said. "We have a face. All we need is a name."

"Not my department," Chang quipped. "I've got a three o'clock upstairs. Hang here as long as you like." He clapped Jack on the shoulder and walked out.

Jack studied the sketch. "Maybe someone he loved died under your father's care. Do you have records from your father's practice, his research, anything like that?"

"My mother kept all his research and the original files from his practice. Active patients got duplicate files sent on to their new doctor. After she died, Max had the house packed up and the contents put in storage in Washington. He thought I might want to go through it when I grew up. I never did. I felt my past was as dead as my parents."

"What happened to it all?"

"As far as I know, it's still locked up in the warehouse where Max put it."

"Do you have access?"

"He gave me a key when I turned twenty-one. It's in a strong-box at home."

In a house I hadn't stepped into since Skyla died. Where her freshly folded jeans were still piled in the laundry room, and a Sub-Zero refrigerator was filled with her favorite foods. Christmas ornaments were stacked in the living room waiting for Skyla to come home, for a tree-shopping trip that would never take place. I didn't want to go back. Not yet. Maybe not ever. Now, Jack clearly expected me to.

"We can make the four o'clock shuttle," he said, putting his parka on and packing up the ThinkPad.

I shook my head.

"What is it, Lacie?"

"I haven't been back since Skyla died. It's too soon. I can't deal with it."

Jack handed me the sketch.

Looking at the face of the man who had torched my daughter gave me courage. "Okay," I said, standing. "Let's go."

We approached D.C. at dusk, as the sun cast a rich gold light over the white monuments below.

"This was the city of my dreams," I said, on our descent. "I was full of hope and ambition when I moved here. Now I can't even think about sitting in front of a camera. I'm afraid I'll never be able to speak a full sentence without fumbling or saying, *My daughter is dead*. As if that's the only real event that matters. Other people endure loss, Jack. Why is it I think I was supposed to have a better deal? Why do I think I had the right to see my girl grow up? That I had the right to die before she did?"

The landing gear touched tarmac. We taxied in. The seat belt light blinked out. Passengers churned around us gathering shopping bags fat with gifts. I squeezed my eyes shut, hid my face in my gloved hands. My body was shaking and my legs felt weak. Jack didn't press. The plane emptied. A stewardess asked him if I needed assistance. Jack said no and bought me some time. He did the right thing, which was nothing at all. The feeling had to go full cycle. I had to reach bottom before I could come up again. Finally, I dropped my hands and nodded.

He helped me out of my seat and guided me down the ramp.

The terminal was crowded. Travelers were frantically rushing, trotting, running to make connections, to get bags, to get somewhere. We moved in slow motion, the swelling crowd parting and then closing again behind us. Jack draped his arm protectively over my shoulder. My head was bowed, and I watched my feet moving one in front of the other, taking me back to a place I had never been without Skyla: home.

We took a cab into the city. It was a long slow ride in bumper-to-bumper Beltway traffic. The driver glanced at me in the rearview mirror so much it made me nervous. I had been a hot tabloid story here. *D.C.'s Sweetheart Anchor Goes into Hiding.* Or some juicy headline like it. Jack got a call while we were stuck there, inching along. His side of the conversation didn't reveal much, but when he hung up, he was happy.

"Ben Freeman," he said. "They found the snowmobile abandoned in the woods. There were plenty of tire tracks from the car he was driving and fresh footprints in the snow. The tire tracks are on their way to the State Police lab. The footprints are easier to read. Waffled-sole hiking boot. He wears a size ten."

I thought of those size-ten boots planted in the slush next to me and my mind went numb.

By the time we reached Georgetown, dusk had turned to night and streets were iced over. We fishtailed once. The driver apologized. He made a right turn then a left. Familiar landmarks slid by. Another left. Two blocks down, my street sign appeared.

He turned right and jerked to a stop at a police barricade. Two squad cars were parked broadside. A sawhorse closed off the narrow point of entry between them. Dozens more police units, ambulances, and fire engines jammed the street beyond. My own WRC News van was right up front. Reporters swarmed the police line, juggling cameras and mikes, angling for prime positions. A chopper whacked through the sky, swinging high-voltage searchlights over an area that was already, strangely, brightly lit up. Sirens whelped. My pulse ticked up.

"Shit," the cab driver muttered.

Jack leaned out the window and showed his ID. A young cop pushed the sawhorse aside and motioned us through at the same instant I saw it.

My house.

Jack's phone rang. I grabbed it out of his hands and let the voice fill my head.

"Lacie bug, Lacie bug, fly away home. Your house is on fire, but there's no children at home. The fire already took her, didn't it? I'm there now, watching my fire. I wish you were here with me. We could watch it together, side by side, hand in hand."

Jack covered the mouthpiece. "I'm going to look for him," he whispered. "Stay here. Keep him talking." He jumped out and locked the door behind him.

"I was inside your house," the voice promised. "I was there. I touched your clothes and I slept in your bed. I smelled you everywhere. I built this fire out of love. Do you understand that? Are you watching? Do you see what I did, Lacie?"

I looked out the window at the packed sidewalks, at the pulsing, shifting bodies, the spectators spilling into the streets. Moths drawn to the flame. He was out there too. I unlocked the door and plunged into the crowd, grabbing shoulders, turning faces, listening to his voice at the same time.

"It's wonderful here, Lacie. I wish we could share it."

Where are you? Where the hell are you? I cursed silently, looking at faces of old men and young men, but never his, not knowing what I would do if I found him. *My house,* I thought, pocketing the cell phone. *He must be up there close.* I ducked under the yellow tape, zigzagged around fire trucks, jumped over the fat fire hoses streaking the road, and raced up my driveway into the billowing black smoke.

"Where are you?" I shouted, but the sound of fire and water erased my words.

"Who are you?" I cried, dropping to my knees as tears rolled out of my smoke-stung eyes. "Goddamn you. Who are you? God fucking damn you. Why me? Why me, you son of a bitch?" I cursed and damned him while my home—Skyla's home—burned and every last thing I had to remember Skyla by burned with it.

What in God's name have I done to deserve this?

A black-coated fireman tripped over me. "What the hell?" He locked strong arms around my waist and pulled me up. "Get back, lady! Get the hell back!"

Windowpanes exploded. Flames kicked out. He ran me down the drive and handed me off to another fireman, who pushed me behind the police line. A second set of windows exploded. Smoke clouded the sky. Ashes sifted down on my coat, light specks of gray, the same color as Skyla's ashes. I heard thundering water, a dozen wailing sirens, bullhorn voices, but nothing was louder than the roar of the fire. The winter north wind blew in, hot with fire and heavy with soot. Spray from the hoses gusted like rain. Jack spotted me and pushed through the crowd. Sweat streamed down his cheeks.

"Get back in the cab, Lacie. Now."

I shook him off. He stayed with me. Water, ash, heat, and smoke hit us full in the face. We stood, side by side, watching my house burn up, burn down, burn orange and red and yellow, burn hot and deadly in the cold Washington night.

Chapter Twenty-three

❧

Jack got me away around midnight and into the nearby Four Seasons Hotel. There was no suite this time, just one room, two beds, and a federal agent standing guard outside our door.

My clothes were damp and dirty. My hair was wet and full of soot. Hours of standing in the wind had frozen my skin. I was overcome with shock from what I had seen. Jack ran the bath, then stripped me down with medical efficiency, and put me in it. I felt shame for a moment, knowing my scars were in plain view. Jack was impassive. When he had my hair washed and rinsed, he changed the dressing on my face, wrapped me in the hotel bathrobe, and ordered me into bed.

The agent standing guard collected my clothes to take to the laundry. Jack fussed in the minibar and poured me a double Scotch straight up. I swallowed it like medicine. It went to my head.

"I'm on the mountain," I said. "And I'm the blind one this time. Jack, please tell me, how the hell do we stop him?"

He poured me another Scotch.

The liquor was strong, but still I tasted smoke.

Jack had the occupants on our floor moved out and when that was done, he had hotel security lock the stairwell door and give him a key. A second federal agent arrived to stand guard at the elevator, and a third stood watch at the lobby entrance downstairs. A pair of agents arrived to pick up Chang's sketch. Jack wanted the face run through the database. Arson and pyromania were the search specifications.

Jack checked the tap and trace on his cell phone next. The incoming call had come from a new number, lifted from a dentist in New York. The dentist was having sushi in Manhattan when the call came through, and the call was placed in Georgetown.

We spent the night with lights on and drapes closed. I drifted in and out of sleep, listening to Jack's hushed voice as he talked on the phone, the steady sound of him walking, pacing, window to door and back again, thinking.

I awoke late morning to the sound of the television.

Jack was sitting in a chair pulled up next to the set, watching a WRC special news bulletin.

"The home of WRC anchorwoman Lacie Wagner burned last night, in a fire of unknown origin. Action News was on the scene."

The camera panned as the fireman pulled me away from my burning house and pushed me back behind the police line. It went in for a close-up on my tear-streaked face, then pulled back wide again and panned over the crowd. He was right there behind me in a black-hooded sweatshirt. The nightmare face. Damp pale skin glistened in the firelight. Deep lines channeled across the broad forehead and his flesh sagged off high sharp cheeks. Dishwater-blond hair was streaked with gray. A ghost of a smile played at his lips. I could almost smell the sickly sweet stale nightmare breath.

He touched my hair lightly and ducked away into the night.

"That was him," Jack said, riveted. The camera went wide again on my burning house.

"Why did he do it?" I asked. That old refrain.

"The house is symbolic," Jack mused. "It's his way of saying if he wanted to kill you, he could have killed you and Skyla any time he wanted, before you ever knew he existed. He burned your house when he knew you weren't there to prove that he could just as easily have torched it when you were there.

"The killing isn't what fascinates him, Lacie. It's the game. He doesn't want you dead, not now anyway. He told you so yesterday. Whatever the Dead Time is, it's not here yet. It's the chase that intrigues him, the game that gives him satisfaction. He wants to play games, so let's play." Jack handed me the phone. "Call WRC."

"Why?"

"You're going on the air."

I dressed in freshly laundered clothes, tied my hair back, and applied full camera makeup. Jack told me we were going to put the sketch and news clip on the air, and that I would make a personal appeal to my viewing audience for help identifying him. Quantico had agreed to set up an 800 number. Skyla's killer had a face, and now tens of thousands of people were going to see it.

"I'm ready," I said turning away from the mirror, wondering if I really was.

Jack opened the door. The agent standing guard escorted us out to a blue Lincoln with tinted windows, government plates, and an armed agent serving as bodyguard and driver. He was trim and neat in a gray suit, with short black hair and a chiseled young face.

"Vic Holloway," he said, as Jack got in. "It's an honor to meet you, sir."

"Call me Jack, not sir."

"It's an honor to meet you, Jack." Holloway grinned.

Jack simply nodded.

Holloway put the Lincoln in gear and pulled smoothly away.

Jack opened his ThinkPad and punched keys.

"What are you doing?" I asked.

"Writing your script."

"I'm capable of writing my own," I countered.

Jack worked all the way across town, intent on the screen, fingers moving fast, and he didn't stop typing until we pulled up in front of WRC. Holloway escorted us inside, bolted the front door, and stood guard.

The lobby was cheerful with a six-foot pine. Presents for the WRC Toys-for-Tots drive were piled underneath. Ornaments were pictures of all the WRC talent. My own face topped the tree. The WRC Star.

The receptionist jumped up. "Ms. Wagner, we are all so very sorry . . ."

"Thank you." I swept past her and guided Jack down the hall to the newsroom.

Typing, phone calls, and conversations stopped. I felt a dozen pair of eyes on me. Harry saw us through his office window. He dropped his cigarette and telephone, and hurried out. I checked the newsroom clock. It was eleven-fifty. Jack wanted me live on the noon newscast. The story would play again at six and eleven.

"This is Jack," I said to Harry. "Jack, meet Harry. Harry, where's the floor crew?"

"Ready and waiting."

"We've got artwork," I said, heading into the studio. "I'll need close-ups of it, and a piece from last night's footage. Do you have the master tape?"

"Cued up and ready to roll."

"Good." I mounted the silver news set and sat in my usual chair behind the U-shaped desk. The city skyline sparkled behind me in a wall-sized mural. D.C. at night. A majestic sight. "Tell me one thing, Harry. Honestly. How do I look?"

"Like hell, Lacie," he said gently.

"That's what I thought." I snapped open a compact and freshened my lipstick. My heavy camera makeup did little to conceal the dark circles under my eyes or the hollows in my cheeks. My pants were loose. I had lost weight since Skyla died. I brushed extra blusher over my one good cheek, fussed with the bandage on the other, then snapped the compact shut.

The noon news producer was busy hooking Jack's computer up, feeding his text directly into the Tele-Prompter.

"Ninety seconds," the floor director announced.

I had a gift for reading script I had never seen and making it flow as if I were speaking straight from my heart. I hoped the trauma of the last weeks had not stripped me of that. For the first time in my news career, I had stage fright. My hands shook. My stomach twisted. My mouth went dry.

"One minute," the floor director said.

"Harry," I called out as the clock clicked over to 11:59:30. "Go to a commercial when I finish the story. I can't do the whole half hour. It's not in me."

"I'm ready to step in," Harry assured me.

"Thirty seconds," the bearded floor director warned.

I emptied my mind and focused on the Tele-Prompter. The first script page scrolled up. "Jack! What the hell did you write?"

"Just read it, Lacie."

"Twenty seconds and counting," the floor director announced.

"What are you trying to do to me?" I stood up. "I can't say that."

"Fifteen seconds . . ."

"Trust me, Lacie. Just read it."

"It's too goddamn personal!"

"Ten seconds . . ."

"The story's personal."

"Nine . . ."

"Baring my emotions in public is not what I do."

"It is today."

"Eight . . ."

"How can you ask me to do this?" Tears of frustration stung my eyes.

"Trust me."

"Five . . . four . . . three . . ."

Harry saw my panic and made a move for the set. Jack held him back.

"Lacie, read it. Please."

I was too shook up to consider ad-libbing. I needed a script and the only one I had was Jack's. I dropped down in my chair and looked at the Tele-Prompter. The words were a blur. My eyes were full of tears. I had never stumbled or fallen apart on the air, and I willed myself not to now.

"Two . . ."

I blinked five times fast.

"One . . ."

The red on-air light flashed on.

"Welcome to the WRC Action News. I'm Lacie Wagner with a special report. Sitting here, night after night, reporting the traumas and tragedies of others, I have tried never to forget the simple fact that people make news stories. The person is the story. And today, I am the story.

"My daughter was viciously murdered over the Thanksgiving weekend. It was not a random event, but part of an older campaign of terror and revenge, one that goes all the way back to my own childhood. There have been rumors and much speculation about my disability. I have never talked about it publicly, but now I am going to show you the truth. I am going to show you my hands."

I tugged my gloves off and held my hands up, thinking only of the copy skimming by on the Tele-Prompter screen.

"They were burned when I was ten years old in a fire that was set to kill my father. The man who destroyed my hands murdered my father but failed to kill me. He has come back after all these years to finish what he started. He has taken my daughter, and now he wants to take me.

"I don't know why, only that he continues a siege against me, against my life, all that I own, and all those that I love. He was responsible for the destruction of my house here in Washington last night. He's out there right now, among you, a stranger you pass in the subway or one you sit next to on the bus. He may dye his hair or grow a mustache, but we know his face."

The camera cut to a close-up of the FBI sketches.

"The picture on the left is what he looked like twenty-three years ago. The picture on the right is what he looks like today. WRC-TV inadvertently got this live shot of him last night at the fire. He was in a crowd of spectators, watching."

The camera cut to the clip of his hooded face.

"I can only imagine that he is a weak man, an outcast, a misfit, of such low intellect that he can communicate only with fire. Fire is primitive. The killer is primitive too."

The camera cut back to me.

"The FBI has set up the dedicated 800 number scrolling across your screen. For the sake of my daughter and all the other young lives that have been destroyed by the primitive men who walk among us, please help find him. When a child dies at the hands of a killer, a little bit of us dies each time too.

"It is my profession to put events into words and pictures. There are no words to communicate the pain and anguish I am feeling. Or the fear. In America, we have a wealth of rights. The right to live peacefully, without fear, is most precious. With your help, together we can work toward that great goal. I want to thank WRC-TV and all of you out there watching tonight. Thank you for your support."

The camera cut to a commercial.

I pushed away from the news desk, grabbed my gloves, and rushed off the set.

Harry stopped me. "That was a hell of a piece. You'll get a network pick-up tonight."

"If it was so good, why do I feel so lousy, Harry?"

"It's not easy to undress in front of millions of viewers, and that's basically what you just did."

"Great." I choked, humiliated, angry.

"It was," Harry promised.

I left the studio. Jack lurked in my office doorway. He had the decency to look somewhat sheepish.

"You sandbagged me, Jack."

"You wouldn't have agreed to do it my way."

"This is your idea of trust? Pushing a blind man over the cliff?" I marched past him and flopped down in my desk chair.

Jack closed the door to give us privacy. "Listen to me, Lacie. We need one of two things. We need someone to step up and ID him, or we need him to make a mistake. You made this a news event by taking your gloves off. That's what guarantees a network pickup. The network will know your piece is a ratings event. They'll promote the hell out of it and that means more people will watch. The more people who watch, the better chance we have of getting him ID'd.

"And, the better chance we have that he will see the piece, wherever he is now. A man like this watches the news closely. He probably tapes the news stories about his crimes, and keeps them as souvenirs. If he wasn't watching at noon, he'll be watching tonight. You challenged and insulted him, Lacie. He'll respond. If we shake him up enough, he'll get mad. When he gets mad, he'll start to get sloppy. Up until now, he's been meticulous and controlled. We need him to make a mistake. But he won't, not unless he's mad enough to lose his cool."

My desk was swamped with mail. Every line of my telephone was blinking. I pitied the receptionist. My private intercom buzzed. Not knowing what else to do, I punched the speaker on.

"Ms. Wagner?" the newsroom operator said. "This call seemed important."

"Who is it?" I asked, tired and drained.

"A Richard Wagner. He says he's your father."

Jack nodded.

"Put him on," I said.

The line clicked over to silence.

"Lacie Wagner," I said, warily.

"*A weak man, an outcast, a misfit,*" he cried. "*Of such low intellect that the only way he can communicate is with fire. Fire is primitive. The killer is primitive too.* You hurt me, Lacie. I thought you understood me. Fire is not primitive. It's powerful! You attacked me. How dare you put my face on the news for the world to see! You've challenged me. Fight fire with fire. I always have."

The line went dead.

"He's mad," Jack said, simply. "That's good. Maybe he'll make a mistake." He put his parka on.

"A few more mountains to scale before the day's over?" I said unkindly.

"Yes. We're going to the storage facility."

"I don't have the key. It was in the house."

"I know. We're going to go find it."

Chapter Twenty-four

There is a violence to the aftermath of fire almost as frightening as the raging blaze itself. It is the utter destruction. My house was no exception.

Firemen had hacked through the front door and left it hanging by a hinge. Ruined furniture littered the front yard, a garage sale from hell. Blown-out windows were dark gaping holes. Shattered glass sparkled in the afternoon sun. What had once been a smart town house was now a roofless shell, red bricks licked black, the beautiful inside turned ugly and tossed out.

We pulled up in front, next to the fire inspector's van. Yellow police tape fluttered in the breeze, marking off the boundaries to my property. Two rookies patrolled the line, keeping curious spectators and tabloid columnists back. Jack and I got out. Holloway stayed behind, standing watch.

Reporters shouted out questions I didn't bother to answer. That old refrain drifted through the air: *A statement, Ms. Wagner! Tell us what you're feeling!* All they had to do was look. How the hell did they think I felt?

The fire hoses had washed away snow in the front yard and turned it to mud. A blackened sofa straddled the walkway. The air was still heavy with acrid smoke and wet ash. Fire officials and police milled in the yard.

We went up the steps, ducked around the broken front door, and into the dim interior. A carpet of ash squished under my feet. Burned furniture littered the living room. Books that once lined my bookcases were gone, reduced to silt. The rear picture window looking out on my small square city garden was blown out. The garden itself was a hideous lifeless patch. The fire inspector approached. Jack showed ID and introduced me.

"What've you got so far?" Jack asked.

"There's no question this was arson," the inspector said. "Hell, the arsonist did everything but leave us a handwritten note. He wanted us to know this was a deliberate torch. And he wasn't interested in setting your average fire. No sir. From the burn patterns here, I'm guessing he soaked the whole place with chemical accelerants, rigged a half-dozen different remote-controlled strikers, then set them all off once he was outside. His goal was swift total destruction and that's pretty much what he got. He was no novice either. His strikers were world-class, and he knew how to fix this for maximum heat. There are two kinds of fires. Hot and goddamn hot. This one was goddamn hot."

"Can we go upstairs?" Jack asked.

"Sure," he said. "Watch your step though."

I stopped at the staircase landing. Closed my eyes. Heard water dripping from the rafters, the fire inspector's deep voice rumbling in the next room, his heavy shoes crunching through the first-floor wreckage.

"Do you want to wait outside?" Jack asked, feeling my fear.

"No," I said, opening my eyes. "Let's go."

The staircase was cement-based and safe, but dark. Water trickled down the walls. We inched up, feeling the way. At the top, I led Jack down the main hall. Much of the roof was gone, a dingy light filtered in. We passed Skyla's bedroom first. The door was burned out. I stepped over the threshold.

White walls were scorched black and wet with water. Her bright brass bed had been seared to a dull iron gray, the mattress stuffing and crisp pink bedding burned away. Bare coiled springs poked up from the heat-warped metal frame. Odds and ends stuck out of ankle-deep ash. Wire coat hangers. Twisted silver picture frames. Melted metal knobs from the neck of Skyla's violin, a spiraled length of gut string, the metal from an old retainer she saved just for fun. Rivets from her sneakers.

This was the final indignity—to take my father, my hands, my daughter, then my home and all of Skyla. To take away every last thing of hers and leave me nothing to remember her by. He had done a thorough job of wiping my girl off the face of the earth.

My room was no better. He had heaped my clothes in the center of my bed. It was the only explanation for the belt buckles and metal zippers hanging into the mattress springs. Bureau drawers had been yanked out and emptied, the contents burned away. My socks. My underwear. My nightgowns. Fire was intimate. It took everything I had.

Jack understood. He kicked through the ash with his big hiking boots, and fished for buried treasure. He came up with precious things. A silver hair clip. A gold-framed picture of Skyla and me. He fished again and came up with the prize.

"Here," he said, "you'll want to keep this."

It was a round piece of fire-baked, glazed clay. Two perfect tiny handprints preserved in ceramic. Skyla's hands. She had been five years old. A kindergarten art project signed and dated. I didn't trust myself to speak, so I just tucked it in my shoulder bag and nodded my thanks.

The fireproof safe was built into the cement wall in the back of the walk-in closet. Jack held a penlight so I could see. I dialed in the combination and opened the little door. Stock certificates and the title to my house were kept in a bank vault. There wasn't much in the home safe. I emptied it quickly. A pair of diamond earrings my father had left me. My passport. My birth certificate, Skyla's too. And the key to Max's storage bin.

"That's it," I said, when I finished.

We picked our way down the dark stairwell and out into the daylight.

I didn't look back, not even once as we pulled away, nor did I think about finding a new place to live. I was living a minute at a time now, knowing that if the voice were ever close enough to whisper in my ear again, I wouldn't survive. Life could be snuffed out with a single squeeze of a flamethrower's trigger. Life was a moment-by-moment event now. This understanding created a fundamental change inside me. A psychic shift, a preternatural survival instinct fueled by rage. Rage kept me going.

How dare he.

I stroked the ceramic handprints. They were so very small.

The storage facility was in an industrial park forty minutes outside of downtown Washington. We arrived late in the afternoon. Shadows were long and the air was sharp. The security guard at the entrance checked the tag on my key, pulled the chain link gate back, and let us drive in.

Five long metal structures were built in rows and numbered. The individual storage spaces were then identified by letter. We found mine in the fourth row, seven spaces down from the end: 7-D. Holloway waited patiently in the car. Jack and I got out.

The lock was old. Jack had to work to get the key in, but it fit and the bolt scraped back. He pushed the door open and found the light switch. Four fluorescent tubes sputtered on. The air inside was as cold as a butcher's freezer. Furniture was piled eight feet high. Stacked cartons were marked haphazardly or not at all. Jack poked through the piles, reading labels where he could.

"Appliances. Formal china. Family silver."

"Open that one," I said, surprising myself. So many years had gone by, I had forgotten about things I had once loved.

Jack hauled it down and slit the packing tape with a pocket knife. I lifted pieces out one at a time: a gravy dish, salt and pepper shakers, candlesticks, a crystal and silver wine decanter. The silver was dull, dark with tarnish.

"These belonged to my father's mother," I told Jack. "Once a week when my mother went to her garden club evenings, my father cooked dinner with me. We dined by candlelight with these silver candleholders and ate with these forks and knives. My father poured his wine from this decanter. He talked to me about politics and world events as though I were an equal. I watched the news so we could discuss it. My passion for the news came from him."

"Why didn't you ever come take the silver?" Jack asked.

"It reminds me of my mother." I sat cross-legged on the cold cement floor and told Jack how every night after my father's death, she set the table for three with my father's silver even though he was never coming home, and lit candles even though they terrified me. Then, the two of us sat in silence, dining with a ghost.

"She never spoke to me during dinner," I explained. "There was just the sound of silverware clicking against plates, candles hissing, an old clock ticking. When she finished her meal, she would put her fork down, look at me, and say: *Lacie?* Then she would run out of the dining room, away from me and the unspeakable words she wanted to speak."

"What words?" Jack asked.

"*Why didn't you die instead of him.* She said it once, when I was still in the hospital." I dropped the silver pieces into the carton and pushed it away

Jack went back to work, moving furniture aside, searching for my father's files. He found them against the back wall in twelve neatly marked boxes.

"Yes," he said, softly, with anticipation. "Let's take these back to the hotel where we can see what we're looking at." Jack carried the boxes out to the Lincoln. Six fit in the trunk. He wedged the remaining six in the backseat.

I slammed the storage room door, leaving the silver to sit in the gloom, tarnished by the years and the unwelcome memory of my mother's hateful words.

At the Four Seasons, Holloway piled the boxes on a luggage cart and wheeled them up to our room. A new federal agent stood at attention outside our door, the bulge of his gun visible under his jacket. Jack unloaded the files, thanked Holloway, and locked us in. He checked his watch. We were just in time for the six o'clock news.

Harry looked smart at the news desk in his signature navy cashmere blazer and red silk tie, thick white hair brushed back from his powerful face. His deep voice was heavy with emotion as he gave the grave introduction to my piece. The camera cut to my own intent face and deeply sad eyes. I turned away and wandered the room, listening but not looking. When it was over, I turned the set off.

"Someone will call the 800 number." Jack said the words like a wish, then tossed me a room service menu. "We skipped lunch. Let's have dinner."

I thought of the way the trigger nozzle felt jammed up against my chin and pushed the menu aside. "I'm sorry, I can't."

Jack came close. I smelled the fresh scent of his soap.

"How much weight have you lost since Skyla died?" he asked.

"I don't know."

"Starving yourself isn't going to bring her back and it sure as hell isn't going to help you work with me. You need to be as strong as possible to get through whatever else he has in store for us." He held out the menu.

I ordered a roast turkey sandwich with fries, tossed salad, and two pieces of chocolate cake. When it came, I ate everything.

I worked with Jack well into the night, pouring through reams of old patient records, not really knowing what we were looking for. My father was the key. He had been a gentle man, and I wondered what on earth he had done, whom he had hurt.

At one in the morning, I lay down and closed my eyes. I woke

around three to the sound of fingers flying across a computer keyboard and file pages turning. Jack was still awake. Despite the late
hour, he was alert and focused, intent on the work in front of him.
He impressed me, much as I hated to admit it. He was stronger
than I was, and I resented that. He needed more food but less sleep.
He gave strength without pity, and asked for nothing in return but
equal commitment.

I sat up.

"Go back to sleep," Jack ordered.

"No thanks." I reached for a file and began to read.

We combed through lab reports and paged through charts checking birth dates, looking for a wrongful death, a lawsuit, a misdiag-
nosis, correspondence from a despondent or angry relative, and we
found nothing at all.

"Your father kept detailed, thorough records right down to
daily phone logs," Jack said when we finished reading the last file.
"He was a focused, orderly man. The problem is, nothing jumps
out at me. Many of your father's patients died. Strokes, cancer, in-
operable brain tumors, head traumas—nothing unusual. There are
no wrongful death suits, no botched diagnosis or insurance problems. One thing puzzles me: Why did he quit research to go into
private practice? That's an odd move for a man whose entire medical career had been built on research."

I wanted to ask Jack what made a young doctor quit his practice
and join the FBI. "Max may know something," I said instead.

Jack sent an e-mail out into cyber-space, knowing it would eventually reach Max wherever he was.

I looked over at the remaining boxes. "You might find something
in his research, Jack. But I can't help you. It's way too technical
for me."

"Good thing there's a doctor in the house," Jack quipped. "Get
some sleep."

I woke up to the buzz of a razor and the whip of denim covering
flesh.

Jack walked out of the bathroom, toweling his hair. "Morning,
Lacie." He wore jeans and a freshly laundered blue denim shirt.
His face was flushed from the shower. "Take a look at this." He
tossed me an accordion file.

"It's empty," I said, looking inside.

"That's the point. There are fifteen research files just like it, all labeled *Durand*. The front of each file is marked with specific dates: five-day blocks, four weeks apart. The last entry was the five days between Christmas 1964 and New Year's, 1965."

"The year I was born. Ten years before the accident. Seems inconsequential."

"Is it? Look at this notation in the margin of his lab phone log dated August 1975, the day before he went to pick you up from camp." He handed the old yellowed log to me.

"*Durand.*" I recognized my father's small precise handwriting. "I don't understand."

"Neither do I. Unless someone or something he was treating at the time of his death was linked to this earlier missing study. The way he wrote the name, it's like he was asking himself a question: Would the Durand study be relevant?

"Or, had he learned something new that might have made the failed Durand project a success? Did he want to replicate the study, start again with the advantage of all the new information and medical progress made in those ten intervening years? Every researcher has a favorite project, a breakthrough they want to make in their lifetime. Was Durand your father's? Did he fail the first time, and was he preparing to try again?"

"This could have just been a doodle, Jack, the kind of mindless note you make while you're waiting for a phone call to go through."

"Could be, but your father wasn't a doodler. There are no snippets or stray words in the margins of his lab notes or patient files or anywhere else in the phone log. Everything is precise and organized, terrifically neat. This stray word meant something to him. It was a reminder or a question or a problem he couldn't solve."

"The Durand files are empty. How will we ever know what or who Durand was?"

"Much as researchers love to keep their work secret, they can't bear to. They brag to colleagues, drop vague titillating hints. Your father must have talked to someone. He may even have confided in one of his fellow researchers. His work was too important, too exciting for him to have kept it all locked up in his own mind."

"What was my father researching?"

"He was very much ahead of his time," Jack said, sitting down on the bed facing me. "In retrospect, he was brilliant. If he had lived, there's no doubt he would have found answers to questions that baffle neurologists today. Your father was deeply involved in researching the electroneural factors of the brain. He wanted to create artificial signals the brain would accept as its own, signals that could be manipulated and directed to troubled areas, arresting Alzheimer's, Parkinson's disease, and a host of other neural illnesses.

"He had designs for micro-pellet implants a decade before the establishment medical community accepted the fact it could be done. His work was highly experimental and never resulted in viable application, but he was on the track, Lacie. His concepts were advanced at a time when neurology was still a dark miasma of misinformation."

"Do you have names of his colleagues at Harvard?"

"A few. And I found this, stuck to the inside of one of the empty Durand folders."

He handed me a small black and white snapshot. A burly man in a white lab coat and a woman in a white lab coat at his side. Two children stood in front of them. The boy looked ten, the girl was a toddler. Three men in suits were lined up behind the man and woman. My father was at the end, on the left, smiling and proud.

"Turn it over," Jack said.

In the precise tiny letters of my father's handwriting, in faded blue ink, were the words *Durand, New Year's Day, 1960.*

"Is your father in the picture?" Jack asked.

"Yes. He's the last man in a suit on the left." I passed the shot back to Jack.

He examined the picture with a magnifying glass. "He looks happy. There's snow on the ground where they're standing."

"It could have been taken at Harvard outside his lab."

"Which reminds me. Let's try to catch the noon shuttle to Boston. I want to go to Harvard and see if any of your father's colleagues are still there."

"What about these boxes?"

"They're going across town to my office at headquarters."

I looked at Jack in his chambray shirt, open-necked and easy. I pictured him walking into the lobby of the FBI building on Pennsylvania Avenue, crossing the huge FBI emblem inlaid on the floor, and striding past all those pale government men in dark suits and ties and short-clipped hair.

The thought of it made me smile.

Chapter Twenty-five

W e left the hotel through a rear service entrance. The Lincoln was waiting. Holloway greeted us, fresh-faced and bright.

"Morning, Jack. Morning, Ms. Wagner. It's a fine day to fly."

He took a circuitous route out of Georgetown, making a series of confusing left and right turns, checking the rearview mirrors as he went. When he was certain no one was following, he shot up an entrance ramp to the Beltway and raced to the airport.

Traffic was light. We arrived with forty minutes to spare. Holloway walked us through security and tucked us in a rear corner of the shuttle boarding area. He posted himself up front. Jack spent time on his phone with Quantico, listening to the rundown of calls logged in to the 800 number.

In the row facing us, a little girl with a cloud of blond curls sat at her mother's feet, playing with Barbies and singing as loud as she could. The tired looking mother shook her roughly. "I told you to stop it!"

I was there in a second, looking her hard in the face. "Take it easy," I warned. "This girl's a gift. *A gift.*"

Jack was closing out his conversation with Quantico and watching me now.

I dropped back into my own plastic chair.

They say when your daughter's dead you are still a mother. The status has simply changed. You are the mother of a dead child. There is no word in the English language for this. We use *widow* to describe a woman whose husband has died, and *orphan* for a girl whose mother has died. But there is nothing special in our language for a woman whose daughter is dead. She is simply, uneloquently, the mother of a dead child. Implying failure. Implying guilt. *What kind of mother were you that you lost your little girl?*

Jack startled me out of my thoughts. "It worked," he said, pocketing his phone. "A gas station attendant saw him yesterday morning, around eleven. He was heading south on I-87 in a dark van. The attendant couldn't remember the make or exact color and didn't catch any plates. Our man was wearing black jeans and a black ski parka. The gas station is one of those places with a mini-mart inside. He bought thirty dollars' worth of gas, a two-dollar cup of hot coffee, a three-dollar extra-large cup of Swiss Miss hot chocolate, a one-dollar pack of Hostess Twinkies, and he paid in cash."

"What did you say?"

"The clothes?"

"No. The drinks and snack."

"Coffee. Hot chocolate. Hostess Twinkies."

"He's doing this to torture me," I said softly. "Skyla loved hot chocolate and Twinkies in the winter. She used to dip the Twinkies in the chocolate."

Jack's words came back to me. *He spent time with her before he killed her.* Enough time to learn the words to my dreams and her favorite snack.

"How long did he keep her alive talking to her?" I said. "How did he get her to talk and what else did he do to her before she died, Jack? What else?" My voice had risen. It was urgent, afraid.

Holloway made a move. Jack raised a hand. Holloway backed off.

"What did he do to her?" I asked again. "What the hell did he do to her, Jack?"

"Stop it," he said, pulling me close. "Stop it. Don't ever think about that."

"I can't help it. I think about it all the time."

"You have to focus."

"On what."

"Moving forward and we are moving forward. We know more than we did yesterday. We know he drives a dark-colored van and that he went south, toward Washington."

"Old news, Jack. We're always one step behind him. We're always one goddamn step behind him when we should be in front."

"We are going to get in front of him. Listen to me. We have thirty-five FBI field offices distributing Chang's sketch to local police and his face beamed across the nation on the evening news. We've got teams of lab workers and technicians in Boston analyzing tire tread and a size-ten shoe print, the FBI mainframe trolling a data bank of faces searching for a match. If he's a felon, a military man, or federal employee, we'll get a hit. We know what kind of car he drove and where he was twelve hours ago.

"He has to buy gas to stay mobile and food to stay alive. Somehow before now, he has worked to make money. He's visible, Lacie. The 800 number has been flooded with calls. It will take time to sort out the crank calls from real leads, but one thing has already jumped out."

"What."

"Some of the sightings have an interesting configuration. They're clustered by several distinct periods of time and in four distinct cities: Knoxville, Asheville, Raleigh, and Norfolk. The names and jobs are all different. A pizza delivery man in Asheville. UPS worker in Raleigh. Drove a florist's truck in Norfolk. Sometimes his hair was blond, sometimes gray, other times black. He's been following you. The dates of the sightings coincide with the dates you lived in those cities. He's been there in every town you've ever lived in."

"Why now? Why wait all these years to come after me?"

"Something happened to him. A stressor. A psychic break. Whatever it is snapped him, and it's no longer good enough to watch you and fantasize. He needs to live his fantasy now, make it come true."

They called our flight. Holloway nodded. Jack walked me to the gate. We took seats in the front row, where Jack could look at each and every passenger boarding. Even though Holloway was standing watch outside, Jack's body was tense and his right hand lay lightly at his hip, near his gun.

After takeoff, I rested my head against the tiny window and watched Jack. He pretended to read a magazine, but he was focused somewhere inside, turning the puzzle around in all directions. He caught me looking at him and flashed a smile.

It was a real smile, not the wry, ironic, or bitter ones I had seen, and it changed his whole face. There was another Jack Stein I didn't know, but that smile promised I might. I turned away, shaken. Over the past days we had slowly been moving out of our hostile corners, toward each other. One gave a little, the other gave back, and now we were standing somewhere near the middle of our strange playing field, still circling, but more or less even. Hostility had faded to mutual admiration. Agitation had turned to consideration. The chilly space between us had somehow turned warm.

An hour later, the shuttle landed.

We zigzagged through the packed terminal and hailed a cab.

"Harvard Medical School," Jack ordered, climbing in.

I slid in next to him. He handed me a list. "These are names I pulled from your father's research files. The top five are doctors he worked and socialized with. The first, Herbert Voss, directed the research group at that time. He also seemed to know your father well personally. There were lunches, dinners at home, and plenty of memos written in the kind of shorthand close friends or partners use. Boston telephone had no listing for him. Neither did the utility companies. I'm hoping Harvard will."

I scanned the list but recognized none of the names. My father's research career was finished by the time I was born.

The downtown Boston skyline sparkled in the distance. Our driver moved through the tunnel and traveled north up Storrow Drive, a long stretch of highway that hugs the James River. Out on the water, rowers slipped by in long thin sculls. Teams of hard-shouldered men moved in perfect harmony and matched rhythm. Dip, pull, lift. Dip, pull, lift. Oars sliced into the winter gray river and spun out again. Joggers trotted on the riverbank, never quite matching the speed of the sculls. Their breaths steamed in the frigid air. Hands were covered with mittens, and bodies were sleek in form-fitting Thinsulate suits, many with hoods.

The hoods reminded me of the WRC footage, the fire-setter's face under his hood as he watched. *I've been there all along, Lacie. Every step of the way.*

Soon we were turning away from the river and pulling up to the Harvard Medical School Quadrangle. Five marble buildings formed a U-shape around the central open space. The administration building we wanted dominated the far end. It was a hundred-year-old beauty; three levels of gray-white marble with a broad sweeping staircase and six columns with curling cornices in the Ionic style.

Jack paid the driver to wait. We got out and walked briskly. In spring and summer, the grounds were lush with well-tended lawns and massive trees. Now, the Quadrangle was barren. A few people moved between buildings. Classes were in recess for the holiday, but the laboratories and offices never closed. We took stairs two at a time, pushed through the administration building doors, and went up to the overheated admissions office on the second floor.

A leggy young woman worked the desk. Strawberry-blond curls brushed her shoulders, wide green eyes sparkled behind wire-rim glasses. Her red Harvard T-shirt was faded and shrunken, revealing the outline of full high breasts and a ribbon of bare midriff. Beat-up Levi's were low-slung and tight. She smiled brightly at Jack.

"Jack Stein," he said, leaning easily against the counter, offering ID.

"You don't look like an agent," she replied, arching an eyebrow.

"You don't look like a secretary," he flipped back, grinning. The Jack Stein charm again. On and off with the flick of a switch. "Let me guess. Med school student?"

"Next year," she boasted, sitting up a little straighter in her chair. "I'm working here this year to help my parents pay the monster tuition."

"It's a good investment," Jack said.

"Sure is. One day you can call me Doctor. Today you can call me Robin." She turned a pencil into a baton, twirling it quickly through nimble fingers. "How can I help you?"

"I'm looking for someone who was on staff here in 1960."

"Tall order."

"Tall or impossible?"

"Nothing's impossible."

"The confidence of the young."

"You're not what I consider old."

"Thank you again."

"Staff of 1960?"

"Yes."

"Did he graduate from Harvard?"

"I don't know. What if he didn't? What are the chances he's in there somewhere?"

"Good," she said. "Harvard Med School Alumni has elevated record keeping to an art. Staff records are archived in the mainframe. If the man you're looking for wrote any journal articles in the years after his post here, his credentials would include Harvard, automatically ticking the article into our system. I'll put his name in on a broad-based search. If he achieved tenure here, got a pension, went to a class reunion, appeared as a guest speaker, or published anything, we'll get a hit."

"His name is Dr. Herbert Voss," Jack said as she swiveled around to the computer.

"Spell it."

"V-O-S-S."

She zapped the request out into Harvard's private cyber-space. Less than a minute later, a reply scrolled across the screen.

"Home run," Robin said, merrily. "Dr. Herbert Voss. Not only was he a graduate of Harvard Medical School in 1950, but he went straight into research, and eventually chaired the Neurology Department in the late sixties. He wrote dozens of journal articles over the years, all cited on the forthcoming printout. Dr. Voss retired in 1990 at the ripe old age of sixty-six."

"Anything else?"

"A clipping in the *Alumni News* says that Voss received a lifetime achievement award for distinguished research, but was unable to attend the ceremony. He suffered a debilitating stroke in 1992 and was put into a nursing home. Huh. Too bad. Crummy way to end a great career. All those years of research and he couldn't prevent his own body from going AWOL." She printed the pages out and handed them to Jack.

"How'd I do?" she asked with a sweet smile.

"A-plus," Jack tossed back, enjoying the game. "Is Voss alive?"

"In 1992 he was. There's no death notice in the file, so I assume he's still at the Brookline Manor Nursing Home."

"Try another name for me?"

"My pleasure."

"Wagner, Richard. Class of . . ." Jack looked to me for help.

"1950."

"He and Voss were classmates," Robin said, stating the obvious. She punched my father's name in. A moment later, a response flipped up on the screen and the printer hummed. "One hit. Dr. Richard Wagner. End of story. Your Dr. Wagner disappeared off the radar or is flying so low, *Alumni* can't catch him."

"What?" Jack said.

"The database came up dry."

"But he worked here for fifteen years."

"Not according to Harvard."

"What about payroll records? Benefits? Employee savings?"

"Nothing," Robin insisted. "Zip. It's like he was never here, which is weird because *Harvard Alumni* notes every little thing. Births, marriages, deaths. Private practice listings too. I got his name by accident."

"How?"

"The information didn't come up with the class roster for 1950. It got zapped back to me from the medical school library, of all places. Dr. Richard Wagner checked out a book in 1958 and never returned it. It's more than forty years overdue. Hate to pay that fine."

"Are you telling me he isn't listed as a med school graduate?"

"If he was, the class list would've been the hit, not the library. It's like he was erased from the whole system. I'll download the list of graduating students in his class and we'll take a look ourselves. Computers do make errors."

She typed in the request. The list popped up. "Three hundred and twelve students. Three women. The rest were men. Times have changed, thank God. The names are in alphabetical order. I'll check R just in case some nerd screwed up and inverted the first and last names. Nothing under R, nothing under W. Dammit. I'll just read the whole thing. Maybe my hypothetical nerd made a typo and entered it as Cagner or Dagner." Robin went down the list reading names out loud. "Gary Zweig," she said, spinning around to face us, "is the final entry. Dr. Richard Wagner just isn't there."

"Maybe we've got the wrong year."

"Doesn't matter," Robin explained. "Even if I punched in the wrong year, his name would have popped back up from the correct graduating class. The search string would've found his name, wherever it was. It's so weird. Like he just vanished." She gave the new printout to Jack. "Guess I flunked that one."

"Nope. A-plus again. Sometimes finding out what isn't there is just as important as finding out what is."

"Cryptic."

"Part of the job."

"Well, good luck, Agent Stein. And Merry Christmas."

"You too," Jack replied, less cheery than before.

Outside, we crossed the Quadrangle in silence. I imagined my father hurrying across the same ground in winter, eager to get to his lab, wondered how a man so accomplished could be completely wiped out of Harvard's records.

Our taxi was waiting. I ducked into the backseat. Jack gave the driver the address and slipped in next to me. As the taxi pulled away from the curb, we were both silent and pensive, wondering what kind of shape Herbert Voss was in.

Chapter Twenty-six

❦

The Brookline Manor Nursing Home was an imposing colonial mansion surrounded by parkland. Elm trees lined the long drive. Wheelchair ramps fanned out to either side of broad granite steps. Double doors with brass knobs opened into a main room that looked more like a Beacon Hill banker's home than a medical facility for the frail elderly.

The young nurse at the reception desk told us we would find Dr. Voss in 3-G. We thanked her and stepped into the elevator. It was decorated like the lobby with brass fixtures, mahogany walls, a good oil painting, and a parquet floor.

"I did an exposé a few years back on nursing homes in the South," I said on the ride up. "They were hellholes. Dr. Voss is lucky."

"No," Jack corrected. "Dr. Voss is rich."

The elevator opened onto a softly lit, carpeted hall. Three-G was five down, on the left. The door was closed. Jack tapped lightly and we walked in.

Heavy curtains were drawn. More brass, more wood, more good oil paintings, but this time the hospital bed spoiled the illusion. Dr. Voss's body looked brittle and thin under starched white sheets. His head was small against the big pillows. As we approached, I saw wispy gray hair combed carefully down, a hooked nose, and full lips. The left side of his face and mouth were slack from the stroke. One hand lay on top of the bedcovers. It was spotted with age and the skin was like crepe, but the fingernails were perfectly clipped and buffed. A thick gold watch hung loosely on his wrist.

Jack pulled two chairs up close to the bed. We sat down.

"Dr. Voss," I said, softly shaking him.

He stirred in his sleep. His lips smacked together on the good side. I shook him again. He gurgled and coughed, then opened his eyes. They were light blue in color, the lightest blue I had ever seen, almost translucent.

"Who's there?" His voice was fragile and thin, high-pitched like a boy's. Age had squeezed the resonance out of it. "Who's there?"

"We're friends, Dr. Voss."

"Open the curtains. Let me look at you." He lifted his hand off the bed and pointed. "Dark as a damn dungeon in here. Open the drapes, I say."

Jack pulled them back. Bright sunlight filled the room. Voss attempted a smile. He closed his eyes and sighed. "That's better. Much better. There will be plenty of darkness where I'm heading. Until then, I want light!"

He opened his eyes again. They slid over Jack and when they got to me they widened. "I must be dreaming! So beautiful! Such hair! Are you an angel?"

"No," I said warmly, "I'm Lacie Wagner."

The name registered instantly. "My lord," he whispered. "Is Richard here with you? Did you bring Richard?"

"No, my father's dead. A long time now."

"Oh, yes, yes. How stupid of me. He died in a terrible car accident in 1975. Goddamn stroke. I get all muddled up sometimes. When they told me Richard was dead, I cried for days. He was such a good man. A gifted doctor. A brilliant researcher. Wagner. God rest his soul."

Spittle dripped out of his mouth. I pulled a tissue from my pocket and wiped it away. Dr. Herbert Voss was a man with pride and dignity. He cared about the way his hair was combed. He cared enough to have his nails buffed. I felt certain he did not want to lie there with spit on his chin.

"Thank you, pretty Lacie. I'm so weak. The right side doesn't work at all. The left side's almost useless. It's a curse, being old, a curse, I say. We can send men to the moon, load all the books of the world onto a single microchip, but we can't take the indignity out of aging. We can't stop the human body from betrayal."

His bony hand trembled. "I'm moving swiftly toward death and yet my brain is alive! Alive, I tell you! I can lie here and run formulas, complex mathematical calculations in my head. I can recite the table of the elements backwards and from the middle on out. But I can't walk to the john, can't take a shower. Can't even eat a plate of spaghetti by myself."

"Do you feel up to answering a few questions?" I asked.

"I just told you. My brain works! It works!"

I glanced at Jack. Was Voss slightly demented? Was his mind really sound? Jack motioned for me to go ahead.

"Why did my father leave research, Dr. Voss?"

"He was bright. Smarter than the rest of us put together. Some of the less talented researchers laughed at him. His ideas were advanced. And, like all things ahead of their time, they sounded outrageous. Implausible. Ridiculous. But Richard never questioned his vision. He had faith and patience. He said he had a lifetime to prove himself right."

"But he cut his lifetime in research short. Why?"

"I begged him to tell me why, but he refused. I felt betrayed. We were more than friends and more than peers. We were together on a shared mission. He owed me an explanation. I got angry, made heated accusations. Richard just turned his back on me and walked away. He never spoke to me again. I tried to call, went to his home to apologize. Nothing worked. When he left Harvard, he rejected everything and everybody associated with it, and that included me."

Jack held up the black-and-white snapshot.

Voss squinted. "Tell me what I'm looking at."

"We were hoping you could tell us," Jack said, holding the picture closer.

Voss inspected it. The right side of his forehead screwed up in concentration. His eyelid ticked. "That's Richard on the left, of course. Look at his face! So happy!"

"Do you recognize the other men standing with him?"

"No. Not a one. They're not part of our team. Haven't even seen them around the medical school."

Jack gave me a look. Voss had reverted to the present tense.

"Damn it all!" Voss exclaimed. "You see what I mean? I *know* I'm not at Harvard now. I *know* I should be using the past tense, but it comes out the present. Goddamn annoying."

"Are you sure about the man in the lab coat?" I asked. "He wasn't at Harvard with you?"

"No. He's much older than we were. Couldn't have been a classmate. Wasn't a professor. Don't recognize him at all. I didn't know everyone, however. Even then, it was a big place."

"The picture was in my father's files," I said. "He wrote the name *Durand* on the back. Does that mean anything to you?"

Voss shook his head.

Jack pocketed the snapshot, disappointed.

A nurse breezed in. "You'll have to leave now. Dr. Voss needs rest."

"I need excitement," Voss protested. "I need a new body. That's what I need! Not rest! I've had enough damn rest!"

She closed the drapes. "He's sensitive to light."

"Fooey," Voss complained, spittle spilling down his chin again.

I leaned in to wipe it. "Dr. Voss, I appreciate your help."

"Fooey," Voss said again. "Damn shame about Richard. He was so happy those last years, hand-picked by the government as he was."

"The government?" I said.

"Yes! I always thought we'd lose him to Uncle Sam, not to private practice. He was so proud when they came asking for his participation."

"In what?"

"Can't really say. I thought at first they wanted him to consult on a medical problem. It wasn't uncommon. When a big political figure is diagnosed with a brain tumor, he wants the best medical talent money can buy. Richard laughed when I told him I thought he was practicing medicine on the president. Laughed! He promised he was doing something better than that. More important. More exciting."

"When did this happen?" Jack asked.

"1960," Voss said with certainty.

"The same year the snapshot was taken," I said. "Dr. Voss, did he ever tell you what he was working on?"

"Nope. Not a word. Claimed he was sworn to secrecy. He couldn't keep his excitement a secret though. His face glowed! It glowed, I tell you! Must've been a hell of an opportunity. He took a week off each month for five years. Never told me where he was going or why."

The dates my father had written on the empty *Durand* files were five-day blocks at four-week intervals from 1960 to 1965. Listening to Voss, I realized that the files must have been filled with the work he did for the government.

"The first four years of the project," Voss explained, "Richard was always happy, smiling and singing, the crazy Frenchman."

"My father wasn't French," I said. "He was Southern. Why did you call him a Frenchman?"

"Did I? I meant to say he was singing like a Frenchman. French songs. In French." He peered up at Jack. "Don't look at me like that! My memory's in perfect shape. It's the rest of me that's falling apart."

Jack pressed. "What happened after the first four years?"

"He changed. Came back from his trips looking tired and drawn, as if something weighed on him. Finally, at the end of 1964, he looked downright broken in two. *Talk to me, Richard,* I pleaded. Stubborn bastard refused. He went away for Christmas and New Year's. Then, in February 1965, he resigned. Looked like he was in a deep depression. You were born later that year, Lacie. I like to think your coming into the world cheered him considerably."

"Thank you." I kissed him lightly on the forehead. It seemed the right thing to do.

"The doctor needs his rest," the nurse announced, holding the door open.

On the way out, I looked back. His eyes were fixed on me. He wasn't smiling or frowning, but thinking. Intently. He lifted two fingers of his good hand in what was supposed to be a salute, then the door whooshed shut, leaving Dr. Voss alone in the gloom with his nimble mind and useless body.

When we were back in the cab, heading to the airport, I sat in silence, thinking about what we now knew. In 1960, my father became involved in a government research project he called *Durand.* By 1965, something had gone terribly wrong. He left Harvard and destroyed the files, as if he never wanted to think about the project again. I was born the same year. Ten years later, in 1975, the day before he picked me up from summer camp, my father wrote the name *Durand* in the margin of his phone log. And the next day he was dead.

I knew intuitively there was something I was missing.

My pulse began to race.

I closed my eyes and went over the facts again.

Then it hit me.

Linda Severino. Not only did she have nightmares like mine, she was at camp with me. And now I had learned that our fathers worked for the *government* at the same time. Too many coincidences? I turned to Jack.

"I know this sounds crazy," I said, "but listen to me. Hear me out."

I told him everything I knew about Linda Severino. I described the burning plane and the pilot trapped inside, Linda's hysterical confession of guilt, and her fatal leap into the sea. I told him that Linda had nightmares filled with whispering voices like mine, and that she had been scared of burning to death. Our lives were linked by fire and fathers destroyed. I talked about John Severino and his dazzling political career, how he started in the Navy, moved on to the Pentagon, and ended up on Capitol Hill with the White House right in his reach. Then, how a fiery car crash left him burnt and crippled, a recluse with a wild mad mind.

"Stranger still," I said, "Linda and I were at camp together the summer I burned. If my nightmare's a memory, then hers was too."

Jack absorbed the new information. "Something happened at the camp. We'll have to go up there, Lacie, and try to shake your memory loose."

The cab dropped us at the terminal. Jack paid. We hurried in. I stopped in front of a concourse lounge and looked at the wide-screen TV over the bar. My WRC special report was running on Tom Brokaw's national news. My gloves were off, my maimed hands held high, twisted frightful appendages that didn't look as if they belonged to me.

Jack was next to me, watching too. His cell phone rang. He flipped it open. I heard the voice.

"You've called in the troops, haven't you, Jack? You've called on able-bodied boys to stand watch night and day. You're wrong to feel safe. Remember this: All the King's horses and all the King's men won't keep Lacie from burning again."

A dial tone droned. Jack and I ran down to the gate. We were the last two passengers to board.

Chapter Twenty-seven

Vic Holloway's New York counterpart was waiting for us in the lobby of Jerry's building. He was as young and trim as Holloway, with the same short dark hair and discreet gray suit.

"Scott Chapman," he said, pumping Jack's hand. "It's an honor, Agent Stein."

"Jack, please. This is Ms. Wagner. Did Holloway bring you up to date?"

"Yes, he did. Ben Tyler's on his way to join me here for the night. You'll have Dick Reed and Alan Curtis on the day shift. They started this morning. How do you want us to work?"

"One of you stands surveillance here with the building doorman. I want the other on ten, outside the front door."

"You got it. Soon as Ben Tyler gets here, I'll send him up."

Jack steered me into the elevator and hit ten.

On the ride up, I realized Jerry's loft was safer by far than a hotel with multiple entrances, hundreds of employees, and strangers spinning through. This building was small, with limited entrances. Jack could control it.

He drew his gun and went into the loft ahead of me. The search was quickly done. Windows were secure. The alarm hadn't been breached. Certain that Jerry's apartment had not been entered or tampered with, Jack punched in the alarm code and locked us in. I had slept in Washington. He had not. His voice was gravelly, his eyes were red. He said good night and disappeared down the hall.

I had an armed federal agent outside the front door, an armed federal agent in the lobby with the armed ex-Marine night guard, and Jack inside with me. I felt safe. I took a long bath, slipped a flannel nightgown on, and sat in Skyla's rocking chair just looking around her room. Day-Glo fish finned across her computer screen, reminding me I hadn't checked my e-mail for several days.

I moved to the desk and logged into my WRC mailbox. Thirty-eight new messages had come in. I scrolled through them quickly. Most were from news reporters and anchors around the country expressing sympathy. Jerry left a long tender letter telling me I could live in the loft for as long as I wanted—forever, if need be.

Max surprised me and called in from his computer. His face zapped across cyber-space in a video download file, filling the screen. "How's my guard dog, Lacie?"

"He's growing on me."

"I knew he would." Max looked smug.

"Considering what's been going on, I'm happy to have him around."

"What do you mean?" Max leaned forward and peered out at me. "And what the hell happened to your face?"

I filled him in. Max glared out from his godforsaken nameless location, scratching his beard as he listened to the latest complications in my already complicated life. When I finished, Max was frowning and angry.

"Dammit all, Lacie. Who would want to do such things? What does Jack think?"

I told him, then asked about my father's research and why he left Harvard.

"Your father was a private man," Max explained. "And in those days I lived most of my life a long way away, before there were faxes or e-mail capabilities or satellites. I wasn't around much. Even so, when we were together, Richard never talked about his work. When he went into private practice, he simply said he'd had enough of research."

"Did he ever mention special work for the government?"

"Never. I'd certainly remember that."

"Max, what about Jack? Tell me what you know about him."

"Jack can speak for himself."

"That's a cop-out."

"It is indeed."

"You sent him to me. The least you could do is tell me who the hell he is."

"Like I said, Lacie, he's a good man. A very good man. To be trusted."

"He said you saved his life. What did he mean?"

"Sorry again. You'll have to hear it from Jack." Max leaned into the camera. "I don't have a good feeling about what's going on, Lacie. Say the word and I'll be there to help you both."

"I'll think about it," I lied, wanting Max as far away as possible from the madman who was hunting me.

"There's no time to think!" Max insisted. "I'm setting out on a training mission in the Canadian Rockies. We'll be there until after New Year's. If the decision were mine, I'd scuttle the expedition and come home to you now."

But the decision wasn't his. It was mine. Max treated me like an equal. He always had. I liked that.

"No thanks, Max," I said softly, touching the screen, wishing I could touch his face. I wanted his help, but the truth was I wanted him out of the line of fire more.

"You sure? One hundred percent sure?"

"Yes. Go on. Don't worry about me."

"I will always worry about you," Max sighed. "I check my e-mail twice a day when I can. Keep me up to date. Stick close to Jack. Take good care. I love you, girl." He blew me a kiss across the thousands of miles separating us. His face dissolved from the screen at the same moment the front doorbell rang.

I pulled a robe and gloves on and went out, but Jack was already there talking to Ben Tyler, a skinny young agent with red hair and freckles. He handed Jack a manila envelope. The big block printing was unmistakable, as was the shape of the videocassette inside.

"This came here today in the morning mail," Ben Tyler said in a soft Southern drawl. "Since it's addressed to you, Dick Reed took the liberty of checking it out to make sure it's not some kind of mail bomb. It's a standard VHS cassette. No booby traps inside. No prints. It was wiped clean."

The young agent seemed uncomfortable, like there was something else he wanted to say. Jack picked up on it.

"Did you look at this tape, Ben?"

"Well, yes sir, I did."

"Jack. My name's Jack, not sir. Is there something on this tape Ms. Wagner here shouldn't see?"

"Not exactly. I was thinking more of you, sir. Jack. This guy's a son-of-a-bitch, if you don't mind my saying so. I'm real sorry you have to see this."

Jack thanked him and closed the door. He opened the envelope and took the cassette out. The same black block printing marked the label, but this time it read, *Stein*. We went straight to Jerry's office. Jack dropped the tape in the VHS machine and hit play.

Snow and blue sky and a lone eagle soaring. Heavenly country morning quiet. Then, a shrieking snowmobile engine and the beat of flamethrower fire hitting air and snow. Images went speeding by, distorted and dizzying, but recognizable. My black frightened figure against the white. A kaleidoscopic documentary of my terror: Lacie running, Lacie freezing, Lacie jumping, Lacie stumbling in a drunken circle, Lacie falling to the ground, Lacie crying, fire whipping all around her. The picture steadied, the engine idled. A black gloved hand reached down and jammed the nozzle trigger high and hard under my chin.

The camera cut to the same black gloved hand ripping open a bag of Swiss Miss instant hot chocolate and pouring it into a cup. Hot water next, and a quick stir with a silver spoon. My spoon. My cup. My Georgetown kitchen before the fire.

"C'mon, Jack, you're falling short!" he cried, stirring and stirring, tiny freeze-dried marshmallows swelling and bobbing in the cup. "You're not as vigilant as you should be! I taped the fun so you could see for yourself the havoc your recklessness brought. What kind of guard dog are you, boy? Lacie trusts you so much. She trusts you with her life."

The hand stopped stirring.

"Aw, shoot, Jackster. You didn't tell her, did you. Shame on you. You didn't tell her about Gabby. Uh-oh, Jackie-O. You should've told her about Gabby! That's not fair, letting our sweet Lacie put her life in your hands without knowing. She ought to know about Gabby!"

His left hand appeared in the frame, gripping a fat fresh Twinkie. He dipped it in the chocolate. "You didn't tell her about Jason either, did you, Jackster?" He reached for the camera and tilted the lens up. Where the nightmare face should have been was a blown-up newspaper photo of a smiling little boy. The gloved hand jiggled the picture up and down. "Tell her the truth!"

The screen went black.

"Jack?" I started.

He shook his head and walked out, fists clenched, face flushed, throat working hard. He was as private as I was. He knew my grief, but the look on his face warned that I would not know his.

I sat for hours in the shadows writing Jack's story a dozen different ways, wondering which one was the truth, and finally at midnight, I got up and drifted down the hall to the open guest room door. When I heard his steady breathing, I looked in.

He was sleeping on top of the bed, fully dressed, stretched out on his back, arms at his sides. His gun was at his hip, the red parka and computer bag on the bed next to him. He slept ready to move fast if he had to. Light from the hallway spilled across his face. He looked younger in sleep, with the tension gone.

I watched the rise and fall of his chest, as I used to watch Jerry's. Jack was nothing like Jerry. He was nothing like any man I had ever met. He had alternately infuriated and intrigued me, and lately he had impressed me. There was something in him I recognized in myself. A stubborn independence. A fierce pride. And now, grief over something lost.

My losses were all public: my hands, my father, my daughter, my home.

What about Jack? Who was Gabby? And the little boy? I doubted I would ever know what had happened in his life to make him the way he was. Loss is a private thing, unless you are a public figure, which Jack certainly was not.

Or was he?

My nightmare man had found Jack's story somewhere. With the right keywords, dutiful searching, and a powerful Pentium processor, I could find it too.

I went back to Skyla's computer and used my password to log into the WRC mainframe. From there, I accessed the archives of the *Washington Post* and the *New York Times*, and filled in the search command with two words: Stein, Jack.

I didn't wait long. The archives delivered material starting with the most recent stories first, working back in time. I skimmed news and features and in-depth profiles dealing with Jack's work. Fifteen years of heroics for the Bureau, hunting killers and finding them, but nothing on Gabby or any boy called Jason.

It all came scrolling up in the last batch of clippings. The facts, all the sad sorrowful facts. I shifted the sort order and began with the oldest article.

A marriage notice in the *Washington Post*: *Dr. Jack Stein Marries Gabriella Vargas, Esq.* Jack, twenty years younger, in a suit and tie and short-cropped hair, grinning from ear to ear, both broad hands holding on to his small lovely wife. Gabriella. Lush lips parted revealing strong white teeth, black brows arching over large dark eyes, black hair tumbling around a classic Latin face. And Jack. Jubilant. Radiant. Things I had not seen in him or ever imagined.

He had graduated with honors from Georgetown Medical School, Gabriella with honors from Georgetown Law. Jack went into private pediatric practice, Gabriella went to work for the ACLU. The birth notice came a year later. Jason Stein. Nine pounds, eight ounces.

Then, I found the rest of it. The magazine profiles, front-page stories, the special reports. The picture of Jack and Gabriella, arms wound around each other, turning away from the camera, hiding their grief. And the last picture of Jack alone, in a dark suit, head bowed, walking in the rain.

I looked at that picture for a long time before signing out of the archives and glancing at the desk calendar.

Christmas Day was two days away.

The anniversary of his terrible double loss.

Chapter Twenty-eight

❧

Oh! *He laughed when he thought of Lacie watching the tape. Swiss Miss and Twinkies. What a clever boy he was to have found that out. And Gabby? Gabby, Gabby, Gabby! Jason too! He had found out how to make the strong fed weak.*

As much fun as he'd been having, the most fun was still to come when the game shifted into high gear, when the stakes were raised, and fresh chips chinked on the game table. What fun when the wager was a young lovely life. He had played with Linda Severino, and there was meaning to her death, a score now even, a debt finally paid. But Lacie was the prize, his bride, his Queen, and he was days away from having her close by his side.

He counted calendar pages. Christmas and then some. The Dead Time was almost here.

He plugged the little electric water heater into the dashboard lighter, ripped open a packet of Swiss Miss, and poured it into a Styrofoam cup.

Swiss Miss and Twinkies. What an all-American snack.

Chapter Twenty-nine

The nightmare came that night, as it usually did, with the face and the voice, but then it changed. There was another sound under the whispering, a *who-whoosh* of heavy wind and the smell of smoke. Smoke has a flavor all its own and I tasted it in my dream. It filled my nose, stung my lungs, left me coughing and choking, gasping for air.

There was so much noise—alarms shrieking and fire roaring. Hands over ears, I shut the noise out, but my hands were pulled away and someone was shouting my name.

"Lacie! Wake up!"

I wanted to slip away from the nightmare and spin back into a deep black sleep.

"Lacie, wake up!"

Arms scooped me up off the bed. I felt groggy and woozy, disoriented.

"Lacie! Lacie!" Desperate, urgent, the way only fire makes a voice sound.

I opened my eyes. The shrieking alarm was there in Skyla's bedroom and the room was full of smoke. I panicked, rolled out of Jack's arms, and landed on the floor. The air was better there. Jack dropped down next to me. He was fully dressed with his backpack and computer bag slung over his shoulders.

"Crawl!" he shouted, herding me out the door and into the hall.

I turned left toward the living room, but Jack held me back. The sleek leather couches and fine Persian rugs were raging fireballs blocking the front door. Drapes were walls of fire, and the fire was unlike any I had ever seen. This fire was white. No reds or oranges or blues, nothing but blinding white, burning fast with a heat so intense it stripped the flames of their own natural color. Fire jumped from couch to wood, wood snapped and sparked, the hallway carpet ignited, and a long snake of white fire came at me, hotter than the fire that had destroyed my hands.

Jack shouted. "Back off!"

I couldn't. I was the deer in the headlights.

Jack pulled at me. "Move!"

The heat on my face. The hiss and spit of white flame.

"Move!" Jack roared, wrapping his arms around my waist.

The smoke was suffocating me. Fire had taken so much from me. I wanted to give up now, surrender.

Jack swung me up off the floor. He stumbled down to the master bedroom at the end of the hall, kicked the door shut, and dropped me on the bed. Smoke turned my head heavy, made me want to sleep. I was dimly aware of Jack yanking a window open and pushing the screen out. Fresh winter air rushed in. Jack pulled me to the window.

"Breathe, Lacie! Breathe!"

My head cleared. My eyes focused. Ten stories down, fire trucks converged in the street. Ambulances and police cars came sailing in around them, sirens whelping, red roof lights spinning. Teams of firemen reeled hoses off trucks. Neon stripes on their black jackets glowed yellow in the dark. They strapped oxygen tanks to their backs, snapped masks in place, and ran into the building, but we were out of time. Living room windows burst like gunshots, and the fire was roiling on the other side of the bedroom door, sneaking up under the threshold, flickering in around the doorjamb edges, leaping in small white sparks across Jerry's good designer carpet.

"Climb out on the ledge!" Jack yelled as more windows blew out and fire raced toward us faster than help.

The window ledge was less than two feet wide and the wind was strong. I looked down hoping to see a rescue ladder from one of the red engines drifting up, but there was no such stairway to safety. A piece of news trivia floated through my mind: *Aerial ladders are built to go to the seventh floor, not the tenth.*

An inflatable air mattress ballooned on the sidewalk. Twenty feet square and black. A small life raft in a sea of cement. Just in case. The window in the room next to us blew out. Jack searched the roofline hoping to see a fireman dropping safety ropes.

I looked up and saw nothing but black.

Behind us, the fire fed on the fresh cold air and the bedroom erupted. Flames skipped from carpet to bedcovers to drapes.

"Climb out," Jack ordered, choking on smoke.

Burn to death in the fire or slip off the iced ledge and fall. Hell of a choice, Jack.

"Lacie, climb out!"

"No!"

He hustled us over the windowsill. The ledge was impossibly narrow. The frigid wind cut right through my nightgown and my bare feet tingled on ice, but my back was hot. The seasons were colliding. Winter in front, Satan's summer behind. We looked at the roof again and saw a fireman belly-down with a thick coil of rope in his hands.

"Tie it down and drop it!" Jack shouted. "There's not enough time to pull us up!"

The fireman tied one end of the rope around a ventilation duct and tossed the coil.

"Climb on my back!" Jack ordered, catching the rope.

I wrapped my arms around his neck. He hoisted me up and locked my legs around his waist. Flames shot through the open window. My nightgown sparked and caught fire, scorching my thighs, and a furious white fireball exploded out across the ledge, but we were already off, Jack speed-sliding bare-handed down the rope, kicking off the building, controlling our descent while the fireball above surged toward the roof in great billowing clouds, engulfing the rope.

If we had tried to go up instead of down, the fire would have killed us.

Jack slid fast, but the rope wasn't long enough. It stopped three stories short of the ground. Dangling, we looked down in disbelief. If we fell together, Jack's weight would crush me.

"Let go!" he ordered.

Fire was eating the rope. We felt it giving way.

"Now, Lacie!"

I let go and dropped, hit the airbag hard and bounced. The fire-engulfed rope split. Jack fell sooner than he wanted to. I rolled to the side. He hit. Bone cracked against bone, but he landed next to me, not on me, and those precious inches saved my life. A fire blanket covered me like a shroud. Hands beat the flames out of my nightgown and lifted me. Jack pulled me out of the flame beater's arms and ran me down the street to the Range Rover.

Emergency vehicles blocked it on all sides. Jack cursed. An empty blue and white police car was parked next to us, keys in the ignition.

Two cops were standing fifty feet away with their heads turned up, staring at the white fire. Jack opened the squad car door, pushed me down and across to the passenger seat, then dropped in and started the engine.

The cops turned around.

Jack put the cruiser in gear and hit the accelerator. We shot forward, weaving through the tangle of engines and ambulances, away from the fire and the press of spectators standing twenty and thirty deep at the police line, away from the bullhorns and radios and gyrating lights, away from the shadows where one man watched. Jack's phone was ringing. I knew who the caller was. I felt his eyes on us and heard his voice in my bruised throbbing head.

And all the King's men couldn't keep Lacie from burning again.

Chapter Thirty

Jack punched up the siren, set the roof lights to spinning, and drove recklessly out of the city, south, west, north, and finally when he was sure no one was following, over the bridge and east, through the ugly press of commuter towns and beyond, to where the highway finally stretched open and empty. He shrugged out of his parka, pushed it over to me. "Here," he said. "Put this on."

I huddled in my seat with my blackened nightgown drawn up around my thighs, twisting a corner of the flannel collar into my mouth and tasting smoke. My legs felt hot. My hands stung.

Forty-five minutes later, Jack left the expressway, flipped the siren and roof lights off, and dropped down to a reasonable speed. Our headlights were the only lights now in the dark night.

The sky brightened. He turned the headlights off and drove on.

Soon, the sun was a full orange ball over a china blue sea. Early morning fog evaporated. Gulls dipped and cried. We went whizzing past the road that led out to Jerry's beach house, through sleeping villages and sprawling silent estates, past sand dunes and out to the far reaches of the island where the weekend crowd never ventured and the thick woods promised us sweet privacy and life.

Jack turned left, down a winding road. Houses here were few and far between, randomly set on generous five-acre parcels of woodland. He turned again and rumbled down a long snow-covered drive.

"Refuge," Jack said, stopping the car.

Refuge was a gray wood house with windows and decks like Jerry's, but this one was soft and warm where Jerry's was huge and hard. It was surrounded by trees, invisible from the road.

Jack got out of the squad car and came around to my side. My feet were bare. The snow was deep. He carried me up the steps and fumbled for keys. The front door opened into a wide entryway.

Beyond that was a living room with sweeping flagstone floors, a stone fireplace, vaulted ceilings, and big comfortable furniture.

"Where are we?" I asked.

"Home," he said simply, slamming the front door, snapping lights on, and turning the thermostat up. He set me down on one of the sofas.

An open country kitchen angled off the living room. Two walls of windows looked out into the woods. Jack put a pot of water on the stove and disappeared. He came back with a wet washcloth and a bag full of first-aid supplies. The burns on my legs throbbed. He covered them with cream, gauze, and tape, then changed the dressing on my face. The palms of his hands were red with rope burns. They must have hurt.

"It will take a while for the house to warm up," he apologized, tossing me a fur duvet. "Coffee and breakfast. Then we'll talk."

Exhaustion washed over me. I fell asleep. When I woke, the sun had swung around to the west. Shadows were long and, according to the clock on the mantle, I had slept until four in the afternoon.

The house was quiet. Jack was sprawled in a big easy chair across the room, sound asleep.

I pushed the fur cover off and stood up. My body was stiff, my skin black with soot. I moved quietly, not wanting to wake him. The ground level of the house was one wide open space with the kitchen, living and dining areas, and walls of windows facing south and east. There was a small powder room by the stairs. On the second floor, I found a comfortable office with a desk, sofa, television set, built-in wood file cabinets, and walls of books. Beyond the office, was a single huge bedroom ringed with floor-to-ceiling windows. The house was clearly built for one person.

I went through the bedroom to the master bath. The shower was a marble walk-in with jets that sprayed out from all sides. I tore my nightgown off, stuffed it in the trash, and stepped in. Warm water washed away soot and sweat and some of my fear. When I finally felt clean, I got out and rummaged through Jack's cabinets looking for his medical supplies.

There were no forgotten tubes of lipstick, no nail polish or women's perfume stashed away. No electric rollers or stray hairpins. There was nothing feminine at all, I noticed, no past or present female in evidence. I found the first-aid things I needed, changed the dressings on my calves and thighs, and helped myself to a robe hooked on the back of the door. Wrapped in terry cloth, a thick towel turbaned around my head, I went into his bedroom to find something more suitable to wear.

A four-poster king-size bed faced the windows. A large oil painting of a snow-capped mountain filled one wall and a massive antique armoire filled another. I opened the heavy armoire doors and found neat stacks of blue jeans, heavy cotton turtlenecks, sweaters, denim shirts, and five pairs of hiking boots. I touched the shirts and changed my mind. It was all male. It was all Jack. Wearing his clothes didn't feel right. It was too intimate, I thought. He would object.

In robe and turban and bare cold feet, I went into his office and sat at the desk. The bookshelves around me were filled with an eclectic mix of mountaineering guides, literature, medical texts, and, oddly, seven good-sized rocks lined up in a row. I touched one. It was cool and smooth, light gray in color. I wondered where it had come from. The desktop was neatly organized with Jack's ThinkPad, a fax, and a telephone.

I picked up the phone and called Jerry. It was long overdue.

"Lacie!" he exclaimed. "Where the hell *are* you?"

"Somewhere safe."

"They told me the loft was a total burnout. Nothing's left. What happened?"

"He's after me now."

"Who?"

"The man who killed Skyla. He burned my house in Washington and he found a way into your loft."

"Why?"

"I don't know yet."

"This is crazy," he said, sounding slightly hysterical. "Fucking crazy."

"It is."

"The NYPD's looking for you. So is the fire inspector. You're the page-one story in the papers today, and the lead story on local and national news. The tabloids have floated a rumor that since Skyla's death you've come completely unglued. They hint that you're torching these places yourself. Running doesn't make you look good."

"I have no choice."

"They say you were last seen—and I'm quoting here—*with an*

unknown male, escaping the scene in a stolen police car. I talked to the chief of detectives. Nothing I do will get you off the hook. They want to hear from you. Go in, Lacie. The NYPD can protect you."

"No, it can't." I thought of Martinez's sweaty face. The NYPD had given up on finding Skyla's killer, and I knew they wouldn't be receptive to my story of nightmare voices coming to life. "The NYPD won't and can't protect me."

"Call Garrett then. Tell him your side of the story over the phone. Fax him, e-mail him, call him, I don't care, but you've got to talk to him!"

I answered him with silence.

"Okay, Lacie," he said, exasperated. "Do what the fuck you want. You always have."

"I'll check in with you tomorrow," I said, but he had already hung up.

I called Harry next.

"Harry, it's me."

"Lacie! What the hell's going on? The police are on their way. They want to monitor your e-mail and tap your phone. I said no goddamn way. They're trying to get a warrant. Won't take them long."

I wanted free access to my e-mail box, knowing *he* would inevitably send something there. I didn't want the police to intercept it. "I need your help, Harry. No questions asked."

"You got it."

"I can't access my e-mail if the police are watching it. Create a phony e-mail box for them to look at. Copy some of my old messages in there so it looks legit. They won't know it's not the real thing."

"Right. I'll do it now."

"Thanks, Harry." I was talking to a dial tone.

I picked up the TV remote and turned on the news. Jack had satellite. The Manhattan stations came in bright and clear. I flipped over to ABC's five-o'clock report. Jerry was right. I was the lead story. My WRC portrait floated over the shoulder of a grim anchorman.

"It was the second tragedy in as many days for Washington, D.C., anchorwoman Lacie Wagner. Fire officials are still sifting through the wreckage this evening, searching for evidence in the fire that broke out in the early morning hours . . ."

The camera cut to a view of Jerry's building and the strange white flames shooting out into the night. I turned the set off. I didn't want to live through the fire again. Once was enough.

I drifted downstairs and settled back on the couch. Jack was still asleep in the easy chair. That uncanny exhaustion swept over me, and suddenly I thought of Skyla, in infancy, the sweet weight of her lying slack and trusting against my shoulder. Outside, the wind whistled and the moon appeared above bare treetops. I closed my eyes and remembered: This was Christmas Eve.

I woke up to the smell of food.

Jack was cooking. A bottle of red wine waited, uncorked, on the counter.

He smiled. "I haven't used the house in a long time. Refrigerator was empty. I had groceries delivered while you were sleeping. And, I put a clean pair of sweats in the bathroom for you. They'll be too big, but at least you'll be warm."

I found them hanging on the back of the door. He had thoughtfully chosen a black FBI sweatshirt and matching sweatpants. The socks were white. My feet were cold. I pulled them on, then went back out to the kitchen and slipped onto a stool at the counter.

Copper pots hung from a ceiling rack. Big glass jars were filled with dried pasta and herbs. Jack was chopping chives, mixing gravy, and looking in on what smelled like a roasting chicken.

"What are you doing?" I asked, not knowing what else to say.

"Making dinner." He poured me a glass of wine.

"Can we talk about what happened?"

"Only if you want to right now."

"I do."

"Okay." Jack sipped his wine, stirred his sauce. "The early word from the fire inspector is that Jerry's loft was deliberately torched."

"They think I did it."

"They considered the possibility at first. Not now."

"Tell me this, Jack. How did he get past an armed doorman and two armed federal agents last night? How the hell did he get into the loft?"

"He didn't."

"You lost me."

"The doorman swears no one had access to the tenth floor yesterday. And he's right. Chapman ran through all the security tapes from the last couple of days. Our man was nowhere in sight. He didn't have to be. He set this one up a long time ago. And that fits what we know about him. He's a planner. A thinker. A gamesman. He set it up so he would never have to get into the loft at all."

"How?"

"The fire inspectors couldn't go in until this afternoon when they were absolutely sure the place was structurally sound. Once inside, they figured it out right away." Jack found a pencil and paper, and pulled a stool up next to me. He sketched the layout of Jerry's living room. Circles were tables. Rectangles were sofas. Bookcases were evenly spaced boxed lines.

"This wall," he said, tapping the pencil on his drawing, "is the south-facing exterior wall. It was lined with bookcases, remember?"

"Yes."

"He hid his strikers between the wall and the bookcase. Next, he taped Ziploc baggies full of magnesium shavings up and down and across the backs of those bookcases. Each striker was made from a pinch of C-4 packed in flammable material. Home cooking kind of stuff, but very effective. Two copper wires ran from the C-4 pack through tiny holes drilled right through that exterior wall.

"Outside, he fed the wires around the wall horizontally and down the back of the building, tucking them tightly in the old cornices and brickwork. He stopped about ten feet above the ground. The wires were invisible to the casual eye."

"Copper is a good conductor of electricity."

"Exactly. Last night he came equipped with a hand squeeze box, a kind of small manual generator. You pump it to generate the electrical current. There's a Dumpster in back of the building. He stood on it so he could reach the wires. He fed the copper wires into the squeeze box and pumped, creating that small electrical current. The copper grabbed the current and ran it up all the way into the bookcase striker. The electrical current set off the C-4 pack. When that exploded, the sparks ignited the magnesium, and *boom*. The bookcases blew out, sending a wall of white fire into the living room. Magnesium burns fast and hot, five thousand degrees kind of hot, and the fire is white."

"How did he get the strikers in there in the first place?"

"Jerry didn't move into the loft until September, right?"

"Right."

"I talked to the construction company and found out the renovation of the building exterior and lobby was going on at the same time that Jerry was doing his loft. My guess is our man got into Jerry's loft this summer during the renovation, when the exterior was still in scaffolds. The scaffolds made it easy to do the placement of the wires. Workmen were coming and going by the dozens. There were five different trades, two different contractors in Jerry's place alone, decorators running around, plus all the specialty workers Jerry used to build the stereo system into the walls, the recessed lighting, the custom bath and kitchen. One more guy in a hard hat working late just wasn't noticed."

"Are you telling me he was planning this six months ago?"

"Lacie," Jack said, tapping the drawing, "I have the feeling he's been planning it for a hell of a lot longer than that."

He set two places at the counter and took the chicken out of the oven. It was gold and smelled of tangy herbs and spices. Jack carved expertly and arranged the meat on big china plates, spooning fragrant herb-infused wild rice to the side, bright baby carrots, and fresh cranberry confit. He pulled fresh sourdough bread out of the crisper and poured us both more wine.

We ate in comfortable silence. When we finished, Jack produced an apple pie for dessert and served mine with a generous scoop of vanilla ice cream.

"That should fatten you up," he said, passing me the plate.

I ate it all and took seconds. Jack was a healer. He radiated a calm strength and, despite all that had happened to me, I felt oddly optimistic for the first time since Skyla's death.

We took our wineglasses into the living room and sank into the deep couch.

"Did you run Durand through the Bureau database?" I asked, casually.

"Yes."

Something in Jack's voice made me sit up straight. "You didn't get a hit."

"Oh, I hit something all right. Unfortunately, it looks and feels like a brick wall. The search never took place."

"Why?"

"When I entered Durand as the keyword, the database was preprogrammed to block the request and notify a higher office of my attempted search." Jack put his wine down and turned to face me. "I've been instructed to offer you my apologies and to tell you the case is closed."

"The case is far from closed," I said, incredulous. "They want you to quit in the middle of an investigation?"

"Remember, this never was an official FBI case. It's not on record and it's not sanctioned."

"But the 800 number . . ."

"It was run through Quantico at my request. The cars and agents in D.C. were doing me favors, as were the men in New York. I operate with a freedom and access to Bureau resources other agents don't have."

"Go on."

"Skyla's murder is still considered an active homicide investigation under the jurisdiction of the NYPD. There is no federal jurisdiction. The snowmobile incident is under investigation by the Stockbridge police. If they ask, the Massachusetts state police will step in. The fire in D.C. is under the jurisdiction of the D.C. fire inspector and local police. Welcome to bureaucracy. Despite my privileged status, I still answer to the Bureau at the end of the day."

"What do they want you to do?"

"Tell you I'm sorry, but it's over. Justify myself. Remind you that I ran the crime details through VICAP and came up with zero. That we tried a dedicated 800 number, made a national appeal, and got buried in calls, people making so many diverse claims, it would take months for us to check them all out. They feel I've done enough. Too much, as a matter of fact. As for your safety? The Bureau does not consider itself a free bodyguard service. They want me to drop it."

"What if you don't?"

"I get tossed out."

"All because you asked for information about Durand?"

"Yes."

"What or who is Durand?"

"Something or someone who, like your father, was erased from the face of the earth."

I got up and went to the window. Clouds tumbled across the sky. Bare trees swayed in the wind. My fragile optimism vanished. Fear and uncertainty filled me, then a stubborn determination. I would barrel ahead, alone. I would use myself as bait if I had to. One against one.

Jack came up close behind me. I smelled the spice of his aftershave, felt his hand gentle on my shoulder.

"I'm not going to drop it, Lacie."

"You really have no choice. You promised Max a favor, not your career, not your life."

His cheek touched my hair. "I promised Max I would find the man who killed Skyla and that I would protect you until I did."

"Max will understand. There's no other choice for you." I wanted to tell him I knew he had lost everything else. I didn't want him to lose the FBI too. "You can't possibly continue."

"You're not listening."

I rushed on, trying to convince him. "There are other people you can help, other children you can vindicate. You don't owe Skyla or me your career. You've already done so much." Tears stung my eyes.

"Take my hands," he ordered.

I shook my head no.

"Turn around and take my hands."

I did.

"What do you see?"

"Smooth skin. A small half-moon scar above the wrist. Strong hands."

"They're strong enough to carry you a while, Lacie. You've done everything in your life alone. I'm asking you to let someone in, to let someone carry part of your load. I'm not asking you to be weak or dependent or needy, only to trust me, let me finish what we started, the way we started. Together. We've stumbled across something big. Questions need answers before you can find peace and a new life."

He wrapped his hands around mine. They were warm and sure. His eyes were the dark blue I had come to recognize as determination, and the storm brewing in them was a wild mixture of strength and purpose and independence.

"You must be one hell of a mountain climber," I said.

"I am indeed."

"Okay, Jack Stein. What do we do now?"

"Just what we've been doing. Go after the answers. Borrow a car. Take you back to the camp. Find John Severino. Figure out what or who Durand was. And somewhere along the way, nail our man. We could both use some rest first. It's been a rough two days."

Jack insisted I sleep in the bedroom. He took the couch.

I climbed into his four-poster bed, fully dressed in the FBI sweats. The sheets were blue-and-red-checked, and a thick eiderdown duvet lay folded at the foot. I pulled it up and watched the snow falling outside.

After a time, I slept.

Chapter Thirty-one

I woke on Christmas Day to bright blue skies and a winter white world. Snowplows hummed in the distance. Jack rattled in the kitchen. The aroma of fresh ground coffee drifted up. When I was showered and dressed in his sweats again, I went down.

"Good morning," he said, pushing four brightly wrapped boxes across the counter.

"What's this?"

"What's it look like?"

"Why?"

"It's Christmas."

"Your promise to Max didn't include buying me presents."

"They're not really gifts. Just things you need. Totally utilitarian, I'm afraid."

I untied ribbon, opened lids, pushed fresh white tissue paper aside. Inside the boxes were two cashmere turtleneck sweaters, a pair of wool slacks, a pair of jeans, five pairs of cashmere socks, fur-lined snow boots, a fox hat, fur-lined kidskin gloves, assorted simple underwear, and a down parka. Everything was black. I was stunned. "Why did you do this?"

"You needed clothes. I didn't want a store clerk to recognize you from the news and I didn't want to leave you here alone. So I called one of the shops in town yesterday. They came by while you were sleeping. Hope it all fits."

"I'll pay you back," I said simply.

"No, you won't."

"Yes, I will. I'm financially independent."

"I'm sure you are."

"It's not right taking gifts from you."

"I haven't bought Christmas presents in a long time. I had fun."

"Expensive ride," I said, fingering the fox hat.

"I'm financially independent."

"That's good, because as of yesterday you're unemployed."

"Not exactly. I told them I'm taking a two-week vacation. What I do on my time's up to me, isn't it?" He smiled and piled two plates with food. "Fuel up, Lacie. We're going for a hike."

We walked briskly through the woods. Jack knew his way, though there were no markers I could see. We came out on the crest of a road. A half mile away, the Atlantic shimmered, a sheet of silver in the late morning sun, flat and calm, not a whitecap in sight. Patches of snow were melting fast in dark gold sand.

"Come on!" Jack called out.

He broke into a run. I followed and matched his pace. We ran down the road, through sand dunes, and across to hard-packed sand. Seagulls coasted on thermals, sleepy waves slapped the shore, and skinny-legged sandpipers darted in and out of the tide line. The cadence of our long even strides, the steady thump of my heart, and the wide open space calmed me, carried me far away from white fire and falling. That new sense of time filled me. There was no past, no future, only the present. Only now.

Two miles down the shore, we veered up to a protected hollow in the dunes and collapsed on our backs, spent. The winter sun was surprisingly warm on my face. The ocean was in full view.

Jack sat up and looked out to sea. "You asked me once if I didn't have somewhere I'd rather be or a family to go home to."

"You don't owe me an explanation."

"I want you to understand why I do what I do."

"It's none of my business," I said, not having the courage to tell him I already knew.

"Yes, it is," Jack said quietly.

He went on to tell me his story, talking softly but evenly at first, when the going was easier, when it was the good part, the happy part about his college years, when he was a headstrong young man in love with a girl named Gabriella Vargas.

The picture he painted was a study in contrasts. Jack was the son of a doctor, blessed with a privileged life. Gabriella was the daughter of Cuban migrant workers, blessed with an intellect that lifted her up and out. She went to Georgetown on scholarship and when she passed the bar, she went to work fighting for the rights of poor people like her own immigrant parents. Jack healed with his hands. Gabriella healed with the law.

"When I finished my residency, we decided to have a child." Jack's voice faltered now, the words came slower, and he stopped often to clear his throat. "We had a boy and named him Jason."

His fingers dug into sand, his voice grew husky.

"The years passed quickly. My practice was growing as fast as my son. I look back and that time was an island, sun-washed and bright. Jason laughing and chattering a mile a minute, Gabby's voice all around, the sight of her rocking him to sleep in her arms, two pairs of big eyes looking at me with nothing but love. Every morning of my life, I woke up feeling proud and confident. I had it all. For a very brief shining moment, Lacie, I swear to God I had it all."

Jack dug in the sand for pebbles and lobbed them out into the waves.

"When Jason was five," he said, lobbing as he spoke, "Gabby took him to the mall at Christmastime. The temperature that day was approximately thirty-eight degrees and skies were clear. A winter storm was blowing down from Canada, but forecasters said it wouldn't hit D.C. until later that night. Shoppers were out in droves, anxious to finish before the storm hit.

"The mall was crowded, so Gabby held Jason's hand. They visited Santa, bought a few gifts, then Jason saw the Häagen-Dazs stand and said he wanted ice cream. Gabby bought him one scoop of chocolate in a small cup. Jason needed both hands to eat it. *If only I had bought him a cone instead,* Gabby said later. They walked away from Häagen-Dazs and Gabby stopped to look at something in a store window. When she looked down, Jason was gone.

"Gabby stayed calm and didn't move, thinking he would wander back. She asked someone to call security. Four men arrived. She told them what Jason was wearing and gave them a couple of snapshots from her wallet. Gabby was good under pressure. She stood on a bench and organized a group of fifty volunteers. They swept through the mall, checking rest rooms, toy stores, dressing rooms, even the midget-sized houses of the Santa Village. An hour went by. Jason was still missing. Gabby called the police and then she called me."

Jack said he must have been crying on his long drive across town, because billboards, street signs and signals were blurry smudges.

He found Gabby standing soldier straight in front of a store window, arms crossed over her chest, telling her story for the tenth time to a new team of detectives.

"*He was right here,* she said, stamping her foot. *He's wearing a red turtleneck, blue jeans, and red sneakers. He wanted to wear red like Santa. That's what he said. He's got a reindeer pinned to his turtleneck. The nose blinks red. It's Rudolph, of course.*"

Then she looked up and saw Jack. All the fight went right out of her. And her eyes. Jack swore he would never forget her eyes. The fear. The snuffed-out hope. The guilt. *Find him, Jack,* she said, sagging against him, pawing his coat. *Find him.*

Jack worked with a team of cops searching a ten-mile radius outside. They issued a statement for the local newscasts, but at eleven o'clock, the storm had hit, the mall was closing, and Jason was still missing. They drove for hours after that, Gabby gripping the dashboard, straining to see through the falling snow. At two in the morning, not knowing what else to do, Jack took Gabby home and waited by the phone.

A ransom note showed up the next day. Magazine letters cut out and pasted on plain white paper, Jason's reindeer pin attached, red nose blinking. The deal? A hundred thousand dollars in hundred dollar bills, double-wrapped in plastic and placed in a nylon gym bag. The instructions were clear. Gabby was to show up at midnight alone at a specific point on the Potomac River bank and wait for the contact. If she delivered, Jack would get a call at home telling him where to find Jason. No police, no tracking devices, no feds, no backup. Not even Jack. Gabby alone or Jason would die.

Gabby wanted to do exactly as the letter instructed, but the D.C. police wouldn't let her. They wired her with a two-way radio and posted backup teams of cops at strategic points near the designated drop site. They were afraid whoever had Jason might try to grab Gabby too. They said it was for her own protection. Jack agreed.

Gabby walked down the riverbank at eleven forty-five that night and waited. It was thirty-two degrees and snowing lightly. Three hours went by. No one showed. The police called Gabby over the two-way and told her to go home. She refused. A half-hour later, they called her again and ordered her to leave. She turned the radio off and stayed out there, hugging the gym bag, walking a slow circle in the snow, turning her head left, right, left, watching. At five-thirty, just before sunrise, D.C. police gave up and sent two plainclothes cops down to bring her in.

I pictured Gabby out there, alone in the snow, and felt her desperation, her need to not give up, to never give up. The approaching cops were symbolic of failure, of the end. One way or another, it was finished and Gabby couldn't accept that.

Jack told me she pushed the cops away and accused them of blowing the deal. Then, he said, Gabby fell apart. She reached in the gym bag, ripped open plastic, grabbed a handful of bills and tossed them in the air screaming, *Give me my son! Take the money! It's yours! They'll leave you alone! I promise! Take the money! Just give me my son.* Falling to her knees, shouting at the sky and the gray rushing river, and finally at the white frozen ground, begging God and the unseen kidnapper to take the money and give her back her son.

"The cops went to get her because they figured it was over," Jack explained. "They figured wrong. Those long hours waiting were the test. The kidnapper was out there somewhere, watching. The minute he saw them trying to take Gabby in, he called the apartment. I answered. *You broke the rules,* he said. *Jason's dead.* We never got another call or another chance."

Jack was quiet for such a long time, I thought he was finished, that he had told all he was going to tell. He surprised me when he cleared his throat and spoke again.

"The police believed the killer wasn't out for money at first. It started as a crime of opportunity when Jason wandered away in the crowded mall, an impulse grab by a man with a fixation on young boys. Then he heard on the news he had the son of a doctor and lawyer and greed kicked in. He tried the ransom deal, but the risk of getting caught scared him off going for a second try.

"The loss shattered us. Gabby quit work. I urged her to go back. She refused and sank into a deep depression. I tried to get her professional help. She wouldn't do it. She crawled into herself, shut me out. She slept in Jason's room and stayed in the apartment day after day, waiting for Jason to come home. I tried a hundred ways, but I just couldn't reach her."

Jack paused again and closed his eyes. He lay like that for a long time, fingers sifting sand.

"Gabby wouldn't let me in," he said, softly. "Why? Why wouldn't she let me help her carry the grief? It was my loss too. We could have gotten through it. And together, we would have. But she was on her own private mountain, all alone, with no safety ropes, no guiding lights, no one to work her down safely. I could have helped her. She just wouldn't let me."

I had read the facts and figures, the events as told by good objective reporters, and I knew the end to Jack's story, what happened next. Now, tears rolled down his cheeks as he struggled to put it into his own words. They were the hardest for him to speak, and I tried a dozen times to stop him, but Jack wanted to talk:

"Three months turned into a year," he said in a voice ragged with new emotion. "The doorbell rang early on Christmas Day. I had just showered and dressed. Gabby was in her nightgown. Two tired detectives, hats in hand, told us Jason's body had been found. A heavy rain washed out a back road shoulder about thirty miles from the mall. He'd been there a long time, probably since the night the drop went wrong. Shot five times in the chest and buried like a dog. Dental impressions established the identity, they said. There was no doubt.

"Gabby ran off into the apartment. I told the detectives I'd be in touch, took their cards, and closed the door. I walked into the living room. There were two sets of French doors that opened on to our big wraparound terrace. We lived on the twentieth floor. The morning sun flared in through the glass. I didn't see her at first, not until I opened one of the doors. She had climbed over the railing and was standing on the outside ledge with her back to me.

"I bolted across the terrace calling her name, but she never turned around, she never answered, she never said I'm sorry or I can't go on or I love you or good-bye. She never said anything at all. She just pushed off with her feet and let go, springing away from the rail, from safety, from life, from me—leaping out, arms wide open, like she was embracing the ghost of our child or her own impending death.

"The wind lifted her hair, and that's the last thing I saw. Her long dark hair blowing out all around her pink silk nightgown. Then, she was gone and there was nothing but the empty air and me, standing breathless and alone, clapping my hands over my ears, afraid to know that she never even screamed, that her twenty-story fall was long and silent, that she was unafraid and happy to die.

"I screamed for her, loud and long, so I wouldn't hear her body hitting metal or cement, that one dull thud, the sound of Gabby dying, but I heard it anyway. A hundred and fifteen pounds of the woman I loved hitting the ground. Her final rejection of me. I heard it and shouted her name again.

"*Gabby!*" Jack said it now in a whisper. "I was two long strides from the railing, she had been just out of my reach. Two long strides, ten seconds too late. I couldn't go to the rail. I didn't have the strength to get there and I didn't want to see. My legs gave out. I folded down on the ground, put my head in my hands, and closed my eyes, but not before I noticed Jason's old tricycle sitting in a corner, rusting in the snow."

Jack's hands curled into fists. His lips tightened, the muscle in his jaw tensed. I had come to know that struggle, the constant battle.

"I had always climbed for fun," he said quietly. "But after Gabby died, I closed my practice, sold the apartment, and spent three years traveling the globe, climbing mountains, the highest ones I could find. The Seven Summits. I did them all, then settled at Mt. McKinley and worked on expeditions, leading climbers to the top. I had to prove myself again, prove that I could be trusted with life, that people could depend on me. I never lost a climber. No one died under my watch. No one got hurt.

"I met Max on McKinley. Come vacation time, he's not the kind of man to sit on a beach and watch the sunset. Climbing is his idea of relaxation. We spent a lot of days and nights talking. Max told me three years were enough. He told me to get the hell off the mountain and get on with living, to deal with my life. He bullied me and he was right. He steered me into the Bureau, said I should put all my rage to good use.

"The man who took my son took my wife too. I couldn't set that straight up on a mountain. So I came down, went to the FBI, and became their self-appointed hunter of child killers. I keep at it long enough, I figure one day I'll get lucky and accidentally nail the one who killed Jason. Max saved my life. I went up to the mountains to find myself. If I'd stayed longer than I did, I would have just lost myself all over again. I have pieces of the Seven Summits. I keep them at home. They remind me of how I felt standing up there, how it seemed as if I could reach right up into Heaven, touch Gabriella and my little boy too."

His fists uncurled, he took my hand. We stayed like that for a long time, side by side, faces to the sun, listening to the steady beat of waves hitting sand.

I thought of Jack climbing in the summer, half nude, bare torso slung in a harness, nimble fingers digging into rock, close to the sun, where the heat of it would dry the tears off his face. I thought of him in winter, hacking his way up glaciers, crying as he climbed, tears turning to ice on his stone-cold cheeks.

I had interviewed a survivor of the Everest disaster in the spring of '96, when eight climbers died on the summit in a sudden savage storm. I learned that most men gravitate to extreme climbing in search of thrills, challenge, a heightened sense of life; most are chasing glory and dreams.

Jack was different.

He climbed for redemption, and he climbed to forget.

Chapter Thirty-two

We walked back in the afternoon as the sun dipped low in the west. The silence between us was easy and natural. Later, I watched Jack cooking with his sleeves rolled up and an apron tied around his jeans. He looked at me and shrugged.

"I like to cook," he said.

Dinner was tender veal pounded wafer-thin, lightly breaded and sautéed in butter with lemon and herbs, served with oven-roasted new potatoes and tender baby carrots. We shared a crisp tossed salad afterward with a ripe Brie cheese and a velvety vintage Bordeaux. Outside, the snowy woods surrounding us seemed to glow in the moonlight, and it was in this peaceful hush we took the last step to one another.

I chose Jack.

I watched him, studied him, measured the hardness of his thighs, the powerful roll of shoulders, the even length of his long able arms. I felt his skin without touching, tasted his lips without kissing, and imagined the bite of his teeth against my breast, the scrape of his cheek against mine.

Jack.

I wanted him then and there, hard and fast and deep. I wanted roughness and smoothness and sure strong movements. I wanted the weight of his body to crush me. I wanted to lie belly to belly with him, pull my knees up, lower myself onto him and ride. I watched Jack's long fingers wrap around the wineglass stem, and I wanted to feel them on me. My choice was sudden and frightening.

"Lacie?"

He knew. What I was thinking. What I wanted. How I imagined what his hands could do, might do, would do. I wanted him but I was afraid. I turned away, closed my eyes, but I could still see his big hand resting on the counter, midway between the wineglass and my body.

Jack was closer now and more certain.

Fear was all that separated us. My fear. I was more afraid of men than fire. Would he laugh at me? Flinch? Recoil from my touch? Wasn't love tactile? Feeling, touching, finding, grasping? How could I do all those things, how could I love him well with such monstrous hands? Fear overwhelmed me.

Leave it, leave it. Let your fear go.

"Lacie?" he asked again, wanting to be sure. His hand was on my arm, at my elbow, then it was under my chin, tipping my hidden face up, touching my closed eyes open so I was looking at him, at the twin hunger and loneliness there in his eyes.

Leave it, leave it. Let your fear go.

I did. Words were not spoken. I slipped into his arms and offered him me. Our lips came together in a long searching kiss as we circled aimlessly across the great stone floor kicking off shoes, peeling off sweaters, shrugging out of shirts, tugging off jeans—everything. Suddenly we were down, rolling on slate, the splendid weight of his fit bare body heavy against mine, and then as if he knew my thoughts and fears, Jack showed me how handless passion can be.

His cheek was next to mine, on my ribs, at my waist. He eased my legs apart with his knee, dropped down and stroked me, working his tongue in a long slow rhythm, driving it deep, taking his time, taking me right to the edge. At the very last second, he pulled away and brought his lips up to mine, sharing the taste of where he had just been.

It was my turn. I locked his wrists together, rolled him on his back and showed him how handless my love could be. Sliding my thighs along the length of his full-muscled legs, I drifted down, brushing my lips across his chest, the firm table of his stomach, to the hard ready length of him. I took all of him in my mouth and moved, taking him right to the limit, right to the edge, and when he was almost there, I pulled away and up, back to his warm waiting lips.

We turned.

Jack. Bringing his mouth down on mine, firm, hard, then softening, inviting, blue eyes open and heated, heavy with desire. *Jack.* Breathing my name, dipping his head and kissing my breasts.

Take me now, now, now, I begged softly, until he did.

He rocked into me.

I cried out once when he entered, the surprise of him filling me, the heady dizzying beat of him moving in and out, his smooth skin gold against my marble white. His hands were free now and bold, roaming my breasts, circling my waist, cupping my hips, pulling me tight up against him, urging me to match his moves until we could not stop or slow or wait and the wild shuddering rush filled us both at once.

Sometime later, we drifted into the big bed and started all over again. The bright moon lit the room, casting shadows on the wall: our two bodies moving together, the hunger, the grace, the strong shared need, Jack kneeling over me, my hips tilting up, his elegant slow move down.

Now, now, now.

Bending, turning, stirring, rolling, rocking, riding, *now, now, now,* in his wide firm bed.

Jack. Taking me up, letting me drop only to work me all over again, slow and sure, sending me up time after time until he could no longer hold back and we stayed up there high and sweet and long and tight, together.

We fell asleep wrapped around each other. I stirred once and opened my eyes to find Jack watching me. I kissed him softly, then fell back into a heavy dreamless sleep, the kind I never had.

The whispering voice I heard that night was Jack's.

Only Jack's.

Chapter Thirty-three

I woke up alone in the morning to the sound of Jack rattling in the kitchen downstairs.

I was relieved. Part of me was afraid to look in his eyes, afraid I would see regret and embarrassment for our reckless night. I lingered in bed. My body was lazy, my lips felt full. I didn't want to shower, not just yet. I wanted Jack's sweat and scent, the feel of us on my skin a little while longer; proof that I was alive.

I pushed tangled sheets aside and went into the bathroom looking for a robe. Under Jack's body, in his hands, I had felt whole. Now, I ripped bandages off and the mirror showed me the truth. Old injuries mixed with new. The burn on my face had turned pale pink. Fresh bright red welts streaked over the ancient graft scars on my thighs. Blisters bubbled up on calves and forearms. I applied ointments, taped new dressings in place, and noticed a red mark high on my breast that wasn't a burn at all. Jack's mouth, or the scrape of his early morning cheek. I touched the mark like a prize and smiled, reached for a robe and belted it.

The rocks lured me into his office. I held them all; one from each of the Seven Summits. Pieces of Jack's journey to save himself. The shelf above them was filled with thick leather-bound notebooks. I pulled one out and opened it.

The notebook was methodically organized by date and case number. This was Jack's private gallery, his collection of angels avenged. Each case began with pictures of the victim: a color photograph of the live child and next to it, a crime scene shot of the dead body in situ. Jack's handwritten notes followed, careful log entries detailing his investigation, and finally, a photograph of the killer.

I paged through the fifteen books. Sweet smiles and broken bodies, and the faces of their executioners. Jack had found them all: the fathers, the brothers, the uncles, the stepfathers, the strangers, the serial killers, the opportunists, the mothers, the blitz attackers, and the methodical stalkers. The child killers were here, and his neat tight handwriting described their fates.

A few were shot down in the arrest, the rest were tried and convicted. Of the convicted men and women, some were put to death and many more were still sitting on death row waiting to die. Those that were lucky enough to escape death row were in prison, locked up for life.

Jack was vigilant with those prisoners. He showed up at their periodic parole hearings with pictures of the dead children—their beaten, bloodied little bodies—arguing against early release, against any kind of release. The locked-up killers were gone, but Jack made sure their crimes were not forgotten.

There were only two entries in those fifteen fat notebooks that did not have the face of the killer pasted in: The first and the last.

The first was Jason Stein. In life, he had been a beautiful boy, smiling and happy, with glossy copper hair and Jack's blue eyes. The crime scene picture showed Jason dead, his decayed body slumped in the shallow muddy grave, hair matted, small white bones visible in the murk. The last entry was Skyla Costello. Her lovely young face in life, her butchered torso in death. No sullen killers pasted in, no names and prison numbers, no careful documentation of the killer's fate.

Fifteen years of work, and these two children alone remained unavenged.

I put the notebooks back and sat at the desk for a long time shaking the images from my mind; helpless babies and hammers coming down, big bare hands around tiny infant necks, ice picks driven into five-year-old hearts, little boys turned to mud, my own sweet girl turned to ash. *There is no justice,* Jack had said. I believed he was right.

His computer was in front of me, screen saver working, hurtling meteors out of space. I touched the mouse and the meteors disappeared. I logged into my WRC mailbox. Thirty new messages had come in. Harry's scrolled up first. It was simple and from the heart. *If there's anything else you need, call me.* The next message stopped me cold.

I am lost. I can recall the exact moment I became lost; a sudden violent shift and there madness was, burrowing into me, replacing reason with rhyme, love with hate, sucking my soul out and leaving a whispering void in its place. I am a fighter, a rebel, a merchant soldier marching to the white-hot buzz of the blankness inside me.

My madness is an electrical current, high-voltage and deadly to touch. Madness runs at its own pace, sets its own course, writes its own rules, sings its own song. The song now is a vicious vibrant hymn, urging me to tear my hair out in fistfuls and stretch my toes one by one until they rip out of my feet. The song is a whisper, an incessant hissing whisper, and it's driving me to right what was wronged.

The whisper was inside of me when I saw Skyla with the sky blue eyes. She was so lovely to watch, drifting along the city sidewalk in spring, winsome and fey, with a sweet easy sway to her hips. She looked at me, tossed her hair, and smiled with so much unintended promise. A split second lock with my eyes and the connection was made.

The death connection.

I knew the time had come to right the wrong.

I have been watching you for years, Lacie, since you were younger than Skyla. You have looked at me too, not knowing who I was or that you would die with me. Your gloved hands brushed mine a dozen times, taking change, signing for a package, accepting flowers. And the agony I felt, wanting to kiss you, to grab you and run away! But the time was never right.

Then Skyla smiled at me and I knew it was a sign that our time had come. To see Skyla see me, not knowing who or what I was, to see her give me a flirtatious smile the way all teenage girls give to men, old men, young men, all men, even dangerous men, bad men, even deadly men like me.

The daughter's daughter. A generation has gone full cycle. Skyla smiled at me and I knew, Lacie. I knew our time was finally here.

I called out for Jack. There was no answer.

"Jack?" I moved to the doorway. "Jack!"

The house was ominously quiet.

A phone rang. Jack's cell phone, on the desk. I picked up.

"Have you read my latest missive?"

"Yes."

"Good girl, Lacie."

"What wrong do you want to right?"

I heard seagulls and waves pounding sand. His shallow raspy breath.

"Who are you," I said.

"You don't want to know."

"Yes, I do."

"Is Jack Stein fucking you yet? If he hasn't, he'll try. He's a scoundrel, a rogue, and a thief. He's stealing you and you're mine. He's keeping us apart, Lacie. But he can't do that forever. I'm learning all about him. I'm beginning to understand his secrets and his sharply tuned mind. I was going to wipe him off the board, but I've decided to let him participate in the last round of our game. He seems to want to play."

"The Dead Time? Is that the last round?"

"Smart girl."

"What if I had died in your white fire? How could you play the last round without me?"

"There's a calculated risk in every game, and, yes, you could have died. But the odds were the fed would get you out, and he did! I'm an excellent strategist. I know my opponent's strengths." He sighed. "It's a beautiful day at the beach. Would you like to come walking with me? The water's cool but the sun is warm. Do you have the sun there in Jack's wooded retreat? Or are you at Jerry's? Did you run back to your conjugal bed hoping Jerry's great wealth would wrap you in safety? Are you walking the big outdoor terrace? Looking at the sea? Scanning the beach left to right now, looking for me?"

He laughed and hung up.

His laugh stayed with me. The hollow chill in it. The promise. All the great glass windows in the house exposed me. I jumped at an odd sound. Was it from the left or right? Was it human? Was it him? Did he get to Jack somehow, lure him outside and kill him? Was he out there now with the flamethrower strapped high and tight on his back waiting for me? Was he squeezing the nozzle, testing the fire? Was he in the basement? Slipping in through an open door? Was he walking up the stairs, coming my way? Was this it? Was the Dead Time here?

He was doing a good job. I was blindfolded and he was turning me in circles, telling me to swing at the piñata, pin the tail on the donkey, making me play terrible childhood games where blindness makes you helpless. I didn't want to die this way; cowering barefoot in the corner, hair matted from sleep, armpits soaked in sweat, hands shaking, and where Jack's loving words should have been, nothing but the nightmare voice beating through my head.

Our time is here. Our time is here.

The seven rocks caught my eye.

Don't let Jack down. Don't lose yourself to fear.

I stumbled into the bedroom, pulled on jeans, boots, and a sweater, raced downstairs, and out the front door. No screaming snowmobiles careened out of the woods this time, no whips of fire danced at my feet. Instead, incredibly, I saw Jack, at the top of the drive, calmly cleaning the windshield of a white Jeep.

"Jack!"

I ran to him. His eyes were full of emotion and the emotion was not regret. His lips brushed my temple. He breathed my name: "Lacie."

"I didn't know where you were." I clung to him and blinked back tears of relief.

"A friend of mine came by to pick up the police car and loan me his Jeep. We talked for a while. He just left. What's wrong?"

"He called, Jack. He's out here. He knows where you live. He knows where Jerry lives."

His soft expression turned hard. "Call Jerry. Tell him to leave town."

"He won't believe me. I have to see him in person."

"No."

"I have to see Jerry," I insisted. "Now."

"Okay," he said, understanding my resolve. "Get your things. We can't come back here."

We packed quickly and tossed bags in the Jeep. Our haven was ruined. He had found us again.

Chapter Thirty-four

A half hour later, we pulled into Jerry's drive. His white Mercedes was parked in front. Music drifted on the breeze. A slow sliding bow over violin strings. Jack drew his gun and walked me up to the wraparound deck, following the music to the ocean-facing portion of terrace. He stopped at the corner, hugged the house wall tight, and edged around to see who was there. His body relaxed. He signaled me.

Jerry was sitting upright on a chaise, playing Skyla's violin, bowing gracefully. He was good. Skyla's talent had come from him. The music was enormous, sad, and elegant. His eyes were closed and the instrument was tucked tight under his chin. He wore jeans and boat shoes, a blue Gore-Tex sailing jacket.

"Jerry?"

The bow lifted. Jerry opened his eyes. "I sit out here and play for her," he said, gesturing to the sea. "I feel like she can hear me. Isn't that stupid?"

"No."

"Even though I know she's dead, I'm waiting for her to walk through that door and say *Hey, Dad, I'm home.*" He slouched back in the chaise. "I'm so fucking sad, Lace."

I sat down next to him, taking in his shadowed eyes and unshaven cheeks.

"A friend of mine picked me up at dawn this morning and took me out to Montauk," he said. "We sailed for hours. My friend said the fresh air and open sea would make me feel better. My friend was wrong." He sat up suddenly and focused on me. "I'm falling apart, Lacie. You should be falling apart too, but you look good. Different too."

"Of course I look different. I have a bandage on my face."

"No," he said, looking at me intently, "it's something else."

I fidgeted, uncomfortable. I could still feel Jack's hands on my skin and imagined Jerry could sense it. Nothing escaped him, especially if it had to do with sex. Jerry nudged my chin up and looked in my eyes. I felt a stab of guilt. *How can I think about pleasure when our daughter is dead.*

"Let me guess," Jerry mocked. "Your live-in FBI agent. Your bodyguard. Whatever the hell you call him. He's taking a few fringe benefits."

"Jerry, stop."

"I hope he's a better lover than he is a bodyguard. Two places gutted with fire, then he steals a cop car and puts you on the run like a common criminal. What the hell's Jack Stein trying to do?"

"He's trying to keep me alive."

"So he can fuck you, Lacie?"

I slapped him.

He pulled back, surprised, and rubbed his cheek. "I deserved that, of course. You have the right to do whatever you want with whomever you please. I'm just sorry it's not me. To the victor go the spoils."

"I'm not a prize and this isn't a contest."

"Everything in life is a contest, Lacie. You just don't know it yet." He rose and moved to the rail. The wind ruffled his hair. "Why are you here?"

"To tell you to leave East Hampton. Now."

"Why?" he asked, amused.

"My house and your loft were torched by the same man, the man who killed Skyla. He's after me. He thinks I've come to stay with you. You're in danger. You have to go somewhere safe until this is over."

"I'm not going anywhere."

"He's real, Jerry, and he's out here at the beach. You have to leave."

"You sound hysterical."

"I'm hardly hysterical. I'm frightened. There's a big difference."

"If he's after you, why would he hurt me?"

"You're linked to me. That's all it seems to take lately."

He smiled sardonically. "I'll take your words under advisement."

"Cut the legal bullshit, Jerry. Just get out. Now. Go to the

Caribbean. Drink piña coladas and come home when it's all over."

"How will I know when *it's* over?"

"I'll call and tell you, or you'll read my obituary. One of the two things will happen and when it does, you can come home."

Jerry checked his watch. "I'm late for lunch in town with my partner. Feel free to stay a while. Enjoy the view." He picked up his jacket and walked away.

"Agent Stein," he sniped, a second later. "You do stick close to her, don't you?"

I moved to the rail and watched Jerry swing down the steps, cross over to his Mercedes, and open the door. He looked up at me before getting in.

"Stein's a lucky man, Lacie. I admire you. And, in my own neurotic way I love you too. Take care. Take good care."

He dropped inside and slammed the door. The electric locks snapped into place. Jerry appeared surprised. He tried the door, but it did not open. A strange line of white flame sprang up on the dash, streaking like a fuse down toward some unseen fuel pack rigged beneath his seat.

"Jerry!" I screamed, seeing the panic on his face, understanding he couldn't get out.

Jack vaulted over the terrace rail. I sprinted down the stairs.

A blinding bright light flared, the interior burst into a roiling mass of white fire, and Jerry disappeared. Windows were rolled up tight, the sun roof was closed. We tugged on door handles. Heat radiated out, buckling paint and popping tires. I backed off, afraid.

Jack pulled his gun and hammered the window. Glass shattered. Oxygen-hungry fire gushed out. He hit the ground and rolled. Hidden fuel loads packed under the chassis exploded, one after the other, and wings of fire erupted, sweeping out and up to either side, enveloping the exterior.

"It's too late," Jack said, getting to his feet and running me to the Jeep. "Jerry's dead." Three minutes had passed from the moment of full combustion. No one could survive more than a few seconds engulfed in white fire like that.

Jack's cell phone rang. He answered.

"Lacie's lucky she wasn't with Jerry," the voice said. "But then again, I have always controlled whether she lives or dies. The power is mine and mine alone. She won't die yet, not while there's dealing to be done." A dial tone droned.

We sped off, leaving the burning Mercedes behind us and slow spiraling columns of black smoke twisting up, dark against the bright noon sun.

Chapter Thirty-five

Jack avoided the main route and raced down empty country lanes instead, whipping through the woods, checking the rearview mirror and talking to someone named Steven Stiller on the cell phone. Jack's side of the conversation was direct and to the point. We needed help. Fast. His explanation was short. I guessed Stiller already knew the basics.

Adrenaline rushed: Fight or flight. Jack chose flight and Steven Stiller had a plane.

His next call was cryptic.

"Look for me at the end of the day," he said to someone he called Logan. "I'm not alone. Lacie's with me."

A short time later, we arrived at the tiny East Hampton airport. It was nothing more than a strip of asphalt in the woods with a small control tower built on the side. A big-shouldered man wearing Ray•Bans and a flight jacket waited on the runway next to a brand-new Cessna. He had wispy blond hair and a choirboy's face.

We piled into the small plane. Stiller settled in the cockpit. Jack sat in back with me.

"Where are we going?" I asked.

"Private airport outside of Boston," Stiller shouted over revving engines. "But the flight plan I filed says we're going to New York. I've got a friend at the Tieterborough private airfield there. If anyone asks, the log will say we landed at the scheduled time. There will be no reason to suspect we haven't."

The plane accelerated down the runway and lifted off. I watched the woods below drop away. Roads were black asphalt squiggles snaking through white snow, the Atlantic disappeared, and droning engines worked, taking us far away from Jerry's sudden fiery death. *Keep going!* I wanted to shout. *Fly us to the West Coast, to China, and beyond.* I remembered Jack's offer of a safe house. Could he get me one for life? Could he slip me into the witness protection program before I witnessed my own hot burning?

You can run, Lacie, but you cannot hide.

I spent the flight staring out the window, silent and afraid.

Stiller prepared for landing. The cabin pressure changed, my ears popped, and a short sweep of runway came into view. Wheels hit, brakes locked. We lurched forward in our seats. The plane taxied to a stop.

"Massachusetts," Stiller said, turning around. "As promised." He handed me a gold Amex card. "Use this. Anyone tracking you won't be looking for credit card transactions under my wife's maiden name."

"Thanks," I said. "I'll pay you back for whatever we spend."

"You two have more serious things on your minds," he said, gently. "There's a dark green Buick parked at the curb. Keys are under the floor mat. Hertz contract is in the glove compartment."

We found the Buick and the keys, tossed our bags in the back, and took off, speeding down a lonely country road, away from the airfield.

"Where are we going?" I asked, twenty miles and three lonely country roads later.

"To a cabin for the night," Jack said. "Tomorrow we'll go up to the camp."

His cell phone rang so often, he finally turned it off. We both knew who it was. Jack was quiet. I saw a new tension in his features; uncertainty too. All those notebooks full of killers, but he had never come up against a madman like this.

We stopped briefly for gas. There were two self-service gas pumps and a news rack with the *New York Times*. I was the page-one story. Jerry would have that privilege next. Jack filled the tank and paid. It was after four. Purple clouds striped the sky, washed in color from the setting sun.

It was dark when Jack finally slowed and turned up a narrow drive. There was no address, no mailbox, or sign, just a quarter mile of bad road flanked with pine trees leading to a cabin nestled in a clearing at the end. In any other circumstances, it would have been charming. Jack parked the car and took the bags. I followed him up the walk.

A short solid man waited on the small front porch. He had a bulldog face that had been hammered by years of wind and sun and shoulder-length silky black hair shot through with white. He wore a sweatshirt and jeans, and black sunglasses even though it was night.

"Jack Stein!" he boomed. "I'd know the sound of those boots anywhere. I hear them in my dreams, the way they sounded when we made the final pitch up the north face of McKinley. Those boots are music to me!"

"Logan," Jack said, embracing him.

"And the second pair of boots there promise something nicer than two old stone-hounds talking shop. She's light but tall, judging by the length of stride. She made it up the walk in ten steps. You made it in nine and you're a giant, Stein. We all know that."

"Lacie, meet Logan."

"Hello," I said.

Logan grinned. "A voice like yours will keep my mind full of pretty pictures for a long time, lovely Lacie. Come in, come in. Make yourselves at home."

He led the way. I was impressed with his ease of movement. He never once faltered or hesitated. Logan knew where he was and what surrounded him, every inch of the way. I trailed in after him, shaking snow off my boots.

The house had a simple layout and a lived-in feel. The main living space was square, with a long overstuffed couch facing the empty fireplace and broad easy chairs to either side. The kitchen, like Jack's, was open and surprisingly well equipped with a six-burner stove and copper pots hanging from hooks. Lamps and ceiling fixtures were plentiful and lit.

"I turn the lights on every night," Logan said, reading my mind. "Can't stand the idea of sitting around in the dark. Crazy habit, I know."

A huge German shepherd trotted in through the open front door, nose to the ground sniffing, until he got to me. Ears went flat. He growled and barked. Dogs, like horses, can smell fear.

"That's Thor," Logan said. "Don't mind him. He's a pussycat under all that canine hair."

There were two bedrooms on opposite sides of the cabin. Logan steered us to the right, down a small hall, and into the guest room. Brightly colored rugs were scattered across wood floors, an old-fashioned quilt covered the double bed, and big oil paintings of pine trees filled the walls.

"I did these," Logan said, tapping a painting, "back when I could see." He snapped a light on in the bathroom. "I'll leave you to wash up. Then Jack can help me with dinner." He backed out and closed the door.

"Your blind climber?" I asked.

"Logan's more than that," Jack said. "He has a way of seeing things none of the rest of us do. He's been helpful in the past on difficult cases. He may be able to help us now."

My throat tightened and all I could think of was the great white inferno that had wiped Jerry off the face of the earth. We had been too busy running for the horror of it to sink in. Now, standing in the quiet cabin surrounded by the night woods, grief and shock hit me hard.

Jack saw it. He crushed me to his chest.

Later, Jack and Logan cooked Italian on the big gas stove.

I curled up on the couch and listened to the murmur of the men talking, but I didn't hear their words. My mind was crowded with words of my own. A terrible refrain, a dark fugue: *Jerry is dead and I will be next.* Fear was a thief, stealing heartbeats and swiping my breath. The shepherd sprawled next to me, his head heavy in my lap, whining his discontent. He smelled the fear but didn't understand the threat.

Jerry is dead and I will be next.

How could he be dead when I could close my eyes and see him so clearly? The way he looked in those final seconds standing by the car, his sad eyes, the new furrows on his forehead. *Take care, Lacie. Take good care.* I wanted it to be a cruel joke. I wanted to race back to the house, see Jerry dust ash off his chinos and play a jig on his violin.

I remembered the expression on his face as he watched Skyla's birth. The anticipation, the fear for me, for the baby, for himself when he first held her, when she was still wet from the fetal sea. The immensity of it hit him, his awesome new responsibility for that life. A new chapter begun. Who would have guessed the surprise ending? The daughter's slow burning death; the father's instant cremation in an oven of white fire.

One minute, Jerry was getting in the car, feeling the good cashmere on his skin, the weight of the sailing jacket, supple flex of boat shoes, and the next second he was gone. No drawn-out agonies, no death rattles in the chest, no knifed arteries spurting blood while the victim floundered like a slow dying fish. No animal shrieking like Linda's young pilot Bratton who knew he was flying straight to his death, no frenzied helpless panic like Richard Wagner's, my father, who lived long enough to feel the pain of fire and watch his own body burn, and by God, no death like Skyla's. Jerry's was fast.

A burst of white; hard cut to black.

The fugue played on. *Jerry is dead and I will be next.*

Logan touched my shoulders. "Dinner's ready," he said.

I nodded and rose.

We sat on stools at the kitchen counter and ate Logan's spicy linguine with fresh-baked bread. When we finished, the blind man turned to me.

"Jack's told me what you look like, but I'd like to see you for myself. Do you mind?"

"No."

He ran his hands over my face. I felt callused fingers, strong nails, skin roughened from years of use and too little care. His hands were like feet, walking him over the surfaces of the world. The irony was not lost on me. He could see with the very appendages I tried to hide.

His fingers spread, probing behind my ears, at the base of my skull, up and around the crown, to the top of my head, and then over and down, walking the arcs, the spheres, the lines from forehead to chin and all the planes in between. He traced and touched, smiled and hummed.

"You're so beautiful," he said. "A woman to love. Serious but sensuous, full of unlocked energies. Your lips are full and your smile would be something if you weren't filled with so much sadness, so much grief. You're sad."

"I am," I said softly.

"Of course you are," he said, going over the bandage several times, measuring the length and width. "You're sad because of Jerry and your girl. And you're scared because he wants you next. Jack sent me a copy of the tape and read me the e-mails. Such exact attention to the symmetry and balance of words. He's an exact man. Such malevolence. He's full of rage and hate.

"Jack tells me his identity is locked away in your memory somewhere out of reach. I'm going to help you, Lacie. Tomorrow, I'm going to help you remember. Tonight you can sleep. Thor and I will be standing watch. You're safe here. And tomorrow, we'll unlock the secret in your mind."

When we left Logan, he was staring out the window with his palms pressed against cold glass, searching the night in his own special way, listening for something wrong; a car coasting down the road or footfalls in the snow.

His ears were so sharp, I hoped he wouldn't hear us too. Jerry's death left me afraid for my own life, and whatever hours I had left were hours I wanted to live. We closed the bedroom door and undressed slowly, taking our time, stopping for lingering life-affirming kisses. Finally, Jack lifted me and moved to the bed. The flesh is a good place to forget fear, the best, and we filled the night hours forgetting.

I hoped Logan couldn't hear the hidden sighs, the muffled cries, the tender words whispered, Jack's groan, my sudden intake of breath, our feet sliding up and down against starched sheets, my hair sweeping over his thighs, his lips drifting over mine, but mostly I hoped he couldn't hear the sound of our bodies moving one against the other, skin brushing skin.

I never considered how noisy love could be until I thought about and feared a blind man listening.

Chapter Thirty-six

We left early the next morning as dark clouds tumbled across a flat-lit sky and tall pines swayed in the first gusting wind of an approaching storm. By the time we reached the main highway, wet sleet was slicing down faster than the windshield wipers could slap it away. The Buick was not equipped with snow tires or chains. Jack drove cautiously.

Logan and his dog were quiet in the backseat. I looked at them from time to time. The blind man kept his palms pressed to the window glass. His head was turned, as if he were looking out and watching the landscape streak by, but behind his dark glasses, his eyes were closed.

An hour and a half later, we were on a two-lane route in the heart of the Berkshires. Sleet had turned to blowing snow, and we slowed to a crawl, looking for the camp. It was marked with a simple wood arrow pointing right: *Lone Pine Camp for Girls—Private Property—No Trespassing.*

Jack turned. The road in was rocky and slippery, slick with ice. The Buick's chassis dipped and squeaked. Overgrown brush scratched the doors and bare branches slapped the windows for so many miles I began to wonder if kids had moved the sign as a joke, if this wasn't the wrong way, a road leading us nowhere. We bounced along, tail skidding out from time to time, Jack pulling on the wheel in quick angry corrections. The road angled up and at the top of the rise, I saw it.

"There," I said, pointing right.

The buildings hadn't changed in twenty-four years. They were the same dark wood cabins lined up in a broad arc on a ridge facing the lake. The lake itself looked different in winter. I remembered it as a sheet of sparkling emerald water, dotted with boats, alive with swimmers and water-skiers. Now, chunks of white ice floated on gray water. The piers were empty, lake banks desolate.

"A woman's memory is a cursed and blessed thing at the same time," Logan said, rolling the window down. "She remembers things she would rather forget, and can't remember what she must. You can tell me the color of the dress you were wearing the day you met Skyla's father, but you can't remember the night your own father died. Is that right, Lacie?"

"Yes."

"Come. Sit with me a while."

I got out and slid into the backseat.

"Place your hands in mine."

I offered my gloved hands.

"No!" he said, sharply.

I took my gloves off and watched him. His lips tensed as he measured my fingers, but he did not flinch. Logan felt the palms, counted the scars, then he put my hands down, cupped my ears with his coarse hands, and began to speak.

"Your memory is as dark as my world. But you have not lost your memory of that night, Lacie. It's simply locked out of reach. The mind is a great repository of sensory information. Much of it is ignored because we depend so much on sight. There are ways to see without using your eyes. I will use your other senses to help you see the past."

He feathered his fingers over my face.

"Drift, drift," he coaxed, thumbing my eyes closed. "Let your mind go. Let it take you where it will." His soft voice puffed in my ear, urging me back, pushing me away from the present, past the frightful time of my own red-hot burning, to the earlier days of camp.

"Listen to the sounds, Lacie. What's different today?"

"Snow falling off treetops."

"Good. What sounds are the same?"

"Wind rippling across the lake, running through the trees."

"Tell me about sounds you heard back then and not now."

"Crickets. Girls laughing in the dark."

"What else?"

"Canoe paddles dipping in water. The steady thunk of tennis balls on hard green courts, the hum of motorboat engines, and the buzz of transistor radios all tuned to different stations."

"Excellent! What now?"

"A hand tapping against glass." I stiffened. "A breath breathing. A voice whispering."

"Go on." The hands were traveling my face again. "Don't stop, Lacie. Let yourself see him. Who is he?"

"He's young. His face is unnaturally white. He tells me something has happened to my father, that I mustn't wake anyone, and to come with him right away. He shows me a badge. I think he's a cop. I slip out of bed, put my sneakers on, and go outside. He promises to take me to my father and hurries me away to a car parked up on the road. Once inside, he locks the doors and takes his shirt off. He's twisted and bent. Horrible. I try to get out, but there's no door handle on the passenger side. He says he's the God of fire and swears he will kill my father if I don't do just as he says. He makes me touch him in all the places where he is burned."

"And?"

"I do, hoping he will let me go. He doesn't. He wants me to kiss him."

"Do you?"

"I don't want to, but he makes me kiss his ugly burned flesh."

"What next?"

"He pulls himself out and he's burned there too. *Reach out and touch the fire, Lacie.* Then, he jams himself in my mouth, forces me to take in the long sliding length of him, but it makes me sick. I throw up. He's furious and promises I'll suffer for that. He tells me I will burn. He lights a cigarette and lifts my hair. He holds the burning end close to the skin on my neck and describes how I will burn if I tell, how I will feel, how I will squeal and scream, how I will beat at the flames with my hands, and how the fire won't go out.

"He promises my father will burn too if I tell anyone at all what has happened. Then, he presses the burning cigarette to my neck while he keeps a hand over my mouth to silence my scream. When he's finished burning me, he drops a pill down my throat and when he's sure I swallowed, he lets me out. I find my way back to my camp bed and sleep a drugged psychedelic sleep. When I wake up, I think I just had a bad dream, but then I feel the burn on my neck, hidden by my hair, and I'm afraid it wasn't. I don't tell anyone what happened. Anyway, I'm going home in two days' time. My father will come take me away.

"My stomach is sick. The counselors say it's just nerves. They promise I'll be okay. I'm not. I'm afraid. I don't sleep those last two nights. I sit up, huddled in the corner of my camp bed, carving my name in the wall, watching the night, waiting for fire, waiting for him to appear. When he doesn't, I'm glad and think maybe I've dreamed him after all. I convince myself the burn is really just a bee sting.

"Finally, it's the last day of camp. My father comes to fetch me. I throw my arms around him and for the first time in days, I close my eyes. Can he smell the sickness on my breath? The terror in my sweat? Apparently not. He whirls me around, tells me I'm a lovely princess and that my carriage awaits.

"I hurry into the front seat of his new red Cadillac, looking over my shoulder, into the dusk, waiting for the one white face to appear. Then we're off, and I'm safe. I throw my arms out the window and laugh. He was just a dream, a terrible nightmare, and now I'm free." I opened my eyes.

Jack was watching me carefully.

Logan nodded. "Good."

"If you saw him here," Jack said, "there's a good chance he worked here. Let's take a look around."

We got out and walked.

"Where are the cabins?" Logan asked.

"To the left, up on a ridge," I said. "Ten in a row, twenty girls in each. Mine was the one farthest out, at the edge of the woods."

We hiked up and went down the line.

"This was mine," I said, stopping at the end. The windows were boarded up. The door was locked with a heavy padlock.

"This lock is new," Jack said, jiggling it. "The locks on the other cabins are old."

We drifted down to the lake and out to the end of the old weathered pier. Wind kicked off ice, stinging our cheeks. We left the lake and went to the main camp buildings, to the director's office. Windows were boarded up. Jack tugged on the old padlock.

"Hey!" someone called out. "What're you doing there! This here's private property!"

An old man limped up to us. I recognized him as the camp custodian. The girls used to make up stories about his leg, how it was bitten by a bear, mauled by a freshwater shark, or made lame by a horse. Then, his hair had been carrot red and his face covered with freckles. Now, his hair was gone and the freckles had turned dark

from age. Pale eyes peered out at us, shiny with suspicion. Jack
flipped open his ID.

"What the heck does the FBI want in an old closed-up place like
this?" the old man said.

"Are you the owner?" Jack asked.

"Hell no. I'm Creech. Jimmy Creech. I just look after the grounds
now, take a tour past once a week or so, make sure no goddamn
hippies or homeless folks have broke in and set up housekeeping in
any of the cabins. Happens from time to time. Camp's been closed
for going on six years now. They finally went and sold it to some
developer. Supposed to rip it down next spring and build some la-
de-da hotel here instead. Damn shame. Camp's been here a long
time."

Jack eyed the fat key ring hanging off the old man's belt. "Do
you have keys to the administration office?"

"I got keys to everything."

"Mr. Creech," I said, "we have to look in the director's files for
information I need about my time here. It's urgent and can't wait.
You can watch over us, make sure we don't leave things a mess."

"You're too late to worry about that. Some dang vandal got in
there a few weeks back, tore the place to pieces. But he didn't get
the files. I'd already moved them out and stored them in the old
dining hall along with a bunch of other things I was going to move
to my own place for safekeeping. When that developer comes,
everything here will be just plain destroyed. I saved the files thinking someone might want them someday and now it looks like I was
right. Follow me."

He took us down the hill to the dining hall, unlocked the door,
and turned on lights.

"The files are in those cartons there," Creech said, pointing to
stacks against the wall. "One carton for every year, twenty-five in
all. I'll be outside. Just shout if you need me."

He limped out. Logan and the dog waited at the door.

We found my summer quickly. The first folders were filled with
accounting—payroll expenses, utility bills, food bills, leasing charges
for the camp horses and powerboats, art supplies, laundry bills, and
the like. Jack rifled through them quickly.

The next file was full of camp applications arranged in alphabetical order. I recognized my father's handwriting, that same precise
script Jack and I had seen in his files. There was a small black and

white snapshot of me, hair split into two high bouncing pony tails, skin clear, perfect teeth revealed in a wide happy smile.

"You were beautiful from the start," Jack said.

My application was stapled to a copy of my school record. Lone Pine was one of the most prestigious camps on the East Coast back then, with a reputation for encouraging "a liberal arts education in a healthful outdoor environment." The camp drew girls from three principal cities: Washington, D.C., Boston, and New York. Competition was stiff. My father had used his Harvard credentials to get me in.

The next folder was filled with daily observations by my cabin counselor. A final report was filed at the end of the summer along with a letter that was delivered to my father when he picked me up:

> *Lacie Wagner is a gregarious, spirited child with social skills developed beyond her age. She shows tremendous ability and promise in painting and drawing. Athletically, she is lean and strong, and should be encouraged to pursue tennis.*

The letter filled two pages. At the end, the counselor mentioned *the incident.*

> *Lacie had difficulty sleeping the last two nights of camp and refused to attend the final campfire. When I asked her why, she began to cry: "I'm scared. I don't want to burn to death."*
>
> *I assure you that Lacie had no traumatic experiences here and certainly never showed an aversion or fear of fire. She attended all of the campfires and was never once even slightly harmed by a stray spark or flame. I can only attribute her sudden fear as a late manifestation of homesickness. Six weeks is a long time to a young girl, and as Lacie spoke constantly of you, Dr. Wagner, I assume her family life is close and that this first-time separation was more emotionally trying for her than you might have thought.*
>
> *If you have any questions, please don't hesitate to contact me. I am an English teacher on staff with Boston University and can be reached immediately after the Labor Day holiday at my office on campus. My card is enclosed.*
>
> *My very best regards,*
> *Katherine Lawrence.*

The last documents on file included a copy of my father's check, emergency phone numbers, and a copy of my school record. Jack put the file to one side and then pulled Linda Severino's. It was as neat and orderly as mine. The picture showed a big athletic girl, with a pretty face and straight, short honey-colored hair. We did not share a cabin, and the only reason I remembered her was because she was the camp star at water-ski jumping. "It's the closest thing to flying," she said one day out on the lake.

"Take a look at this," Jack said, handing me a page from her counselor observations.

> *Linda is fearless. She takes the most challenging ski jumps and chooses the most aggressive horse at the stable. There is no apparent reason for the inexplicable and sudden onset of nightmares. She tells me she dreams of a white face watching her. She sleeps next to the cabin window. I reassigned her to a bunk away from the window, but one night later, she awoke with the same nightmare.*

"And look at this," Jack said, handing me another page.
I read it and looked up at him, confused. "It's from my file."
"It *could* be, but it's not."

> I read the words again: *On the final day of camp, she refused to attend the farewell campfire. When I asked her why, she began to cry: "I'm scared. I don't want to burn to death."*

Jack placed Linda's file to one side with mine.
We started back at the beginning, reading every girl's file, searching for another incident of nightmares or fear of fire, and finding nothing.

"Let's run through the personnel files," Jack said, pulling A for himself and giving me B.

Barker, Teri. Cabin Ten Counselor. I tossed it aside.

Baxter, Arthur. Head Chef. I smiled, remembering him. He was a portly red-faced man who walked through the dining room doing magic tricks with a coin.

Beane, Edward. Camp Doctor. I opened the folder and looked at the small black and white photo. It was the face of my nightmare, the nightmare face. Beard and mustache could not hide the eyes, the cheekbones, the wide forehead. The face was here and it had a name. Beane. Edward Beane. "Jack," I said. "It's him."

Jack looked at the picture. "Why didn't you recognize him? Why didn't you know it was the camp doctor?"

"He didn't look like this. At camp, he had a beard and a mustache and wore his hair pulled back under a baseball cap. The man that night had long stringy hair and a clean-shaven face."

"What about the voice?"

"He whispered to me. I couldn't have recognized it. But this is him, Jack."

Jack flipped through Beane's file. "He went to Harvard Medical School. There's a lot of information. A name, Social Security number, the works. We'll find him."

We took the three files and went outside, to Creech.

"We're going to borrow these," Jack said. "When we're finished, I'll see that they get back to you."

Creech picked at his teeth. "Don't see where it matters much now. They being so old and all. Camp's closing. Might as well keep 'em."

I showed him Beane's picture. "Do you remember the doctor that summer?"

"Yup. Couldn't forget him."

"Why?"

"I caught him sneaking around in the woods the last night of camp. He had white stuff on his face, and the beard and mustache were gone. I grabbed him and said I'd kill him unless he told me what he was doing. He swore he was just playing a joke on one of you girls. Told me some story about how you all believed the forest here was haunted. I didn't trust him. Told the director not to ever hire him back. Course we didn't have that problem, because he just disappeared. Didn't even take his last paycheck. That's mighty strange."

An owl hooted in the woods.

"Listen to that!" Logan said.

The owl hooted again.

"It's an owl," Jack said.

"Exactly!" Logan exclaimed.

Jack turned to Creech. "The cabin on the end there has a new lock."

"Sure does," Creech said. "Came by after the Thanksgiving weekend and found the door open. Someone had been living inside there. Eating, sleeping, the works. The old lock was busted right off. They'd gone and replaced it with a new lock of their own, and when they left, they just left that new lock hanging with the key in it. I figured they were the ones who busted into the director's office."

"You said they?"

"I'm guessing there was two of them in there, judging by the amount of food containers and trash."

"What did you do with the trash?"

"Hauled it away. They must've been burning it up right until the time they left, though."

"Why do you say that?"

"Off to one side of the cabin, about two hundred feet down the slope, I found the leftovers from some kind of big bonfire. Smelled like someone used a hell of a lot of gasoline too."

"Is it still there?" Jack asked, hoping for evidence.

"Nope. I washed it all away, then churned the earth up good to get rid of the burn mark. Hell, it's all covered with snow now anyway."

"You have the key to the cabin?"

"Sure do."

"I'd like to take a look inside."

Creech shrugged and walked us up the ridge. He unlocked the shiny new padlock, opened the door, and flipped the lights on.

"Nothing much to see," Creech said. "I threw all the trash out."

I went over to my old bed. Although the window next to it was boarded up from the outside, I remembered seeing the woods and the face. I remembered the open window and Beane's voice whispering to me in the dark, drawing me out, then later, his ravaged torso, unzipped pants, that terrible scarred manhood.

That's what fire does, Lacie. And it's going to do it to you. Reach out and touch the fire.

And me, sitting up all night scared, carving my name in the log cabin wall.

I pulled the bed aside. The carving was still there. Next to it were three freshly gouged words: *Skyla was here.*

Chapter Thirty-seven

Let's finish our work," Logan said, laying his warm hands on my shoulders. "The ride home, Lacie. Close your eyes and feel that last long ride home. The smells. The sounds."

His hands touched my face, his voice filled my ear, my fear dropped away, and I remembered.

I spoke fast as my memory opened up, spilling images. I told Logan how our Cadillac whizzed down the road, carrying me home. I remembered the rich smell of new car leather, the feel of it against my summer-bare skin, the glowing radio light and the sad violin, the rumble of heavy tires rolling over smooth asphalt, and the speedometer tipping up to eighty.

My father liked to drive fast with all the windows down. On that balmy summer night, I stuck my head and hands out the window. I remembered the night air rushing against my face, pressing my eyes closed like a puppy's, whipping my long hair back, a red-gold jet stream in the dark. My skin tingled. I felt young and free and happy, until I saw the bright headlights in back of us, the white sedan riding up fast and hard, tapping our bumper.

Lacie? Get back inside. My father took a hand off the steering wheel and tugged at me.

The sedan tapped us again. A gunshot cracked the night. The Cadillac jerked to the right, out of control. We rocketed over the soft shoulder, down the embankment, and straight ahead into the glade. We hit the tree. Metal ripped, glass shattered, my father's head cracked against the steering wheel, my head slammed into the dash. Stunned and scared, I turned and saw headlights up on the rim of the road. My father was slumped over the steering wheel, moaning. I shook him and begged him to wake up.

I looked behind us again and saw a man running down the slope, carrying big cans in each hand. He started at the rear of the

Cadillac, dumping liquid over the trunk, then he yanked the back door open and soaked the seat. Gasoline fumes choked me. He drenched my father, tossed the empty can in, then picked up a full one and tossed it in the backseat. My father came to. He was pinned under the crumpled dash. Trapped.

Sweet dreams, Lacie, the man outside whispered, pale-faced and grinning.

He lit a match, tossed it in on my father, and ran.

My father's white lab coat went up in flames. He slapped at them, but his arms ignited, then his legs, then his shoulders. My father was screaming now, great whelping howls, an animal in agony. I reached into the fire, wanting to pull him free, wanting to save him. The flames drafted up, engulfing his face, consuming him, searing flesh from bone as I was suddenly yanked out and carried away.

He pulled me out. The man with the pale grinning face. Beane pulled me out and used his own body to kill the fire on mine. He rolled me, beat at the flames, sealed his lips over my mouth and breathed life into my smoke-filled lungs. When the burning stopped, he carried me a good distance away, and lay me down in the cool summer grass under old elm trees. I looked up. His face was right over mine, lips curled up in a smile. His breath was sickly sweet and he said:

Lacie, you reached out. You touched the fire and lived. You are blessed with life.

He crossed my hands over my chest and kissed my cheeks.

I saved you, Lacie. I saved you because I love you. I'll be watching you. I'll always be there, even if you don't see me. I'll come for you one day. You'll be my bride. You're blessed, Lacie. Don't ever forget that. You're blessed.

He ran off. An engine jumped, tires churned gravel, he roared off into the night.

I lay in the deep wooded gully, staring at tree leaves fluttering in the light summer breeze and the white moon floating high. I heard the endless blare of the Cadillac's horn and knew it was the weight of my father's dead body pressing it. Fire roiled up and caught on the trees, birds scattered, and then the blaring horn stopped. The faint sound of sirens came next. They were too late for my father. Shock wore off and I finally blacked out.

My eyes opened later in the hospital when the doctors were lifting me onto a gurney, wrapping and masking me, sliding tubes into my arms and racing me down the hall. I watched the IV dripping life, and felt the stunning pain where my wrists ended and my new life began.

Blessed? I thought not and closed my eyes.

"I didn't tell anyone," I said to Logan. "I thought I dreamed him."

Chapter Thirty-eight

W e left Lone Pine at dusk. Jack drove slowly. Branches were Beane's bony-fingered hands reaching for me. Every slap and scratch sent me shrinking away from the window. The night pressed in as dark as my own memory had been. How blessed the tight black vault of impenetrable memory suddenly seemed. I wanted to forget what I now knew, wipe the terrible pictures from my mind.

Was Beane an avenging angel? Was fire the flame of justice? Was Skyla the price for saving me? Or was my father the price for someone else? Why not me? Why didn't Beane just take me?

We dropped Logan at the cabin and waited until he and the dog were inside. He appeared at the window, palms pressed against cold glass, head cocked, listening to our departure.

Jack drove tirelessly through the storm, high beams shooting small holes of light into a world gone white. Highway signs flipped by. We were heading for Boston, to Harvard, the one and only clear link between Beane and my father. Hours later, city lights appeared and soon we were on the road out to Cambridge, the river silent and empty on our right, an obsidian streak cutting between two white banks.

There were no rowers now, not after midnight, not in the snow. I missed the sight of them, the steady tireless pace of them, and wanted the simplicity and purity of their thoughts for my own. To just row, stroke after stroke, to not think ahead, to not think back, to be so wonderfully lodged in the present, in the here and now, warm with the good work of honest exertion, not cold with fear, mixing up dreams and reality.

A motel vacancy sign winked green in the night. We pulled up and took a room for the few remaining hours until morning. The Eagle Mountain Inn had none of the grace the name implied. Tired furniture and dingy drapes. A push-button lock on a flimsy door. I thought of Beane with his size-ten shoe. One well-placed kick and he could walk right in.

Jack saw it too. He wedged a chair between the wall and door and pulled the drapes. I showered alone, soaping myself with the tiny motel bar, scrubbing with a cheap square of washcloth that was rough against my skin, wishing memories could be washed away.

Jerry engulfed in flame. The white fire roiling. Beane's timeless promise of death by fire.

They say you don't know what alive is until you fear being dead.

I wanted to feel alive and Jack could do that. Hungry for all the time we had never had and for the future that might not be ours, I walked out into the room. He was sitting on the edge of the bed unlacing his boots, pulling them off.

"Jack?"

He looked up surprised to see me without a towel and soaking wet.

He rose, lifted the wet mass of my hair off my face, tasted my tears, and instantly understood. His body was warm and alive and very close to mine. We moved back to the bed, stripping off his clothes. He caressed the small of my back, rounded my hips, parted my thighs and stroked. His free hand traveled up to my breasts, my throat, my face, sweeping my eyes closed, urging me to focus on feeling. My right leg traveled up along his left, he eased me down, then just as I wished it, Jack was there inside. I wrapped my legs around his waist, inviting him deeper.

The night hours were ours and ours alone. Edward Beane, I swore, would never have those.

Chapter Thirty-nine

There was a moment like this each morning, when he woke feeling whole. His hands traveled down before his eyes opened, reaching for the heat, wanting to touch himself, to jerk himself calm, to grab and rub and slap his hunger away.

But his hands rarely made the trip down without skating over torso along the way. The feel of it was enough to shock him fully awake, to scare him conscious, and dampen all erotic charges. They touched torso now.

His eyes blinked open. The first watery light of day turned the sky the color of steel. His body was cramped and stiff from sleeping in the front seat of the van. Hoping the nightmare was not a memory, hoping he was waking up whole, he looked.

He was a freak, half-eaten by fire. His torso was twisted and cratered, his scarred penis limp and soft. He fingered it. How could he be hard when he was a burned man, a ruined man, a man no woman would want to touch? Not so! he admonished himself.

Lacie would want him, he swore, slapping the soft thing hard. Lacie would love him well.

Chapter Forty

Jack's cell phone rang at dawn. He sat up and answered.

"There are only so many places left to go," Beane gloated. "You're running out of havens, harbors, and homes. All your worlds are going up in flames. But Jack is nimble, Jack is quick! You've moved off the board, out of my sight. You can't stay hidden for long. You have to travel to learn the truth you want to know. So where to now? Where are you taking the lovely Lacie next on your single-minded quest?"

"We've found the truth, Beane," Jack said.

"Beane. Very good. I'm impressed. Jack and the Beane Stalk. I've always known you'd excel in this game. You're the finder of truths; you've found my name! But is the name a name or simply a rhyme? My name changes like the weather, one day this, the next day that. I was Beane once and now I'm someone else. There have been many other names and faces in between."

"You're not as invisible as you think. People remember you in Raleigh, Asheville, Norfolk, and Knoxville."

"Yes! I was always there, right next to Lacie in a clever disguise. I never looked the same twice. It's so easy to hide who you really are. I've spent a lifetime practicing. People are gullible. If you have gray hair, they think you're old. People take you at face value. Cover your burns and they think you're whole. Lacie knows that.

"So search all you want, my good tall fed, comb through the federal databases, the phone book, city hall. You'll find plenty of Beanes, but not one of them will be me. Follow the Beane trail back in time, follow it all you like. It leads to one place and one place only. The Edward Beane trail stops cold at a wall of fire."

"What is it you want?" Jack asked.

"You've got it all wrong. What does *Lacie* want? You'll soon know the answer to that riddle. Until then, love her for me, Jack.

Love her hard, love her well, make her come, and when you're done, tell her I have something she wants."

Beane cut the connection. Jack put the phone down, wrapped his body around mine, and spoke softly, but all I heard was the echo of Beane's last cryptic words.

Tell her I have something she wants.

It was a double entendre, an erotic threat and teasing promise at the same time. There was only one thing I wanted and Beane couldn't undo what he had already done. I lay with Jack for a while longer, but the spell was broken. The sun had risen and Beane had stepped in to claim our day.

We got coffee out of a lobby vending machine and went back to the room.

"Beane's job application," Jack said, opening the file. "He graduated from Harvard Med School in 1974 and was finishing the first year of his residency when he wrote this application. There's an eloquent statement here explaining why he wanted to work at the camp. Lots of flowery stuff about the fulfillment of helping children.

"He went to Lone Pine for an interview with the director. She filed her notes from that meeting: *Edward Beane is a bright young man. I consider the camp fortunate to have such a high-caliber physician for the summer.* She had a point. No Harvard med students I ever heard of wanted to take time off from residency to go patch scraped knees at a summer camp."

"Why did Beane want to?"

"Because he needed access to an individual or individuals he knew would be there."

"He went to Lone Pine to be next to me."

"And Linda."

"So the obvious question is, what did Linda Severino and I have in common?"

"Besides the camp."

"Nothing. I never met or saw her again."

"Harvard will have more information on him." Jack checked his watch. "Admissions is open now. Let's go."

Robin sat at her desk sipping Starbuck's coffee and picking at a bagel. Same snug jeans, but the tiny shrunken Harvard T-shirt was green this time. Her face lit up when Jack walked in.

"Well, well," she said. "The secret agent is back. What are you looking for now? Something more exciting than an old doctor, I hope."

"A young doctor this time."

"Plenty of those around here. My mother always said the best place to meet eligible young doctors is to work with eligible young doctors."

"Was she right?"

"Numerically speaking, yes. There are hundreds of them running around. Problem is, not a single one has asked me out."

"Maybe you should do the asking."

"Not my style, Agent Stein."

"You seem aggressive enough."

"Strictly passive-aggressive, that's the problem." She smiled sweetly and swiveled around to her computer. "Who are you looking for?"

"Beane. Edward Beane. Class of '74."

She typed in his name. "Wow. Graduated with honors. Wow again. Your young doctor was some kind of genius. Killer test scores. His academic record was just as stellar. And, he paid tuition with cashier's checks. I could never do that. He must've come from a good family."

"What else do you have?"

Robin scrolled down and paused. "Huh. This is weird. Med School keeps track on where grads do their residencies and where they go practice after that. One year into his residency, Edward Beane quit. Never took his boards or anything. He's got an M.D. degree, but he never bothered to get licensed."

"Or, Harvard Alum just missed it," Jack said. "If he ever did get licensed, the American Medical Association will know."

"I'll get the number for you."

Jack made the call and paced as he talked.

I considered Beane's brilliant mind, all the wasted potential. The line between genius and madness can be razor thin. Were monsters born or created? And what about Beane?

"The record is right," Jack said, when the call was finished. "Edward Beane, Harvard class of 1974, isn't a licensed doctor. He never moved to another hospital, not after leaving his residency." Jack looked at Robin. "Where did he do his residency?"

"Right here in Boston," she said, blinking at the computer screen; "ten minutes away, at Mass General with Dr. Francis Fleming, head of the burn ward. Your young doctor worked in Fleming's farm."

"What was he farming?"

"Skin, Agent Stein. Human skin. The file here has hyper-links to a clipping from the *Alumni News*." She clicked on the link and the clipping popped up. "Hard copy?"

Jack said yes.

She hit print and passed him the page.

A black and white picture topped the article: Edward Beane doing the honors at a ribbon-cutting ceremony. A white-coated doctor looked on.

> *Dr. Francis Fleming Unveils New Burn Research Center at MGH.*
> "It is a momentous day," Dr. Francis Fleming said this morning at the official opening of the MGH Burn Trauma Research Center. "Thanks to our generous patrons, we now have a state-of-the-art lab and a high-caliber staff to run it. With brilliant young doctors like Edward Beane, we look forward to making great strides in the treatment of critically burned men, women, and children."

"Did Beane publish any articles from his research?" Jack asked.

"Let's find out." Robin worked the keyboard and printed out a stack of articles. "Five hits, layered by date, oldest first." She gave them to Jack.

"Beane wanted to create a *universal dermis*," Jack said when he finished reading. "The goal was and still is to manufacture a readily available permanent skin replacement."

"What about skin bank dermis and artificial skin?" Robin asked. "Aren't they permanent?"

"No," Jack said. "The body rejects both in just a few weeks' time."

"Then why use them at all?"

"To keep the patient whole while the places destroyed by fire are rebuilt, a little at a time, by grafting with the patient's own healthy skin. The burn victim must suffer through dozens of operations as the rejected bank and artificial dermis is replaced with fresh patches. Soon those too will be rejected and the whole process started all over again."

"The skin grafts are permanent," Robin said.

"Yes, but they leave severe scars and work only when the burn victim has enough healthy skin left to graft from. Most critically burned patients don't."

"Then what?"

"A tiny piece of unburned skin is harvested and grown in a laboratory skin farm. The human body will only accept its own skin."

All those squares of donor flesh, I thought, that could make a burned man whole again. I have seen it in great sheets, frozen like bacon, the color of Band-Aids and twice as thin. I have seen farmed skin too, eight-by-six-inch squares grown from pieces of skin the size of seeds.

As I listened to Jack go on, I couldn't help but be impressed with Beane's vision.

He dreamed of a raceless, genderless skin genetically adapted for each recipient: farmed living tissue that would be permanently accepted by all bodies. His dermis would enable doctors to rebuild critically burned patients immediately, without destroying what was left of their own unburned flesh. Burn victims would be spared the savage graft scars like mine, the countless agonizing operations.

Beane's dream dermis. To rebuild whom? Himself? Someone else?

His papers included pictures of the practical application of his prototypes. Shaved dogs, nude mice, bare rats, bald monkeys, the occasional hairless cat—all patched up, stitched up, puffed up with samples of his universal living skin.

"No creature escaped Beane's testing," Jack observed.

"Including people?" I asked. "Is that why he didn't finish his residency?"

"Could be. Unauthorized testing on humans would have been enough to get him tossed out and banned from practicing medicine. But there was nothing like that on record at the AMA. The doctor who caught Beane would have filed a complaint, and made sure Beane would never get licensed in this state or any other."

"Not if that doctor had something to protect."

"Like a new research facility, grant money, trustee money, and his own reputation?"

"Exactly."

"The prodigy turned prodigal son." Jack turned back to Robin. "What does your computer tell you about Dr. Fleming?"

She punched the name in. "This is your lucky day, Agent Stein. Fleming still runs the burn unit at Mass General."

*   *   *

A half hour later, we stepped off the elevator on the thirteenth floor of the Bigelow Building in the hospital complex and walked into the burn ward, the very white world I had never wanted to see again.

Doors were wide open on both sides of the long hall. As we passed, I couldn't help looking inside. Four beds to a room and a computer screen suspended over each, blinking with heart rates, blood pressures, body temperatures; vital signs of fragile lives. IV's dripped. Machines pumped air into smoke-ruined lungs.

These fire victims were much worse off than I had been. After all, fire took just my hands. But this was the critical care wing of the burn ward, and the patients in it were the badly burned, the mostly burned, the burned up, the burned out, the barely alive, all wrapped from head to toe in yards of white gauze. I looked at the motionless white cocoons, and imagined torsos and legs and arms burned away as my hands had been, my pain multiplied by a thousand.

We passed the children's ward next. I paused at the open door. Eight beds instead of four, each with a tiny cocoon. It devastated me to look at the silent prone children, wrapped and waiting for their own strange spring to come. They wouldn't emerge as butterflies. Their new bodies would be patched red and raw, terrible to behold. There were no cartoon animals on the walls, no brightly painted colors, nothing at all. These young patients didn't know what was around them or that they were even still alive.

Jack led me down the hall to the nurses' station. While he introduced himself and asked for Dr. Fleming, I watched the tank room across the way.

A large steel bathtub was tilted up so water ran easily from head to foot. The tub was occupied by a badly burned man. A young nurse eased him from side to side, moving a hand-held shower head over his body, rinsing off burned dead skin and washing it down the drain. She tried to be gentle with the black-charred white man, but I saw the glint of his teeth when he grimaced, his back stiffening and arching up, fists curling tight at his sides. He cried out once, a piercing animal shriek. I turned away.

"Where's Fleming?" I asked Jack.

"In there," he said grimly, pointing to a patient's room.

There were no doctors inside, only bandaged victims.

"I don't understand," I said, looking.

"Second bed on the right. He came in last week."

It hit me. The doctor was now the patient, wrapped in one of his own white tombs. Beane, I thought. Beane had put him there.

Jack steered me out. He understood how afraid I was of waking up in one of those cocoons, or worse still, of dying in one and never waking up at all.

Walking across the hospital parking lot, I wondered what wrong Beane was trying to right the night he burned my father. Then, I thought of my father and how little I really knew of him. He was fixed in my memory in a thousand snapshots, patiently listening or teaching me. He knew all of my hopes, dreams, ambitions, and disappointments, such as they were at age ten. I knew nothing of his. I knew nothing of Richard Wagner, the scientist. He was always the gentle blue-eyed man whom some called doctor and I called Dad.

I thought of his commitment to research. Had he, like Beane, committed a terrible wrong in the name of science? And if so, how was it tied to Beane? My father explored the human brain, Beane invented skin. Brains and skin, a decade apart. And fire? There was no logical connection, none at all.

"So Beane gets thrown out of his residency," Jack mused, "and shows up next at your summer camp."

"Assuming Fleming did kick him out," I said, "why did Beane wait all these years to get his revenge?"

"Same reason he waited to come after you. A psychic break, some kind of new stressor that's pushed him over the edge. He's suicidal now and wants to clear the deck before he dies. He's going after every person he perceives has wronged him."

"My father ended his research a full decade before Beane started his, and their areas of expertise were entirely unrelated. How can they possibly be connected?"

"There's only one answer." Jack opened his backpack and pulled out the photograph of my father standing with a stranger in the snow, behind the man and woman in white lab coats, two children lined up properly in front. My father's precise handwriting on the back noted the year: *Durand, New Year's Day, 1960.*

"According to his admission files," Jack said, "Edward Beane was twenty-two in 1970. He would have been twelve years old in 1960." He flipped the picture over. The boy wore heavy black-rimmed glasses and his light hair was shaved down in a crew cut.

Preadolescent fat blurred his features. The lips were narrow, and the forehead high. It was not obvious, but it was possible.

"Durand is a French name," Jack said. "Durand was French, and Edward Beane is his son."

"Beane spoke to me of *righting a wrong*," I replied, excited. "The wrong was his father. Something happened to Durand."

"If the man in the lab coat is Beane's father, and the man behind him is your father, then there's only one person the last man could be," Jack said, pointing.

"Linda Severino's father."

"Yes. And he's the only one who can tell us what happened. We have to get to him before Beane does. Jeff Hoag will know where he is. Call him."

I did. We were lucky. Jeff was home and anxious to see me, face-to-face.

Chapter Forty-one

We flew to Washington on the shuttle, and used Steven Stiller's American Express card to rent a four-wheel-drive Cherokee. Midday traffic on the expressway was light. We were soon cutting across metropolitan D.C. and passing the white dome of Capitol Hill.

The sights were familiar, yet I felt like a stranger. My face was no longer on the big WRC billboards, and I had no house to go home to. Everything I owned was packed in a small bag in the backseat, and suddenly I could not imagine life without Jack, a man I had known for less than two weeks. I could not see beyond the present, and the present was now narrowed down to an hour-by-hour existence. The night hours with Jack were heaven. The daylight hours thinking about Beane were hell.

We pulled up in front of a three-story colonial building on a quiet side street in Georgetown, not far from the burned-out shell of my house. The front door was painted glossy white and worked on a buzzer system. I pressed the button marked 3B. Jeff's voice came scratching through the little speaker. "Ms. Wagner?"

"Yes," I said.

Jack pushed the door open and followed me into the lobby. A tiny fake Christmas tree sat on a low coffee table. Silver tinsel and bright blue balls looked garish under fluorescent ceiling lights. Jack passed the elevator and opened the stairwell door. We climbed three flights up, pushed through another door, and found Jeff Hoag waiting in the hall.

He was a short stocky man with a boyish face and light blond hair buzzed down military-style. His ears stuck out enough to look comical, but there was nothing funny about his eyes. They were red and swollen, and ringed with dark circles from sleepless nights. He wore a dark green U.S. Navy sweatshirt, baggy sweatpants, and heavy wool socks. A sleeping baby girl in a pink snowsuit lay slack on his shoulder.

"I'm Jeff," he said simply, waving us in.

The living room was sparsely furnished. Wood floors, no rugs. New blue sofa. A glass coffee table cluttered with a phone, answering machine, framed pictures, and baby bottles. Playpen full of furry creatures. Moving cartons were stacked three-high against the walls.

Jack drifted to the window, checking the street, the car, the sidewalk.

"I just got back from a week in Tuscon," Jeff said, flopping down on the sofa, stroking his baby's silky blond hair. "Took Kristy to see my folks for Christmas. Didn't check the answering machine while I was gone, so I didn't get your messages."

"Are you moving out?" I asked, looking around.

"Sorry about the boxes," he said. "We moved in right before Linda left for the Bering Sea. Haven't felt like unpacking. Shit. I haven't felt like doing anything since she died. I just keep thinking about how it must've been for her in that freezing water. Was she scared? Did it take a long time to die? Is that why she took her flight suit off? So she would die faster?" He rubbed his eyes. "Friends keep telling me it'll get better."

"They're wrong," Jack said. "It doesn't. You just learn to live with it."

"Who are you?" Jeff focused on Jack for the first time.

"Jack Stein with the FBI. I'm investigating the murder of Ms. Wagner's daughter."

Jeff turned to me. "I'm sorry. I forgot you lost someone too."

"I'm not here as a reporter," I said. "We think there's some connection between Linda's death and my daughter's."

Jeff whistled softly. "How can I help?"

"The last time we talked you said you had some crazy theories about why Linda jumped."

"Yeah. Crazy's an understatement. A couple of months before she went out to sea, she changed. All of a sudden, she was afraid of everything. Afraid to answer the phone, afraid to go out, afraid to stay in. It wasn't right. Linda was basically fearless. And those nightmares I told you about? She was getting them every night. Her nerves were shot. She finally admitted it was more than the nightmares. She said she was getting strange phone calls."

"Define strange," Jack said.

"Linda swore she heard the voice from her dreams talking to her for real."

"Did you ever hear the voice?" Jack asked.

"No. It always happened when I wasn't around. She said she couldn't tape the voice because she got the calls in weird places. The gym, a restaurant, a grocery store."

"Did you believe her?" I asked.

"Not for a second. I thought she was imagining it. Other than saying she was getting the phone calls, she wouldn't talk about it. Wouldn't tell me what the guy said or what the calls were about. Whenever I pushed her, she just clammed up.

"Then she was offered the chance to teach in a special training mission. That's what they were doing out there in the Bering Sea out of season—practicing tactical moves in a place where no one would see them doing it. Linda said she wanted to go. She took leave when she had the baby and tried to stay home afterward like a regular mom, but I knew she missed flying.

"I thought that was the reason she was acting so strange. I figured all she could think about was the big blue sky out there, of jamming through it in a three-million-dollar fighter plane. I knew she had to finish it, get it out of her system, and then she'd be okay. I thought Linda went because teaching new Navy pilots all her tactical wartime tricks was her idea of heaven. I was wrong. I know that now. Linda went because she was scared to stay here."

Jeff shifted the baby, patted her back.

"Anyway," he continued, "I fly commercial so it's easy for me to look after Kristy. American Airlines calls me out on two- or three-day runs. My sister Andrea stays over then. Way it works, I end up being home most of the month.

"I was out on a three-day trip the day Linda died. My sister was here. The super showed up and told her she had to leave the building for twenty-four hours. They were doing heavy-duty extermination. He said there was a health concern for babies. Andrea took Kristy over to her boyfriend's house for the night. Next thing you know, Linda calls here. The machine recorded two messages."

"What kind of messages did she leave?" Jack asked.

"You tell me. I saved them. Listen to this."

Jeff dropped a microcassette into the answering machine and hit play.

"Jeff? Andrea? Are you there? Please pick up! Please!"

The tape played back the click of a receiver being picked up, then the machine shut off, as if someone did not want the conversation recorded.

"I wasn't here," Jeff explained. "Andrea wasn't here. But someone answered the phone. The second call came in four hours after that, two hours before the plane went down." He punched play.

Linda's sobbing voice filled the room. "Pick up, goddamn you. I know you're there. Pick up the phone! You son of a bitch. You mother fucking son of a bitch. You win. I did it. Now get out. Leave my baby alone. Get the fuck out. Just get the fuck out of my life and leave my baby alone." There was a soft click of the phone being picked up and the sound of the machine being shut off.

Jeff stopped the tape.

"Who else have you played this for?" I asked.

"No one."

"Why?"

"Because it proves Linda did it. It proves she rigged the plane. And it sure as hell proves she was whacked out. Crazy. Lunatic fucking crazy, just like the tabloids say."

"Despite this tape, you don't believe that."

"No, Ms. Wagner. Someone was in here. You heard it yourself. I believe Linda now about those weird phone calls. I'm just sorry I didn't take her seriously back then. I wouldn't tell this to any other reporter, but you're different. I thought you might understand."

Jeff Hoag had no idea how well I understood.

"Linda loved flying more than she loved me," he explained. "And the only thing she loved more than flying was Kristy. I think whoever scared her here, got to her out there."

What's real? What's not? That was Beane's game. A manipulator of minds. I picked up a framed picture. Linda on the flight deck, swaggering and proud, swinging her helmet at her side, grinning ear to ear, sunglasses glinting in the sun, blond hair rippling in the wind. She looked strong-willed and confident. I looked at her sleeping baby. *Why?* I thought. *Why our children?* Beane had threatened to kill her daughter and he had succeeded in killing mine.

Jack showed Jeff the Durand snapshot. "Do you recognize anyone?"

"Sure. The man on the right, in the dark suit. He's real young there, but that's Linda's dad."

"Where can we find him?" Jack asked, urgent, ready.

"This is so weird," Jeff said, blinking. "You're the second person this week to ask me that."

"The second?"

"Yeah. A guy called yesterday. Said he was an old friend of the family. Just got back in town, heard about Linda's death. Wanted to know where he could find Mr. Severino so he could offer his condolences in person."

"You told him?"

"Sure. Ordinarily, I wouldn't have."

"Why?"

"Linda's dad's got some crazy ideas about privacy. We weren't supposed to tell anyone where he lived. He said he was hiding."

"From what?" Jack asked.

"Hell, I don't know. He never said. He cooked this whole thing up right after his car accident."

"Was Linda in the car that night?" I asked.

"No, thank God. Her dad lost control. Sixty miles an hour, right into a cement wall. The gas tank blew and a monster fire broke out. He got fried. Totally fried. John Severino was and is a proud man. If you ask me, I don't think anyone was ever after him. I think he just couldn't stand the idea of people seeing him as an invalid, all scarred up and pretty much useless. So he made up this jerky story about being hunted. Salvages his pride and makes him feel important all at the same time."

"Where does he live?"

"Out in the boonies in Virginia. He bought an old horse farm. It's falling down around him, but he doesn't care. He says he feels safe out there. Never leaves the place. Hell, the old man wouldn't even go to Linda's funeral. When I asked him why, he said: *Because I'm scared.*" Jeff laughed softly and patted Kristy on the back. "When I asked him what he was scared of, he broke down crying and said: *Why didn't he kill me instead?* I think the old man's lost it. I think somewhere along the line he went completely fucking crazy. Hell, what do I know? Maybe Linda did too, for that matter. Maybe the tabloids are right. Maybe she just fucking lost it out there."

Chapter Forty-two

W̶e left Georgetown at dusk, one in a stream of cars inching across the Key Bridge into Virginia.

John Severino's cleverly chosen retreat was two hours out, in sparsely populated countryside. A small sign identified the property as *Higgin's Horse Farm. Training and Breeding.* Jeff had not exaggerated. It was falling down. Long rows of stables stretching across the fields were roofless sagging shells, and the jumping courses were nothing more than rotted wood posts dotting the land. A large two-level crumbling house faced the horse fields. Two first-floor windows glowed yellow. The rest of the house was dark.

We eased up the long unplowed drive and parked behind an old van. A wheelchair ramp ran up one side of the front steps. The acrid smell of fireplace smoke drifted on a breeze. Frigid night air stung my lips. Jack rang the bell. A peephole scraped open. Jack held up his shield.

"Federal agent. I need to speak with John Severino."

The peephole scraped shut, a bolt snapped back, and the door swung open.

A huge old black man in overalls and slippers faced us. He had broad shoulders, thick arms, and a double-barrel shotgun aimed at Jack.

"Come on in, mister, slow and easy, keeping your hands up neatly, where I can see them. Same for the young miss there. Kick the door shut with your foot."

"Jimmy?" a voice rasped from the adjoining room. "What's going on?"

"Fellow claims he's FBI, sir. I'm holding him in my sight. He's got a lady with him."

"Mr. Severino?" I called out. "Lacie Wagner, Richard Wagner's daughter."

"Wagner?" the rasping voice repeated, incredulously. "Let me see her!"

Jimmy jerked his head and followed us in, keeping the rifle aimed at Jack. We walked into what was once the living room. Now it was a hospital room, cluttered with swiveling bedside tray tables and the requisite institutional bed cranked up to a sitting position. Heavy drapes were drawn. A fire burned brightly in the hearth.

I walked on the rim of the room farthest from the fire, eyes riveted on John Severino. I never would have guessed he was the same man in the snapshot. Twenty-five years of paralysis had turned him into an oversized cartoon head on a stickpin body. Most of his hair had been burned away. The little that was left was wiry and gray. Old burn scars mottled his face. His caved-in cheeks looked cadaverous, as if death were close, but then I saw his eyes, piercing green and bright with life.

"They're okay, Jimmy," he announced. The rifle nose dipped. Jimmy backed off. "Sit down," he sputtered, darting eyes directing us to two chairs at his bedside.

Jack took his parka off. The room was overly warm, but I kept mine on. This was the last stop for us, and I felt cold and afraid.

"How did you find me?" Severino croaked.

"Jeff Hoag gave us your address," Jack replied.

"Jeff Hoag is an idiot," Severino spat. "A military man should obey orders. Hoag does not obey his orders. The last man Hoag gave my address to came here to kill me."

"Was his name Edward Beane?" I asked.

"Beane!" Severino exclaimed. "Then you know the story."

"No, sir. I'm learning it bit by bit."

Jack leaned in and showed Severino the old photo. "Is this you?"

"Yes," he said sadly. "That's me when I was young and ablebodied and stupid."

"Stupid?" Jack asked.

"Stupid. I've paid for my stupidity. Unfortunately, so has Richard. We've all paid for our stupid greed, for feeling inviolate and invincible, for thinking we were giants walking among mere mortals, for believing our commitment to science was more important than life itself. How wrong we were. How terribly wrong we all were."

"Who's he?" Jack asked, pointing to the man we guessed was Beane's father.

"Brilliancy gone mad. There's nothing more to be said." Severino closed his eyes.

"Mr. Severino," I said gently, "Edward Beane wants me dead."

He opened his eyes. "Yes. Beane's a killer, and your father and I made him that way."

"Why?"

"Does it matter?"

"Very much."

He was quiet for so long, I thought he would never speak. A log in the fireplace shifted. Then, he looked at me and started in. "To understand the story, young lady, you must know what took place between 1945 and 1965. The government funded countless numbers of top-secret research projects. A premium was placed on techno-medical research that could have military application. Most of those studies were morally repugnant, like the plutonium projects from 1945 and 1947. Do you know about those?"

"Of course," I replied. The files had recently been opened under the Freedom of Information Act and it had been a big news story. I remembered the footage of President Clinton standing in the Rose Garden, squinting in the sun, apologizing on behalf of the government for things that had happened fifty years before. "Cancer patients were injected with plutonium, without their consent or knowledge. The purpose of the study was to learn how cancer reacted to radiation."

"Oh," Severino cried, "the goals were lofty and the intentions good! But people have a right to be informed and the right to choose such deadly experimental treatments. The desire to learn does not outweigh the obligation to inform. But the government didn't care. Those cancer patients were going to die anyway. So what if we hurried them to their graves? It was done in the name of *research*."

"The government didn't work alone," Jack pointed out.

"True," Severino said. "The academic world was a willing and able partner in many of those dirty deeds. In the fifties, for example, Harvard University supervised a secret federally funded project in which mentally retarded children were fed oatmeal laced with radioactive milk at school. They were injected with radioactive calcium and iron too. The parents were never informed. The purpose of the study? To find out if and how the body metabolizes radioactivity. Again, lofty medical goals, all done in the name of research."

"Those studies," I said, "were conducted under the auspices of the Atomic Energy Commission. The files have been made public and the government has been forced to admit its wrongdoing."

"Right, young lady. But the Atomic Energy Commission experiments are child's play compared to what the Pentagon did, and those projects will never be made public! Anyone who tries to find out will be stopped."

The speech exhausted Severino. He fell silent. His eyelids fluttered closed. Beads of sweat dotted his forehead and his breathing sounded labored. A ticking clock counted the seconds. We waited through thirty ticks for Severino to speak again.

"I'm sorry," he mumbled. "I feel so tired sometimes."

"What did my father do?" I asked.

"Richard?" Severino laughed bitterly. "It's what I did to him. I ruined him, broke him, destroyed everything he lived for. Dr. Richard Wagner would have stayed at Harvard for the rest of his natural life, working happily on legitimate controlled experiments. He was a man of great conscience. Unauthorized testing repulsed him. Human rights were more important than the scientific desire to learn—until I came along and dangled the carrot.

"Long before I ran for public office, when I was a high-ranking officer in the Department of Defense, I worked on a special task group assigned to stay abreast of radical medical advances that could have military application. In the postwar years, Europe was full of scientists with great ideas and no way to fund them.

"One man in particular found his way to us. He was a brilliant French neurologist working in unthinkably poor conditions. Basic lab equipment was antiquated and in disrepair. He needed money, equipment, assistants. He needed someone to believe and support his theories. He needed America.

"One night, he appeared at the Paris apartment of an American intelligence agent, begging for safe transport to the U.S. and government support. It was much to arrange on short notice, but he was persuasive, desperate, and ready. He had already cleared out his lab and stuffed his research into five battered suitcases. His family was waiting on the sidewalk. A wife who was also a doctor, a son, and a little daughter. They were delivered to me in Washington."

Severino's eyes fluttered closed again. His jaw dropped open and he began to snore. The man called Jimmy shuffled in and checked Severino's pulse.

"The visit's worn him some," Jimmy said. "Give him a bit, then you can talk to him again."

Jack and I sat side by side, willing Severino to wake up. I wondered why Beane had let Severino live and why he wanted the old man dead to begin with.

Severino snapped awake and talked as if he had never drifted off. His eloquence and clear train of thought reminded me of Voss—two great minds trapped in useless failing bodies.

"The Frenchman was decades ahead of everyone," Severino explained. "He envisioned things we are only just starting to hear about today. I admit, his work was crude and far from perfect, but his concepts were stunning. There were promising applications for the military and even greater possibilities for the betterment of mankind. He was a gifted man."

"Durand," Jack said. "He was a man named Durand."

"Philip Durand," Severino confirmed. "He had ideas for electrical adjuncts that could manipulate brain waves. He had designs for microchips thirty years before Bill Gates ever set up shop in his garage. He promised I would live to see the day when we cured Parkinson's disease and Alzheimer's with electrical chips placed in the brain. Durand walked the rim, the furthermost edge of scientific thought. I needed the help of someone as brilliant as Durand to follow his research, to understand it, and to guide it for military application. I called on Richard Wagner."

"How did you find my father?" I asked.

"It was easy. He was one of the brightest, most respected brain researchers in the country. Young, enthusiastic, open to new possibilities. I took Durand to see him at Harvard. They shared many of the same theories. He and your father had an instant rapport. It didn't take much to convince Richard to work with us. Durand's enthusiasm was contagious.

"I moved Durand to a remote compound up in the woods in the north of Maine. It was federal land, with power and water paid for by the government. Richard helped him build an elaborate lab with the most modern equipment. Then, we had to supply Durand with subjects. Your father objected to the plan. I pushed him into it."

"Who were the subjects?" Jack asked.

"Children," Severino sighed. "I reached into orphanages across the country and took twenty-one young children ages three to five. They were hopeless unadoptable children with terrible birth defects, but every one of them had a healthy young brain. I gathered those twenty-one young healthy human brains in their deformed young bodies and handed them over to Durand and Richard. It was a living brain farm.

"The children were divided up into several areas of research. Some were induced with brain tumors. The ability to study a tumor from the onset and to experiment freely with innovative treatments was an indescribable scientific liberation. Some children were used for pharmacological experiments. Others still for electromagnetic charting, and thereafter, as subjects for crude brain implants.

"When one child died, I brought in another. Twenty-one young brains to help take us into the twenty-first century. The children had no homes, no parents to miss them, and no futures to jeopardize. Furthermore, they wouldn't understand what was being done to them."

"My father agreed to this?" I asked, astounded.

"At first, Richard was outraged at the thought of using innocent children as guinea pigs, but he quickly calmed down. The project was too exciting. In those days, a living human brain was the most coveted yet most forbidden research tool. He couldn't resist.

"The first years went by splendidly. Durand seemed happy and productive. We, the government, lavished him with cash and equipment, anything he wanted. His family adapted well. His wife was happy to work with him. The daughter was six when they arrived, too young to care. And then there was the boy."

"Beane," Jack said, softly.

"Yes. He was twelve and as brilliant as his father. His name was Edouard, spelled the French way. He was already educated to the fourth-year university level in mathematics, science, and physics, and worked side by side with his father for the next four years. Richard took a liking to Edouard and gave him medical textbooks. The boy devoured them, asked for more. By the time he was sixteen, Edouard could have passed a medical school equivalency exam.

"Four years into the experiment, Philip and his son changed. Richard said they seemed to be turning against us, against America. We hoped it would pass, but it didn't. Philip grew secretive, refused Richard access to research data, and eventually locked him out of the compound. Maybe it was the isolation, too many years alone.

Philip became irrational, psychotic. I suspected he was testing chemical compounds on himself. We learned he had been quietly acquiring guns and ammunition with the money we sent him. Richard and I decided the time had come to shut the project down.

"On January first, 1965, we traveled to Maine with a small elite team of soldiers intending to scare Durand out. If that failed, we were going to take him out with force. Remember, this was three decades before Waco or the Freeman ranchers, before CNN and satellite TV. We had no one to answer to and the freedom to handle the situation as we saw fit.

"Durand had barricaded himself, his family, and the children inside. He was heavily armed. We went in at night so we could surround the compound without Durand knowing. Richard and I tried to talk him out. Durand refused. He ranted and raved about a U.S. conspiracy to take his research away from him. And then, he fired the first shot.

"Our team fired back, and lobbed a few grenades in to shake Durand up. The grenades did more than that. They hit the oil supply in the rear of the lab where Durand was hiding. The explosion was horrible. We just stood there, helpless, and watched the place burn. It burned all through the night. The soldiers went in at dawn and searched for human remains. A mass grave was dug. It was a frightful grave mostly filled with bits and pieces of children: mandibles, femurs, skulls, legs, arms, hands, feet, and torsos. We left the compound that night. The Durand *situation* was solved and the files were sealed. I kept one photograph to remind me of my mistake. It's there by the clock."

I picked it up. Philip Durand faced the camera with a proud smile on his face. His adopted children were lined up in neat rows in front of him. Some with fins for arms, some born without legs, some without any appendages at all, just torsos and heads, they were all bald and grinning, not knowing their healthy brains were Durand's property to harvest, mutate, and ultimately destroy as he saw fit.

I thought of my father's dedication to science, his hunger and burning ambition to understand the human brain. He was vulnerable. Lured by the promise of new knowledge and the potential of new discoveries, he allowed himself to step out of bounds, to forget right and wrong. I thought of the moral anguish that must have ripped his soul. Yes, it would have been Richard Wagner's greatest shame: children stolen by the government, brains practiced on at whim, and a mass grave filled with their broken burned bodies.

I put the picture down.

Severino went on.

"We didn't know that Edouard Durand survived the fire. He was in a different part of the compound when the lab exploded and raced back to try to save his family. He got his sister out, but it was too late for the others. They were flaming human scarecrows jerking wildly in the inferno. Edouard watched them dance and die, then he fled the compound on foot and disappeared into the woods."

"How could you possibly know what Edward Beane saw that night?" I asked.

"Simple, my dear. He told me himself. But I'm getting ahead of the story. Edouard knew those Maine woods well. He hiked and hunted in them for years. He had a secret shelter, stocked with supplies in anticipation of something his father called 'the Dead Time.' Durand had parceled some of his government funds out into a dozen different bank accounts using a dozen different phony names. And, he gave cash to Edouard to bury in the shelter.

"Edouard tended to his own wounds, nursed his sister in those cold long lonely hours, and made his plan. His mind was already poisoned against us by his father, then by watching us murder his family. Whether his sister lived or died, I don't know. He wouldn't say. I assume she died. Edouard Durand was sixteen years old. He was old enough to stay alive in the woods, hitchhike out, and lie his way into a new life.

"Why didn't he go after you and my father then? Why wait?"

"Beane found thinking about his revenge gratifying, exciting. He became obsessed with it. His was a madman's logic: If he killed us right away, what would he have left to live for? So he didn't. He kept tabs on us instead, knew when our daughters were born, what they were named, where we lived and what kind of soap we used to shower. He watched us even as he went on with his own life.

"He adopted the English spelling of his French first name, changed his last name to Beane, and faked a high school record. He sailed through four years at Boston University, excelling in math, economics, science, physics, and, of course, French. Then he went to Harvard Medical School and graduated. He dreamed of achieving medical glory, of making a name for himself, but he never finished his residency."

"He was like his father," Jack said. "He did unauthorized testing on live humans."

"Worse than that," Severino warned. "Beane created his own burn victims to work on. He bragged to me. Claimed he set fire to hobos, whores, vagrants—people no one would ever go looking for. He burned them and used their charred bodies to practice on."

"Francis Fleming found out," I said.

"Yes, but he foolishly did not have Beane arrested. Fleming feared for the reputation of his lab and burn ward. They made a deal. Fleming agreed to keep quiet if Beane quit his residency and never tried to get licensed anywhere else. Fleming had sworn testimony on file with his attorney, ready to go to the AMA if anything happened to him. Disappear or go to prison; Beane had no choice. Fleming held the trump card."

"And that enraged Beane," Jack said.

"Of course. His new anger fueled the old. He lied about his medical credentials to get on staff at Linda's summer camp as the resident doctor. It was a sheer accident that Richard Wagner's daughter was at the same camp, and the coincidence thrilled Beane.

"He relished the idea of being so close to our children and planning their deaths even as he put Band-Aids on their scrapes. Beane sought atonement for his family. He wanted Richard and me to suffer. Killing our children was better than killing us."

"But he took my father instead," I said.

"He said he changed his mind that night and decided to kill you both. He told me he followed your car, fired a shot at the rear tire, and forced it off the road, set it on fire. At the last minute, he pulled you free, Lacie. Only God and Edouard know why. Edouard wouldn't tell me and I haven't talked to God lately.

"He tried the same thing on me. I was alone in the car and should have died, but someone drove by in time to save me. Beane called once after my accident. He told me who he was and said he would come back one day to finish what he started. He swore I would burn to death one day. I went into hiding.

"He let me hide. I was half dead anyway. I tried to alert officials in the Pentagon. My warnings fell on deaf ears. They thought I was crazy. So I hid. The irony is, all those years I spent thinking he was coming after me, he was really following Lacie and Linda, planning for his final revenge. It was them he wanted, not me. Something set him off this spring and, suddenly, it was time. He put his plan into action. He got to Linda."

"Linda was in the middle of the Bering Sea," Jack said. "How could he get to her there?"

"The answer's right in front of you." Severino's eyes blinked at the bedside telephone. "Beane stood here and told me how easy it was to get Andrea and the baby out of the apartment. Then, he placed an emergency call to Linda at sea.

"He told Linda he had Kristy. His deal was this: a plane in exchange for Kristy's life. He wanted one plane to go down in a raging fireball over the Bering Sea that very night, and said he had ties with the military, ways of knowing if she did what he wanted. The plane or her child. Edouard left her no choice. Linda had nowhere to go for help. He said if he saw any police or federal agents sneaking around, he would kill the baby."

"Why didn't she go to her commanding officer?" I asked. "Why couldn't the Navy put out a false news bulletin? Buy her enough time to get help?"

"You're naïve," Severino sputtered. "It would have been next to impossible for Linda to convince the Navy to agree to a false dissemination of information, and she didn't have the luxury of time to try. When Beane disconnected, Linda's first move was to call her apartment. I'm sure she hoped to talk to Andrea or Jeff, find out it was a hoax and that Kristy was okay. But when she called her own home, Beane answered! At midnight, D.C. time! He was in her apartment and swore he had Kristy! He had a tape of a crying baby playing while he spoke!

"He got Linda with the one and only thing she would never risk losing—her child. If it had been me or her husband or even her own life, Linda would never have given in. But her child? The mother in her was far stronger than the soldier."

Knowing what Beane was doing to me, I guessed he had stalked her, terrorized and hunted her, then pushed her to the limit and broke her mind. I could hear Beane taunting Linda and I pictured her alone in her small stateroom with the phone in her hand, Beane's whispered threats bouncing off a satellite and going right into her ear. I imagined Linda's pretty face dead white in shock when her nightmare voice found her on the Great Bering Sea.

I imagined the words he used and the way he spoke them, his voice trilling and gloating as he spun his own utterly convincing version of reality. The ragged whisper, the raspy voice speaking the words every mother fears: *I have your baby.* Then, the ransom: *Do just as I say, Linda, and your baby won't die. Are you a solider or mother first? Where do your loyalties lie?* A deadline deal and no margin for error.

"So she rigged the plane," I said, understanding her logic, terror, her panic, her desperation. I would have done anything to save my daughter. Anything.

"Yes," Severino said. "I'm sure she thought the pilot would have time to eject, but something went wrong and he died. I'll never know for certain why she threw herself overboard. Perhaps she believed if she took herself out of the game, Kristy would be safe. Perhaps she sensed that Beane would kill her in the end, and she wanted to deprive him of that. It doesn't matter now. Beane got his revenge. Linda's dead. Richard's dead. I'm a vegetable. But Beane's madness has run wild. He's on a murdering rampage and he won't rest until all of us are dead."

"You said he found you a few days ago," Jack said.

"He waited until Jimmy went to town, then broke in and stood right where you are, bragging about Linda's death. He stayed a long time and walked all over the house. I don't know what he was doing and he wouldn't say. He came back in here, threw my bed-covers back, and opened my pajama shirt. He ran his hands over my hideous body, over all the burned places and scars, whispering as he touched me, describing what my death would be like." Severino choked. Tears leaked out of the corners of his eyes.

"Why didn't he kill you?" Jack asked.

"Edouard said it gave him pleasure to think of me lying here helpless. He said: *I'm going to give you your own living nightmare, Severino. One night, not tonight, not tomorrow night, but one night, you will wake up to the smell and sound of fire. You will wake up to find yourself surrounded by flame. And that night, you will die like my father died.*

"Then, he lit a match, flipped it onto my bed, and left. Jimmy came home soon after. He got to me before the blanket burned much. But Edouard was right. I lay here at night, with my eyes wide open, watching, waiting for the first spark."

The speakerphone next to the bed rang. Severino's eyes widened. "Answer it."

I punched it up, knowing who it was. "Beane."

"Are you warm there in the farmhouse, Lacie, my love? Does the fire at your back feel good? Did Severino tell you the story?"

"Yes."

"The sins of the fathers are visited upon the daughters. You were supposed to die, but I changed my mind. I couldn't imagine life without you."

"Why?"

"I love you." He hesitated, sucked in air, then said softly: "And, you reminded me of someone."

"Who?"

"Oh, no," he said, veering away from me, suddenly defensive. "Time's up. No more rhymes or poems or games. Let me talk to your mountain man."

"Durand," Jack said.

"You've learned some French. Well done, *Jacques,* but too little too late. You can't keep her from me. You can't keep her alive, the way you couldn't keep your wife from jumping. You're death on women, Jack. Ever notice that?

"The only question left is this: Will you go down with her or will you step aside and let me take what's rightfully mine. How much do you love her? Do you love her enough to die? Because that's the game now. It's life or death, so think hard about your next move."

"Take me!" Severino sputtered. "Take me, for God's sake!" But the line was dead and Beane was gone.

"It isn't safe for you to stay here," Jack said to Severino. "Come with us, now."

"No. I'm too old and sick to run."

"I won't leave you here," Jack said.

"You have no choice!" Severino insisted. "It isn't safe for *you* to stay. I've got Jimmy to look after me. Go. Take Lacie and go. That's an order, young man. An order!"

We were walking to the car when the explosion hit. I felt it first, a huge vacuum sucking air, then the night cracked, a shock wave punched us to the ground, and Severino's house burned in a madman's wild pyrotechnic display. The Fourth of July in December. A private show for two. Beane had seeded the house with fireworks and his fire now was setting them off all at once.

Rockets and geysers and Roman candles, glittering anemones

blooming in the sky, Aurora Borealis on a psychedelic trip, a thousand shooting stars streaking the night, dazzling trails of colored fire, ruby and emerald and amethyst dreams, aerial torches, blinding celestial fountains, man-made comets hurtling high, brilliant and bright, whistlers and screamers and hot colored streamers all raining down in a heated shower of riotous color mixed with glass, wood, and mortar. A thousand hot needles danced on my exposed skin, stinging my mouth, my upturned face, my head and neck.

Then, suddenly, it was over, the night sky was starless and black, and Aurora Borealis was sparking in the snow around us, tiny pinpricks of color sputtering to white. Severino's house crackled and snapped with less vengeance, a steady slow burn now that the wild stuff was spent.

Jack's cell phone rang. He flipped it open.

"Jackster!" Beane shouted, jubilant and thrilled. "What a sight, Jackie-boy!" He was exuberant, gloating, and gay. "What a wondrous sight! You ain't seen nothing yet. I'm saving the best for last. Put the lovely lady on. Now, Jack! Do it!"

"What do you want," I said in a new dead voice.

"No, no, no!" he cried. "You've got it all wrong. What do *you* want?"

"For you to die. For you to burn in fucking hell."

"Not so fast, Lacie. You don't want me dead yet. *I have something you want.*"

"Impossible."

"You watched Skyla burn. You watched the bright flames lick her flesh. But was it really her, Lacie? Was it your child you saw burning in the night or was it a trick of the eye? A sleight of hand? A devious deceit. Was it a different girl dressed up in Skyla's clothes who burned in the bonfire? Am I a chess player or magician, the master illusionist? If Skyla isn't dead, whose was the body in the box? Was it a hoax, a sham, a fraud, a trick? Was it all done with smoke and mirrors? What's truth and what's a lie, Lacie? Can you tell? Did you watch the truth on that tape or is Skyla alive?"

The dial tone buzzed.

Chapter Forty-three

Get in the car," Jack ordered, rising and ducking around to the driver's seat.

I slid in and we were off, the Cherokee pitching and rocking as we sped down the unplowed road and away. We sailed along dark empty rural routes, switching often, checking the rearview mirrors for someone following, but seeing nothing but black sky and white country.

"Skyla's alive," I said, as we raced through the night. "She's alive!"

"She's dead," Jack said. "You saw her burn."

I knew the tape by heart and played it back in my mind. "He cut from the close-up of Skyla's face to a wide shot of the burning. It could've been someone else in Skyla's clothes and a wig for her hair."

"She's dead, Lacie. You saw her body."

"I saw *a* body. Her bracelet and ID were in the box with it."

"You buried her at sea. You told me so yourself. I saw a copy of the death certificate. The M.E.'s office released the remains and they only do that when legal identity is established. Beane's playing with your mind."

It hit me. NYPD homicide had never released the case files to Jack, and I had never told him about the foul-up in the M.E.'s office, the accidental cremation of the remains. There had been no reason to. I was convinced the charred and butchered torso was Skyla's. I told him now, and explained how Jerry used his connections to get a death certificate signed and the ashes released.

Jack hit the brakes, made a sharp U-turn, and headed north, toward New York City. I didn't ask where we were going. I knew. The city morgue in the Chief Medical Examiner's building never closed. It was open all night long.

My mouth went dry. Skyla. Beane's cruelest joke yet. To watch me bury my daughter and grieve. To put me through hell and back again only to whisper that Skyla was alive. Alive, alive, alive. A sleight of hand. A trick of fate. A magician's joke. Saw her in half, cut her in pieces, set her on fire, then pull her out of a hat alive and in one piece.

Beane boasted that he was a master of illusion. Was he good enough for that?

We arrived in the morgue receiving bay at 3:00 A.M. and walked past two rows of pine coffins stacked five high, waiting for early morning transport to potter's field for city burial. These were the unclaimed dead, the indigent dead, the unidentified and the unwanted. The smell of death was thick in the air. I pulled my turtleneck up, buried my nose and mouth, and eyed the bio-hazard waste container in the corner. Jack brandished his ID and bullied a hound-faced night guard into taking us up to the administrative offices.

Two levels up, two full floors above the pine coffins and cold steel storage bins, I still smelled death. Its unmistakable odor clung to my clothes, a ghastly perfume. We followed the guard down the hall to personnel. He unlocked bolts and opened the door.

"Make it fast," he mumbled, wiping a sweaty hand over his flushed face, hiking uniform pants up over his basketball belly.

We squeezed past him. He smelled like death too.

The air inside was sickly sweet, heavy with floral aerosol freshener and old floor wax. The stark office was in shadow, with rows of tall metal cabinets lining the walls, filled with weights and measurements of the dead. Jack turned the lights on. The office didn't look eerie now. It just looked sad. I imagined the employees stuck here with no windows and wondered how they did it, how they spent weeks and months of their lives breathing recycled air that was candy-coated to mask the smell of death.

File drawers were organized alphabetically. Jack started with A. I started with Z. We worked in silence, flipping folders open, checking ID pictures stapled to the files. The night guard grew bored. He wandered off.

I found Beane filed under S. He had used John Severino's name, but it was Beane's face grinning out at me from the ID snapshot. He listed an address in Manhattan and a social security number. We knew both were fake. Beane was too smart to leave a trail.

According to the file, Beane had started work in October as a custodian. He had keys. He had access. He knew how to fill out the paperwork, call the funeral home, switch ID tags on the remains, and ensure that the wrong body was sent out.

A hundred and fifty employees worked in the six-floor building, including assistant M.E.'s, secretaries, and maintenance. The M.E.'s office processed five thousand bodies a year. It had been child's play for Beane to get the torso destroyed. I looked again at the snapshot. Beane looked malevolent and secretive, thrilled with his own self-invented game.

He had burned and butchered someone, but it wasn't my girl.

Skyla was out there with him.

"She's alive," I announced, closing the folder.

"Not necessarily," Jack gently warned. "You have to think like Beane. His game is psychological manipulation. What's real and what's not. Remember what he did to Linda. He's going for your mind, using uncertainty to make you do what he wants."

"Uncertainty?"

"He convinced you Skyla was dead. He offered you a body, evidence, the burning itself, and then amused himself by watching you go through pain and grief like he did when he lost his family. Now, he has planted hope. *What if?* He has purposefully left enough loose ends to make you believe Skyla *could* be alive. Hope without proof. What better game—to bring Skyla back to life after you've already mourned her, only to kill her off, if he hasn't already done so. The horror of that would be irresistible to him. Don't set yourself up, Lacie. It's a cold hard fall. Please. He's using Skyla to reel you in."

I didn't answer.

Jack turned my face and looked into my eyes. "It's too late," he said, dropping his hand. "You've already bought into it. He's got you. You'll do anything he asks."

I nodded. Beane had a very willing player.

Jack's phone rang. He flipped it open and held it so I could listen.

"Have you thought about what I said, Jack? About Skyla being alive?"

"What do you want," Jack said, flatly.

"Lacie, of course. A simple trade. Tit for tat. Skyla lives, Lacie dies. I saved her once. It's my right now to watch her die. The choice is yours. Tell Lacie this is her one and only chance. There

won't be a second. When I call next, I'll tell you where and how."
He hung up.

Jack pulled me close. An odd calm washed over me. I had always
known it would end this way. I had known this from the start.
Beane was after me. And now, he wouldn't even have to chase me or
hunt me down. I would walk willingly into his arms. I loved Skyla
more than my own life. And I hoped Jack would understand that.

Chapter Forty-four

The nightmare woke him as it often did, scaring him awake to the sound of his own voice crying out, his heart slapping hard, his breath shallow and dry, his body shaking with fright.

The nightmare never changed because it was really a memory that haunted his sleep. And the memory frightened him more than any invented horror ever could.

On that night, that New Year's Eve, his job was a big one. The biggest. Acting sentry for the whole compound. His father trusted him and treated him like a grownup, which at sixteen he almost was. A man, he reminded himself, palming the new soft whiskers sprouting from his cheeks. He was the man of the house while his father was sleeping, responsible for all the young lives and his parents' too.

His Swiss Army watch ticked over to midnight and the second-hand swept him into New Year's Day. The full moon outside hung fat and low in the winter sky. He yawned once, and then he heard it, at 12:02. Twigs snapping, branches slapping, leaves crackling under heavy military boots. His father warned him they would come one day. Was that them now? He crawled across the floor to the window and looked out. He saw nothing but trees.

A twig snapped in the woods. Squirrel or soldier? A barn owl hooted. Soldier again? Whistling out some kind of code? Giving the kill signal?

His heart kicked hard in his chest. Cold sweat rolled off his forehead, stung his eyes. He shimmied back, away from the window, belly to the ground, out of sight. The Death Squad soldiers had night vision goggles on their faces and night scopes mounted on their guns. They could see him, even if he couldn't see them, and they could shoot him down, pluck him off with one silent shot, though they would probably use ten—just out of spite. His father *had warned him that the Dead Time was coming and now it was here. They were prepared to fight back. They had to fight for their lives and their work.*

Chin to floor, he slithered into his father's room. The big man lay sleeping on his back, thick lips open, cheeks warbling with each deep snore. His mother lay next to him, one arm thrown across the burly male chest next to her. He inched up along his father's side of the bed, tugged the sheet, brought his lips close to his father's ear and whispered: "Papa, ils sont là. *Father, they are here.* Ils sont là."

His father's eyes blinked open, instantly alert. "Oui. Je t'ai dit. *I told you so. I told you the day would come.*"

Five minutes later, they were all belly-down on the floor, all twenty-five. Even the youngest children were perfectly trained, quiet as mice, docile and obedient. Twenty-five hearts, twenty-five pairs of sweating palms. A family of fear. His father whispered to him, ordering him to act as sentry at the front of the compound.

"Oui, Papa."

He slithered across the hard lab floors, down the hall, and up to the front window.

The barn owl hooted again. Man not bird. The siege began and the world went red.

When he crawled out later into the dense Maine woods, he was able to take only one child. The choice had been easy. Only one was alive. His sister. He had pulled her out before she died. She was a human torch, jerking and screeching, flaming hot. He took his pajama top off and ripped it into three pieces. Using one to protect his face and the others to protect his hands, he ran into the fire, pulled her from the belly of the burning beast, and rolled the fire out of her with his own young body. He beat it down, out of her hair, off her face, and off the scorching cotton pajamas. He dropped a blanket over her and beat and beat, and rolled and rolled. When the fire on her was finally out, he picked her up and hurried away.

His own torso was scorched and blistered, parts of his skin were seared off the bone, but he had no time for pain. He took his sister and ran.

Soldiers swarmed around the burning compound, weapons dangling at their sides, sweaty faces slack-jawed with awe, watching the fire, while Edouard dragged himself and his sister to his secret hiding place in the rocks along the river. He tucked her deep in his *cave, boiled water from the river and used it to cleanse their wounds. His cave was packed with a full supply of medical equipment, drugs and tools, all plastic-wrapped and sterile. A survival kit.*

He was prepared. He had always been prepared for this day. His father had promised the time would come. His father had warned him. Now he and the girl were the only survivors, the only ones left. The soldiers wouldn't miss them. There would be enough charred bones and skull and seared bodies to satisfy. Twenty-three was close to twenty-five. In a fire that hot, the last two might have been reduced to dust. He knew the chemistry of fire, the temperature of it, and how an intense blaze could turn a human to two pounds of powdery ash.

He looked down at his own ruined body and cried. His sister moaned in the dark. There were two left now, but by morning, there might be only one.

He opened his eyes. He was safe in his van. The nightmare was a memory he would never forget. Now, there were many miles still to be traveled. He was racing the clock. He had to reach his new hiding place because the Dead Time was almost here. This time, however, the tables would turn, the victim would play the Devil's role and the Devil herself would die.

Beane put the van in gear, pulled out of the highway rest stop, and headed west, away from the rising sun.

Chapter Forty-five

We holed up in a small hotel in downtown New York. The cell phone lay on the table, ready to be answered on the first ring.

While we waited, Jack worked on his computer, looking for the last piece to Beane's story. He sailed through cyber-space, accessing files, records, asking questions, and finally getting answers. At the end of the first day, he sat back and ran a hand through his hair. "I think I know why Beane pulled you out of the fire."

I stood behind him and looked at the computer. The news article was two columns wide with a black and white photograph. The picture was grainy and slightly out of focus, but nonetheless shocking. Beane's ten-year-old sister, slumped in a wheelchair, claws for hands, teeth bared in a quasi-smile for the camera. Her skin had the pale waxy look of rebuilt flesh, and I guessed her twisted mouth was the result of a careless or inexperienced surgeon's knife. Her eyebrows were burned away, her cheeks asymmetrically seared.

"Rescuing you from the fire was gratifying," Jack explained. "It made him feel strong, in control, as if he was rescuing his sister again."

"What's her name?" I asked.

"Anne. She was left at the front gate of the Westbury Ridge Hospital in northern Vermont in February 1965. It must've taken Beane a full month to work his way out of the Maine woods and get her there. A custodian found her. She was wrapped head to toe in sterile white dressings and was wearing a gold bracelet with her first name engraved. She had no last name. The hospital records simply called her Anne Doe.

"According to the article, she was blinded in a fire of unknown origin. The trauma broke her mind. She functioned at the level of a three-year-old and talked gibberish. From the look of her, I'd say Beane tried to graft her skin himself. At sixteen, he didn't have the experience to do a perfect job. He was able to graft well enough to save her life, but not her appearance. The local paper ran the picture and story several times that year hoping someone would show up to claim her. No one ever did." Jack saved the photo to his hard drive.

"Why did he wait all these years to come after me? Why now?"

"Anne died this summer. It's the emotional trigger we've been looking for, the final stressor that set Beane off. He's suicidal, but he wants to settle the score once and for all before he dies. Wrecking the plane vented his rage against the U.S. government. Linda was the perfect conduit. He didn't care how or if she died. You're a different story. He wants you to suffer the way he did."

"What's the difference between Linda and me?"

"You were burned in a fire and she wasn't. Beane bonded with you. You're both survivors."

"He set my father's car on fire that night intending to kill me too. Why did he rescue me?"

"My guess? He had a sudden change of heart. You were ten years old, the same age as Anne had been. He looked at you and saw Anne."

"Do you think Skyla's still alive?" I asked, afraid to hear the answer.

"I honestly don't know. Beane's tipped right over the edge. He's near the end, close to his own self-destruction, capable of anything right now. Anything. That's what scares me."

"Say what you mean."

"Lacie," he said reaching for me. "He might want to burn Skyla in front of you, to make you witness the horror in person, the way he watched his family die. In his sick mind, it would forge the strongest bond between the two of you. This time, he may want to burn her for real."

If she's not already dead. It hung there between us.

Jack held me in the dark hours, but night like day now belonged to Beane too. Two days went by and Beane was ominously silent, but he was with us, sleeping or waking, he was all we were thinking about. Was Skyla with him? Was Skyla alive? Or had she burned in the bonfire after all?

Jack was right. Beane was playing me perfectly. Just enough doubt. Just enough hope. He was reeling me right in.

* * *

The call came early the next afternoon, December thirtieth.

"Life and death are math, Dr. Stein, or didn't you realize that?" Beane announced. "How hot is the fire that turns bone to ash? I know, I know! One thousand seven hundred and twelve degrees. And how hot is the white fire that can melt you from two feet away? An even five thousand degrees. Here's one for you: How fast does it take a hundred-and-fifteen-pound woman to fall from the twentieth floor? Do the math, Jack! Do it! Don't know? I do! I do!

"Twenty floors, at 128 feet per second. The 256-foot drop takes four seconds, 87.27 miles per hour, facefirst. A sweet wingless swan dive into the hard D.C. cement. Four seconds and it was over. Her brain shut down. Oh, it might have taken a minute or two for her reflexes to quit. Her toes might have wiggled, her arms might have twitched, but her organs were surely smashed flat by a drop like that, incapable of functioning at all."

Jack. Hard-faced and angry. Trying hard to not slam the phone down, to hang on, to wait it out, because Beane had warned this was my one and only chance to get Skyla back.

Beane rushed on:

"Did you ever consider the carnage inside? The splintered pelvis, twelve wrecked ribs, the internal hemorrhaging, noxious gases in the blood? The heart, liver, and kidney broken like eggs? Did you ever look down from your slick penthouse balcony and wonder how the savior of lives lost one as precious as that? Poor Gabby. Fine Cuban cheekbones pulverized by the drop, black hair soaked through with red warm blood. If only you had been a little less strong when Jason disappeared. If only you had showed her your own wrenching grief, she might not have felt so terribly alone.

"But you were a man's man, weren't you, Jack! I'll bet you took Jason's disappearance like a soldier, stayed stiff-lipped and dry-eyed while your pretty wife died and died and died a thousand times over inside. You tried to be strong for her when what she really needed was weak. The irony is that Gabby's death made you harder still! You dug your hands into solid rock, scratched at ice and stone, and for three long years you climbed alone.

"Oh, you helped blind men and dreamers scale those craggy peaks, but you were turned inward, Jack, lost inside yourself. You climbed high then higher, McKinley, Kilimanjaro, Everest. You led brave men up to soaring summits, but when you looked down, you never saw the great winter vista, just Gabby's poor broken body covered in blood."

Jack. Pulse ticking hard in his neck. Unable to hang up. Jack. Eyes squeezed shut, jaw clamped down tight, throat and fists working.

Beane was pushing him hard.

And Beane bantered on.

"Bad as death by falling is, death by fire's a thousand times worse. You witness the dying. Gabby was lucky. She was dead the second she hit. But when you dance and jerk the burning man's jig, minutes to death feel like hours. Your face melts. Your eyesight goes fast. Despite the intense light, you're blind. Despite the frightful heat, you're cold. Death by fire lasts a very long time. You make desperate deals with a deaf and dumb God. Anything to end it! *I promise, I promise!* A thousand promises hurled at Heaven, while the godless fire eats you alive. When they dug Jason up, there was still flesh and bone and hair. When Gabby jumped she still had her own soft skin. But fire, Jack? Fire takes it all. It eats you, gnaws you down to your very bones and then melts those too."

Beane sucked air through his teeth and blew it back out again, whispering words in the exhale. "I am fire and you, Jack Stein, are ice. I've got you nailed. You're my opponent. I know you inside and out. And now, I'm ready to play."

"What's the deal," Jack said, flatly.

"Lacie for Skyla?"

Jack looked at me.

"Done," I said.

We listened to his instructions.

Wyoming. Beane had crossed the country. He was in Wyoming, in the great wilderness where there were countless places to hide, hole up, and burrow in out of sight with a helpless young hostage.

"Go to Jackson Hole," he ordered, "as quickly as you can. Run! Fly! Hurry! Skyla's waiting. Don't let your guard dog blow it, Lacie. No troops or cops or teams of stiff-backed agents. Come alone. The two of you. No more, no less. When you get there you'll learn how perfect a game this is for Jack. See you soon!"

The phone went dead.

"He drove," Jack said. "He wouldn't have risked a plane with Skyla, if she's with him at all. We still have no proof she's alive."

I paced the room. "What is *proof*, anyway? A photo that's been altered or fabricated by a computer? A voice that might be a recording? I can't believe what I hear and see. I don't need proof. I'm going."

"We can do this the smart way, Lacie. One phone call and I'll have a hostage rescue team in there, ready to back us up. The Bureau instructed me to quit investigating Durand, but they would never turn away from a hostage situation."

I knew about hostage rescue from the Waco disaster. I had done my fair share of follow-up stories on Waco and knew HRT had let that *situation* get out of hand. They brought on the fire of the century there. I thought about the small burned bodies of the children at the Koresh compound and I knew that if HRT showed up, Jack would no longer be in charge. I didn't trust HRT to get my girl away from Beane alive. I only trusted Jack.

"No," I said. "No HRT."

"We *need* them," Jack said, incredulous. "It's their job to do hostage rescue, and they do it pretty damn well."

"Do they? What about Waco? I'm not taking the chance they miscalculate."

Like the D.C. police did. I didn't say it, but it was there between us.

"Beane's as crazy as Koresh was, and he's one step ahead of us," I rushed on. "He always has been. What if we get there and he's got Skyla rigged to blow? Did you think about that? What if he can turn her to dust with the flick of a switch, just like he did to Severino and Jerry? Think like Beane. We have to play it straight, the way he wants. And that means no HRT."

"If he gets to you," Jack warned, "he'll never let you go. With backup you'll have a chance to walk away from this alive, maybe with Skyla."

"There's a bigger chance it will go down wrong. Our job is to get Skyla out alive. We have to do this alone. You and me. No one else." I took a deep breath and then I said it: "What about Jason. Did backup help you then? Wouldn't you have been better off doing exactly what you were told to do?"

Jack blinked.

"No HRT," I said softly, reaching for him, hating myself for the low blow.

He twisted out of my arms.

Kicked the wall.

Ran his fingers through his long hair.

Paced and fumed and cursed.

I waited it out.

When he finally calmed down some, he packed his computer and shrugged into his parka. "Okay. No HRT. Let's go."

Chapter Forty-six

Beane zigzagged his way up the mountain, using a series of chair lifts. His pretty pet was docile at his side, mouth taped closed, face hidden beneath a ski mask, telltale silvery-blond hair covered by a hat, memorable eyes invisible behind ski goggles. Beane gripped her elbow in one mad hand, and fondled the gun in his pocket with the other, ready to shoot her like an animal if she bolted.

The last chair lift let them off at the summit. They drifted across the face of the mountain and down, ducking under red barriers and around signs that marked hazardous off-trail terrain. The old lift was his destination. It sat hidden on this unused side of the mountain, shut down and forgotten by everyone but him. It was a speck of brown far away in the white snow.

This side of the mountain was off limits, and was not blasted or plowed. Snow wedged dangerously deep, ready to avalanche. Beane stepped out of his skis, made the girl do the same, then strapped both pairs to his back. He led his pet step by careful step through the drifts, keeping tight to the tree line. An hour later, they arrived at the old lift. Beane unhitched the skis and hid, waiting for the full safe cover of night to make his final ascent.

The girl shivered at his side. He watched the summit. At dusk, just as he expected, two Mountain Patrol skiers drifted over to the barriers. They peered down into the long afternoon shadows, sweeping binoculars side to side, looking for the odd skier who might have tumbled off the edge, who might lie hurt, waiting for help.

Beane was a long way away, but he took no chances. Sound traveled great distances in the mountains. He held his breath and gripped the girl hard, keeping his weapon shoved into her ribs. She didn't make a sound. His pet. His perfect pretty pet.

Mountain Patrol lifted their skies, arced neatly around, and *disappeared. Beane relaxed. The last leg of his long journey was about to begin.*

Daylight faded from the sky, twilight turned to night. When the sky was black, Beane drove his pole through the small glass observation window of the lift control hut. He climbed in, switched a flashlight on, and found the power switch. He flicked it up and an instant later, machinery groaned. Metal screeched. The row of chairs lurched and moved slowly forward.

Beane crawled out and stepped into his skis. The girl did the same. He led her to the starting position. A double chair made of old wood slats reeled around. When it touched the backs of their legs, they sat back. The chair swung up and their skis lifted off the ground. Beane dropped the safety bar. They were airborne, sailing through the sky.

Clouds split, revealing a full moon. God was a Cyclops and this was his glowing night eye. For an instant, the snow below was bright as day, bright enough to see a deer loping through trees, then the clouds slammed together and the moon was gone. The lift creaked. The girl whimpered. The chair rocked wildly in the heavy winter wind.

Up, up, up they rose, along a new mountain face with a ninety-degree pitch and a narrow gully of avalanche-ready snow snaking down through ice-covered rock. The girl was hunched up against the bitter cold. Beane's own hands and feet were frozen. He thought of fire, a hot red fire to warm him. The wind sliced down from the north, the chair dipped and creaked, and the hard mountain in front of them was black, invisible in the dark. Twenty minutes later, Beane looked up and saw the pinnacle station silhouetted against the sky. He lifted the safety bar and edged forward, ready to dismount. Next to him, the girl tensed.

"Move!" he hissed.

She shimmied to the edge of the chair. Their skis touched ice.

"Now!" Beane shouted, pushing off from the slatted seat, holding the girl's arm and pulling.

She hung on to the lift.

Her skis lifted. The chair reeled up preparing for the return trip. Beane yanked. She tumbled down, skis clattering and popping off on impact. She lay still, crying softly. Beane nudged her with his foot. "Idiot. You'll die out there on the mountain, on a night like this. Stand up."

She tried to stand, but her ski boots skidded on the slippery ice and she went down.

Beane left her lying there and turned his attention to the station control hut. No one had bothered to lock it. He shrugged the big pack off his back and ducked inside. He shut the power off and emptied a portion of his pack on the floor, setting aside two pairs of heavy alpine hiking boots and a pair of clippers. He took his clumsy ski boots off, put the hiking boots on, then used the clippers to cut the main lift wires, shutting the lift down for good.

When he was done, Beane shouldered his pack and went back out to the girl.

"Put these on," he said, dropping the hiking boots. While she changed boots, Beane pitched the skis one at a time over the edge and grinned. They were alone on the peak and there was no way down. He helped the girl up. She slipped again, but steadied herself and moved slowly at his side. To the back of them, where the useless chair lift swayed, there was nothing but that avalanche-ready gully. And to the front, plunging seven hundred feet down, was a sheer vertical ice face. Above them was a broad plateau.

A tight, narrow path, like a rocky spine, wound up to it. To the right and left of the serrated spine were sheer vertical plunges dropping off thousands of feet into the night. To fall here was to die.

Beane and the girl picked their way up the ridge slowly and carefully, on all fours. They came out on top at the edge of a massive snowfield. It was a miraculous sight. At the eastern rim of the field was nature's anomaly and Beane's very good fortune: a thick stand of limber pines, scrawny and bent from the wind, but woody. Many were dead and fine for burning.

In Colorado the tree line rose to 13,000 feet. In these northern, more bitter heights of Wyoming, 10,000 feet was the norm. Trees disappeared higher than that. But here, at 11,500 feet, these stubborn limber pine had grown tall. Slim trunks made them easy to cut. Over time, on previous trips in his preparation for the coming days, Beane had cut down half of the limber pines. Tonight, the wood lay neatly stacked and ready, covered in a tarp.

On the far end of the snowfield was a rough-hewn timber structure with a steel stove pipe jutting up from the roof. It was a warming hut, an old shelter, put there to protect summer climbers when sudden violent storms hit. Beane knew the shack. He had spent great time and care choosing this spot, and bit by bit, tirelessly, over the year, he had horsed up tools and supplies.

Now, he clapped his hands together once and inhaled the sharp summit air. A blizzard was on its way. The first snow was just starting to fall. It was deathly cold outside, but Beane knew it would be warm inside, when he lit the fire. He chose this peak because it was all but impossible to reach in winter without the lift. And it was high. Beane wanted to be close to heaven when the Dead Time came. He wanted the stinking smoke from his own burning flesh to rise up and blind God, sting him in the eye.

Chapter Forty-seven

❦

We made the last flight out of New York to Salt Lake City and waited two long hours for the connection to Jackson Hole.

Beane has won, I thought, sitting in the deserted terminal lounge, watching snow feather down across the runways outside. He's won. None of the tools of the trade had helped us find him. Not the sketch or the shoe size or the name. We had figured out who he was and why he wanted me dead, but it made no difference now. He was in control, calling the shots, just as he had always been.

Our flight boarded. I stared out another dark window and saw nothing but Beane's face. We landed in Jackson at midnight. A tired girl waited at the Hertz counter with keys to a four-wheel-drive red Jeep. Jack signed the papers, and we were on our way.

We cut west across the valley, through a driving snowstorm, toward mountains we could not see but knew were there looming up ten, eleven, twelve, thirteen thousand feet. Plows worked the highway, lights spinning, rolling steadily in both directions, but snow swirled down as fast as the big blades pushed it out of the way. Visibility was dropping by the minute. Jack fiddled with the radio and found the weather update.

The airport was now officially shut down until the next afternoon. Many secondary roads were closed and the main road we were taking into town was on the verge of closing. We made it to the outskirts of the mountain base village and stopped at the first hotel we saw—three levels of Western ranch-style charm with a vacancy sign blinking out front.

A fit young night clerk let us in. "You folks just made it," he announced, taking our bags. "Everything will be shut down tomorrow, including the mountain."

Upstairs, the room was lovely, with horns on the wall and a deep brass bed, but its beauty was wasted on me. I closed myself up in the bathroom, stripped off my clothes, and twisted the shower faucets up full. I stepped in, rested my forehead against tile, and wished the beating water could wash away my fear. Two weeks ago I had nothing left to lose. Now, I had everything. Then, I cared nothing about dying. Now? I was alive and I wanted to stay that way. I hated Beane for this final torture.

My own death was one thing, but the fear of Skyla burning in front of me, or Jack knifed or shot or gutted while I watched, was too much. My mind sped through all the versions of how it might go down, all the ways it could happen. I was accepting Beane's death sentence, Skyla for me, and believed nothing Jack or I could do would change my fate. Mine was the numb acquiescence of a victim: *Finish it quick and don't make me hurt.*

But fire hurt. My father knew, Severino knew, Fleming and Anne and how many more? A world of walking wounded. Survivors of fire. A separate race wrapped in wedding-white gauze, and Beane wanted me now for his bride.

I slid down the shower wall, looped arms around legs, buried my face, and hoped the rushing water pounding on my back would drown out the sound of my choking sobs.

It did not.

The shower door opened. Jack stepped in and dropped to his knees. Water sprayed over his soft denim shirt, hard hiking boots, leather belt, and worn blue jeans, but he didn't care. He held me in the false warm rain and listened to me confess my fears, then he lifted me up, carried me out, wrapped me in towels, and put me in bed. He left his clothes in a soggy heap and slid in, shush-shushing, stroking my hair while he swore: *We're going to make it through. We'll get her back. I won't let you down. We'll get her back. We'll get you out. I won't let you down.* I finally believed him enough to close my eyes.

When I opened them again, morning had come and the world was still white.

Jack called the local police, gave a description of Beane's van and asked for a search of the area. He left his cell phone number. We tried to walk outside, but the bitter cold and wind drove us back in again. Jack glared at the sky, his handsome face angry and grim, silently blaming God. Morning slid into afternoon, afternoon into night. It was New Year's Eve and the snow was still falling fast.

The first call came at 10:00 P.M. An officer named Quinn said he had found the van parked in the main ski area parking lot.

"I want to be there when you open it," Jack said curtly.

Thirty minutes later, we rolled into the ski village, past the deserted aerial tram station, ticket windows, and into the main lot. A blue and white police cruiser waited on the far side, headlights on high, drilling through the blowing snow, illuminating the van. It was a gunmetal gray Ford, and judging from the amount of snow piled on the hood, it had been there for a while.

Jack pulled up next to the cruiser. He rolled his window down. Quinn stepped out. He flicked a burning cigarette into the snow and ambled over. He was a big V-shaped man, ruddy faced and rugged, dressed in jeans and a dark blue alpine parka with the fur-trimmed hood pulled tight around his head.

"Jack Stein?" he asked, squinting in.

Jack offered ID.

"Glad to meet you," the burly cop said, shaking his hand. "I'm Quinn. I did an external visual inspection. Both the driver's door and the passenger's door are unlocked. There's no one up front and nothing out of order. Couldn't get a look into the back area. It's blocked off from the front seats by a sheet of solid metal. That's not standard in a Ford like this. I'd say it was put in afterward, sort of a do-it-yourself custom job. There aren't any windows in the rear doors. Doors themselves seemed to be unlocked. I jiggled the handle, but waited for you to get here before actually opening it up."

"You have a chance to run the plates?"

"Yup. District of Columbia. Registered to a 1995 red Porsche. Obviously stolen."

"You have any forensics men we could call in?"

Quinn laughed and brushed new snow off his hat and shoulders. "This is Jackson Hole, son, not New York City. I've got a Polaroid camera, plastic gloves, tweezers, and a trunk full of evidence bags and tags. You and me. We're the forensics team. You want fingerprints, you'll have to wait'll the snow lets up. The one and only boy who can do that kind of thing's stranded up in Coleville."

"What about the Teton County sheriff's office?"

"Forget it. Their boys all live an hour or two out of town, and the main roads are closed. There's no way to get in tonight."

"You take the pictures then," Jack said, "and I'll collect the evidence."

"Sounds good to me." Quinn stepped back to the cruiser and rummaged in the trunk.

"Stay here," Jack said to me, opening his door.

I didn't have to ask. He was afraid of what he was going to find inside. The missing pieces of Skyla? The ones that weren't in the box? Evidence of torture? Of rape? My young girl's blood?

"Jack," I said, holding him back. "What if he's got it rigged to blow?"

Jack shook his head. "He doesn't want you or me dead right now. He needs live players to play his game. And his game starts tomorrow. Not today."

"Still, just to be on the safe side . . ."

"Best I can do is a surface search, but I won't be able to catch any sophisticated kind of bomb work. There are a hundred ways he could have set it up, nearly all of which require a bomb squad to find. We don't have the luxury of waiting. And, as I said, I believe Beane wants to meet us face-to-face."

"But you will look, just the same."

"I will," he promised.

Jack got out, slipped on a pair of plastic gloves, and took Quinn's flashlight. He swept snow off the van's windshield and worked the flashlight left to right, looking inside. He moved to the passenger window, then the driver's window and repeated his search. He blew on his hands to warm them, gently brushed snow off the hood, and felt his way up and down, left to right. Next, he dropped down to the ground and slipped under the van. His feet disappeared. He slid out the other side and walked a full circle inspecting the door frames and windows, feeling around for telltale wires.

He worked a long time, slow and thorough, running his fingers over nooks and crannies, and even standing on top of the police cruiser hood to study the van's roof. When he was as satisfied as he could be, he signaled Quinn. The big cop snapped pictures. I counted five pops from the Polaroid flash.

Jack walked around to the rear doors, holding his gun in a ready position. Quinn yanked on the handle and the doors swung open. Quinn aimed his flashlight in, arced it left to right, up and down. From where I was sitting, I couldn't see inside. Jack said something to Quinn and they climbed in.

I watched the Jeep's dashboard clock and waited five full minutes before getting out. I walked up to those wide open doors, readied myself, and looked.

It was a rolling prison, a windowless hell, padded and dark, access to the front seat cut off with a wall, just as Quinn had described: the perfect place to stow a hostage. I catalogued the objects inside. Winch for lifting a snowmobile in and out. Bunched-up sleeping bag on the left. Cell phone scanner and jumble of equipment to work it with. Video camera, tripod, boxes of tapes. Porta potty. Mini-fridge. Styrofoam cups. Twinkie wrappers. A cheap violin.

And sitting in the center was a Video Walkman powered with a battery pack, playing a tape of my last WRC newscast. There were my bare twisted hands held high, my eyes locked on the camera, and my lips moving, but the voice coming out wasn't mine at all. It was the hoarse whisper, the gleeful cry, distorted and warbled by batteries running low, its two-syllable chant drawn out unnaturally slow: *Ga-bby, Ga-bby, Ga-bby*. He was hitting us both with this endless loop of tape: *Ga-bby, Ga-bby, Ga-bby*, as my lips moved and my finned fingers trembled in the hot studio lights.

Jack shut the player off.

I looked away from the screen, down to the right, and saw a fistfull of long blond hair. I made a sound.

Jack turned around. "Go back to the Jeep, Lacie. Please."

I stepped closer. "Tell me."

"The hair looks like hers," Jack admitted, crouching inside. "I'm guessing he cut it off and used most of it in the videotaped bonfire."

"What else?"

He held up a pair of new tiny-waisted jeans, extra-long length. My girl's size.

I nodded. "What else?"

"This entire rear area has been customized with soundproofing. There are restraints. Handcuffs. Ankle cuffs too. But there's food and water in the refrigerator, and the space is relatively clean. He left the keys in the ignition and all the doors unlocked, like he didn't care if these things were stolen. He's not planning on coming back. I can't tell you more than that."

"Say it, Jack. Just say it. You can't tell me if he raped her or killed her in there."

"Don't do this to yourself."

My eyes filled with tears. Skyla's prison blurred. "You can't tell me if she's alive or dead. You can't tell me he didn't press his burned body next to her every night and whisper horrible promises in her ear. You can't tell me he didn't hurt her in there before he burned her or butchered her."

"Lacie, for God's sake."

"I'm sorry, I'm sorry." I stumbled back to the Jeep and slouched in my seat.

Snow covered the windshield; I couldn't see the van. I didn't want to. There were no answers there, only bits and pieces from Beane's magic trick. The master illusionist was long gone and who or what he took with him, I did not know. It was the uncertainty that rattled me, and the irrational fear that, despite Jack's assurances, the van was Beane's best booby trap, cleverly wired and rigged to blow. I closed my eyes and waited. The blast never came. Jack was right. Beane wanted us alive.

A half hour later, Jack dropped into the seat beside me. "Quinn's going to impound the van. He's also going to canvass all the hotels in a fifty-mile radius on the off chance Beane's holed up somewhere. But I don't think he would have left the van in plain sight if he was in town. It's almost like he's flaunting it in our faces. *Look all you want, but you'll never find me.*" Jack flipped the wipers on and looked out toward mountains that were hidden behind the curtain of falling snow.

"Up there?" I said, reading Jack's expression.

"Yes," Jack said, putting the Jeep in gear. "It's the only place he could be."

Jack slept fitfully, out of sheer exhaustion. I traced the warm plane of his cheek, touched his lips, felt the heat of his soft breath warm on my chest, and remembered his strong words on our first day together: *I don't give up and I don't fail.* Back then, he had never come up against a killer like Beane. I rolled away from him, stared out the window at the unnaturally white night, and silently talked to Skyla.

When he slammed those double doors on you and darkness closed in, did the winter chill seep through the hard metal floor? Were you cold in your prison, Skyla? Did you count the days, scratch the wall with your fingernails to keep track? Do you know how much time has gone by? Or was time meaningless to you,

hours like minutes, as the van bumped and chattered along, speed-
ing you through the weeks and finally across the country to this
Western wilderness. Did your heart twist, did fear kick your breath
away? Did you wonder if he was going to keep you like that for
years and never let you go?

Were you there when he burned the body and butchered it down
to a torso? Did he make you watch? Did he shove it in next to you
for the long ride back to the city? Did you look at it and wonder
when your turn would come? Did he show you your death notice
in the New York Times *and tell you that Skyla Costello was offi-*
cially dead? Did he make you play that cheap violin?

How could you spend six long weeks with him and still be
whole? How will you survive this last long night with him out there
in the cold? Skyla, Skyla, Skyla. All this time locked in the back of
a van, alive but scared. Did he break your mind, sweet girl? Your
body too? Wherever you are, hold on. Keep it together, baby. We're
coming soon.

Skyla was strong, determined, and competitive. I remembered how
she was on the basketball court when the opposition blocked her.
Body loose and fluid, face tense, she would take a wide stance,
bounce the ball, evaluate the threat, and chant quietly to herself while
planning her next move: *Deal, deal, deal.* Was she breathing those
words now up there, cowering in the cold with Beane at her side?

Deal, deal deal. How did she deal with knowing she was officially dead?

I made my own deals with God, desperate promises. *Me for her.*
How many mothers had cried those same words? And how many
times was it too late, the child already gone from cancer, a car accident, a murdering hand. *Take me instead.* It's the black side of the
lullaby, the mother's instinctive choice. *Take me instead.* It's pro-
grammed in.

Me for her, I whispered now a hundred times straight, knowing
the call we were waiting for would not come until night turned into
New Year's Day.

Chapter Forty-eight

Morning dawned bright and clear. Outside, I saw the ring of mountains for the first time, jagged peaks jutting high and sharp, piercing a vivid blue January sky. The call came early, at quarter past six.

"Jackie boy! Welcome to the Wild West! You've been a good soldier, obedient and on time."

The connection was bad. Beane's voice dropped in and out.

"We're here," Jack said. "Where are you?"

Beane laughed. "High in the sky, Jackie-Oh! Up with the birds. I can touch the stars, taste the wind, pluck feathers from an eagle's wing. The view's splendid, Jackster! Simply splendid!"

"Come on, Beane. We're ready to deal."

"Tell me something, Jack. Tell me this. What would you do if you found the monster, went face-to-face with the creature who killed your little boy? How would you feel? What in the hell would you do to the man who took your son to hell and never ever brought him back again?

"I'll tell you. I think you'd kill the monster. Rip his throat out, fire twenty-five shots into his face at close range. You'd wipe him off this earth, make him vanish without a trace, as if he'd never lived at all. As if he'd burned to ash. Ashes to ashes, Jack. That's where all this is heading. You'll never be able to look your nightmare man in the face. You'll never find him. He's long gone, nameless and free. But Lacie's found me. What will she do if Skyla's really dead?"

"Why do you want Lacie, Beane? You got your revenge. You got it a long time ago. Richard Wagner's dead. Severino's dead. Linda is too. The score is settled."

"What's odd isn't even, Jack. I keep thinking about that. All these years since I watched Richard burn, I wondered why I didn't feel good—didn't feel right—then I knew. It's because I dragged Lacie out of the fire. I let her live. And because of that, I let Linda live. You see, I gave those two girls life and that made them my very own. I watched them grow up. I was always there watching, like a big brother. I loved them both, but I loved Lacie most. I've chosen Lacie."

"Why?"

"Because she's marked by fire and that means she's my bride."

"If it's Lacie you want, why did you take Skyla?"

"For Lacie to understand me, she has to feel what I have felt. We're bonded now. Scars on the inside. Scars on the outside. Lacie and me. We've both lived through fire and grief."

"Killing her won't get your family back."

"No, but it will even the score."

"Four for one, Beane? What kind of math is that."

"New math. My math. One for each. One for my father, one for my mother, one for Anne."

"That's three, Beane. Who's the fourth?"

"Why, I am, Jack! You'll see my body. You'll see where I've been touched by flame, kissed by fire, the pretty boy turned freak. You'll look at me and know the hell I've been through—burning while the Devil himself looked on from the outside and waited for us all to die. The Devil was wrong. I cheated him and ran naked through the woods in my new ugly skin.

"The fire blinded Anne. I'm glad it did. She never had to look in the mirror and see what happened to her face. I look at my body every day. I'll show you, when you bring Lacie up. I'll show you then. It's not a pretty sight. The fire took Anne's mind, burned her mad. I'm happy for that too. She never remembered the terrible night. Now Anne's gone. The Dead Time's here. It's my time to die and I want Lacie to die with me.

"But I'm going to love her first. Love her like a man. I'm going to kiss her in secret places and drive my burned body into hers. We're going to be one. I know you've fucked her, Jack, and that makes me mad. But I accept it. The fire will cleanse my bride and make her pure. I'm going to strip her down to her bare burnt skin, and when I'm deep inside her, in the place you've been, I'm going to step into the fire with her in my arms. We'll burn as one, Lacie and I. It's my dream, my fantasy, my God-given right."

"Where are you?"

"Of course you want to know! You're the bodyguard, the night watchman, the lover of my bride! I know all about you, Jack Stein. You're the kind of agent the feds fear most. You're a wild card. A one-man band. You're not a team player. You go it alone, by your rules. We're not so different. We play different games, but essentially we're the same. I play chess. You climb mountains. Both are cerebral endeavors. Climbing requires a nimble body, but you need a nimble mind too. You need strategy, to think ahead, to know where you're going four steps before you get there. Same as chess.

"Well, it's checkmate now, my federal friend! The king's got the pawn and he's willing to trade for the queen, but there will be no castles or royalty of your own. It's just you, Jack! The white knight with his queen. Come alone. No hostage rescue sneaking along, no federal police or soldiers or such. No cheating. It's just you and Lacie, or Skyla's dead."

"Where."

"Flagg's Peak. The summit. There are two parts to this final round. First, you have to get to the foot of the peak. The weather's not on your side. Fifty-knot winds are blowing in ahead of a new storm. A chopper can't fly and chair lifts aren't running. You can't even travel by snowmobile. Avalanche danger's too high. You'll have to hike. Once there, the real work begins: getting to the summit.

"I disabled the old lift, but that shouldn't bother a mountain man like you. The main southern face is closed and the steep gully run is ready to avalanche. There's only one way up to the summit and that's to climb the north face. It's a solid ice wall. You'll need ropes, axes, ice screws, and a fine sturdy step. You'll have blizzard conditions and zero visibility by nightfall. Search and Rescue won't be able to pick you up when it's over, so pack your pajamas and get ready for a long cold night. Bring Lacie. Be here by dusk or Skyla burns with me. The bonfire starts at sunset. Game, set, match. I win."

The line went dead.

Jack called Teton County Search and Rescue and asked dozens of technical questions. When he had the answers he needed, he hung up and plugged the hotel phone line into his computer. Moments later, the Teton mountain range filled the screen. He pointed and clicked his way up, through gullies and valleys and gulches, up, always up, and north. Geographic detail rolled by. A river gorge, timberland, steep narrow ski runs, wide snow bowls, the main ski summit, and there at the top right, a stand-alone peak. A tiny speck against the whole sweeping range.

Jack highlighted the speck with the mouse and clicked. The map enlarged.

"Flagg's Peak," Jack said. "Eleven thousand five hundred feet and isolated. Beane went up before the storm hit. That means he's been there for two nights now. There's an old warming hut at the top. He must be using it for shelter. His rundown on weather conditions was accurate. Another blizzard's blowing in from Canada. Winds are already pushing fifty knots ahead of the storm. It's just going to get worse. Mountain Rescue choppers can't fly and the avalanche danger's too high to risk snowmobiles."

"How do we get up there?"

"We'll have to hike. Count on a good five hours to reach the foot of Flagg's Peak. From there, the southern ski face is unapproachable, just as Beane said. It has one run down, a narrow gully with a ninety-degree pitch called Devil's Slide. There's an old abandoned chair lift that used to service the peak. It was put in for locals who liked life and death thrills, and was never marked on ski maps. The lift was closed ten years ago when a couple of hotshot young skiers were killed coming down the Slide.

"Beane disabled the lift. Without it, there's only one way up. Again, just as he said. The north face ice wall. It's a grade-three, class-five climb to reach the summit. Seven hundred vertical feet. Traveling alone, I could do it in ninety minutes. It will take work to maneuver you up. I'm estimating three hours for us both to make the ascent. We'll need ropes, harnesses, crampons, and ice tools."

"I can't," I said, panic rising fast inside me, thinking of hands that couldn't tie swift sure knots, hang on to rope, or scramble for holds. "I can't climb."

"I'll get you up there."

"How?"

"One step at a time, just like I did with Logan."

"Logan has hands," I said through tears.

"A blind man trusted me to be his eyes. You have to trust me enough to let me be your hands."

"It's impossible," I whispered.

"No, it's not." He came close and gripped my shoulders. "It's difficult, scary, and dangerous as hell, but not impossible. We have no choice."

He let go of me and called Search and Rescue again.

Even if I made it to the top, I assumed I would never make it down. Suddenly, I thought of Max and I wanted to say good-bye. Jack's computer was still on-line. I tapped out a short note describing Beane's final move. I told Max I loved him, and asked him to look after Skyla. Jack stood behind me, reading the screen. When I finished, he sat down in my place and added on to my e-mail to Max while he talked.

I moved to the window and pressed my face against the glass, looking up at the great white wilderness.

"I need access to an equipment shop in town," Jack was saying on the phone. "Can you do that? Good. No. We're going in alone. He so much as sees the shadow of anything he thinks is backup and he'll kill the girl. The way we're going to work it is this . . ."

Hold on, baby, I thought, looking out and up.

"Emergency support," Jack went on. "Yes, I know there's a good chance you won't be able to send a rescue team up tonight. I'll carry basic medical supplies and survival gear, but I want a Medevac chopper ready anyway in case the storm blows itself out. This girl could be hurt."

I thought of all the things Beane might have done to her in the six long weeks he had held her captive. What if he had raped or beaten her? I would know the instant I saw her. If her eyes were flat and dull, doll-blank, and her body stiff, ready for the next blow, I would know she had been brutalized.

Keep it together, I willed her, looking up at those unapproachable peaks. *Be strong, baby.*

Jack's final words drifted my way. "I want the air ambulance at Jackson airport standing by and the trauma team at the burn center in Salt Lake City on alert. Yes, you heard me right. The burn ward."

I was still staring out the window, but instead of white peaks and slopes all I saw were thick gauze cocoons. The burn ward was on high alert, ready and waiting for my hot, blistered body to come smoking in.

Chapter Forty-nine

An hour later, we were at the mountain base surrounded by the solemn five-man team from Search and Rescue. Radios were checked and double-checked. Snowshoes and a pile of climbing gear filled the back of the Jeep.

We were dressed in bright red windproof, waterproof climbing pants and down-filled hooded parkas, the same bright red for maximum visibility. Neoprene masks covered our faces from cheek to chin, protecting skin against the bitter wind and cold. We both carried two-way radios wrapped in long-lasting medical heat packs to keep the batteries from freezing. We wore double-thick plastic shelled climbing boots on our feet, goggles over our eyes, and avalanche detectors around our necks. Jack had given me a crash course in mountain survival.

If an avalanche swept him under and I was left standing, I would snap the detector from signal-send mode to signal-receive mode, let the beeper guide me to the right place, then dig like hell. If I were the one swept under, I would have to remember to push my arms forward, creating as big an airspace in the snow as I could, and wait for Jack to come dig me out. We didn't talk about what would happen if we both got swept under.

Instead, he gave me a large oblong metal clip called a carabiner, and showed me how to work it like a door handle, using both of my hands to spring it open where a normal person used only one. My index fingers were the strongest, so I used them, right index finger bending at the knuckle and hooking around the clip, left index finger pushing against right, to help pinch the steel open. Hook, pinch, open. Hook, pinch, open.

Jack made me practice without gloves, then with gloves, over and over, until I could do it with my eyes closed, ten times fast. I would understand later just how important that one manual move would be. I lacked the dexterity to tie and untie knots, but I had enough strength to hook, pinch, and open my way up the ice wall.

Jack sheathed a squat, sharp hunting knife and strapped it to my ankle. Next, he equipped me with a seat harness. Kevlar straps circled my thighs and waist. He tugged at the straps until they were tight, then eased a chest harness across my shoulders and under my arms, pulling the straps into a secure fit. The chest and seat harnesses were linked together with a short length of rope. Jack's fingers moved fast, deftly working the rope into a series of expert knots. Finally, he snapped that super-sized steel carabiner in the center of my chest harness, and watched me do it one last time. Hook, pinch, open. I was ready to climb.

Jack wore the same kind of harnesses. He carried two full coils of climbing rope at his left hip and a webbed nylon belt around his waist slung with steel ice screws, carabiners, pitons, rope clips, and pulleys. His gun was secure in a holster under the parka at his right hip, and he wore a heavy-duty watch with built-in altimeter and compass on his left wrist. The heat-wrapped cell phone and two-way radio were tucked in an inner parka pocket. A second gun was strapped to his calf, invisible under climbing pants.

I didn't have the manual dexterity to fire a gun, and doubted I had the strength or training to wield my own knife with accuracy. Jack was my weapon, I thought, watching him.

He hoisted a pack over his back and secured it. Inside were high energy bars, liters of fresh water, and three thermoses of hot chocolate. He also carried three sleeping bags rolled up tight and basic survival gear to help him weather the night if Search and Rescue could not make the flight up. Two sets of crampons, a lightweight aluminum shovel, and a set of ice axes were strapped to the outside of the pack. Jack slapped our snowshoes down, checked his watch, and touched my hair.

"Seven-thirty," he said. "Time to go."

I stepped into the snowshoes. The bindings snapped into place.

I looked up the mountain at the windswept crests and jagged peaks jutting impossibly high above us. The base temperature was ten degrees Fahrenheit. The summit temperature was twenty below zero.

A fat cumulus cloud crossed the sun.

*   *   *

We hiked up the gentle base slope at a steady pace. The aluminum snowshoes were light and had steely-toothed crampons on the bottom that gripped snow crust well. Walking flat-footed across deep drifts felt awkward at first, but after the first hour my thighs warmed and the walking style was natural.

The second hour was even better. Movement and breathing were rhythmic. I hit a cadence and let my mind go blank, thinking of nothing but moving forward, always forward. Traveling with the wind in our faces, we dipped our heads and hiked straight up, hugging the tree line where there was forest enough to do so. It was safer there from free-falling slabs of snow that might slide off and avalanche across the open mountain face. We steered clear of gullies too and any narrow channels where snow seemed likely to slide off, fast and deadly.

The crystalline air was pure and smelled sharply of pine. Wind in the trees roared like rushing water, drowning out the thump of our snowshoes slapping snow. High above, sunlight struck the peaks. Ribbons of snow gusted off the wind-raked summits and glittered white against a cobalt sky. Jack and I moved side by side, close enough to touch. From time to time, he turned and looked at me.

"Good work," he would say. "You feel up to moving a little faster?"

I would nod, give a smile he couldn't see under my neoprene mask, and increase my pace.

The slopes quickly changed from gentle to steep. Jack stopped to rope us together. I didn't have the experience needed to keep myself from sliding if I fell on a steep incline. The rope was a safety line. Jack would use it with his body weight to counteract my fall.

When the knots were tight and we were ready to move, Jack pulled an ice ax from the pack and gripped it in his uphill hand, pick head pointing forward. He used it like a cane to help him walk. He changed tactic, moving diagonally now instead of straight up, zigzagging up the mountain face, step-kicking with his feet, driving the ice ax in with his right hand, pulling it out again, and working us both forward and up. Always up.

The flank of the mountain angled sharply and suddenly the ice ax was no longer useful as a cane. Jack held it across his body, horizontal and perpendicular to the hill, driving the pick end into the mountain sideways. My job now was to stay put and feed out the twenty-foot length of rope linking us together. When it grew taut, Jack stopped moving, buried his ax in the snow, and helped pull me up. The steeper the pitch, the slower we moved.

We lost time on those sharp inclines where I slowed him down considerably. My body was not conditioned for high-altitude exertion. I sucked bitter cold air into my aching lungs, but under the down, fleece pullovers, and silk underwear, I was sweating. We stopped a dozen times to clear my fogged goggles. I asked for water so often, Jack finally rigged a liter bottle inside my parka with a long sipping straw that ran straight up to my cotton-dry mouth.

We trudged on, moving ahead even as thick clouds rolled across the sky, masking the sun, leaving us in a flat gray light.

Jack looked up at the clouds, then at me. "You feel up to moving a little faster?"

I nodded and increased my pace.

The first flakes fell at ten.

They were powder-light.

The wind picked up, kicking loose snow around our ankles, blowing it off the bluffs into our faces where it stuck on the goggles: a white shroud worse than fog. I brushed the goggles with my gloves, smeared the snow, and never saw clearly again. Moisture and wet flakes dotted the yellow plastic shield, turning the world into soft focus. My body was no longer hot or even warm. It was cold. I shivered, tightened my hood, and drank more water.

At eleven, Jack stopped and took out the first thermos of hot chocolate. We finished it. Warmth from the hot drink flooded my body, the sugar gave me a boost of energy. I moved faster for a while and felt good, until the warmth wore off, leaving me cold and stiff.

A blister bubbled up on my heel. My upper thighs were burning now, and my ankles ached in the tight confines of stiff new climbing boots. Visibility was ten feet at best. The clouds had dropped or we had simply walked up into them. Peaks, summits, and trees were all invisible. Wind drove the snow down sideways in near-solid sheets. Jack shortened the loop of climbing rope between our harness clips and we walked on across the featureless terrain, unable to tell where land ended and air began, listening to the frequent rumbling thunder of nearby avalanches.

At eight thousand feet, we stopped, devoured chocolate bars and bananas, and finished off the second thermos of hot chocolate.

At noon, snow was hitting us like ice pellets, and we were so high up, the bitter cold cut through to the bone. Silk long johns wicked my sweat away, but not fast enough to keep it from freezing to my skin.

Dragged up against gravity, into thinner air, I cursed the driving stinging wind, the dense swirling clouds, and wished for sun to light our way. My goggles were hopelessly fogged. My fingertips and toes were frozen. My strength ebbed. I slowed, fell behind, lagged, stumbled to my knees. Jack's red parka vanished in the whiteout. The rope between us went taut.

Jack dropped back. He helped me up. I walked like a blind woman, letting him guide me. Carabiners and pitons clanked on his webbed belt. His breathing was deep and regular. My own was ragged and uneven. Wind ripped down from the shrouded summits. We wrestled against it, hunching shoulders, angling up, making slow stubborn progress. Suddenly Jack stopped. Clouds swirled apart, revealing the wide-open bowl that separated us from the foot of Flagg's Peak.

"Avalanche risk here is high," he called out. "I don't want to cross tied together. If a snow slab goes and pulls one of us under, the other goes by default if we're tied up. We stand a better chance of one of us being above ground when it's over if we cross separately." He unhitched the rope from my carabiner. "Stay close and move with me."

We stepped away from the tree line. Jack used his compass to guide us. From time to time, he stopped and listened. Finally, we emerged from the bowl. Jack tied us together again, took another compass reading, and zigzagged up, digging the ice ax head into snow as he went.

An old trail sign poked out of a drift. Jack checked it against his map and nodded. We changed direction and, ninety minutes later, at five after two, we hit the ice wall. Jack pulled his goggles off and looked up. Snowflakes caught in his eyebrows, ice crystals formed on his lashes. Snow collected on his shoulders. He took a compass reading, wiped ice from his face, and turned to me.

His eyes were so blue in our white world, and from the expression in them, I knew he was worried. It was late and the hardest work still lay ahead. Beane had left us no margin for error. Our ascent had to be technically perfect and swift. Dusk fell early in the northwest, in winter.

Jack slipped his goggles on, removed his snowshoes, and motioned for me to do the same. He slung the backpack to the ground and unhitched the two sets of crampons, steel skeletons that would attach to the bottoms of our boots. Like the snowshoes, long razor-sharp steel teeth stuck out from the bottoms of the crampons, but these teeth were longer and sharper, made for ice. The crampons had an extra pair of teeth the snowshoes did not have and they jutted straight out from the toe at ninety-degree angles. Jack strapped a pair on my boots, then a pair on his own.

He removed a thick coil of yellow rope from his belt, and tied one end of it through the waist and leg loops of my harness, securing it with a tight figure-eight knot. He tied the free end of the rope through his own harness in the same way and placed the rope coil at my feet.

He unpacked two fiberglass climbing helmets, a double-pointed ice pick and ice hammer, and the last thermos of hot chocolate, then swung the pack, now lighter by ten pounds, up over his back again. He opened the thermos, gulped down half of the chocolate, gave me the rest, and tried to explain how he was going to get me up the steep ice wall facing us, but the wind ate his words. I listened dumbly, half blind, and just shook my head. The only thing I heard him say was, "One foot in front of the other. Hold your arms straight out at your sides."

He stuck his arms out scarecrow style and I understood. "Balance?" I shouted into the wind.

I saw him nod yes.

He crossed the one-foot distance between us and took me in his arms. He pushed my hood aside. The bitter wind stung my ears, but now at least, I heard Jack's voice.

"This is the last greatest distance, Lacie. We're going to make it up. Trust me. We will ascend in three distinct stages called *pitches*, of roughly two hundred and thirty feet each. I'll go up first, and set rope pulleys that will keep you safe and help you climb. When it's your turn to climb, you won't see me, but you will feel me taking up the slack and keeping tension on the rope.

"It will take thirty minutes or more for me to get to where I can set up the first pulley. If I can't find a natural ledge in the wall to work on, I'll have to carve one and that will take more time. When you feel me tug three times, turn your face to the wall here, dig the toes of your crampons in, and walk up. Hold your arms out-stretched to each side. It will give you balance, keep your body from swinging around, keep you from losing your toehold.

"Think of it as walking, Lacie. You are simply walking, one toe dig at a time, face to the ice. Keep one foot planted in the ice, then pull the other free and dig it in as high up as you can reach. One, two. One, two. Don't think about where you are, or that you're walking vertically without a floor to hold you. The wall will hold you. The ice is strong, deep, and hard. It will hold you. Dig into it. Don't panic. I'll be up there with the rope. If you lose your footing, you can't fall. I'll always have you by the rope."

"What happens if you fall?" I asked, imagining a climbing part-ner who did not exist, one who could grip rope in powerful hands, one who could yank on a pulley and stop his fall, one whose hands were strong enough to twist ten-inch steel ice screws into this tow-ering wall of ice and able to pull a fallen climber to safety, one who could hoist Jack out of a crevice or off a ledge or out of thin air or any one of the other dozen places he might tumble into or onto. With me, helpless at the base, he was climbing unprotected. "What if *you* fall?" I said again. "What happens then?"

"I won't fall."

Jack radioed in our position to the rescue team at the base, just in case. Finally, he fit the helmet on my head, adjusted his own, and shouted out a recap of instructions, reminding me how the two hundred and forty feet of coiled rope would feed out slowly as he made his ascent. He ordered me to watch it and make sure the coil didn't tangle.

When the coil disappeared and the rope was right against the ice, I would feel the three sharp tugs and know it was my turn to go. Jack pushed my neoprene mask down, his too. Our lips met, warm and moist in the frigid air. It was a long hopeful kiss and though I did not want to think it, I knew too, if something should happen, this was our kiss good-bye.

He worked the neoprene back up, cupped my face, then turned to the ice wall and began to climb.

Holding an ax in each hand, Jack kicked his right foot into the ice and swung his left arm up, slinging the ax into the wall in a long reach above his head. He kicked his left foot in next, swung the right arm up high, slinging the second ax into ice. Spread-eagle against the ice, slinging axes, right and left, one after another, digging steel-toothed crampons toe-first into the wall, Jack crawled vertically up.

Chunks of ice scuttled down, hitting my shoulders and helmet. I looked up. A fine frozen powder sifted through the air, dusting my goggles. One moment Jack was a bright red smudge against the stark white wall and the next he had disappeared into the clouds. I listened to the sound of his feet kicking ice and his axes swinging. I kept watching and listening long after the sounds were gone and the wall above was silent and still.

I tucked my body against the wind, finished off the chocolate, and watched the bright rope at my feet uncoil. Snow swirled, fog whirled, the wind battered me. I tried to think of warm things: sultry D.C. days, torpor and opaque August skies, still summer nights in small Southern towns, screen doors slapping, flies buzzing. I tried to think myself warm, but my body was cold.

I had no sense of direction, no sense of right or left, or down. Only up, and that from the vivid yellow rope slowly reeling out, a sure sign Jack was above me, moving. Time was lost in the whiteout. I didn't have a watch. With the howling wind and the whipping snow, there was only one measure of time and that was the cold. Hands were numb again, feet turned to wood, I shivered uncontrollably. More than half the rope was still there at my side. I feared hypothermia and wondered how long it would take to set in.

"No!" I shouted, rebellious and rising. I clapped my mittens together, jumped up and down, tried to jump myself alert, but the merciless wind beat me back into a tiny crouch. As my core temperature dropped, my senses dulled and my thoughts drifted to Linda Severino, to what her last minutes must have been like in the Bering Sea. Hypothermia makes no distinction between land and air. Cold is cold—and enough cold can kill you.

I braced myself and waited.

I knew the warning signs, the slowing motor coordination, slurred speech, sluggish brain. Then, the split second change, bliss striking and cold snapping, leaving the exposed victim giddy and warm with hypothermic madness, chasing hallucinations. Would I, like Linda, rip my protective clothing off and swim bare-skinned into an ocean of snow?

Would I see apparitions? Ghosts? Jerry skimming across the white powder sea? Harry trim and tailored on this final frozen set? Max scudding by? My father standing tall, folding me to his chest? *Listen, Lacie, listen. This is the sound of life.* I shook my head clear. The rapid thump-thumping was my own hardworking heart. Would the cold shut it down? How could Skyla survive two nights in weather like this? Was the old hut on the summit shelter enough against this savage chill?

Three sharp tugs jerked the rope. I took a deep breath, straightened, turned to face the ice wall and panicked. *I can't do this.* I pressed my forehead against ice. Hot tears dripped into my goggles. Heavy fear inside made me dizzy and sick. The rope ran from my harness straight up the wall, tight and ready for me to move.

I can't.

The rope jerked again. Three times. A sharp rebuke.

No! I can't.

Then, I thought of Jack up there alone, spread-eagle, chin to the wall, crawling belly to the ice, swinging his way up to save my daughter, and I readied myself. One step at a time, he had instructed. One step at a time.

This one's for Jack.

I took a tiny baby step up with my right foot and dug those steely crampon teeth into the wall. When I was sure the hold was solid, I picked up the left foot, kicked it in, and began to climb.

Right toe, out and up and in. Left toe, out and up and in. Arms out like a tightrope walker, nose to the ice, I began to inch my way up. Ice tinkled around me from somewhere above where the yellow rope chafed Jack's ledge. Chunks bounced off my helmet, more frozen shavings sifted down in a fine crystal powder. I dug one foot in, pulled the other foot out, and climbed handless up the white ice wall.

The harness straps dug in under my arms and around the backs of my thighs, creating a seat for me to lean into. I was afraid to look up, afraid to look down, so I looked straight ahead into the blinding white. I saw so many shades of white. Blue white. Violet white. Gray white. Marble white. Gardenia white. Milk white. Jasmine white. Alabaster white. Lily white. Ice white, smooth and hard as glass.

Punishing physical effort started to warm my body. I could feel my feet. My toes tingled. The wind raced around me, over me, under me. My arms began to ache, terribly, as if I were holding fifty-pound stones in each outstretched hand. I dropped them to my sides and in that one simple move, lost balance. My torso twisted to the right and the weight of it yanked my right foot out of the wall, then my left foot jerked free, leaving me dangling, a plaything for the malevolent wind. Ferocious gusts slung me into the side of the wall, tossed my body until I was spinning, spinning, spinning like a top, reaching stupidly into the mist, grabbing nothing but clouds and falling snow.

Toes. Toes were the answer. Those saw-toothed toes.

I kicked my right foot out and hit air. I kicked my left foot out. Steel pierced ice and the spinning stopped. I kicked the right foot in hard and staked myself to the mountain. One leg was hiked up way higher than the other, but I was stable now and ready to move. I stretched my arms out at my sides and started again, one foot at a time, kicking ice. There was no top, no bottom, no left or right, just up, and somewhere in the white windy world, I finally heard Jack calling.

I dug in, more determined than ever, foot over foot, arms out winglike at my sides, walking vertically up the side of that strange winter earth.

Jack's voice grew louder. I heard the sound of the rope scraping. More ice dust and snow sifted down. Suddenly, his words were clear.

"Throw your arms over the shelf," he shouted. "Keep those toes dug in."

A narrow ledge was right above me. I reached high and dropped my arms over the lip. Jack grabbed me under my armpits, pulled me up and over, back from the edge. He clipped my carabiner to a rope that was fixed to an ice screw, anchored in the wall. I had made it up the first pitch, handless as I was. I had made it.

Jack dismantled his crude pulley system and coiled the rope. When he finished, he stood close, nudged my hood back, and explained why I was clipped to the ice screw.

The ledge was slender and made of ice. If it should give way, I would hang safely by my harness, hitched to the ice screw, until the three rope tugs came. Then, I would dig my feet into the wall, hook my fingers into the carabiner clip, pinch it open, and set myself free to climb the rest of the way. Hook, pinch, open. It was harder now with numb fingers, but somehow I made it work. Jack watched. When I could do it five times in a row without fail, he started up.

I waited longer this time for the three tugs to come, so long I knew Jack had not found a natural second ledge to set his pulleys, and that he was hanging from an ice screw like mine, but with nothing solid under his feet to hold him while he hacked a ledge in the wall.

I kept my index fingers hooked around the oversized clip and waited, afraid my hands would freeze too much for the fingers to work. Finally, the rope jerked three times. I kicked both feet in, pinched the carabiner open, freed myself from the ice screw anchor, and started to climb.

I was bolder now, taking wide steps and holding my arms diligently out at my sides. Total concentration kept me sane and unafraid. *Sky-la. Sky-la. Sky-la.* One toe dig for each syllable of her name. Chanting softly to myself, I kicked my way up to Jack. He was pinned to the wall, clipped to an ice screw contraption like the one he had made for me. His boots were dug in hard and his hands were working the pulleys that kept me safe. He clipped me to a second ice screw anchor, nodded once, and tapped his watch face.

Time was precious. It was four o'clock and somewhere to the west the sun was dropping low in the sky. Jack worked fast, preparing for the third and final pitch. The one tap on the watch said it all. Beane's bonfire started at dusk, and dusk was less than an hour away. Jack spidered his way rapidly up the wall. I hung poised, clipped to the mountain and Jack's yellow rope, keeping my fingers hooked around the carabiner, ready to move.

There was no need for hand-hacked ledges now. When the rope spooled out, Jack had reached the top where there was solid ground to anchor himself and set the last pulley. The rope jerked three times. I freed myself and climbed. Kick, pull, kick, pull, huffing hard, working to find extra oxygen in the thin air, pushing through cramped thigh muscles, spasms in my back, and those thousand-pound arms.

I kicked and cursed and cried, racing against the clock, moving as fast as I could, which was maddeningly slow. At the top, the sheer ice wall wedged in, giving way to a gentler incline. I was able to gradually straighten and walk right over the rim, to Jack.

We were above the clouds and the summit was in sight.

The ridge leading up to it was a narrow rocky spine of mountain with sheer vertical drops to either side. Ice and snow filled the deep pockets between rocks. The ferocious wind tearing across the spine would toss us over like pebbles if we tried to stand straight. Jack tied us together with a short length of rope, and we scrambled on all fours like animals over knife-edged shale and slippery ice as night rushed in.

At the top of the spine, Jack untied the rope linking us and drew his gun from the holster. He tucked it into his parka pocket, where he had easy access. Moving slower now, afraid of traps Beane might have set, we crept over the last steepest portion of the notched ridge shoulder and stepped out on a broad-bellied plateau. A shimmering white snowfield stretched in front of us, loose snow gusting up like fine sugar. A thick stand of scrappy limber pine crowded the east rim. They were bent by the wind and skinny. Some of the trees had been crudely chopped down. At the far end of the snowfield was a long pile of wood, and beyond that was a tiny ramshackle wood hut. The summit shelter. Smoke curled out of a chimney.

We stood, side by side, scanning the field for Beane or Skyla, searching the white for some sign of life, fearing that despite our very best efforts, we had arrived too late.

Chapter Fifty

Deep inside his parka pocket, safe in the heat packs, Jack's cell phone rang. He pulled it out and flipped it open. We crouched down together, backs to the wind, straining to hear the voice.

"Jackster!" Beane greeted. "You've made it! You've brought the lady up against all odds! Good work! Impressive and bold! Just in time for cocktails. I have a perfect view here and watched you crawling up the ridge. No one followed. That was good, Jack Frost. Smart. But maybe you've got white-coated Ninjas somewhere below, sneaking up as we speak."

"No, Beane," Jack promised. "We did as you said. We came alone."

"Lacie's precious to you, isn't she? But the girl's more precious still. So young. So innocent and untouched. Or is she. Is Skyla well? Is she even alive? And if she is, are her maiden days over?"

"If you raped her . . . ," Jack choked.

Beane laughed. It was a hollow sound. "Rape? You still don't understand me. I'm not talking about carnal lust, but something bigger, hotter, brighter. I'm talking about fire. Do you read me, Jack?"

"Maybe."

"Skyla was a maiden, pure and untouched by the burning flame. Time has passed. You no longer know what's real and what isn't. Whose was the body in the box, Jack? Was it a stand-in, a fake, a different dead girl? Or was it Skyla who burned in my independent film production? Is that the final joke, that you climbed all this way for nothing, to save someone who doesn't exist? And if, by the grace of God, Skyla's alive, is she untouched? Or, like Lacie and myself, does she wear the mark, carry the scar, is she now a lifelong member in the club of freaks?"

"We made a deal."

"We did indeed. But no promises were made regarding the condition of the merchandise. It seems right that we trade one set of fire-damaged goods for the next. Tit for tat. An even exchange. A fire sale to beat all fire sales. The question remains: Does my fire sale merchandise live and breathe? Or is she nothing more than a blackened charred corpse."

"Come out and talk to me face-to-face, Beane. Show us Skyla."

Beane sighed. "You're right. I'd like to chat all night, but the sad fact is I can't. Time ticks by. It's New Year's Day and the Dead Time is here. I'll show you the girl, and the last round will commence."

The line went silent.

We watched the cabin.

What machinations of evil were yet to be revealed? What game now? What would he spring on me now that I was here? A thousand yards of pristine snow separated us. I had no doubt this last short distance would be the most treacherous yet in my journey to reach Sky.

The cabin door opened. Beane stepped out, steering Skyla in front of him, using her as a shield. He had a gun to her head. Her hands were behind her back, apparently bound. Her body was bundled in a man's heavy parka and thick ski pants. Cruel gifts from Beane, I guessed, like the brand-new jeans in the van. Skyla's long blond hair had been cropped short. It glowed silvery in the twilight. Her face appeared untouched. That was a relief. She was able and walking, her face unmarked by fire.

My girl was there, a phoenix risen from the ashes, arms and legs and torso all together in one perfect splendid piece. *Skyla.* Standing tall, walking, moving, breathing cold winter air into her live warm body. *Skyla.* My girl was alive.

Keep it together, I willed us both. *Steady. Don't fall apart. Not now. Keep it together.*

Next to me, Jack tensed, ready to spring. One hand clutched the phone to his ear, the other dove deep into his pocket and gripped the gun.

Beane wore only jeans and hiking boots. His upper body was bare. In the last light of day, I saw where fire had chewed half of him away. I saw spindly upper arms, stick-thin from where flame had devoured muscle, then the concave hollows at his belly where full fleshy tissue should have been, and the chest, bare and waxy, one nipple burned away, the asymmetrical bend to his body—right side never matching left.

He was a gruesome patchwork of multicolored scars, of gorges and gullies. He pulled a cell phone from his waistband and cupped it to his ear.

"See?" Beane whispered. "She's good as new. The gun's loaded, Jack. If you break the rules, Skyla will die. Is Lacie listening? Can she hear me speak? The game starts now. Take your gloves off, Lacie, and hold your hands up high!"

I tugged my mittens off and held my hands above my head.

"Good!" Beane chortled. "I see the proof! It's you! An even trade, that's what I said. Now look at Sky."

She brought her hands out from behind her back and held them out to me.

They were mummy-wrapped and huge, white gauze mittens, bandages for gloves, the kind of bandages I had worn after the accident. The kind you wear when your hands are burned down to bone.

"Goddamn you," I spat, lurching forward, body shaking, feet digging sluggishly slow in the heavy snow. "Goddamn you!" I screamed, mind and spirit breaking, snapping cleanly in two. Without snowshoes, I fell through the snow crust and sank in up to my thighs. I pushed ahead, fighting drifts as though they were waves, as if the snow had an oceanic push, a tidal pull. Legs churning, arms thrust way out in front, I reached hopelessly for my poor burned Sky.

Beane laughed.

I stumbled and fell. There was no up or down, only white in my ears, in my eyes, on my tongue, numbing my cheeks. I thrashed, arms spinning, feet kicking, wishing snow was water, wishing I could swim my way to my mutilated daughter.

Jack's arms were around me, pulling me out.

"He burned her," I coughed. "He burned her!"

Jack swung me over his shoulder and bulled through the deep drifts, driving forward, closing in on Beane and that long woodpile.

Suddenly, Beane struck a match and dipped down, swiped it from left to right. The wood burst into flame. Fifty feet long, three feet high, an extraordinary wall of fire sprang up, cutting us off.

Jack backed away. Set me down.

Wind fanned the fire. Through the flickering orange flames, Beane chortled and trilled while holding Skyla tight to his bare bent body.

"The rules are set," he gloated. "You can't go around the fire. You can't run to the right or to the left, only straight ahead. You want to save Sky? Walk through the wall of fire and set her free. Walk, Lacie, walk."

The flames jumped and wavered, and on the other side, Beane's grinning victorious face, Skyla's huge wrapped hands.

"Walk through the fire or watch Skyla burn," Beane cried. "Come, Lacie, come!"

At what price Sky?

A walk through fire?

Her grossly bandaged hands were a flag. My rage rode high.

I shot ahead, moving crazily toward the white waxen face, toward the whispering voice that had spoken to me in a lifetime of dreams. Beane was there, coaxing me, urging me on, inviting me into his nightmare. I made it to the edge of the fire wall, then stopped short. Flames kicked ten feet high, warming my face, my wooden limbs, my stump feet. The fire was hot. The neoprene mask was suffocating me. I ripped it off.

Walk into the fire. Do it, Lacie! Now! Do it!

Beane's order filled my mind, but those dancing flames paralyzed me.

An explosion cracked the thin mountain air. Beyond the wall, the cabin erupted. A geyser of white fire shot up, and white burning wood littered the sky, fast-falling sizzling confetti, magnesium snow, five thousand degrees Fahrenheit, bright in the dark sub-zero night. Beane was caged now by two fires of his own making: one white, one orange, both smoking and deadly. He beckoned, dared me to join him in his trap, his fiery pen.

Walk, Lacie, walk! Walk through the fire!

Jack appeared at my side and shook me out of my stupor. He pulled his neoprene mask off.

"We have to go through," he ordered over the howling wind and the roaring fire. "Then, you have to play his madness against him. Play his game. Use his own fantasy to lure him away from Skyla. Tell him what he wants to hear. Make promises. Use your body if you have to. Get him away from her, do you understand? I need a clear shot."

I nodded dumbly.

Jack shielded his face with his arms, bolted up the woodpile and into the fire. Flame licked his clothes and caught. His hood flared, turning into a blazing helmet. Then, he was gone and there was nothing but blistering orange, blue-white sparks, and the stink of freshly seared flesh.

My legs carried me into the fire, after Jack. It was me now plunging into Beane's furnace, screaming and scrambling over the woodpile. Flames lapped at my outstretched arms. The fire was all around. My eyebrows burned, my lips blistered, my parka shriveled, but oddly, my bare hands felt nothing. Timber shifted, logs gave way.

I leapt out of the fire and rolled, killing fire in the melted slush. Jack had rolled too. He was on his feet now, a wild scarecrow with singed hair, swollen lips, and a red parka burned black.

"Now, Lacie," he whispered, pulling me up. "Tell him what he wants to hear."

Skyla was a human shield, pinned in front of Beane's body, locked in a chokehold, the gun ground into her head.

"Edouard!" I shouted. "I'm here. Ready to go with you."

I edged ever so slowly to the left, forcing him to turn to track me, wanting him to turn his back on Jack. It did not work.

"Stop moving!" Beane cried. "Stop right there!"

"I came just as you asked," I called out, stopping. "You must trust me, Edouard!"

"Prove to me you don't carry a weapon."

I took my parka off, tossed it aside. "See? I'm preparing myself. You're right. We were meant to be together, you and I. You're the only one."

His expression changed and, sensing that I had him, I rushed on. "You're the only one who will find my body beautiful. You understand, don't you? The ridicule, the shame I've lived through because of my burned body."

"Yes!" Beane gasped. "Men like Jack lied to you! They hid their repulsion and pretended to love you, but they didn't! It was nothing more than a curiosity, fucking a freak."

"I knew you'd understand, Edouard. You won't laugh. You won't call me a freak. You'll love me like a real man, won't you?"

Beane's eyes were wild. Jack was right. Beane's own madness was going to hypnotize him, draw him into my game, away from Skyla.

I pulled my sweater over my head and backed off, placing myself behind Jack, hoping now to lure Beane between the two of us and give Jack the clear shot he needed. I pulled layer after layer of clothing off my chest, calling to Beane as I went.

"The fire feels good, Edouard. You built a beautiful one. I want to share it with you. I do. Come. Touch me. Kiss me. Come and touch the fire with me."

"Prove to me you have no weapon!" he cried.

He inched toward me, Skyla in front, the gun nose ground to her head.

I pushed my ski pants down far enough to show him the graft marks on my belly.

"Come stroke me, Edouard. Touch me here. Reach out and touch the fire."

He edged, inch by inch, closer to me, closer to Jack. Then, he sensed the danger and froze. Eyed Jack. Eyed me.

I was stripped down to the last silk undershirt. Jack's instructions echoed in my head.

Give him what he wants. Get him away. Get me a clear shot.

I went for it, pulled the shirt off and faced Beane, as bare-bodied as he was.

"Hurry, Edouard!" I urged. "Hurry! While your fire is hot! Come touch me!"

It worked. He inched closer, until he was even with Jack. He stopped again, anguished. He wanted me, but he did not trust Jack.

"Toss the gun, Jackster! Into the fire! Now! Do it!"

Jack hesitated.

Beane jerked his arm against Skyla's throat. She cried out. Jack threw his gun into the fire and held his empty hands up high.

"Good," Beane shouted. "Now, take the pack off slowly and toss it in too."

Jack removed the pack filled with all his survival gear and threw it into the fire.

"See, Beane?" he called out. "I'm playing by your rules. Now, let the girl go. Let her come to me, and Lacie is yours. Just as we agreed."

Beane nodded yes, but in one split second, broke the deal. He tipped the gun away from Skyla and fired two shots. Jack went down. Skyla screamed. Beane cracked his gun across her head. She crumpled at his feet.

And now Beane was alone with me.

I fumbled for the knife. Beane knew what I was doing. He came at me, ripped the knife out of the sheath, and tossed it into the fire along with his gun.

I turned, tried to run, slipped on slush, and scrambled up, but Beane was on me, grabbing me, locking my body against his, kneading my breasts, clutching my sex, moaning and crying, trying to kiss me. Sweat streaked down his sunken cheeks, his thick lips, his ravaged torso, and his breath was hot and sour in my face. Under the twisted skin and scars was steely muscle; Beane was strong. He tugged on his zipper, freed himself, ground his pelvis into mine. I felt his excitement rising hard.

"We're going to burn now, Lacie," he promised, slapping himself, then rubbing against me, driving me step by deadly step, backward to the fire. He slipped his left hand into my ski pants.

"Take them off," he whispered hoarsely, working his nimble fingers through layers of cotton and silk, touching me, driving one then two then four fingers into me. "Take them off. Now. It's time, my bride, my beautiful bride." He locked his lips over mine, thrust his tongue deep into my mouth.

I bit down hard and tasted his blood. Beane howled, reared back, and slapped me. My head snapped to the left. I spit out a chunk of Beane's tongue, jerked my elbow up, and struck his chin. His teeth cracked together. He backhanded my cheek; knuckles were bullets against fragile bone. My head snapped to the right. His fist crashed into my jaw. My head snapped back to the left. I choked on my own blood and vomit, and fought to stay conscious.

Beane shoved me down next to the blazing woodpile. He loomed over me, jerking his newly limp penis, ready to drop his twisted body over mine and roll us both into the fire. He wanted to die coupled like lovers, and although he could not do that, he still wanted to burn and die with me, on top of me, as close to being part of me as he could get.

My vision doubled. There were two Beanes leering and jerking, four of his coal-dark eyes wet and glowing. Windblown flames whipped my bare skin, searing, stinging, and the heat—the sweltering, mind-numbing infernal heat—overwhelmed me. Thick smoke swirled all around, suffocating me, spinning me into a blackout.

I gave up. Thought it was over. Believed I could not win.

Then I saw the reflection of fire glinting off steel and my head cleared. Those sharp teeth were still strapped to my boots. Instinctively, I smiled at Beane and spread my legs as if in offering. He knelt between them and in that one vulnerable moment, when he was off balance and unprepared, I snapped my right knee back and kicked up hard, catching him in the chest. He shrieked.

I pulled my left knee back and kicked again. Steel claws ripped his scars, pulled them apart. *Right foot out, pull back and kick. Left leg out, pull back and kick.* Just like climbing, only now I was driving those jutting steel teeth into Beane's warm flesh instead of the cold ice. I kicked and kicked, shredding his body, ripping white waxy tissue and graft gullies apart, tearing skin from bone, then cracking the bone itself with my vicious steel teeth.

I caught the side of his shrieking face and raked it as though the crampon teeth were the sharp strong fingers I didn't have. I dug into the roll of his shoulder, sheared the one remaining nipple off his chest, dragged the steel teeth down in a long deadly line to his groin, pulled back and kicked one last time, straight and hard, right into his sex, the thing he had once forced me to take in my young mouth and later touch with my ruined hands. I impaled him as he had intended on impaling me, and despite the sweat and tears salting my eyes, my kick was right on target.

Beane roared in pain and arched away from the deadly crampons, spurting blood. He tottered on his knees, then rose impossibly and stood, doubled over, swaying from left to right. My booted foot snapped out and up on its own, catching him in the chin with razor tusks, thrusting him off balance. I kicked again. He lurched back. I kicked again. He collapsed into the fire.

I dragged my body close to the flames and watched Beane burn.

I wanted to see every last second of it with my own eyes, to know that he was dead, that he was destroyed, that he was not ever coming back, that he would never again whisper to me or touch me or burn me or steal my daughter. I crawled as close as I could and watched.

Beane was trapped in his own pyre, engulfed in flame. I watched fire eat his pants, his legs, his arms. I watched flesh shrivel, white bones turn black. I watched him jerk and twist, holding one flaming hand out to me. I simply lay there and watched the bloodied, shredded nightmare face smear and melt and finally, disappear.

When he was gone, when all I saw was a charred bent form crackling in the fire, as black and brittle as my own father's had been—when I saw that—I crawled away and searched for Sky.

She was sprawled in the slush, next to Jack, crying.

I will know, I thought dragging myself over, *if your eyes are flat and dull, doll-blank, and your body stiff, ready for the next blow, I will know you have been brutalized, raped or beaten, that Beane broke your spirit in those long six weeks. You're my girl, my flesh and blood, and I will certainly know. If your eyes are flat, doll-blank, if you flinch from my touch, I'll know that Beane has won.*

I tipped her face up. My second pair of indigo eyes looked out at me, wide open and huge. They were brimming with tears and fear and hope. Skyla was terrified and tired, but full of life. He hadn't touched her, not in that way. He hadn't raped or broken her or turned her into a version of his own mad sister. I hugged my daughter tight to my beaten body and wept while my crippled hands traveled over her, touching her hair, feeling the shape of her skull, counting ribs, arms, legs, eyes, and ears, inspecting her as if she were a newborn, which in a way she was. I pressed my burned lips to the pulse point at her neck and felt life thumping there.

Skyla's alive. She's alive! I rejoiced, not having the good human decency to care that someone else's girl had died brutally, painfully, terribly in Beane's bonfire. Someone's daughter had kicked and screamed while the fire burned her alive that night. Someone's child, but not mine. I thanked God selfishly, shamelessly, for that.

Melted snow around us ran red with Jack's blood. I let go of Skyla and pushed his burnt parka up, working my way through fleece climbing clothes and silk underwear.

Jack, Jack, Jack. Spread-eagle against the ice, swinging one hand over the other, reaching for Sky. Risking everything to find and save my one and only Sky.

I wasn't a doctor, but I knew enough to understand the luck of two bullets lodged up high on his left shoulder, away from the heart and lungs and life-giving arteries. Jack opened his eyes. His left arm was immobilized by the gunshots, but he was able to stand and herd us to the end of the burning woodpile, out into fresh snow, safely away from toxic smoke, dangerous windblown flames, and the fierce heat of Beane's white magnesium furnace.

The air was bitterly cold and I was exposed. My sweat- and blood-streaked skin had turned numb. Jack eased out of his ruined parka and gave it to me. He took Skyla's hands one at a time and loosened her bandages. White gauze fell away. This was the last of Beane's cruel games. There, where I had feared total destruction would be, were two perfect hands untouched by fire.

"Thank God," Jack said.

"Who are you?" Skyla asked, through tears.

"Jack," he answered, breathing deep and gathering us close. "My name is Jack."

We had no shelter, no provisions, and Beane's fire was dying down. The two-way radios were destroyed by our run through the wall of fire, and Jack's cell phone was buried somewhere out in the snowfield. The full force of the storm was howling in around us. I knew that a night exposed on the mountain would be deadly, and I was afraid.

I thought fear and exhaustion had driven me to hallucinate, to mistake the thundering wind for the sound of propellers coming our way. I listened again and heard nothing but wind. Jack thrust his right hand up high in the sky, and for a split second I believed he was reaching for Gabby and his little boy. There was a certain look on his upturned face that made me sure, then the look was gone and the strangest aircraft I had ever seen was rising up over the summit and Jack was simply flagging it down.

It was a chunky combat gray turboprop plane with wings that were in the process of folding up, rotating the propellers to an upright position, instantly turning the plane into a wild kind of helicopter with huge beating rotors on each side.

"V-22 Osprey," Jack said, smiling through his pain. "Boeing's invention and the Delta Force's dream."

I learned later that it was a new military hybrid that could fly like an airplane, but take off, land, and hover like a helicopter. The Osprey remained totally stable in the kind of high winds that flipped standard search and rescue choppers, and came equipped with new advanced-generation radar enabling the pilot to fly in zero-visibility conditions. It was the only aircraft in the world that could have made the trip.

That night at the summit, like the hawk it was named after, the Osprey hovered rock-steady in the high winds.

Max did not need searchlights to find us.

The bright glow from Beane's last fire was light enough.

· A NOTE ON THE TYPE ·

The typeface used in this book is a version of Sabon, originally designed in the 1960s by Jan Tschichold (1902–1974) at the behest of a consortium of manufacturers of metal type. As one who began as an outspoken design revolutionary—calling for the elimination of serifs, scorning revivals of historic typefaces—Tschichold seemed an odd choice, but he met the challenge brilliantly: The typeface was to be based on the fonts of the sixteenth-century French typefounder Claude Garamond but five percent narrower; it had to be identical for three different processes, working around the quirks of each, such as linotype's inability to "kern" (allow one character into the space of another, the way the top of a lowercase *f* overhangs other letters). Aside from Sabon, named for a sixteenth-century French punchcutter to avoid problems of attribution to Garamond, Tschichold is best remembered as the designer of the Penguin paperbacks of the late 1940s.